The Court of Silver Shadows

Books by Beatrice Brandon:

THE COURT OF SILVER SHADOWS

THE CLIFFS OF NIGHT

The Court of Silver Shadows

by Beatrice Brandon

DOUBLEDAY & COMPANY, INC.
Garden City, New York
1980

All of the characters in this book are fictitious, and any resemblance to actual persons, living or dead, is purely coincidental.

ISBN: 0-385-09629-1
Library of Congress Catalog Card Number 75-40713

Printed in the United States of America

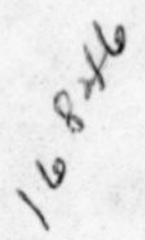

In loving memory
of M. Roberts and John Setton
of Will Burke and his friend Will
of Monty Druitt
and of L. A. B.

Nobody dies.

1

ALL THE WAY FROM TAMPA'S AIRPORT MICAJAH HAD MADE A FOOL of himself, yowling and spitting in his carrier and paying no attention to my futile soothing. At last I buttoned the flap over the screen and left him to wail in the dark. Micajah was one of those rare cats who dislike heat and loathe the sunlight; his first plane trip had done nothing to sweeten his disposition.

The cabdriver did not like cats, and told me so, and we rode twenty miles in a mute irritation with each other. Finally he cleared his throat and, obviously thinking of his tip, said, "That's Blackbeard's Bayou." Between houses I saw the dull silver sheen of placid water. "Your address is two more blocks."

Micajah let out a plaintive cry, echoing with resentment.

"Say," the driver threw over his shoulder, "that wouldn't be Sablecroft Hall you're going to?"

"Yes."

There was silence except for Micajah. Then, "My God," he said, shaking his head.

"Why?"

"That's the weirdest place in St. Pete."

"Why?" I repeated. I do not care for strangers who tell you that they hate what you patently love, especially cats.

"You'll see in a second. It's like one of them old movie theaters we used to go to before the talkies."

"Oh?" Anyone old enough to recall the silents, who still used the word "talkies," must be forgiven some outspokenness on his dislikes. "It sounds fascinating," I said.

"And people *live* in it," he said. "Nobody could pay me to. There it is."

Micajah gave a heart-rending screech, as if he understood the words, and shut up.

The house was enormous, absurd, a welter of towers and crenellated walls and decaying buttresses all in light blue stucco, looming behind a seven-foot wall of the same material. It did resemble one of the "motion-picture palaces" that had gone up all over the country in the first half of the 1920s, heavily influenced by all the books and films of romantic-desert-sheik blather. But Sablecroft Hall had been built, about the same time, in the prevailing Hispano-Moresque mode for which we could thank primarily the wild architect Addison Mizner. It had its similarities; it had sprung from the same remote ancestor as the theaters, but the educated eye could see all the differences too.

"Amazing," I said.

"Ain't it?" said the driver, stopping before a pair of broad wooden gates set in the heavy wall. He got out and opened my door, and in our newfound amity even held the cat carrier while I emerged. He set my two suitcases on the cracked old pavement. I paid the tab and tipped him.

"Is it haunted?" I asked lightly.

"People will tell you it is." He stared at me oddly. "Not that I believe that kids' stuff . . . but the old boy that built it was just ornery enough to stick around and play jokes after he died."

"Did you know him?"

"Me? No! But a cabby hears things. You want me to wait?"

"It's all right, they expect me."

He glanced around. "Well, this is a good neighborhood, you'll be okay," he said. Did I only imagine that his tone was dubious? He drove away, leaving Sablecroft Hall to sunlight and to me.

The gates were filigreed rather primitively with a multitude of holes in a paisley pattern. I stared through one of these gaps at the house, for the barriers were taller than I. Micajah in his black box gave a lonely coo of inquiry.

There is a certain kind of sunshine that is more ominous than darkness. It usually accompanies sultry heat, and it gives you the feeling (if you analyze it) that our yellow star has just this moment increased in power and, like an old electric bulb, is about to flash and go out for good. I hate it. It reminds me of how powerless we are before the great forces of nature. Who, after all, will screw a fresh sun into the socket when the dark explodes over us?

Was it this, and the fact that I was tired and far hotter than I cared to be, and the sweat that was making my vision blue, and the cabdriver's libel of the place that stuck in my memory—or was there really a queer, forbidding air to Sablecroft Hall that caused me to hesitate before going in: as though it came from a dead time, and belonged back there? As though the door might be opened by Valentino himself, gone these fifty years.

Funny, I'd never felt any such emotion on viewing one of the leftover Moorish theaters, which are only delightful anachronisms.

Micajah asked for me again, sounding abandoned and helpless. "The time is out of joint," I explained to him. I found the bell push, six feet from the pavement, and shoved a thumb onto it irritably, provoked at my silly reaction to a house as intriguing as this one. I'd looked forward to coming here. I'd be living within those blue walls for many months, and the photographs I'd seen of the Hall had appealed to me. There was no reason for a third dimension to reverse my feelings so strongly.

But my first impression was that I was definitely *not* coming home. If the cab had still been there, I might have fled. . . .

Nothing moved beyond the gate, and the only sounds I heard were the mewing of sea gulls and the hot frying sputter of some insect sizzling away to himself in the distance. A tiny brown lizard, no more than an inch long, ran in spurts down the blue gate and after gaping at me for a moment, darted off. I rang the bell again. And again.

The man who finally opened the huge door to peer out was entirely unexpectable. "Yes?" he called, and went on without pause. "Yes, what is it? What do you want? This is a private residence, no solicitations!" He squinted at me under his hand, trying to make me out in the glare. "I am going to release several gigantic dogs, very savage and spiteful dogs," he roared angrily. "You'd better be off!"

"I'm Mrs. Warrick," I said loudly, for we were speaking across ten yards of ground. "I'm one flight early."

He wallowed toward me, an overweight porpoise struggling against a heavy sea. Three or four Great Danes came out and slouched after him. At sight of them I felt a gust of irrational fear, like a sudden clammy puff of wind from across the steel-colored water behind the house.

I recognized the plain truth: I did not want to go in. Only a foolish pride kept me from snatching up my cat and running.

"Pay no attention to the brutes, when they see you're welcome they'll pay *you* no heed," said the fat man, and slid back a two-by-four that held the gates. "Come in out of this appalling heat at once, Mrs. Warrick. I'm sorry you've had to wait." He dragged back one of the openwork blockades and picked up my bags, which were heavy, as though they'd been empty. He was very powerful, obviously, which surprised me. "I presume your kitty's in that odd-shaped case? You'll feel better if you carry it, then. Get away, Roderick or whoever you are"—this to one of the dogs—"Mrs. Warrick's come to stay and you mustn't annoy her."

I walked toward the front door beside him, the big dogs pacing us sullenly, watching me from the corners of their eyes.

"I am Pierce Priam Poole. My father wished it on me out of spite, but I think it rather fits me, don't you? Do go off about your business, Thunderer or Elfenstein or whatever. Go and guard the place as you're supposed to." He went on talking in an impetuous, nonstop fashion with a deep rumble of a voice, saying nothing with a great many words, and I thought he was strained and worried and trying to conceal it. Micajah at last was mum, but I felt him shifting around in his prison. Between jet lag, fear of the dogs, and complete discomfort I felt no need to interrupt Mr. Poole, or even to nod intelligently, because he was gazing at the Hall as if he too were seeing it for the first time. He was an unwieldy behemoth of a man, perhaps six feet tall, perhaps in his early fifties, certainly over three hundred pounds fat. His neck was thicker than his head, which was itself of imposing bulk. His eyes bulged whitely from sockets of suet, and he was very pale.

"What do you think of our sanctuary? Rather imposing in its quiet way, *I* always think." Somehow he managed to wave one of my suitcases in a vast arc. "Flamboyant, some people have said. Rubbish! Has a house no right to a unique personality? What a very dull world it will be when at last we all live in little squalid squares of plain brick and mortar. Ticky-tacky, that's the term, yes. Welcome to Sablecroft Hall, Mrs. Warrick," he said, his joviality forced and hollow; he might have rehearsed the speech a hundred times, his thoughts were so clearly on something else. "We hope you'll be, ah, happy here," he added without conviction.

"Thank you."

"In, in, away from this beastly brilliance." He ushered me into a crisp, cold dusk that made me gasp. "You'll grow accustomed to it, it's the air-conditioning," he said. "Besides, you have come from rather far north. Like it cool, I expect."

"Yes." After the cab from Tampa, its metal just below boiling point, I found the dry chill almost painful in my lungs.

He set down my bags. "I'll be back in an instant, I must bar the gates or curiosity seekers and prying barbarians will overrun the grounds." He hastened off. I sank Micajah's carrier into the velvety pile of a deep green rug. The Danes ambled in one after the other and stood watching me.

"Hello, boy," I said to the nearest, a magnificent harlequin. It looked at me with opaque eyes that showed no more emotion than two brown marbles. I reached to pat its head and it moved away sharply. None of them even glanced at the cat's traveling case. An incurious lot, with an air of impartial hostility.

Mr. Poole returned and closed the immense door, which was pegged and studded and as thick as a castle drawbridge. "My word," he panted, sounding more Edwardian than ever, "the Malay jungles can't be more smoldering than this ghastly state! If Gilbert Sablecroft had built his mansion in Alaska, I might have enjoyed an occasional ramble out-of-doors." He slid a massive bronze bolt into its double staples, shutting out Florida. "I'll take you to your room, Mrs. Warrick. Would you like luncheon? Or will you wait till four-thirty tea?"

"Tea, thanks. I ate on the plane."

"Baskerville, Shandygaff, Camberwell, do please move aside," he said to the dogs. "There's good fellows. I hope that you like dogs, and Puss does too?"

"He'll tolerate them if they'll tolerate him," I said, going at his heels from the twilit hall into a gigantic two-story-high room that was lighted, not much more brightly, by two chandeliers: a big multicolored Tiffany and a 19th-century forty-branch crystal. Everywhere stood cabinets, statues, and objects that my tired eyes saw without identifying. We threaded a path among them.

"We call this the great hall. The library has about the same dimensions. You're imagining that everything is constructed on a Brobdingnagian scale—rooms, dogs, myself? Don't worry, you'll find your bed-sitter quite a normal size."

We went to the east wall, where a stairway with a wrought-iron railing rose to a balcony beyond which I could see several doors on the second floor. We tramped upward. The "great hall" should not have surprised me after the immensity of the house, yet it did. It was more like a gigantic museum gallery than a room. Micajah squalled suddenly, and I saw the dogs below, five of them now, gaze up at us, their big cropped ears turned toward the sound. I'd always believed that my cat, who weighed eighteen pounds and was a mass of truculent muscle, could hold his own in any company. A slight tremor of apprehension went through me. That was more than a quarter of a ton of dog down there.

"I hope you've brought your autumn clothing," said Mr. Poole.

"Yes, I wasn't sure how cold it might be at night."

"*Out there* it will plummet to eighty," he said with loathing. "Safe in our fortress, it's the same day and night, winter and summer: a refreshing seventy-two. It seems colder to you just now; indeed you might have guessed sixty, eh? That's the admirable dryness. You'll grow used to it shortly, and of course if you keep the door shut you can regulate your room to your own taste. I'd do that if I were you, Mrs. Warrick—yes, shut and bolted at night? No one's ever broken in, but you can't tell when it may happen."

Pierce Priam Poole seemed to have a siege mentality. Sablecroft Hall against the world. And here I was, a stranger from *out there*. Invited, but a stranger.

"I will," I assured him. We had walked along the balcony into a corridor and after five closed doors had now come to a large, sunny, pleasant bed-sitting-room. "Your lair," said the fat man.

"If I were you, I'd have a bath and a lie-down, to shed the effects of such a dreadful trip. Your bath is just through that door."

"It wasn't a bad trip, really," I said, smiling weakly, aware that I looked as if I'd been running for blocks.

"*All* journeys are outrageous and fearful, to be avoided whenever possible," he replied heavily. "Someone's put down a kitty pan and a bowl of water, what a nice welcoming touch. Well, until teatime, then, Mrs. Warrick—"

"Laurel, please."

"Laurel, of course; you must call me Pierce." For the first time he seemed to focus all his attention on me. "I do hope you'll feel at home in Sablecroft Hall, Laurel, that you'll become acclimatized soon and grow used to us. We're not the most everyday lot in the world, but search for the good in us and take the bad with a smile of forgiveness," he said as though he meant it. "The gong goes three minutes before tea. You can't miss it, it's on the intercommunication system. Wander anywhere you like so long as the doors are open." He left me alone.

I unlocked the cat carrier and swung its top open. A pair of golden eyes like hot buttercup petals regarded me from the middle of a round mass of tousled white fur. Micajah, never the most patient cat in the world, was in a bleak fury. "Hi, old fellow," I said tentatively. He flattened his head in a snake imitation and hissed malevolently.

"I warned you that you'd be in that box a long time," I said helplessly.

He uncoiled and stepped out, leaving a nest of shredded newspaper, bits of which clung to his long semi-Persian coat. He gave the room a brief once-over, scorned it verbally, and walked under the bed. A paw came out at the end of a very long leg and swiped at my shin; having expected it, I jerked back in time. He swore at me, extravagantly guttural. "Okay, you know where the pan is."

I went to the windows, three of them set side by side in an arched alcove, the black marble sills waist-high. There seemed no way to open them. I looked out and saw a palm grove and beyond it part of a small yellow house. To the northeast was a long swimming pool, blue-tiled, empty. I thought of that first terrible sight of Norma Desmond's clogged, dry, rat-infested pool in *Sunset Boulevard*. Southward ran the tall stucco wall, which circled the whole property. I could almost see the heat, too, lying along the earth, enfolding everything damply, a malignant, elemental beast. Even though it was turned too low, I was grateful for the air-conditioning, for I am a cold-weather person. But I found the thermostat and pushed its wheel to seventy-eight; the energy required to keep such a monstrous house at seventy-two must be staggering, and I hate waste.

Perhaps the ancient art of cross-ventilation was unknown in St. Petersburg. Perhaps all the denizens of Sablecroft Hall had medical reasons for avoiding warmth. Perhaps they were simply so rich and self-centered that they could ignore the world's dwindling fuel supply.

I put the cat carrier in the closet and unpacked a bag just enough to find my amber jersey dress. Then I ran a lukewarm bath, stripped, and slid into it. I'd had about four hours sleep, packing far into the night and then lying awake with apprehensive fidgets; and flying dulls me at the best of times. I dozed off, dreamed chaotically, and awoke gasping with cold and confusion. The water had iced. My watch on a stool beside the tub said I'd slept for an hour.

There was a movement high and to my right, half-seen, half-sensed. I jerked my head around and saw against the translucent glass of the small bathroom window a repulsive shadow, like the silhouette of a gargoyle traced in hoarfrost. I'm ashamed to admit that I gave a choked scream. The thing turned its head inquiringly. It was a pelican, perched on some ledge or balustrade just outside.

"I'm a long way from Connecticut," I said aloud with a rickety laugh. Scrambling out of the azure porcelain tub, I toweled hurriedly, took a few swipes at my hair, and dressed. The bedroom temperature had gone up only a few degrees, and I found it invigorating, like a New England wood in deep autumn. I wondered whether the terrible consumption of energy would ever stop worrying me. After a few moments in the depths of a lovely big armchair covered with yellow-and-black Art Nouveau fabric, I said good-bye to Micajah, sullenly uncommunicative under the bed, and went out and shut the door. The great hall was still empty. I walked down the staircase and into the midst of its treasures.

Paneled in a ruddy brown mahogany all the way to the painted cypress ceiling, nearly thirty feet above the dark green rug, it engulfed me like the museum gallery I'd thought it, overwhelming a lone student on an empty Sunday. There were no windows, but the dozen easy chairs and sofas each had its handy table with reading lamp, and the two immense chandeliers cast their individual rainbow and prismatic white auras over either end of the room. Huge, dark bookcases stood here and there against the walls, crammed with such a profusion of volumes that I hardly dared imagine what the library itself held.

These books were the reason for which Mrs. Sibella Callingwood had brought me from Connecticut. I went toward the nearest collection, intending to scan the titles and make some estimate of how complicated my job would be. I'd save the multiple glass-topped cases and glass-fronted cabinets for later. It was those that had given me the notion of a museum, with their legion of unknown contents. I was aware of the portraits, the armor, the statues, but ignored them until, as I was crouching down to begin reading jackets and spines, one of the sculptures cleared its throat and spoke.

"So you came after all!"

I started, turning and rising so quickly that I almost fell. Of course it was not a sculpture, but a man, who had been standing quietly near the center of the room. One of the Great Danes, a beautiful pure steel-blue animal with light, piercing eyes, sat at his feet like a majestic lion of marble.

"Oh!" I said. "You startled me. This place is so big that I didn't see you."

"Why did you come?" he demanded. His voice was low and carrying, with a threat in both tone and words. "I warned you, damn it."

"What *are* you talking about?"

"I'm Sheridan Todd," he said impatiently, as though that explained everything.

"I'm Laurel Warrick, and you obviously think I'm someone else."

"I know who you are right enough, and you know who I am."

"You're an ill-bred young man who enjoys startling strangers and making mysteries," I said, too pertly; but I was not going to begin here in the role of the introverted librarian who dares not lift her voice. He was walking slowly toward me, the dog pacing him. I stood straight, my eyes on a level with his chin, wishing I'd worn high heels. A six-foot man with a dog more than half his height take a lot of facing down.

"I will be hanged," he said slowly. "The postal system has done it again, hasn't it? You don't know me. You never got the letter. I knew I should have called you."

"What—" I began, but he waved me intolerantly to silence.

"I wrote to you, Mrs. Warrick. I told you not to come. Well, then, I tell you again. Turn around. Go home to Moorington. Flee to your snug stacks and your safe files and your tidy borrowers' cards and unhaunted reading rooms. Watch your four seasons change and forget you saw this place. Do it today, this afternoon. I'll drive you to Tampa."

I looked at him levelly. He was somewhat too heavy for his height, with a paunch and a fleshy look about the cheeks and jowls; his bone structure was not broad or heavy enough to carry this excess weight with any sort of flair or grace. He wore a thick, dark mustache that disguised his mouth, and his straight hair was cut collar-length. The irises of his eyes were green, their whites shot with red veins. They were too deeply pouched for a man who appeared to be no more than thirty. A heavy drinker? His expression and the lines in his tanned face were either of world-weariness or of insomnia. His finest feature was his nose, high in the bridge, narrow and aristocratic, dominating his face though not unpleasantly. Despite his arrogant intonation, I liked his voice, which had a deep, resonant timbre.

"Are you master here, then?" I asked him.

"There is no master of Sablecroft," he said, "only a mistress. Some day, perhaps. You haven't answered me."

"I wasn't aware you'd asked anything."

"I told you that you must leave."

"You didn't hire me, Mr. Todd. Who *are* you, anyway?" I shot at him angrily.

"I'm the man who's telling you to go home," he said between his teeth, and the Dane, catching his mood, gave a growl, staring at my face.

"Certainly not," I said, as calmly as my heart's fluttering would allow. There was a kind of electric charge radiating from him, a force that made me long to back up. He was actually frightening me, he and his satanic dog.

"Oh, damn!" he said abruptly, taking his gaze from mine for a moment and giving the Dane a couple of sharp slaps on the shoulder. "Don't tremble like that, I'm not going to hit you. I want you to abandon this place and this position for your own good, and that of —some other people."

"Just like that?"

"Just like that. Of course you'll be compensated for your fares and your time."

He and his beast seemed to be crowding in at me, pressing me against the tall case of books, yet none of us had actually moved since he'd stopped within two paces of me. I thought I had never felt such raging energy poured forth at me. I said, controlling my voice with difficulty, "You're too kind, Mr. Todd. But I resigned my job for this one."

"Ah," he said, gesturing sharply so that the Dane snarled again, "they'd take you back!"

"No they would not. The position's filled. You may think a small library's budget can be expanded out of charity, but it can't."

"Leave this place, Mrs. Warrick. Leave the dead to the dead, and don't root around in graves." He hooked his fingers under the brute's collar, apparently to keep it from my throat. "I suppose you've no idea what I'm talking about," he said, sneering.

"I think you're crazy," I whispered.

"This house is crazy and full of madness. Mad people and mad shadows. Get out. You're not wanted here."

"Then why was I hired at twice the salary I'd have dared to ask, and without references?" I demanded, anger answering insult.

"Irresponsible caprice. Hrolfengar!" he shouted at the growling dog, who cowered down at the name. "Why did you ever come?"

And then a voice snarled out above us, so unexpected, so impossible, that for a moment I was sure I was losing my mind. Because it was the harsh, wrathful voice of Humphrey Bogart, and it demanded, on the instant that Sheridan Todd ended his question, "Whyn't ya starve first?" Then I did step back, amazed, and banged into the bookshelves.

"Ignore that," said the man sharply, as I looked around a little wildly. "What do you think you have to gain here?"

I blinked at him. Gradually I took hold of my wits. "An extremely good salary, six or eight months of fascinating work in my specialty, and if I'm satisfactory, a favorable reference."

"Nothing more?" he asked. He was taunting me, cryptically, his debauched eyes baleful. He waved a hand, indicating the exotic riches of the great hall. "Is that all, really, Mrs. Warrick?"

"If you imply that I'm a thief, you'd better make your accusations to my employer," I said coldly, while a detached piece of my mind was dredging up the origin of the Bogart quotation: *Dead End*. But how . . . ?

He sighed. It was loud, theatrical, and evidently sincere. "Go away, Laurel Vane Warrick," he said. "For your own sake. Out of kindness to us." He watched me for a moment. "For the love of God," he said quietly, "if that is all that will move you. Go home." He turned on his heel and stalked away, loosing the dog, who followed him without a glance behind.

Thunderstruck, I stood there until they had vanished. I felt more icy of skin and bone than the air-conditioning could account for. Sheridan Todd had left a venomous warning to hang there in the many-tinted dusk like a tangible fog. Unconsciously I rubbed my hands across my bare arms to warm them.

"Get thee to a library, go," said a voice so like Todd's that I looked to see whether he had come in again by some other door. "It isn't bad advice. I think you should take it, ma'am." One of the armchairs swung to face me on its swiveled base. The occupant pressed his fingertips together and smiled at me. "I wasn't eavesdropping. I was asleep. Sorry. Didn't like to interrupt when he'd wakened me. I take it Sherry wrote you not to come. Might have done it myself if I'd thought of it."

"Perhaps you'll tell me why, since he won't," I snapped.

"He seemed to think you'd know." The young man unfolded himself and stood up. He was a little taller than the first one, and quite good looking, as slim as a weasel and apparently as boneless, for he moved with a sinuous beauty. His nose and jaw were long and lean, his hair curly and almost black, his eyes the light bright blue of Egyptian enamel. He came and shook hands with me, his fingers long and flexible and pleasantly warm where mine were glacial. "My name's Daniel Cavanaugh. Sibella, your employer, is my grandaunt and Sherry's grandmother. You see, we're all related here. Even Pierce Poole stems from the decayed English branch of the family tree. Callingwood, Todd, Poole, Cavanaugh, Abbott—all Sablecrofts together."

"How do you do," I said, wondering who Abbott might be. "Why should I leave?"

He inspected my face carefully. "Pierce said you were damned pretty, and you are," he said. "This is a strange enough house, Mrs. Warrick, but I don't believe you scare easily, do you? All right, wait a few days and see. Perhaps you'll remain beyond the wicked influences, and mind your own business, and survive nicely, though I doubt it."

"You both talk as though the place were crawling with danger."

"Psychically it may be; depends on your temperament. It's also possible that we have a dangerous lunatic on the loose. We'll see how he or she is affected by your presence. Promise me one thing?"

"If it's reasonable."

"Should you be in—shall we say *doubt,* about anything, come to me. I'll try to help." I mistrusted that suggestion at once, and he sensed it. "Or Pierce Poole," he said. "He's the true British granite under that flab."

"And Mr. Todd?"

"Make up your own mind about him. And oh . . . look out for shadows."

I regarded him with what I hoped was serene remoteness, although a better actress than I might have found it hard to seem aloof while recovering from a fit of trembling. "Mr. Cavanaugh, you and your cousin both talk like the opening of a bad horror movie out of the early forties."

"You don't believe that occasionally life *is* a rather poorly plotted horror movie?"

"I never did till now. 'Leave the dead to the dead,' 'mad people, mad shadows,' 'a dangerous lunatic,' 'wicked, psychic danger'—when do you bring on the sinister old family retainer and the clutching hand from behind the tapestry?" I asked him scornfully.

He laughed. It was a mischievous, charming sound, like the merriment of an elongated leprechaun, which he resembled. "Quoted all together they do sound ridiculous, Mrs. Warrick. But don't you believe that under the wrong circumstances a house may indeed be a little mad, let's say from an accumulation of harmful emotions? Or that a close-knit family may be dangerous, even unintentionally, to the intruder?"

"Are *you* intent on harming me?" I challenged.

"Good Lord, no!"

"And Pierce made me feel welcome." He hadn't, really, but he'd seemed to try.

"Well, well," said Mr. Cavanaugh, "then forget it. Soon we'll have a long, analytical, profoundly reasonable conversation on haunted houses, haunted families: causes of, defenses against, and cures for. Meanwhile, it's nice to have you with us, whatever Sherry says. I understand you have a cat. I love cats. I look forward to meeting him." He gave a parting wave of one long hand. "Oh, and by the way—there *is* a sinister old family retainer."

"You're joking!"

"No, no," he said over his shoulder with a grin that seemed broader than his lank face could hold, "I always speak truth, I'm too guileless to lie successfully." Then he too was gone, whistling.

Not the most everyday lot in the world, the Sablecrofts, as Pierce Poole had said.

I spent a while reading the titles of books, occasionally taking one out and riffling through its pages. Slowly I began to forget the warnings of Messrs. Todd, Cavanaugh, and Bogart, and to grow excited. I had never dared dream that I would one day hold some of these volumes in my hands, let alone be able to study them. There were rarities here for which enthusiasts would have paid extortionate prices. And this was a small part of the collection, obviously, since there was another room called the library. For the sake of working with these books, if for nothing else, I was already glad that I'd come. . . .

It had all begun three weeks ago, when I'd read the classified advertisement in the back pages of the *Library Journal* under "Positions Open—Southeast." A librarian was wanted, live-in, full-time though short-term; comprehensive knowledge of the cinema necessary, preferably from within that profession; salary generous; write qualifications to Sablecroft Hall, numbered-street address, Blackbeard's Bayou, St. Petersburg, Florida. When I'd answered the ad, wording it cautiously, and received by special delivery a long letter of explanation and a stunning pay offer in the beautiful, ageless italic script of a Mrs. Sibella Callingwood, I'd gone to my head librarian and resigned.

She'd read part of the letter aloud. "'Extensive book collection on motion pictures, total number unknown; a library of audio tapes on the same subject, about two thousand reels; a large assemblage of manuscripts, papers, films, memorabilia, diaries, and holographs, in both calligraphy and cacography; and, well, *things.*'" She'd peered at me over her gold-rimmed half-eyes earnestly. "It's certainly in your line."

"How much notice do you need?" I'd asked.

"Two weeks will do." So more letters had flown back and forth, the last with a check for my flight ticket, and here I was.

And here, too, was the huge harlequin Great Dane, lying some ten feet away in a sphinx pose and watching me as enigmatically as the sphinx herself is said to do. What was his name? It occurred to me that Pierce had used at least half a dozen names, and Sheridan Todd another. How many of the brutes were kept here? "Roderick," I said tentatively. "Roderick?" He cocked his head. "Come on, boy." He rose, appeared to think, and padded off through an open arch in the north wall that led to what looked like the dining room.

Then the teatime gong went off, resounding deep and hollow in the great hall. I followed the dog and discovered another two-story room, this one cheerful with the north light of many windows high in the wall and paneled halfway up with satiny maple, the rest covered with a figured maize paper. A table resembling a banquet board surrounded by a dozen large chairs bore a variety of filled platters, bottles, utensils, and crockery. No one was there, not even a servant: only myself and the Dane.

I stood waiting for some minutes. Then Daniel Cavanaugh thrust his long head in a door and said, "Look here, Mrs. Warrick, we're all up to our ears in a job, so would you just go ahead without us? Sorry to be so inhospitable, but we'll see you at dinner. Eight-thirty suit you? Fine!" and withdrew.

I filled a plate with hot buttered scones, caraway cheese, radishes, peppers, and a few slices of roast smoked turkey; opened a bottle of Perrier water and sat down. The harlequin took up a post about six feet off. After having a few bites of scone, I offered him a piece of turkey. He looked at me sideways, his dark eyes suspicious, and would not touch the meat. I ate it myself. His cool gaze indicated that *that* didn't prove anything.

I had finished the plateful of luscious food and the bottle of bubbly water, and was having a small glass of cream sherry, when I began to sense that someone was watching me. Turning, I saw but did not quite believe in a life-size oil portrait of Erich von Stroheim in Prussian uniform. Eccentricity takes numberless forms, and in a house full of thousands of books on cinema it was not really strange to find a painting of one of the greatest directors in history. But the monocle in the right eye was a piece of real glass.

I don't know precisely what it was about that ridiculous lens, yet as I sat half-turned on my chair, exchanging stares with arrogant old Erich, who'd been painted with the pupils centered so that his eyes would follow you around the room, I began to feel eerily frightened in a more clammy and less rational way than the direct threat of Sheridan Todd had produced. It seemed to me at that moment that the enormous house was impregnated with an atmosphere like that of *Alice in Wonderland,* where nothing was what it seemed; where animals watched you in preternatural silence, and people appeared from thin air to speak to you and vanish, never to be seen again. Where the air was like that in a bubble of ice, yet you could sense the sweltering heat without, ready to rage in at the first pin-prick. Where a really first-class oil portrait was desecrated by someone with an eight-year-old's notion of humor. Where every door had its lock and bolt or bar, and the very grounds were armored behind a thick blue wall. Where you were welcomed by a distracted Edwardian gentleman and ordered to leave by an enigmatic boor who probably drank—certainly scowled—too much. Where Humphrey Bogart snarled at you, and he twenty-three years dead. Where you were left alone, but had never felt less secluded.

I set down my glass of half-tasted wine and fled, almost running, to my own room. If the dog had pursued me or if I'd met another human soul, I believe I might have shrieked. I flung myself across the bed, and in a few minutes was sound asleep. Remarkably enough, I did not dream.

I AWOKE SLOWLY WITH THE PRICKLY FEELING THAT I WASN'T alone. I remembered that I had not bolted the door. Gradually I opened my eyes, to see the cat Micajah washing himself on the black-and-yellow armchair. I sighed with relief, and he paused in midlick to glower across at me. I checked my watch: a little after eight. "Are you hungry?" I asked him. He frowned and arched his ears as though I were some ancient enemy. I sat up, swinging my legs over the side. "Come on, forgive me," I wheedled. Gathering his huff about him like a cloak, he jumped to the floor and marched under the bed.

"Going to be a long pout, then." I unpacked the bag that held his personal dish and a box of his favorite dry food and put it beside the drinking bowl. I'd just finished dressing for dinner when the gong crashed out, brassily spectral and, I noticed this time, a little vague and furry around the edges, like an old sound too often repeated.

"That's a strange thought," I said aloud. I'd always talked to myself, but during the last two years I had pretended that I was addressing Micajah, possibly to stave off the fear that I was growing crotchety from too much living alone. "What does an *old* noise sound like?" The cat did not reply, but dwelt in silence under the bed.

The great hall seemed rather less gloomy now, I suppose because of my extra sleep. It was really splendid in its sunless way. On the balcony, looking out over it with hidden eyes, stood a suit of sixteenth-century parade armor, etched and fire-gilt, its ventail and visor projecting in that stupidly malignant fashion characteristic of medieval helmets. As I passed this grotesque image, it said suddenly, in a crisp, rasping, familiar voice, "Now you're a silly little girl. Here you're in the lion's mouth."

To say that I jumped is an understatement. Then, nailed in my tracks, I stared and stared, recollecting Bogie's voice ringing out earlier. At last I shook myself and said angrily, "Melodramatic hokum!" to dispel the Wonderland aura.

I looked all around but saw no one on either level. Then, on a hunch, I walked back toward my room. Within three steps the speech growled out again. I had triggered the beam of a photoelectric eye—the gadget that opens doors when you pass it. And this had set off a looped audiotape on which someone had recorded one sentence each from two speeches out of the movie *Caesar and Cleopatra*. The voice was that of Claude Rains, playing the first role ever to earn an actor a million dollars—his finest hour, dramatically as well as financially.

I searched for a moment, and found the source of the photoelectric beam, low in the wall opposite the armor. Someone's idea of fun, childish, mildly amusing. Except that so far as I could tell, nobody had witnessed its success. The player would have to visualize the effect.

I walked past the metal figure once more, and Rains' marvelous tones rolled out. "Now you're a silly little girl. Here you're in the lion's mouth!"

Only then did it occur to me that again I was being warned off. I'd been too startled and engrossed in the mechanics of the trick to realize what was being said to me.

"Yes, Caesar," I murmured, "and I'm staying, too." Then I went downstairs and into the dining room.

"Here is Mrs. Warrick now!" exclaimed Pierce Poole. He was bent over a hot cart, agitating an enormous pan rapidly over the flames as he sautéed a savory mess. "Sibella Callingwood, I give you our new librarian, who comes to us from the outside world." I looked toward the head of the table.

She was tall and lean and imperial. Under a tight cap of dark chestnut hair was a pale face like a handsomely skin-covered skull, networked with tiny wrinkles but somehow disdaining them. She had a sharp, beautifully carved nose and hard-looking eyes of a deep gray. The firm mouth had obviously never gone slack for long with any weak emotion. Her gaze, returning mine, was level, and friendly in moderation.

"How do you do, Mrs. Warrick. Please sit here on my left, so we can become acquainted. My, you're prettier than I'd expected. Why should one envisage librarians as plain and old-fashioned, even mousy? I've no idea. I trust the house is comfortable for you?" Like Mr. Poole, she seemed to speak in shoals of sentences without pause. "If we were to let in that damnable tropic air, it would be as detrimental to the books and films as the miasma of a swamp. You must dress warmly and take plenty of vitamin C. But then you come to us from New England. You don't crave the wet warmth, do you?"

"No," I got in.

" 'Fear no more the heat o' the sun,' " murmured somebody.

"Not in *this* house," another agreed.

I sat down. The plates were Wedgwood Queen's Ware, the silver massive, the linen damask blinding white, the crystal heavy and brilliant. Sibella Callingwood did not stint.

"Have you met everyone?"

"The gentlemen," I said.

"Well, the child there is Wendy Abbott," she said. Her voice was a whiskey contralto, like a fine old viola da gamba. "A second or third cousin of the boys, once or twice removed."

This was a dark-haired girl with lavender-blue eyes, who just missed being lovely because of a perpetually half-open mouth which gave her a vacuous look. She was about my own age. We smiled and said hello.

"How does Sablecroft Hall strike you by this time?" asked Pierce across his huge frying pan.

"It's incredible," I said. "Even the armor talks."

"You blasted buffoons," husked Sibella, looking round the table. "I hope you weren't frightened?" she asked me.

The slender Daniel Cavanaugh said quietly, "Mrs. Warrick is not easily spooked, Aunt Sibella. I imagine she talked back to it," and glanced at his cousin, Mr. Todd, and chuckled.

"No, I wasn't frightened. There's either a medium-size player behind the breastplate with a speaker in the helmet, or a miniature cassette machine in back of the visor, with an endless circle of tape timed to click on for one revolution and repeat the same speech whenever the photoelectric beam is broken."

Pierce shouted with approval. "Brava, Laurel! A keen and analytical mind, by heaven!" Removing the delicious-smelling concoction into a hot serving dish, he deglazed the mahogany residue with what the label said was an excellent sherry. "Which speech was it?"

"Rains' Caesar—"

"Ah! Before dinner, so *I* should have chosen his hearty 'Peacocks' brains, Apollodorus!' and Stewart Granger's answer, 'I prefer nightingales' tongues.' Was that it? One could do it even on that tiny machine because the tape moves slowly, one and seven-eighths ips."

I told them what the suit of armor had said to me.

Sibella Callingwood leaned forward, her tall frame absolutely stiff, and said fiercely, "Which of you had the damned effrontery to do that to an invited guest?" No one moved; even Pierce's busy hands froze above the sauce in the pan. "Daniel?"

"Not I, Aunt."

"Sherry? Wendy?" They shook their heads. "Insolence!" said Sibella hoarsely. "I'll have no more of it! Lion's mouth, for God's sake. Pay no attention to it, Mrs. Warrick. A dim prank. We suffer from them spasmodically. Look here, shall I call you Laurel?" The hard gray eyes rested on my face as she slowly went bolt upright again. " 'Mrs. Warrick' is terribly formal when we'll be working closely for so long."

"Laurel, please. And you?"

" 'Mrs. Callingwood' will do nicely."

"Informality is a one-way street," said her grandson, Sheridan Todd, languidly.

"You're very young to be a widow, Laurel," she said, ignoring him. "In my day, of course, we expected to outlive our husbands by a matter of thirty or forty years."

"Aunt Sibella has—" began the girl Wendy, and was overridden.

"I have lasted considerably more than half a century longer than Mr. Callingwood, and enjoyed every minute of it. I don't imply that *you* are, Laurel, I was only anticipating Wendy. Mr. Callingwood perished in the Great War, doubtless while doing something supremely irrational. Was your late husband a librarian too?"

"Yes, we took our masters' together before we were married in seventy-seven. He died a year later." I heard myself say it steadily. I'd wondered if I could.

A narrow, long hand, exquisitely kept, rested on mine for a moment. "I'm sorry for that, Laurel. Those aren't empty words. Eventually you're bound to be told that I have no heart, only a well-preserved icicle in my breast. You won't believe it. No," she said, watching me, "I rather think you'll know better. I like those clear hazel eyes of yours, my dear, I fancy they see farther through a stone facade than most. You wrote this to me, but now will you tell the others, why you're so particularly qualified for the business of cataloguing my library?"

Watching Pierce drench the sauté with the condensed sauce, I said, "My grandfather was Alfred Vane, the film editor."

"So what?" said Wendy.

Pierce scowled at her. "Alfred Vane ranks with Jimmy Smith, Dorothy Arzner, Robert Wilson. They were film editors. Quite possibly Laurel's grandfather was the only craftsman fit to make a fourth in their exalted company. But then one should not expect anyone under the age of fifty to have heard of the great pioneer film editors. Unless it's Sherry here, who's quite bright about such matters in his vague fashion."

"Vane, yes, none finer," said Mr. Todd, a little grudgingly.

Sibella began to eat as the rest of us were served. "Pierce, this is divine. Daniel, open the Taittinger's. You see, you people, I knew Laurel's grandfather, and when she wrote about the job, I wanted her at once. Good blood." She gestured at me with her fork. "Alfred Vane came down here in nineteen thirty-three, to stay at Sablecroft Hall and sit at my father's feet and learn. I'm sure you know that." I nodded. "Mind you, they'd both retired by then, but they were flint and steel, hard, sharp, both still gathering knowledge, both ornery, opinionated cusses. Shout! They'd roar at each other for hours. I still recall one argument over who'd invented the fade-out, Griffith or Bitzer. They were both wrong, it was Méliès who did it, and Griffith admitted it; but tell them that!"

"Pierce," I said, swallowing, "this *is* superb. What is it?"

"Veal Laughton," said the fat man proudly. "A trifling concoction of mine, christened in honor of Charles. It's based on lemon-butter veal, with audacious modifications. I prefer a light red wine to accompany it, but Sibella's partial to chilled magnums of Taittinger with everything. Not that I'm averse to a touch of swank now and again—"

"Swank! Damned if it's swank, you discourteous slug," she said, with great good humor. "I love champagne and champagne loves me." She laughed, throwing back her head and pronouncing *ha, ha, ha* distinctly on a descending scale. Oddly, it seemed an expression of genuine amusement. "Laurel, I'm eighty. When I was about your age, I swore that I'd give up the pleasures of the palate when they began to lose their savor. In spite of the slight deterioration—more like a mellowing, really—that comes with middle age, my taste buds persevere. Thank God!"

I looked at her. It was almost impossible to credit her with eighty years of living: She sat straight and narrow as a poplar, head high, her whole frame radiating pride and discipline.

"You remind me ever so faintly of your grandfather," she told me. "Touch of the same blast-your-eyes expression. Guts. Laurel, you may be the only soul at this table who isn't scared dust-dry of me. I like that." She drank a remarkable quantity of champagne in a swallow. "You're not to think of taking advantage of that, though. I'll fire you if you aren't as good as you claim."

"I'd expect that."

"Ah, professional! And that's the highest praise in my book."

"Speaking of professionals," said Pierce intently, "we must all know at once, who are your favorite actors? I believe that's the question uppermost in all our minds, eh?"

I saw Sheridan Todd grin sardonically. I put down my fork. "Robert Newton, Laird Cregar, Wallace Beery, Edna May Oliver," I said briskly. "Bogie and Rains, if that pleases the tape magician, Una O'Connor, Huston, McQueen—"

"Stephen?" asked Pierce.

"Butterfly. And Katharine Hepburn and Donat and Colman and Landi, and Sir C. Aubrey and Martita Hunt. For starters."

"Capital choices, capital!" He beamed at me. "First the characters, the grotesques, the magnificent originals, and then the great gentry! Are you quite certain you're not fifty years old, Laurel Warrick?"

"I'm twenty-five, but I've seen a movie for just about every day I've lived. It was a requirement for belonging to our family. Grandfather, after all—and Dad was a stunt man. He was killed making a picture."

Sibella frowned, and "Oh dear, I'd no idea," said Pierce Poole, looking really shocked. "But it's how a chap would wish to go, in his boots. How did it happen?"

"It was a fire gag," I said. "The timing was off, or the rig defective, and he inhaled flame."

"How ghastly," Pierce whispered, his round bulging eyes aglisten. "That's a touchy gag at best. I think I would actually prefer the loose gags if I were in the profession myself. Of course, I can't drive a car, so there's no question of the choice ever coming up."

"What a double you'd have made for Greenstreet!" said Daniel Cavanaugh, admiring the notion.

"Yes, shouldn't I have? Well, your actors now, Laurel. I'll wager no one has a topper for that list."

They all looked at one another. Then from over my shoulder an aristocratic voice said through its nose, "You're wise in your generation. We must have a long talk."

If Bogie, and the old armor speaking in the voice of Caesar, hadn't prepared me, I'd have been too startled to carry it off; but I never hesitated. "Ernest Thesiger, *Bride of Frankenstein,* nineteen thirty-five," I said casually.

There was a dead silence, so that for the first time I was aware of some giant air-conditioner purring away in the distance. Then Sheridan Todd said, biting off the words, "Good Lord, another Poole!" and Sibella laughed, *ha ha ha.*

"What's wrong with a second orderly mind in the house?" Pierce demanded. "Give Laurel some more champagne, she's earned it."

"Thanks, I haven't finished this."

"No head?" Wendy said in a rather nasty voice.

"I like wine in moderation," I said, trying not to sound priggish.

"Pity," said Daniel, grinning. "You've never lived in a house like this, where the wine flows like wine."

"No one's ever lived in a house like this since the world began," said Wendy, staring at me. "You'll find out," she added, in her voice a definite warning, perhaps a threat.

"I hope you appreciate secret passages," said Daniel.

"And can tolerate spasmodic attacks of disjointed dialogue clamoring at you when you least expect them," added Sibella. "We have several thousand movies on tape, and the children enjoy playing with their hidden machines."

"But exquisite foodstuffs, mind," said Pierce. "Always the culinary jewels at the end of a hard day's work!"

"And numerous other good things," said Sibella, closing the subject firmly. "Tomorrow you'll be shown over the Hall before you begin your job, Laurel. There's nothing really *strange* here. A toast to Sablecroft Hall," she said, raising her filled glass.

We drank, and another disembodied voice, tantalizingly familiar, came ghosting at us from a mirror on the east wall. "To this household! To life! And to all brave illusion!"

Pierce said, "Well? Well?" looking at me.

"I know. The accent throws me . . . Fredric March," I managed.

"The flick?"

"I don't know."

"Thank heaven, not quite another Pierce Poole," said Daniel.

"*Death Takes a Holiday,* nineteen thirty-four," supplied the plump man.

"I haven't seen it in years," I said lamely.

Pierce rose to prepare a dessert involving pear halves, sugar, and warm white crème de menthe, which eventually was flambéed spectacularly and identified as Poires Gable. I asked whether he always planned his meals around dishes named for actors who had played in a particular picture together, and Pierce affirmed it. "System, tidiness of mind," he said. "Qualities sadly lacking in these times. Had I prepared a salad, I would have used—" and he paused, expectant.

"Franchot Tone Sauce?" I hazarded.

"Dressing Digges."

"Nothing lost, Mr. Christian," I said automatically. Daniel smiled, Wendy looked blank. I felt a brief surge of that sneaky pleasure that comes from sharing an in-joke. Dudley Digges, of course, had played the drunken old surgeon to Laughton's Captain

Bligh. It served me right when Wendy said that she couldn't remember what Dressing Digges tasted like, but that she did know it was based on cardamom, oil, and vinegar; and would Pierce perhaps make it tomorrow night, as a special favor, to be eaten with Pork Chow Coop? By the time I'd figured out that Gary Cooper and Dudley Digges had both had roles in *The General Died at Dawn,* the conversation had left me far behind.

Sibella said quietly in my ear, "Never underestimate her, Laurel, in anything," and I knew that she'd followed my thoughts exactly. I smiled feebly at my hostess. Was I that easy to read? "Things are seldom what they seem," she murmured.

"Skim milk masquerades as cream," added Sheridan Todd, "and vice versa." His tone and the look he gave me were malicious. *He* had rigged up those first two tapes to frighten me, I was sure.

It astonishes me to look back upon that first evening at Sablecroft Hall and realize how devoid I remained of any sensible fear. I had been given warning—obliquely by the cabdriver, flatly by Mr. Todd, pleasantly by Daniel Cavanaugh, ominously by a couple of tape recorders, and in a sort of mean prophecy by Wendy Abbott. I was unwelcome here. Yet, instead of being on my guard and watchful for further indications of menace, I found myself in a fascinating argument over dessert about symbolic meanings in the images of Orson Welles' *Lady From Shanghai,* which was about as far as one could go past the silly little game we'd played with our flashy quotations and trumpery identifications.

This turn of the talk delighted me, especially so because it had been a long time since I'd conversed seriously with anyone in my own field. I felt myself drawn into their family circle, and as the summer sky beyond the high windows had gone flat black, we seemed to have consolidated into a kind of unit, compacted in a thickened atmosphere of bright light and harmony of ideas, snug in this room behind our solid walls. A great breadth of imagination was at play around the table now, as the great dogs wandered back and forth, giving the lofty room the aspect of a garrisoned castle.

At eleven, Sibella rose and said good night, having first told me to report to the library at half past eight in the morning. We scattered, Daniel and Sheridan Todd to the great hall for a last drink, the rest of us to our quarters. In mine, pleasantly warm now at 77°, I undressed, picked up a nightgown, and went into the bathroom to get ready for bed.

A couple of minutes later I opened the door on a quite different scene. The soft white bulb in my bedlamp had been changed for a dull red globe that threw a wash of thin scarlet like blood over my sheets and pillows. Two big old-fashioned revolvers had been wired upright to a board, which lay across the foot of the bed so that the muzzles were trained on the place where my head would have rested had I been in bed. Instead of my head, though, a large color photograph lay on the pillow.

I looked at this singular setup, then went to the door and bolted it. My mind for the moment was as nearly blank as it could be, and I felt no fear, only irritation at the fact that someone had followed me into my room and played this apparently pointless trick.

I lifted the small board with the pair of guns. They were cap pistols, imitation Colts, both cocked.

Two guns pointing at you—someone's trademark. Another movie reference. Oh! William S. Hart, naturally, the lean hard face above the twin equalizers, world-renowned in its day as a symbol of menace. Was it another piece of intimidation? Or just a bad joke?

Leaning over, I picked up the photograph. Against a background of stone pillars, instantly recognizable as the library of Moorington, Connecticut, a girl stared at the camera. Blondish hair in a long bob framed a face with prominent cheekbones, bangs touching the heavy brows. A wide full-lipped mouth, a good enough nose a little longer and higher in the bridge than beauty would demand, a broad jaw. Quizzical expression, as if she were about to ask, "Who the devil are you?"

It was a photograph of myself, and I had never seen it before; although this photo was no older than a month, because I was wearing my new beige dress.

Consternation gripped me now, and I hurled the cap-pistol contraption one way and the picture another and scrambled into bed. I clicked off the odious red light and snuggled down beneath the cold silky sheet and light blanket to think.

Someone had gone so far as to have my picture taken before I'd come down to Florida. Why? Surely not for *this* childish charade? Why, he—or she—must have hired someone to snap me! Possibly even a private detective. Intolerable! And what else had they done, what insufferable prying and snooping into my affairs? I felt myself flush with anger. My life was as open a book as anyone's could be, I had nothing to hide, but the notion of somebody spying on me was unendurable.

With little to go on except for Sherry Todd's notice that I must return home, I worried at the problem until I fell asleep.

I remember that I woke once during the night, unsure for a second of where I was (the blackness was almost total), to hear a small steady grinding noise somewhere beyond my bed. Crunch crunch crunch . . . it was Micajah at his bowl, secretly breaking his fast. I didn't speak; it would have embarrassed him to discover that I knew he was eating. He prided himself on being able to stay mad and hungry longer than any other cat in the world.

I fell asleep again.

By the next morning the great hall had begun to seem familiar; which was odd, for I hadn't examined any of the contents of the glass cases or cabinets, or even looked directly at any of the statues, busts, fantoccini, and bronzes that formed such a crowd of still presences.

Again I walked straight through them into the dining room, and to the door that I knew led to the library, followed all the way by one of those damned, silent, ominous Danes. I knocked and went in, closing the door before he could get through after me. It was the steel-blue beast with the pale eyes, and he seemed to be keeping watch on me for his master, the enigmatic Sheridan Todd.

Or else it was *one* of the steel-blue brutes. I had no idea how many dogs lived here. They were like a gang of lurking, interchangeable mutes, and they stared at me in such a condescending, sinister way that I was beginning to thoroughly dislike them, though I ordinarily love all animals.

"Good morning," said a ragged chorus. The family had already gathered, and I felt like an indolent drone, even though I'd been punctual. I resolved to get up half an hour earlier tomorrow. Sibella sat perpendicular on a Victorian throne of smooth unornamented teak, a cup of coffee in her hand. She wore a superb black silk caftan splashed with gold lace, which suited her wonderfully. Pierce and Daniel were high on a couple of sliding library ladders, Wendy lay on her stomach with her face pushed into a book, Sheridan Todd was carrying a double armload of volumes toward me. He looked as though he'd stayed up too late and drunk too much, and was bitter at being out of bed. The rest of them absolutely glowed with vigor and alertness, even the dark-haired girl with her book.

I put on the brightest face I could manage—difficult enough, for I'm not really a morning person—and clicked across a parquet floor whose geometrically patterned inlaid woods were polished to a fantastic gloss. "Good morning, Mrs. Callingwood. Sorry, I overslept."

"You were told eight thirty; it's eight thirty."

"I simply hate to be last. I won't be again."

"Suit yourself. You won't need the Dewey decimal system, there's only one basic subject here. How'll you go about the job of organizing?"

"I don't know," I said. "I'll have to examine the books and ask a lot of questions first. Especially, what's the purpose of the cataloguing? Is the collection to go ultimately to a public library, or be donated to a foundation, or set up by itself as a historical library somewhere?"

"I never heard such drivel in my life," said Sibella, and Wendy looked up and frowned at me. "Get yourself some breakfast, there's coffee, tea, rolls, and things over there, and sit down beside me while we go into matters. A public library!" she snorted, and shook her head as at a question proposed by the village idiot.

With an apricot Danish and a cup of strong tea, I settled myself on the parquetry beside her chair.

"Give a lot if I were that limber," she said, nodding at my crossed legs. "Never was. They didn't encourage young ladies to fold up on the floor in nineteen fifteen—slacks let you do many things we couldn't. Yours is a lucky generation in several ways, Laurel, though I wouldn't trade with you for all your youth and beauty and freedom."

"Nor I with you, for all your strength and experience."

"That's good. You'll age fast enough on your own. How about my money? Trade a year or two of your life for that?"

"No."

"I believe you. Good." She looked at me more sharply. "You aren't really a beauty, are you? You give the impression of prettiness without being actually pretty. I think it's your nose, that at least is damned fine. And you've got good laugh lines, though I haven't seen you smile much. Are you unhappy?"

"No. I suppose I haven't laughed a great deal in the last two years. I haven't thought much about it."

"Still mourning?"

"No. I feel sad for his sake when I remember Steve, but my existence isn't glum." I ate, thinking, and she waited. Wendy eyed me over her book as if I were some lavish-legged creature crawled in from the swamp. "We had a good marriage," I said to Sibella, "and it would have lasted, but you can't drizzle your life away after a wonderful part of it dies. My friends don't laugh for the joy of living. My husband *did,* and before him, Dad; and so I did."

"Haven't laughed aloud once in two years?" Sibella demanded.

Then I did chuckle. "Yes! Usually with my cat. Just not as often as I should." I looked up at her. We were far enough from the others that this conversation could be private. "I haven't known many people who crowed for the sheer pleasure of being alive, Mrs. Callingwood. But I think that, sometimes, you do."

"What a pleasant thing to say, Laurel. Not that I encourage personal comments, mind you, but a sincere compliment is welcome. You're damned right I rejoice," she said forcefully. "To fling up your hat, to let out a burst of merriment now and then for the pure fun of living, that's a triumph of the spirit. Fewer people realize that fact every year. We've become a nation of glum, long-faced pessimists."

"Maybe you have more reason to be happy?"

"Laurel Warrick," she said coolly, bending a little toward me and lowering her voice to a husky sibilation, "if half the folk in the country had *my* curse, they'd never grin again, let alone laugh."

"Your curse?"

"Silly melodramatic word. Remember, I had a Victorian infancy. But one can't say 'my burden,' after all. Not when one's bragging. No," she said, thinking, "I'm not bragging. I was created as I am and it's my good luck, not to my credit at all, that I can live comfortably beneath a Damoclean sword. I find too much in life to be glad about . . . Pollyanna!" she shouted, with a snort of wry amusement.

"Hayley Mills," said Pierce Poole on his ladder, "honorary Academy Award, 1960." He looked down and gave me what used to be called an unfathomable stare.

"All I mean," said Sibella, quiet again, "is that whatever trouble dogs you, you should laugh now and then anyhow. Either with gratitude to the gods, or in their teeth. I'm glad you laugh aloud with your cat. When shall I meet it?"

"I imagine that Micajah will come out and act half-civilized in a day or two. He's under my bed, still grumping." I went to refill my teacup and came back. "Your curse?" I said.

"Oh, never mind that. But you ought to know, because you're to be one of us. Somebody wants me dead, and they're trying to kill me." Her face revealed nothing.

"To kill you," I said blankly, for a moment wondering if perhaps she were the lunatic Daniel had mentioned.

"You will not discuss it with any of them. I haven't admitted awareness of the fact—except to Pierce, who doesn't count. He is as dependable as the coming of the heat in Florida."

I glanced up at the fat man again. There was a certain incoherency of manner about him that did not reassure me on his dependability. "Why is someone trying to kill you?"

"Because they want me dead," she said reasonably.

"For money?"

"I think, for hatred." She waved her hand, impatient, dismissing an unimportant topic. "There's still plenty of laughter to be used up, and no reason to sulk. That's all I meant."

Just an example in a philosophic monologue? I doubted it. I dismissed the notion that she was crazy. Sibella Callingwood, I believed, said precisely as much as she meant to say, and radiated cool sanity even as she spoke of improbable things. She wanted me to—what? To know she was to be pitied? Not she. She'd scorn pity. To be aware that the warnings I'd had yesterday might be serious? She knew only of the one. But that might be it. *Did* we have a dangerous crackpot roaming Sablecroft Hall? She and the two men appeared to agree on that.

"Now the books," said Sibella firmly. "You asked the ultimate purpose of their cataloguing. It's for the convenience of me and mine. Give this collection to a public library, to be dogeared and stolen and underlined, and chucked away when some fool thinks it's outdated? Nonsense! These are *mine,*" she said, gesturing with both long hands at the vast wall of shelves behind her. "When I'm gone, twenty or thirty years from now, they'll be Sherry's. There'll always be Sablecrofts to care for 'em, even though none of the younger generation *has* had the foresight to spawn yet. Anyway! I want to be able to *find* things, to know what I have and be able to lay my hands on anything at once. Especially when I grow old and take to reading a good deal," said this astonishing woman.

"I understand. I only thought that perhaps you meant to make the collection available to scholars. It would be a kind of immortality. The Sibella Callingwood Library of the Cinema."

"Rubbish! This is my immortality I'm living through right this year, this minute, and I intend to relish every second of it, even if someone's trying to shorten it for me drastically. I don't *want* a lot of grubby oafs pawing in my books. I couldn't care less about 'em. Let 'em stay ignorant of how Lombard died and how many versions Capra shot for the last scene in *Meet John Doe.* If that's too selfish for your stomach, say so. I can buy a cataloguer anywhere."

"Mrs. Callingwood, I'm still deeply in debt for college loans, I can't get my old job back, and the market for librarians isn't booming these days, but that isn't why I say this: From what I've seen of your library, I'd work on it for room and board, period."

"A splendid omen. You'll do a bang-up job, then. Sherry," she called, "bring me coffee! Now then, what will you do first? Examine the lot? Arrange them? Whatever it is, you've only to ask—demand!—and anyone will help you, with hard labor or information or whatever. They all have their jobs around here, nobody loafs, but your needs come first. What will you do? Say."

"I want a good general idea of the total contents," I said. "That'll take a week, I'd guess, for the books."

"You can save the diaries, manuscripts, and so forth till later."

I looked across at the great double-storied north wall, which was entirely covered with built-in shelving of several exquisitely beautiful woods ranging from dark red to light yellow-gray. "Yes. I think there'll have to be an enormous amount of cross-indexing. You don't want a simple listing of your books by author and title, you want groupings by subject, cross-references on personalities—stars, directors, producers, writers, moguls—and individual films and studios and countries of origin. Am I right?"

"And topics: symbolism, equipment development, styles in direction, a hundred more," said Sheridan Todd, who'd come with a fresh cup of coffee for his grandmother. "If you're up to that?"

"I am," I said shortly.

"Time will tell."

"It often does, doesn't it?" I retorted just as nastily.

"One for her, Sherry. Don't you pick on Laurel, she can handle herself as well as I can," said Sibella. "What's wrong? You nursing a hangover?"

He shook his head. "I resent the whole idea of your Mrs. Warrick, dear," he told her. "I could do the same job for nothing, as could Daniel and Pierce. Hardly a crying need here for a librarian."

"I think there is, and that's what counts," she said, the steel ringing beneath the big dark tone of her voice. "If there weren't, the matter would have been handled long ago. By the way," she said, staring up at his fattish, thickly mustached face with its heavy tan (the only tan among them, I suddenly realized, and wondered why), "you're to do whatever Laurel wishes, you know. Haul books to and fro, build new shelves where she wants them, anything. And you, Laurel, you're not to be timid about ordering this lot around."

"I'm not generally timid."

"Not afraid of anything, this one," said Sheridan Todd. The sneer was open.

"I didn't say that! I'm a little frightened by your dogs, for instance. One followed me this morning, looking as though he longed to gnaw on my liver."

"They won't hurt you," he said briefly. "Not unless you attack one of us."

"What about my cat?"

"We'll introduce them and find out. We'll be careful, and I think they'll accept him. We've had cats before and no harm came to them." I heard another sound in his voice: the sneer gone, a genuine concern surfacing. The man cared for animals. I was glad, for I had to live in the same house with him for a long time and would hate to dislike him in toto.

"I kept seven cats," said Sibella. "The best cats in the world, I used to tell them, and by gad they were! I'll never have another. But yours is welcome, Laurel. What's his name, again?"

"He has three," I said.

"'I tell you a cat must have three different names,'" said Wendy, startling me. I glanced down and back and saw that she wore soft moccasins of deerhide. She had moved across the wood in utter silence. "Donat recorded that."

"It's also in a book," said Sheridan Todd dryly. "What's the one that the family use daily?"

"Micajah."

"Unusual. And the special one?"

"Attila-the-Hun-the-Scourge-of-God."

"And the third name?" asked Sibella.

Sheridan knew Eliot's poem if she didn't. "'The cat himself knows, and will never confess.' It's like the camel, who's the only creature to know and keep secret the hundredth name of Allah."

"Is your puss as terrible as his namesake?"

"He thinks he is."

"As to the built-in shelves," she said, wheeling us back to the proper subject, "I want them in here. I want to get the books out of the great hall and my quarters and have them all together. Where do you fancy the shelves, Laurel? We can put them above those on the west wall, or cover that south wall entirely, or both. What's your opinion?"

I looked around. The library was only a little smaller than the great hall, another enormous barn of a place quite without windows, and while the wall behind us was covered with bookshelves, that to my right bore them halfway up—that is to say, only one story high. The air-conditioning system's exhaust fan, as large as an old bomber's propeller, was set in above them. The south wall, paneled in some gorgeous light wood, was featureless except for a huge silver-ornamented door. "If I can judge the number of books, you'll need at least one more full wall of shelving. But it's a dreadful shame to hide that wood."

"The books will look just as fine as the wood. There's almost too much paneling in this place."

"Well, it's your house. Anywhere will be okay with me."

"South wall, then, and we'll see if it's enough. Daniel! Order what lumber you need for the south wall, floor to ceiling," she called.

"Right away," said Mr. Cavanaugh happily. "Take a few days to get the proper stuff."

"Who builds your shelves for you?"

"The boys do it."

"Did they install all this?" I asked, gesturing at the magnificent spread of ledges and brackets towering behind me.

"And their fathers before them. They're fair carpenters, and Pierce is a craftsman without peer." Sibella drank her coffee. "We need no one from outside," she said complacently, "though the house requires constant maintenance, and everyone puts in a six-hour day at one or another of his specialties. Even Wendy. We have the stuff sent in, plumbing, air conditioning, stucco—let 'em send us their wares, but keep themselves away. Sablecroft Hall doesn't like outsiders."

"I'm an outsider," I said, louder than I'd intended.

She regarded me for a full minute. So, I think, did the others, Wendy and Sheridan, but I was watching Sibella. Then she said, "A house may embrace an outlander and make her one of its own. I hope the Hall will do that with you."

"Why?"

"It's a house of shadows," Sheridan interposed. "Your main interest in life is shadows, isn't it? Black and silver shadows on great flat surfaces. You'll be accepted—or engulfed—if you stay."

"Why shouldn't Laurel stay?" asked Sibella angrily, sitting up even straighter than usual. "Did *you* arrange that stupid tape threat, Sherry? I shall be disappointed if you did."

"No, Grandmother. Word of honor," he said formally, archaically. "But it wasn't quite a threat, was it? Just told her that she was in the lion's mouth."

"Implied warning: Get out. All right, I take your word. But the toast last night, from *Death Takes a Holiday,* that was yours, eh?"

"How'd you guess?" He smiled at her.

"Everyone knew I'd propose a toast," said the old woman, "but you're the Freddie March buff."

"You pressed a switch," I said, "but where?"

"Find out," he said. "I'll get back to rearranging books." He walked off slowly. He did look as though he had a hangover—or needed sleep.

"Be an obliging child and open that door," said Sibella to me. "The dogs like to come and go at will. You might check on that switch, too. Mustn't start work with a distracted mind."

I laughed and went into the dining room, sat where Mr. Todd had been sitting last night, and felt below the table. Sure enough, there was a push button anchored there—the alternative would have been a foot pedal—with a wire leading toward the middle of the huge board. Experimentally I pressed it.

Cary Grant said in a playful tone, "Now don't you know that's very naughty?"

I kept my finger on the button, but nothing else followed. This was not an endless audio tape, meant to repeat, as in the suit of armor. I knelt and peered under the table. There were several push buttons scattered here and there at the edges, the wires going to the center and then in a bundle over and down the inside of one of the eight heavy legs to disappear into the thick rug and evidently lead beneath it to the wall. These monomaniacs must have four or five recorders hidden behind the wainscoting, so that they could top one another with appropriate quotations from the motion-picture archives.

I went back into the library, preceded by the harlequin Dane. "Hello, Roderick," I said. It glanced back at me, remote, contemptuous.

"Good morning, Reichenbach," said Sibella. The dog laid its vast head on her lap and whined. She scratched it behind the ear. "Good boy." She nodded to me. "I heard Mr. Grant reprove you. Sherry set it up for you, of course. Rather a clever line."

"Do you fool with—I mean, do you play with the tapes too?"

"Now and then. It's really irresistible when one has all those millions of speeches in cans, and the equipment's there. Naturally, I don't do as much of it, the tomfoolery as you correctly almost said, as the children do. They can negotiate the passages more easily than I can. And Pierce is adept at it too. He's large, but he moves as silkily and lithely as Fatty Arbuckle used to. So many really imposing men can handle their bulk like that. Look at him," she said, jerking her head sideways. Pierce Poole, high on a ladder, was leaning far out as he inserted a couple of books between others: A captive balloon lashed precariously to a pole. "None of it's meant to insult anyone, Laurel. It's only a game."

"I don't like being called a silly little girl—even in Claude Rains' voice—by total strangers."

"No. I don't understand that part. It isn't like any of them, such a slip of taste. You'd be justified in thinking you've come among a pack of Our Gang graduates. And losing your celebrated temper," she added, "as your superior felt it necessary to mention in her recommendation."

"I wrote you I was on the point of being canned," I said, "as—how would she have put it?—too irrevocably dedicated to defending my own rights."

"Almost word for word." She laughed her three syllables. "I didn't mind that, Laurel, there's no one here who can't stand up to a quick gust of angry passion any time you feel you're not getting justice."

"Chief librarians regard it differently. Since I never worked except at Moorington, I'll be unemployable if I can't earn a glowing recommendation from you when I leave," I said.

"Don't go thinking that far into the future, girl. Who knows how many years I'll need you? And I am sorry about the insulting armor."

"It's all right," I said. But of course it wasn't. The tape hadn't been a joke. Neither had the toy pistols trained on my photograph been funny.

"Look here, would you like a tour of the house first, or would you rather familiarize yourself with the books? It's all the same to me." She rose. "Want a guide?"

"Not just yet. I'll examine the books, so we can set up a system together as soon as possible."

"Zeal! I like it. We don't have lunch here, we're geared to breakfast and tea, but if you get hungry there's always something."

"I don't eat lunch either," I said. "I hate to stop for it. Tea's a new meal for me."

"Necessary one, I'd say. You can stand fattening. Good-bye for the present, then." She stalked off—her habitual mode of walking couldn't be called anything less than a stalk, in the sense of a stiff and rather haughty marching gait—and vanished through the big silver-studded door that led evidently to her quarters. The dog watched her leave and then transferred its opaque brown gaze to my face. I blinked at it slowly in cat signals; it didn't recognize the courtesy.

"Need any help?" asked Daniel Cavanaugh. "May I point out the rarities to you, extoll the first editions, explain who the Barrymores were, and tell you which actors had their autobiographies ghostwritten?"

"Gee, thanks," I said. "Could you just keep the dog from biting me?"

"He won't, really. He absolutely will not harm you. Are you afraid of dogs?"

"No. Yes, of some Dobermans, I guess. But he *stares* at me so."

"It's his job. They'll all slack off after a few days, assuming that you're simply one more damn Sablecroft. Here's another. Hi there, Beaconsfield."

"How many are there?"

"An army. An insane number. The kennels are just outside this wall, at the back of the house, with a gigantic chain-fenced run, but they have the freedom of the Hall whenever they like through their own door. Soberly, Laurel, can I help you at all?"

"Not yet, thanks. I'll shout if I need you."

He bowed. I could almost *see* the cape swept back, the sword tipped easily so as not to tangle with the legs. I chuckled, and he cocked an eyebrow inquisitively. I said, "Even if I hadn't known it, nobody'd need to tell me that you grew up in a theater."

"How so?"

"Do you think that anyone today, in the last quarter of the twentieth century, bows like that, except a full-time, impressionable, unconsciously imitative, flamboyant hambone of an old-movie fan?"

His leprechaun laughter rang out, echoing in the big room.

"Bogart showed you how to hold a cigarette," I went on. "Gable, how to look at a woman. Edmund Gwenn, how to twinkle. Doug Fairbanks—Junior, that is—how to take everything in stride with a grin. Dirk Bogarde, how to levitate that brow."

"I took my flair from Flynn," he extemporized, "my grace from Astaire, or was it Chaplin? Timing of Hope, solid worth of Fonda, insouciance of Grant, blarney of Fitzgerald—"

"Eye of newt, tongue of frog," said Wendy, misquoting with a superior air.

"*Your* eye is educated, Laurel Warrick, and your tongue unabashed—the bow was pure Rathbone, long-practiced and sure-set. I think we'll enjoy having you among us."

"But won't you miss your family?" asked Wendy, voice sour.

"Micajah's my family."

"How sad," she said, the words dripping with insincerity, and I saw Daniel throw her a look of admonition.

"Adoptive families can be much the nicest kind," said Pierce loudly, "as I trust you'll find us."

"Even to the little boys who play with cap pistols?"

There was one of those gravid silences in which one could just hear the deep thrum of the air-conditioner. Then Wendy said, "How'd you know that?" from where she now sprawled sideways across both arms of the teak chair, her really fine legs dangling. "Daniel and Sherry haven't done that in months."

"And then only when too much drink's gone down," said Daniel. "I believe it was Christmas when we re-enacted *Shane* . . . we used to fence, too, up and down the great hall staircase, but after—but we don't do that any more."

Again no one spoke.

"The owner can find his cap pistols in my waste basket," I said into the stillness, and walked down toward the corner to begin my survey of the books.

"What the devil are they doing there?" demanded Daniel. "Those are historical pieces, we played with them when we were kids."

"Someone left them in my bedroom. I didn't know they were heirlooms," I said coolly.

Sheridan said, "Belle will rescue them."

"Yes, but look here—"

"Drop it, Dan," said his cousin sharply.

"Right. Still, how'd they get in Laurel's room?"

"One of life's quaint mysteries," said Mr. Todd. Everyone shut up, uncomfortably, I thought.

I went through a dozen volumes quickly, registering them on my memory under three headings. Then Sheridan Todd drifted down beside me. "What was it, some kind of joke?"

"The usual obscure, pointless Sablecroft joke," I snapped, "involving a photo. But I imagine you know as well as I."

He glared at me. "Look, Warrick, I'm sorry if you took what I said yesterday as an unfriendly act. I was upset that you'd come against my expressed wish. How was I to know the letter never reached you? Please don't be so primly sure that everything that happens in this house is my fault. There are, after all, six of us who live here, counting Belle McNabb, with six quite varying senses of humor, or of malice, among us. What photo?"

"One of me, shot before I left home. I'd never seen it till last night. That's all." I took a deep breath, realizing that I was growing too indignant. "It was a continuation of your warning and the armor's message."

"And I did it?"

"I don't know that."

"Well," he said, "that's something, isn't it? I'm not to be entirely condemned without a hearing. Thanks for that." He went away, to be replaced by a Great Dane who lay down two yards off to keep an eye on me.

"Who is Belle McNabb?" I asked it, answered by the customary empty, hostile stare. "Another Sablecroft, I suppose."

The place was knee-deep in Sablecrofts, none of whom was named Sablecroft. I *had* lived in more conventional houses, with more comfortable atmospheres. Yet here I had to remain.

"Further adversity with our Sherry?" asked Daniel, sidling over with his wicked grin. "Don't take it personally, he's often unbearable before tea. It's only the way he's geared timewise. He's really a decent fellow, as long as you don't compare him with me." He squatted, ostensibly looking over my shoulder at a biography of a French director. "Something about a photograph," he muttered. "Long-eared men can't help overhearing things."

I told him about it under my breath.

"I think I've seen that picture," he said slowly, at the same pitch. "Some time ago, only for a second, and I can't remember where. Must be why I thought I knew you when I first met you in the great hall." He slid his bright blue eyes sidelong toward me. They were almost like an Egyptian cat's; they made him most attractive. "Laurel, simply because I grew up in this house doesn't mean I'm unaware that it often exudes a sort of grim malevolence. I mean to say, it *is* haunted, we all admit that, and it's built like some freakish movie set—it was deliberately designed that way—and it's crammed with odd things and unusual people, one of whom is probably certifiable, which I told you. May I ask an impertinent question? Why do you obviously plan to stay?"

"I've nowhere else to go. Don't you want me here, Daniel? Don't you like me either?"

"I like you very much indeed. I like you fully as much as I liked Eva Marie Saint when I was seven, a man of the world. I simply believe that for an intelligent woman you're a little too brave and foolhardy to be real."

I pretended to read a title page, noticing dimly that the book was upside down. "I can show you my library credentials. And the legal papers on my debts and Steve's—my husband's—which are morally mine now too."

"Let's play Honesty for a minute. I'll answer your questions—shall we set a limit of three each?—if you'll answer mine. Are you connected in any way with a detective agency?"

"No!" I said loudly. Then, hushed again, "Who haunts Sablecroft Hall?"

"My great-grandfather, Sibella's father whom your granddad met, Gilbert Sablecroft himself, for one. We all hear him now and then, and Grandmother saw him several times after he died. The dogs evidently see him too. Watch your cat for the signs. Cats are more sensitive to ghosts than dogs, you know. Number Two: Aren't you frightened at the unfriendly aura cast by all those items I mentioned?"

I considered. "I am a little. It's not comfortable, to say the least, to feel unwelcome. But nobody really harms a poor librarian for no reason whatever, do they? It isn't as though my diamond were twenty carats"—I touched my engagement ring with its small, cherished stone—"or I posed a threat to anyone. Why did you agree with Mr. Todd yesterday, even though far more nicely?"

"I think there *is* danger here, because of a puzzling death a couple of years ago, and an unexplained accident that's occurred since then. I think they were both engineered, and since they were aimed at two innocuous people, it would seem there's a quiet, dangerous maniac at large in Sablecroft Hall. We must live here, but there's no excuse for bringing in strangers till we discover the culprit."

"I'd have had doubts about coming," I acknowledged, "if I'd been told that before I took the job. But I can't turn tail from a fascinating piece of work, leave myself out of a job and badly in debt, on account of oblique rumors and cryptic cautions. Have you any idea who engineered the accidents?"

"Yes, though not a firm belief yet. And that's your third question."

"No fair! You know I meant to ask—"

"The suspect's name. Ah, but you didn't. Lady who deal exclusively in words should phrase query correctly," he chanted. "Charlie Chan *must* have said that some time or other. Number Three for me: Are you in love?"

"No!"

"Splendid. No simple village lad back in Connecticut?"

"No," I repeated. He smiled, put his book on the shelf, and walked away to chat with Wendy. I set to work in earnest, and the hours flew by. I was still reading along the lowest two rows, sitting on the parquetry, when the tea gong clashed out and startled me, for by then I'd completely forgotten where I was.

Having put in nearly eight hours already, I had the time till dinner to myself. So, after the best scones I'd ever eaten, with butter and honey, and some of the marvelous bottled water, I told Sibella I'd like to explore.

"Good. You'll be easier in mind when you know exactly where you are, what's around you—"

"Contrariwise," said Wendy, "you may be edgier than ever."

A bull must eventually be clutched by his horns. "I'd like to know what you mean."

Daniel Cavanaugh said, "Take the fifty-cent tour, Laurel. Verbal explanations are weak and confusing. I'll show you what's meant . . . by some of the remarks, anyway."

Playing with her lusterless jet-black hair, which was cut into a short, thick heap, Wendy asked, "Shall I come too?"

"Or perhaps I?" Pierce Poole said.

"Nobody knows the passages more thoroughly than Daniel," said Sibella. "Better one guide than two or three talking simultaneously

—go along, Laurel. He can probably be trusted, in spite of his wild romantic good looks."

"The devil I can," he said cheerfully. I followed him through the great hall and into the dusky twilight of the vestibule. He opened a large closet and stepped in, shoving apart a collection of raincoats, sweaters, and jackets on hangers. He raised a hand in the gloom and the entire back of the closet slid sidelong with a minute squeak. "Have to oil that," he muttered. "These things should be perfectly noiseless."

"Where's the trigger? If I'm allowed to know?"

"Right here." He picked up a three-cell flashlight from the floor and showed me a tilted bronze clothes hook; he turned it upright and the back of the cubicle came into place again. He reopened it. "Ask anything you like. I don't want to make mysteries, but to clear them up. We all know these details, even Belle."

"Who is she?"

"The servant, Belle McNabb. She laid tea, but you were long ago and far away in that novel of von Stroheim's."

"Yes, I never saw one of his books before."

"We have all the editions somewhere. At any rate, Belle McNabb is the sinister old family retainer I mentioned; does the shopping—by phone, in this day and age! Imagine!—the cooking when Pierce isn't in the mood, and as much of the cleaning as Wendy doesn't handle."

"Why 'sinister'?" I asked, trailing after him into the blackness beyond the closet.

He pushed a silent mercury switch and a short aisle lit up on our left, all cement toward the outside of the house and rough wood opposite, which would be the back of the paneled hallway. "Oh, it's an unfair slur, but she is sinister till you know her. Maybe even when you *do*. I've never made up my mind. She's a tiny black woman, brightest eyes you'll ever meet, all the troubles of her race etched into her face and borne with pride. She moves mysteriously here and there and frowns. Her word's law, and don't forget it when you meet her. She's been with the family . . . I don't really know how long. Maybe as long as Sibella herself. I believe her parents were born slaves. Look here, Laurel, have you the least dread of enclosed spaces?"

"None whatever."

"Good. Some of these corridors are like great interminable coffins." Having closed the entrance behind us with another lever which worked the mechanism electrically, Daniel walked to the end of the passage and turned at a right angle into another, putting on two more lights and extinguishing the first. The bright naked bulbs hung on long cords from a concrete ceiling eight feet or so above our heads. This aisle was longer. "Now we're walking due east, the front of the house is on our right and the great hall on our left. Notice the roof's only one story high. Another identical passage is above us." His voice had a curious short-term echo here. "The tunnel above opens onto the balcony that fronts our bedrooms at its far end, and this door," he jerked a thumb right, "leads into an outside buttressed tower, about fifty feet tall, with a crenellated lookout platform."

We turned left, illumination dying behind and springing up before us at his touch. For all my vaunted lack of claustrophobia, I was uneasy, and found my hands clenching tight enough to hurt. I wriggled the fingers and deliberately let them hang loose, glad that Daniel was ahead and wouldn't notice. It was not a cheerful place to be.

"Now we're heading to the back of the house. Here we go right for a few dozen paces . . . curve around another tower . . . and we're aimed due north. The palm grove's out there—you can see it from your window. Left is the kitchen. Here comes the garage, and now we either leave this part of the 'secret' passageway and go through the garage and into its continuation, or climb to the second-floor corridor, outside the bedrooms, which is more interesting."

"It's a lot warmer in here than in the house proper," I said, "but nothing like as hot as I expected." As Daniel tugged at a rope, bringing a ladder sliding toward us from a square hatchway above, I glanced down. "It's quite clean, too."

"Sometimes Wendy or Belle goes through the whole system with vacuum tank and mop. Otherwise it'd be like the floor of a badly kept forest. Lizards, poor little things, and moths and palmetto bugs come in and die, and when the high winds howl we get dirt and even palm fronds blowing in through the open lancet windows and the loopholes and chinks that haven't yet been mended in the towers. Sherry does the outside repairs and I handle the interior cracks, but we're always behind in the work. As to the heat, these walls are thick reinforced concrete faced with stucco. That, and the double walls with more-or-less-dead air between them, were a primitive try at air-conditioning. After you, Laurel."

I trotted up the ladder and stepped off backward onto another cement floor. Following, he drew up the ladder, which then swung on big steel hinges against the inner wall. The open hatchway closed with a thud, and we walked on.

Shortly we came to a block, a flat concrete slab at right angles to the walls and reaching from the roof to just below my waist. "The windows?"

"Right. We creep under." He scrambled through ahead of me, the carpeted crawlspace being about as long as I judged the triple-set windows of my own bedroom were wide. I scraped the top of my head slightly as I came after. "This is the room next to yours. It's empty now."

"Whose was it?"

He hesitated a breath. "My grandmother's. It's a duplicate of yours. Sibella's quarters downstairs are gigantic—they used to be Gilbert's—but Grandmother always said she wouldn't sleep in a damn auditorium, so she chose this one. Look," he said, tapping old, raggedly wrapped wiring that came from behind us and vanished into a hole in the board of the interior wall. "That's the system that lets us send a message all through the house at once, like the dinner gong."

"Speakers in every room?"

"Yes. You'll see a grille high on the wall near your door. The source is a tape deck and microphone near the arch of the dining room."

"Your family is electronically minded to such an extent—what will you do when the world's oil runs out?"

"Install solar energy cells. I'm working on the plans. My father and Sherry's, both dead now—that entire generation's gone, by the way; the famous long-life genes of the Sablecrofts unaccountably skipped a whole step in the line, and we hope they haven't deserted us entirely—our fathers set up the first system in the late nineteen fifties, with the enthusiastic and probably irritating help of the pair of us. I remember there were a dozen Wollensak player-recorders, extinct now. I was about seven and Sherry nine. We've been adding and improving ever since. Most of the equipment's miniaturized by this time, and dreadfully sophisticated. I don't imagine that you find the entire conception particularly sophisticated, do you, Laurel?" He looked over his shoulder, smiling.

"It seems to me it would be fun to play with for two or three days, after which it would be pretty stale," I said honestly.

"I think we continue to like it, not because our imaginations are so restricted," he said, going to hands and knees again to crawl under the massive concrete barrier that housed my bedroom windows, "but because our whole lives have been so tangled with cinema, so molded by it and obsessed with it, that we don't care to stray too far afield. I daresay we have creative streaks that were shunted off their proper tracks, so that we became collectors and appreciators rather than makers of anything artistically important. I know Sherry intended to go to Hollywood when he grew up and be a star, a director, or a writer, depending on what day of the week it was . . . but the house got him in the end. I don't remember myself-when-young ever wanting to do anything but stay here and—"

"Play?"

We stood up on the far side of the bulky window enclosure. "No other word for it, is there? But this isn't the spot for philosophical chitchat. If I don't have you back in a reasonable time, they'll send the dogs after us."

I said sharply, "What's this?" and pointed to a ten-inch square of darker wood let into the wall. There were old hinges and a bolt, which had been rusted once but now shone with polishing and oil. "Is that a peephole?"

"Say rather a disguised aperture, a covert—"

"Don't yammer!" I said furiously. "What sort of house *is* this, with spy windows in the bedroom walls?"

"A madhouse. I told you that! Built by a man so eccentric that you could call him cuckoo with justification. A mansion erected to order by a very peculiar practical joker with a single obsession, the motion picture. The great folly of a bizarre crank. Or the magnificent sport of a man who genuinely knew what he liked and got it come hell or hurricane. It's all in how you look at it. Laurel," said Daniel, soberly, "there are viewports in every room in the Hall excepting the baths. They were made for practical jokes, and are still used when someone thinks of a new trick. But they were never used, are never used, to spy on people, to watch pretty girls undress, or for any other disgustingly infantile purpose. Gilbert Sablecroft was in his fashion a gentleman, and so are his descendants. I give you my word of honor on that." The members of this family were, it seemed, addicted to swearing on their honor; I remembered Sheridan Todd doing so this morning. "You haven't seen the giddiest lunacy yet by a long shot," Daniel told me levelly. "If you can't take the chill, Laurel, as the saying goes, then get the hell out of the icebox."

"You can hardly blame me for being shocked to find that I have, potentially, no privacy."

"Since it worries you—and there's no reason for you to accept the word of a comparative stranger, I realize that—I'll board up this hatch myself. We won't be able to slip in the rubber snake, of course, while re-enacting *The Speckled Band,* and how we'll ever introduce the clutching hands and the pygmies with their poison darts I can't conceive, but I'll close it permanently for you. Okay?"

"I'd like that, yes."

He rubbed his long jaw thoughtfully. "I doubt that any Sablecroft ever thought twice about the Peeping-Tom possibilities, but we know us, and you don't. Consider it done. Would you like to see your room from this angle before the chance is forever lost?"

I said yes, and he slid back the bolt and pulled the tiny door open. I squinted in. There was a sheet of slightly milky glass between me and the bedroom. "What's the glass? I don't recall it."

"Two-way mirror."

"But nobody ever spies in *this* house."

"Don't be cynical. The mirror's on a piece of furniture, makeup table or whatnot, that was moved in there from my grandmother's room for you. All the furniture was rearranged then. What a two-way mirror was doing in Felicity's room I'll never know. Some gag or other, years back."

"Felicity?"

"Felicity and Sibella, twin daughters of Gilbert. Felicity's gone these two years," he said shortly. I had the impression that he had loved her deeply, though how I gathered this I couldn't explain. Hers must have been the "puzzling death" he'd mentioned.

I noted also that Daniel Cavanaugh might be a pathological liar.

That glib brush-off of the observer's mirror held as much water as a ball bearing. Whatever the truth, this window was going to be sealed up for good. I closed the thick little door and bolted it. The iron ran silently through its loops; the fastening hadn't been neglected, in recent times anyway. We walked on, ducking under what he told me were two high bathroom windows and creeping below another big enclosure. "Pierce's room," Daniel said. "Now we circle round the stairwell of another tower and come to the back of the Hall." He unlatched a casement in the outer wall, which slid on steel rods and opened toward us. The inner face was wood and the outer stucco. "There's Pierce's greenhouse below us. All the lavish flowers come out of it. Over to the left is the dogs' run." He closed it and opened another one opposite. I gazed down into the dining room.

"Queer sensation, seeing it from so high. A little godlike, perhaps? It's even eerier if there are people down there. Different, somehow, from standing on a balcony. Do you feel it?"

"Some, yes, now that you mention it. It would seem natural to have a pot of boiling oil ready."

"To pour on the heads of the unwashed rabble, yes! Or molten metal." He chuckled. "Should be a gargoyle jutting below us. Maybe Wendy and Sherry can make us one. They're handy with their fingers; they sculpted some of the waxworks in the great hall."

I pointed to one of the Danes ambling into the room. "I noticed a medieval atmosphere last night—enormous refectory table, yellow wallpaper almost like thatch, maize-colored scatter rugs for the mats of rushes, and now the castle dog. And the height. All very Middle Ages, as long as we can't see the portrait with the monocle."

"We'll go on and view the library." The tunnel took a sudden jog to the left, shortly to the right, and then one of the long stretches lay before us, lighted as usual by two bulbs at this end and extending into gloom and finally intimidating darkness.

I paused at one of the spy holes and unbolted it, but found only a lump of tangled wiring and a large walnut-sided hi-fi speaker set tightly into the aperture. "One of our secret startlers," said Daniel. "Except for the communication-system grilles, they're all camouflaged. The cloth mesh screen that's the front of this speaker is painted *trompe l'oeil* to look like two rows of books, lined up with the real books and with the actual shelf matching the painted shelf."

"But when you all know where the speakers are," I objected, "and almost no strangers now ever see the inside of this house, what's the point of such elaborate disguise? Why not just a speaker?"

"Oh, Laurel, can you bear to do a thing slapdash and halfway? I don't believe it. You must have a compulsively methodical mind for your profession. So do we all. One makes things shipshape or not at all."

"If one has oceans of time."

"Well, we all work, but we play too. And do both equally hard, I suppose. Here's the lookout post for this side of the library," he said, pulling it open. The first thing I saw below was a big black leather easy chair with Sheridan Todd sprawled in its depths, head tipped back to face us. Even more than twenty feet up and halfway across the room, I could see the scowl on his face.

"Hello," I called.

He waved a hand listlessly. "How d'you like our ridiculous movie set now? Find any skeletons behind the wainscoting?"

"Not even a deathwatch beetle. It's one vast priests' hole, with the fugitive priests all gone."

"Leaving only their priestly peekaboo loopholes behind them. Now you know how much privacy to expect," he said, and shut his eyes wearily.

Daniel closed us in again. "I begin to wonder if Sherry actually wants you here," he said airily.

We came to one of the curves that indicated a tower. He led me around it, opened a door, and we stepped onto a narrow, tightly compressed spiral staircase with only a thin iron railing separating us from the fifteen-foot drop down the central shaft. "Easy does it," he said above me, closing the door and lighting his flash. "Don't open the first doorway, but the second. I'll take you back along the ground floor and show you the tape mechanisms."

"Where does the first lead?"

"Into the library. The unlocking device is a false book that tilts forward and slides the door, which doubles as a panel, into the wall. From inside you simply do it by a handle."

"What's the book?"

"The autobiography of Alan Ladd."

"He didn't write one."

"Well then, don't catalogue it, love," said Daniel logically. "It's made of steel, with a painted dust jacket, and used to be Lon Chaney's own story until someone, I think my grandmother, repainted it."

We entered another long aisle. I asked, glancing back, "What did we skip on the west side?"

"Sibella's quarters. It's understood that nobody ever uses those passages. *Lèse majesté*. I imagine all the peepholes and doors have long since been permanently sealed; I haven't been in those galleries since I was a kid." After progressing fifteen or twenty feet, he said, "The three tape decks for the library speakers are just on your left. If you know where the triggers are out there, you can activate any one of three messages. Or you can do it from here." He showed me the starting mechanisms and a perfect Gordian knot of wiring. "The equipment's all solid state." He tapped a key. "Long live the dead!" shouted Noël Coward, and Peter Ustinov replied sedately, "Thank you very much indeed."

"I wonder what that was meant for," said Daniel. "At least we must have wakened old Sherry conclusively."

We went on down the strange alley and around a sharp dogleg, and emerged into the cool north-lit dining room, where two Danes got to their feet with the odd clumsiness of horses rising, all angles and stiffness, and after seeing that Daniel was behind me and in control of the situation, lay down again with great thumping collapses.

"Ah, Cardigan," said Daniel mildly. "Cheers, Otterberg."

"How do you know which is which?" I asked. Both names were new to me, and the enormous black creature with his lolling red tongue seemed the twin of one I'd seen yesterday.

"Ah, cousin Daniel knows. Come, Cardigan." He pointed to the black and then to his own chest. The beast scrambled up, padded over, and reared up to put its forepaws on his shoulders and gaze down at him. He patted its huge barrel affectionately. The ears came forward, furrowing the forehead, and the dark eyes grew warm. "You beauty," he said, touching the long face above him. "You fine great beast!" He made a signal with one hand and the dog went back to all fours.

"If he does that to me, he'll squash me like a grape."

"He'll never do it except on signal, don't worry. Their manners are beyond reproach. Give the lady your paw, Cardigan." Another sign, and the black extended his right leg, watching me. I took it, feeling like a peasant shaking hands with royalty. The eyes were blank, yet watchful. The gesture was no more than a mechanical compliance.

"So all that oblique talk only meant that Sablecroft Hall is entirely surrounded by what one might term a continuous ambulatory," I said, as we strolled into the great hall. "A walled-in ambulatory, but still I imagine you could call it that."

"You could call it Herman for all I'd know," said he. "Shall I seal your room now? I'll just pick up the tools." He went through a door under the balcony, and I headed for my bedroom.

"Wait till you see what I've seen," I told Micajah. He was eating and didn't glance up, but his ears went flat. "The longest, wildest cat-run in the world. I hope you never get into it." He ignored me. I sleeked fingers along his hunched back; he moved sideways and kept eating. Anyone unfamiliar with cats would have sworn that he loathed the sight of me.

Someone had officiously unpacked and put my things away; a lot they'd learned beyond my taste in clothes and cologne. I rearranged a few items, put everything of Micajah's—current catnip mouse, steel comb, rubber spool with a sleigh bell in it, and three spiders made of pipe cleaners—into a special drawer with his photo album. I'd have to go shopping for him soon. His appetite was back.

Shortly I heard drilling and then hammering against the east wall near my windows. Soon there was a knock on my door. "Come see," said Daniel cheerfully. "Your walls are blinded, even if they still have a voice." He saw Micajah. His lean face softened. "Hel*lo*, sir," he said, tone pitched low. The cat stared at him. "May I address you by your name? Micajah . . . may I presume to call you Micajah? Will you consider me impudent if I don't stand on formality? I intend nothing but respect, Micajah, believe me."

I might as well have been in Tibet for all the notice either of them paid me. The big white cat, ears pricked forward, went to the man a step at a time, his eyes immensely round. Daniel knelt gradually till he was hunched on his heels, one hand low in front with the knuckles outward. His voice went on and on, telling the cat how splendid a creature he was, using his name now and then, saying all sorts of nonsense in the most deferential intonation. Micajah stretched his neck and sniffed the hand suspiciously. The hot-gold eyes squinted up. The cat retreated a step and thought about it, while the voice soothed and questioned and lapped round him like syrup. Then Micajah went to Daniel, walking on his toes, and stropped himself against the man's legs.

"Bless my soul," said Daniel quietly, not touching him. "I am honored, sir, highly honored." Micajah smelled his hand again. Then I could hear him begin to purr.

"What coven do you belong to?" I asked.

"I love animals, and they know it."

"That's guff. A friend of mine adores cats, and Micajah won't stay in the same room with her. She has a tiny scar on her wrist where he bit her once when she picked him up. Conversely, my husband could take 'em or leave 'em, and Micajah would curl on his lap and whine with pleasure every time he caught Steve sitting down."

"Then I really don't know. Ask Micajah." He put his fingers just back of the big white head and ran them gently to the plumed tail (Micajah was three-quarters Persian). The damned cat simply roared with sociability.

"This is the crusty old creature who hasn't spoken to me since he hit Florida," I said. "Micajah, you're fired. There's a cat job open."

Daniel stood up. "I'm a new friend, and haven't done anything yet to aggravate him. Want to check on the carpentry?"

I picked up Micajah and dropped him on the bed. He was at the door before we'd closed it, but I fended him off; I didn't want him getting into the maze of passages, or meeting the Great Danes without me along. Daniel took me down the hall past his grandmother's old room and opened a slender door on the far side, which had appeared to be a double walnut panel with a tall narrow oil painting of orange, green, and blue bird-of-paradise plants; there was no handle to it, he simply pushed at the outer edge and it swung open, showing the now-familiar dim corridor of Gilbert Sablecroft's hidden ambulatory.

"There are three of these access channels leading off this hall, Laurel. You see that both walls are wooden here, the backsides of paneled rooms—on our right is my bedroom." We went on, dodged under two of the massive window shields, and Daniel pointed to the hinged and bolted square of dark wood that covered the viewport to my room. He had nailed a couple of metal straps across the whole thing. "Feel better?"

"Thank you," I said, "I hope you won't think I'm unduly suspicious, asking for this."

"No, you just don't know us well enough yet." We retraced our path to the bedroom corridor. "See you at dinner then."

I went in to Micajah, who was lying on his black-and-yellow armchair, staring hard at the mirror behind which he'd heard us talking. I shoved the vanity aside, exposing the light blue paper of the wall behind it, which was flocked in a random geometrical pattern. I would never have noticed the square that disguised the borders of the peephole; the junction was almost invisible.

I tore a sheet of my cream-colored stationery into four thin strips and slid one into each of the cracks around the little door. If it were ever opened from the passageway, at least a couple of these would fall on my rug where I'd notice them. Metal bands can be removed without much difficulty. I was in a house of strangers, and I hadn't seen all those hundreds of mystery movies for nothing.

I manhandled the vanity table, which was old and heavy and moved grudgingly on the deep-piled rug, back into its place. "That's done," I said to Micajah. He got up, humped, turned around and lay down with his nose shoved against the chair and his tail toward me. I had taken away his new friend. "Can you give me a good reason why I put up with you?" I asked. But I knew the answer: Micajah, had he recognized the necessity, would have died for me. He was simply being Cat.

Dinner that night was exotic and delicious again, and the conversation afterward dwelt mainly on cinematic animation, on which I found both Sheridan Todd and Wendy more knowledgeable than I. Pierce rather disdained the whole subject except for Tom and Jerry, and Sibella was in an introspective mood and didn't talk as fluently as usual. Several times I caught her eyes on me, speculating. Daniel spent half an hour arguing passionately against all Disney films save *Pinocchio*. Then we went to bed. There had been no intimations of jeopardy and no audio-taped quotations.

But I was not to escape the latter entirely. Just a moment or two after I had put on my nightgown, the voice of Rex Harrison insinuated itself, catching me completely off guard. "Me dear, never let anyone tell you to be ashamed of your figure!" And Spencer Tracy added briskly, "Not much meat on her, but what's there is cherce."

I'm afraid I cried out with surprise and indignation.

I flew to the vanity, but my cream-paper intruder alarms were in place. I turned up all the lights (the miserable red bulb of last night had vanished and the white one was back in the bedlamp) and inspected the walls. The pictures were innocent, for I lifted each one down to check. Only the communication grille was in evidence. The ceiling was flat white and blameless. The voices must have been piped in through the grille, but there absolutely could *not* now be any way of looking into this room except through the windows, which were covered for the night with their purple-blue shades. I thought of the tiny scopes in doors through which one can see visitors before answering the bell; nothing of the sort here. My door had a keyhole, but I couldn't imagine someone kneeling to peer through it at a time when any one of the family might have appeared in the hall. Besides, I'd been out of range of the keyhole since entering the room.

The only conclusion I could reach was that some inveterate jester had waited for what he or she presumed was the length of time it would take me to undress, and then clicked a switch.

It was a particularly megalomaniacal joke, for the joker would have to believe that he couldn't go wrong on the time span. What if I'd come in and sat in an armchair to read? The whole buffoonery would have fallen flat on its ugly face. And also he'd have to *imagine* the result of his prank, which seemed to me to drain it of most of its savor, at least for a sane person.

Someone in the Sablecroft family was indeed mad.

I turned out all the lights and crawled into bed. I wished that I had never come to St. Petersburg.

THE FOLLOWING DAY I WORKED IN THE GREAT HALL, NOTEBOOK in hand and pencil between teeth, giving myself a preliminary grasp of the scope and specialties of this part of the collection. In an hour or two I had concluded that anyone who'd been reading a book simply thrust it into the nearest open space when he'd finished with it, because there was no order whatever. My work was cut out for me.

Every so often the resident dog would get up, shake himself, and go out with a long springy stride, whereupon another would take his station, all fresh and vigilant. I was no longer afraid of them, precisely, but found it hard to warm up to a horde of such reserved beasts. They reminded me of tigers in captivity: They were aware of me, my presence was perhaps somewhat distasteful to them, but I didn't speak their language and so was unworthy of either love or hate, only of suspicion. I wondered how they would take to Micajah.

Toward noon I began to notice the figures scattered in some abundance among the furniture of the mahogany-lined hall. It seems odd even to me that I waited till the third day to look at them—after all, how many homes include a room as huge as a barn and full of waxworks? Perhaps I'd been a little frightened of the silent throng of alive-looking dead things. And one of them had once turned into Sherry Todd, to welcome me with the demand that I go back where I'd come from. . . .

I wandered away from the bookcases, through the forest of figures, glancing at moody John Garfield, Nanook in his furs, Doug as Bagdad's thief, and Conrad Veidt as the somnambulist in *Caligari.* I saw the row of glass-topped cases and glass-fronted cabinets lined up against the western wall, and headed first for them. As in a luxuriously appointed museum, there lay behind the spotless glass a salmagundi of treasures, not only of the silent film era, but also of the stage's great days: a program of Yeats' *Countess Cathleen*, which had opened the Irish Literary Theatre in 1899, a lush purple-covered brochure extolling John Barrymore's *Hamlet* in 1922, many others.

Of course there were souvenirs of the movies—rubber arrowheads from some long-forgotten Western; shooting scripts in longhand, yellowed, edges curling; an enamel snuffbox flourished by an English aristocrat (born in Pittsburgh) in a Parisian comedy (shot on Long Island); on and on down the long row.

And there were relics of both still photography and pre-cinema moving pictures, usually one to a case. These cases were often encrusted with ormolu, less often of lovely natural woods, and had plainly been made to fit their contents—a tall rack with a head clamp used by a daguerreotypist whose subjects had to sit steady and unblinking for agonizing minutes, a gigantic camera of the Brady Civil War period, a magic lantern, a revolving Wheel of Life, a mirrored Praxinoscope, many more that even I did not recognize.

After a while I strolled back to the statues, nodded to Elsa Lanchester done up as Frankenstein's Bride—one of the rare moments of true beauty in the movies—and then stood staring at the nearest piece, a life-size Nazimova in a great swirling Beardsley-inspired gown all violet, sea-green, and gold, looking like an enormously enlarged *fin de siècle* statuette by Lalique. Slowly I walked around it. The soft wig was the color of flax, the glass eyes were focused on something ethereal above her (the balcony, actually); she ignored me, she ignored everything of the earth earthy. The head and bare arms were of delicately tinted wax.

"Nazimova," said Sheridan Todd behind me.

"I know," I said, and it flicked through my mind that only a day or two ago I would have jerked, startled, at the interruption. Sablecroft Hall quickly accustomed one to sudden voices. *"Salome,"* I said.

"Any idea who designed the gown?"

"Valentino's wife, what's-her-name, Rambova. Don't tell me this is the original?"

"It is. Gilbert acquired it, and Wendy a few years back impregnated the cloth with a preservative so we could use it here in the open instead of keeping it folded in cedar and darkness."

"Who did the figure?"

"I did. I've never been satisfied with it," he grunted, coming over to me and squinting at the image of the long-dead actress. "It has a sickness about it. I can't quite define it, but it's wrong."

"I don't agree. I've seen stills from the movie. You've caught the spirit nicely. There *was* a sick decadence to the Wilde-Beardsley period stuff. If you didn't mean to reproduce it, your subconscious knew better. You're an artist."

"No I'm not. All I can do is copy."

"But copying flat black-and-white in three-dimensional wax—"

"Any fool could do it." He had the most ungracious way of acknowledging a compliment. The omnipresent Dane sat down beside him, and he patted its head absently.

"If you're not an artist, what is your profession?"

"Handyman and landscape gardener. We're all laborers, cooks, and servants in this place. We do our housework, dabble and putter, read and watch movies and listen to tapes a bit, and then we're dead. We hide from the world and form representations of old ghosts, like this object." He touched Nazimova's hand with his forefinger, gently. "Maybe it isn't so bad," he said. "Maybe the degeneration, the sapped vitality, ought to be there. You have a fresh eye, and you don't flatter, do you?" He looked down at me almost anxiously.

"No," I said, "I try to say what I think."

"Never lie about anything?" he pursued it. "Not even by implication?"

"For heaven's sake, I'm human. What are you driving at?"

"You know. Skip it."

After an uncomfortable silence, I asked if he'd done all the wax figures. He shook his head.

"Wendy's better than I am. Felicity, that was Sibella's twin sister, was marvelous with papier-mâché, and almost as good with plaster. The best of the models here are hers, made when she was in her sixties. Wendy's and mine are likenesses—Felicity's are art, sometimes almost symbols. Look at her H. B. Warner over there, his Christ in *King of Kings*. Why, *I* look as much like Warner as that does, and still you'd never mistake the figure for anyone else. I don't even know why, but it's true. She was a sculptor. I'm about at the level of a good photographer."

I stared at the figure of dear old Warner. It radiated agony and majesty. At last I said, since he wanted the truth and I could empathize with that, "You're right."

We walked around the hall together, examining the effigies. There were thirty or more of them, excluding the suits of armor and the smaller works like busts and puppets. "These people are much of your life," I suggested, tentative. "That's why your images are done so well."

"Yes. But I've no patience with a pro whose real job isn't a major part of his life," said Sheridan Todd angrily. "If I'm a professional anything, it's a landscape gardener, and by God, I am good at that. You believe I think solely of movies. You can't imagine the hours in a week when my head's full of nothing but trees and soil conditioning."

We stopped in front of a tabled group of two-foot-tall fantoccini, which were in this case puppets that moved by mechanical contrivances—most fantoccini are manipulated with strings. They were made of painted metal and looked very old, but I recognized Harold Lloyd hanging from a huge broken clock, W. C. Fields juggling numerous tiny cigar boxes, and Buster Keaton entangled with a Keystone Cop. Sherry set them in motion one by one. It was fascinating. The little man with the glasses scrambled hopelessly forever up the wobbling face of time, the supreme juggler did impossible tricks with his boxes, the great stone face underwent ultimate indignities without a ripple to mar that beautiful visage.

"Who made them?"

"Nobody knows. Sibella acquired them, for some fantastic sum, in the thirties."

"From whom?"

"Keaton," he said, leaving me speechless with reverence. Before we moved on I touched Buster's flat little hat. Sherry nodded. "Yes," he said, "homage where it's due."

We walked across the terrazzo floor, the marble chips of its ground and highly polished surface winking in the blaze of the two chandeliers. Yesterday I'd raised a racket on terrazzo and parquetry, not to mention sliding once and nearly breaking my neck. Today I wore soft leather oxfords with heavy all-rubber soles and heels, and because I was conscious of moving in silence on the hard mosaic between the scattered Oriental rugs, I noticed that Sherry Todd did so too. I saw he had deerskin moccasins like Wendy's.

Very handy for sneaking up on people.

"Who wore the suits of armor?" I asked. "Fairbanks and Rathbone and Taylor and Power?"

"No, they go back in the Sablecroft clan for generations. I'd claim them for ancestral helms and hauberks, but there's heavy doubt of any knightly blood in our line. My remote forefathers more likely wore hay-padded jerkins and ran at the heels of the horses."

"Sir Geoffrey Sablecroft," I murmured. "Lord Harcourt Sablecroft. Scarcely a peasant's name?"

"Before Gilbert changed it, about eighteen-ninety-something, it was rendered *Blackfield*. We don't know of any noble Blackfields. No, about two leaps back from Gilbert, the family acquired money and bought things—armor, porcelain, plate, sets of unread books, houses—until the family wastrel, Gilbert's papa, took over and they began to sell things—houses, sets of still-unread books, and so on—till there wasn't much left but, miraculously, the armor. Great-great-grandfather obviously had a thing about mail and crossbows, the bloody-minded old rascal. He hung onto it all the way down the ladder. When Gilbert made his fortune in the States, he sent to England for the lot, which had been stored in a cousin's attic after his sire had guzzled himself to death."

"Tell me about Gilbert," I said. I'd never heard Sherry in a talkative mood, and wanted to prolong it, for he seemed in a far pleasanter frame of mind than usual.

"He was stage manager for England's Independent Theatre in the nineties; he worked on Shaw's first play. Then he came to this country, got involved, usually as producer, in early motion pictures in New York and New Jersey, and eventually sailed down to St. Pete on the crest of a perfect river of cash that he gained by hard work, speculation, or peculation, depending on which stories one believes. He'd seen a few of Addison Mizner's Florida houses, caught the bug, and himself designed Sablecroft Hall."

"He must have been, well, something of an eccentric?" I suggested.

"You mean a crank, a rip-roaring madman, don't you? But then so are we all. We love the Hall." We stopped before a suit of armor of the English Civil War period, its lobster-tail pot helmet shadowing one of the meanest, most scowly plaster faces you could imagine, and stood looking up at it. All the figures were raised on black wooden platforms, or we'd have been gazing down, for the warriors of that time were not tall men.

"No," I said, "I mean a Victorian eccentric, which was much more delightful than a madman."

"Yes, he was a pretty typical oddity of his period, old Gilbert. I wish I'd known him better, I was barely five when he died . . . there aren't nearly enough original characters around these days. He built the Hall for his amusement and that of many guests, people who were fascinated by films, follies, practical jokes, or anything *different*. You know what a folly is, an architectural folly?"

"How did Sansovino put it? 'The aim of the folly is greatly to surprise the stranger,' " I said pedantically.

"And to delight its builder," said Sherry.

"Gilbert succeeded. It's worth coming a long way to see it."

"Have you had a tour of the grounds?"

"Not yet," I said, realizing that I'd been here for nearly three days without poking my nose out-of-doors.

"I'll show it to you. Where are your sunglasses?"

"I don't own any. I have very strong eyes—"

"Not for Florida sun, you haven't. I'll get you a pair. Wait here." He walked quickly toward the staircase, the dog at his side.

I stared at the helmeted figure, which glared over my head scornfully. I wondered if he had a loudspeaker concealed behind his dented old cavalryman's breastplate. Whose voice would be most likely to issue forth? I thought of Sir Guy Standing. *Lives of a Bengal Lancer*. "We come to it. We all come to it." That would be appropriate.

"All you old soldiers come to it," I murmured, and shuddered abruptly as though a fox had jumped over my grave. The line referred to retirement, but in my imagination it had suddenly taken on the darker color of death.

" 'Nobody dies,' " I said aloud to the big armored doll, quoting Richard Conte from *A Walk in the Sun*. The habit was easily picked up in Sablecroft Hall.

The many-tinted rays of the Tiffany chandelier must be affecting my eyes, for the plaster object seemed to be rocking back and forth. Then there was a crunching, splintering sound from beneath it, a voice shouted *"Look out!"* and I shifted to one side with a jerk that must have been wholly instinctive, for I had no time to think. The old soldier came down like a rotten tree trunk, stiff and terrifying, to land with a ghastly clangor of metal and a brittle crumpling sound that was the plaster disintegrating on the terrazzo.

For a moment, I felt the ice of an awful fear congealing in me; then I bent to lift the smashed statue experimentally from its prostrate ruin. The armor was the only heavy part of the thing, and as this consisted simply of the breastplate and backplate, worn over a thick velvety-finished coat of buff, it was not especially weighty. The whole effigy did not exceed fifty pounds. But if it had struck me, it could have hurt me badly, even broken my neck.

I heard Sherry calling. He was coming headlong down the stairs, the dog barking behind him. I only glanced at them. Then I looked at the square black platform on which the personation of Cromwell's man had stood.

Much of the wood had dissolved into dust, like some decayed old stump under a bear's swat. Its interior, corrupted by time or termites, had not been sturdy enough to support the imitation soldier another minute.

"What a coincidence that it should happen just when I was standing here," I remarked casually as Sheridan Todd arrived with his Great Dane, though I was shaking and felt my face bloodless and cold. "Look, the wood's decomposed, the whole front half of the base has collapsed."

"Coincidence," said Sherry, with scorn dripping from every syllable. He knelt, poking with a finger. "The thing's honeycombed—powder-post beetles did that." He shook his head, looking up at me. "My God . . . my God. *Now* will you go?"

"Why?"

"Mrs. Warrick," he said between teeth clenched to the fusion point, "do you honestly suppose that this was an accident?"

"I'd guess not—except I can't see how it was accomplished."

"This damage was done before the wood ever left the lumberyard. Sometimes you don't notice the small signs of infestation, and you varnish or paint your wood, which is futile when the inside's full of tunnels." His finger stirred a spilt heap of finely packed powder. "We always buy kiln-dried lumber, so I don't imagine this platform came from our usual source. Can't you see the meaning of it?"

"I think you're drawing a far-fetched meaning," I said. I picked up what remained of the base, which was so extensively tunneled that it was little more than a shell. "There isn't any apparatus here for causing the final collapse. How could anyone have 'set it' for the precise instant?"

"I don't know. But it happened."

"Life is full of coincidences," I said dubiously. I looked closely at the top surface of the stand I was holding. The faint marks of two feet, one slightly advanced before the other, showed as I turned it to the light. I set the thing down and stared at the soles of Cromwell's man, which were evenly aligned. I lifted the lower part of the torso;

there was no way in which that stiff fellow could have stood with his left toes two inches ahead of his right toes. I said, "Hmm."

"What is it?" asked Sherry, scowling up at me, his fingers still absently shoving the dusty grains of wood about.

"This was the base for some other statue," I said. "Look at the marks on the top." I watched his face as he did so. It told me nothing.

"You're right. It's been exchanged. It must have been. There are several figures mainly of wire and wax that don't weigh more than fifteen pounds. Still think it was accidental?"

"I don't see how it could have been timed," I repeated, impatience at last creeping into my tone as shock receded.

Gingerly he turned the body on its back. The face was gone, and one of the hands, but the armor was intact. "This was one of Felicity's people," he said. "What a vicious, stupid waste! All to spook a foolish girl who's too stubborn to be spooked."

"Why did you do it, then?" I asked him abruptly.

"Why should I have done it?"

"Why should you be the one to keep telling me to go back to the North?"

"Oh, never mind. We'll play it your way," said he. "You have no hidden motive whatever, you're here for the sake of a well-paying job, and so forth and so on. But I assure you, Laurel, I'm not in the habit of hurling statues at librarians, however excellent the idea might appear now and then. Nor would I have smashed this wonderful face to atoms for any consideration." The dog growled, sitting on its haunches beside him. "Do shut up, Rosenkrantz," he said. The beast, who was looking past us up toward the west wall, made a whimpering noise in his throat. Sherry said, "There's nothing there now, fellow."

"What was there before?" I asked.

"I don't know."

Was he implying that someone in the hidden passages between the great hall and Sibella's quarters had somehow caused the soldier to topple? "One can't push over a fifty-pound model from a distance of thirty feet," I said.

"I suppose not," he said reluctantly. He got up and brushed the dust of ruined wood and plaster from his trousers. "Nevertheless, it fell."

I recalled how the thing had appeared to sway backward and forward before falling. I said nothing, however. All around me was a mystery, to which I would not yet trust anyone far enough to hand over a clue. "What shall we do with it?"

"Leave it. Whoever destroyed it should have the decency to clean up the mess and see about a new model, but of course they won't." He handed me a pair of sunglasses. "I'll show you the outside, if you can walk comfortably with your knees knocking."

"My nerves are in fine shape," I said.

"Pity the same can't be said for your judgment. Come along."

I was about to put on the glasses when I saw a tiny dark wormlike object dangling from the three-barred face protector that hung down from the peak of the lobster-tail helmet. The head and helmet had been wrung to one side on impact, as though he'd been *thrawn,* as they called it in his time. I bent as if to touch the spoiled face in farewell, saying something like, "Poor old fellow," and twitched it loose. It was a thin silver-black thread, so strong that it cut into my fingers before breaking. So Sherry'd been right, no coincidence had occurred.

I palmed the thread and walked beside Sherry across the room and through a door into a large kitchen, empty of life, which we crossed to go into the garage, there being no opening from the kitchen directly to the outdoors. In the garage sat a gorgeous automobile, its white paint glowing in the sunlight reflected from an open door. "A Cord," I breathed, forgetting fright for a moment.

"You're expert on cars, then."

"Most of them are only a blur of headlights and whitewalls to me."

"Yet you recognize this as a Cord," he said, a little impressed at last, I thought.

"Dad inherited Grandfather's when he'd learned to drive. It died in an accident when I was five or six. But I never forgot what Dad called its coffin-nose."

"One of the most beautiful, roadwise cars ever built," he said. "I modified it to use modern gasoline, but otherwise it's just as it was forty-odd years ago."

"Does the chauffeur have a German accent? And wear a monocle, and play a pipe organ?"

"Don't be mischievous with me, I'm the chauffeur. And usually the only passenger. We Sablecrofts don't venture out much."

"The peasants are seething with rebellion out there. And you have everything you want right here inside."

"Yes." He gave me a sharp glance. "Why not?"

"But you have a tan."

"I *told* you I'm the landscape gardener. I do all the yard duty. Gardening, policing the grounds, Dane-training. The occasional outside termite-proofing. Trimming of dead palm fronds. That sort of thing."

"Poor Sherry."

"I enjoy it!" he snapped. "We all chose our jobs here. I like manual labor, if I can produce neatness and symmetry."

"You sounded so downtrodden."

"I did not! If anything," he said, glaring at the garage floor as though it were an enemy, "I was boasting. Because I don't look as if I stirred around much, do I?"

I didn't answer. If he was asking to be insulted, I wouldn't take the bait. "Can I have a ride in the Cord some day? It's been a long time."

"Certainly. You're one of the family now," he said, irony in his voice. We strolled out of the garage and Sherry pointed ahead. "Thirteen kinds of palm trees in that grove. Some are older than the house. Blackbeard's Bayou wasn't very thickly settled when Gilbert bought his two acres here, and the little yellow house belonged to a man who'd planted about a hundred palms. It's Belle McNabb's place now, as you probably know."

"I haven't even seen her yet," I said.

"That's quite possible. She sets her own hours and her own chores, which works out well for us because she's a compulsive toiler, like you."

"Really, I'm not compulsive. I simply like my field."

"I wasn't insulting you. My, you *are* a prickly customer, aren't you?" said Sherry, grinning behind the curtain of mustache. I had not seen him smile very often; you could detect a resemblance to Daniel when he did. "Put on the sunglasses," he said.

I did so, and we stepped into the full blast of the light. It was the hottest, wettest sun I had ever felt, and I almost shrank back into the shade, indeed, would have, but that I'd have been ashamed of my weakness.

"Warm day," grunted Sherry, striding toward the back of the house. I gasped some inarticulate agreement. "Of course," he went on cheerfully, "it'll be hotter in a few weeks."

How smug I'd been about keeping my bedroom at seventy-eight; to cool it off that much would require an immense expenditure of energy. And they held the rest of this enormous castle at seventy-two!

"The rooms we're passing are storage places," he said. "The bedrooms are just above. Are you oriented?"

I nodded. We went around a tower that needed some stucco repairs and he showed me the medium-sized greenhouse, attached to the back of the Hall. "Sibella had that built after Pierce arrived from England, because he likes to garden. Some lovely flowers, but mainly vegetables."

"Does that need a greenhouse?"

"It needs better soil than we have here, but this was built principally because Pierce prefers artificial heat to natural heat . . . or maybe it's enclosed heat to open heat . . . anyway, controlled heat. Says he doesn't melt quite so fast in there."

"I've noticed that yours is the only suntan in the family."

"Sablecrofts aren't nature lovers in the main. I don't suppose we'd be so devoted to cinema if we liked God's own creation a little better." I was thinking that he himself must love it, to acquire a mahogany tan and do landscape work, when he cleared his throat and said, "You don't strike me as a romp-through-the-fields, jog-a-mile-before-breakfast type yourself."

"I surfed in California. I ski almost as well as I play softball—between mediocre and rotten. But I'd rather have my nose in a book, I admit, as long as I play at something enough to keep limber."

"Here's the dogs' run," said Sherry, as we came to a long chain-link fence. "Kennels over there. Dog door to the house beside them, so nobody has to be forever letting them in and out." I asked about five foot-high stone pillars, each topped by a stone bowl. "Dining area. They're so tall that it's uncomfortable for them to eat off the ground."

We strolled along the vast length of the back of Sablecroft Hall, the sun heating my scalp like a flame, Sherry silent now; turned another towered corner and saw the shine of water through a broad gate, this one of wrought metal, in the west wall of the grounds.

"Blackbeard's Bayou," I said.

"Though Blackbeard never saw this coast," he nodded. "At least it's one thing around here that's named for some pirate other than the overrated Gasparilla."

"Gasparilla, no Anthony Quinn he?"

"Gasparilla, hardly even Don Knotts. Yet there are eternal Gasparilla Days, Gasparilla parades, Gasparilla Avenues. . . . Well, at least we have Blackbeard's name here, sluicing past the old homestead full of mullet and the occasional stingray that's blundered in from Tampa Bay. Would you like to go stare at the water for a while? We might even see the jack jumping. Or several dead detergent bottles," he said bitterly.

"Some day when I'm not strangling on the humidity." We crossed the front of the Hall and came to another tower, a great thick monster of a crumbling blue column looking like Miss Havisham's rat-infested wedding cake extended upward to a nightmare degree, with a slender lancet window every couple of yards up to the parapeted, cone-shaped pinnacle. A wooden catwalk ran above our heads from the stucco tower to a distant second-story door, which he told me opened into our bedroom hallway. "I think I'd better go in," I said. "I'm woozy."

At once he brought out a ring of keys and thrust one into the lock of an azure wooden door; then he was shutting us into deep gloom and stagnant heat. "Susceptible, aren't you? Never venture out again without a hat." He moved me bodily up a few steps into the diffuse light from one of the narrow thirteenth-century-styled windows. "You've gone dead white. I think we almost lost you."

"Would have been satisfying for you—"

"I don't want to be rid of you that way, stupid," he said harshly. "I want you to leave under your own power." He let me go experimentally. "Better . . . are you possibly allergic to sun?"

"Not that I know of—I had my share in California, with Dad."

"This is different. This is the bloody tropics. Let's go in where it's cool and dry." He opened the library door that Daniel and I had gone through yesterday. A marvelous rush of cold enveloped me. "I came all the way from Tampa in a cab. I don't understand why this happened today," I said.

"Direct sun acts differently. It's a great weapon up there. I passed out from it when I was a kid, two or three times."

"When may I try the outside again?"

"Next time it rains!"

We were walking slowly toward the great hall. I realized that no one else was in the library. "Where are they all? Surely it isn't tea-time?"

"Never try to keep track of anyone here. It's like minding a herd of mice in a labyrinth. Daniel, especially, often vanishes for a whole day."

"Downtown, perhaps?"

"No! In the passages. There's a story—nobody admits hearing it from any reliable source—of a hidden room, or even two, full of all kinds of splendid things. Original prints of lost cinematic treasures! I doubt it, really. If there's a cache it's more likely manuscripts than films. The old nitrate film stock crumbled into chemical litter, just as that wood platform went to powder. Gilbert lived long enough to know that it would—till 1955—so he wouldn't have hidden films."

"The picture I get of Gilbert is fragmented and contradictory."

"Show me a man who's all of a piece," said Sherry, "and I'll show you an extremely dull clod. What exactly can't you match up?"

"His intelligent early interest in a new art form, witnessed by all the old books in such first-class condition that he must have bought them as soon as they were published; and this ridiculous blue edifice with its wraparound maze, peepholes, clashing architecture, and perfectly insane air-conditioning which makes one think that the Sablecrofts would turn moldly if the temperature went up."

Again he laughed, or grunted; it was difficult to guess whether he was amused at me or at himself and his family. "The air-conditioning system is post-Gilbertian. It would have been pretty warm here in his time, of which I have dim memories. It must have been a constant fight against mildew and damp rot and dry rot and pests, and how he must have worried for his books! But the rest of it, the Hall itself, is a vast toy, don't you see that? The broader the intellect, the greater the necessity for relaxation. He had hordes of friends from New York and Hollywood and Europe who'd vacation down here in preference to—well, even Pickfair or Falcon's Lair. When he died, the influx of guests dwindled and finally stopped. His daughters were not the most sociable of souls." Sherry frowned. "I'm not criticizing. Some like company and some like solitude, and who's to judge between them?"

"Several of the nicest people I know are loners," I agreed. We were standing by the closed door to the great hall, and now he opened it and we heard voices raised in anger and despair. "Oh," I said, "they've found the soldier."

"And I think I heard my name mentioned," said Sherry, truculent once more. We went forward. Everyone was there, including a tiny, gray-black old woman in a polka-dotted cotton dress, who had the most brilliant dark eyes I have ever seen. She had to be Belle McNabb. She cast me a single look, about as friendly as she'd have bestowed on a palmetto bug (which is what they call a cockroach in Florida), and then gripped Sherry by the arm.

"Honey, they're blamin' the dogs. You know it wasn't the dogs, don't you?"

"It was absolutely not a dog," said Sherry.

"How do you know that?" demanded Daniel. The cords of his neck stood out like ropes, and he was dark red with anger. "Were you here?"

"We both were," I said quickly. "It almost struck me when it fell."

"Look at the platform," said Sherry. "Do you think a dog was tunneling in that? Don't be a pack of imbeciles—sorry, Sibella."

"Powder-post beetles," said Wendy, on her knees gathering up the fragments of the plaster head.

"Exactly," said Pierce Poole. "It is the work of the Lyctidae. We must examine all the bases closely, we can't afford this sort of destruction. What manner of caretakers are we? Look, here are the typical shot holes all over this end where the females have bored in to lay their loathsome eggs, but the black paint's camouflaged them. This was a case of sabotage."

"Begun quite a while ago, too," said Sherry, and pointed out the marks of another pair of artificial feet.

"I *said* it wasn't the dogs," cried Belle, her voice carrying over several angry shouts as they all looked at the evidence.

"But what the devil made it buckle in on itself?" asked Daniel. "What if it *was* under another figure?"

"The other was far lighter. My guess is it was Gish, she's all wire and wax, can't weigh a third what this fellow does."

"You must have shoved it," said Wendy to me, and added after a pause that was just long enough to be insulting, "accidentally." I didn't even answer her.

"Gish, that's sensible," said Daniel, ignoring Wendy too. "But who'd *do* it? Why trade her stand for his? He was Grandmother's work, he's absolutely irreplaceable. Sabotage! My God, it was murder!"

"It was very nearly that," said Sherry quietly. "If Laurel hadn't been fast on her feet, she'd have had a broken head herself. It's too bad about the model, of course, but we should be grateful to have our librarian with us and unhurt."

Pierce suddenly grasped my hand in his big powerful pillow of a fist. "I didn't realize. When you said it almost struck you, I took it for exaggeration. Laurel, how frightful! There's more than a smashed sculpture to consider, indeed there is."

"I was here," said Sherry, as if defying them to accuse him.

"Up on the balcony with a dog," I added, to be fair.

"And no one else?" asked Sibella. "Leaving, arriving, lurking?"

"We didn't see anyone," said Sherry.

"I think *we* can all alibi one another," said Wendy, still putting chunks of plaster into her handkerchief. "Nobody left the library till a few minutes ago."

"Oh, how can we swear to that?" said Daniel impatiently. "We were all bustling around, paying practically no attention to anyone else." He glared down at the wreckage. "I'm very glad you're safe, Laurel, but this sickens me. There's no innocent explanation; those footprints prove it. It was wanton destruction."

"Possibly," said Sherry, who seemed far less concerned than he'd been just after it happened, "Wendy might be able to repair it?"

"I think so," said the dark-haired girl, holding the twisted helmet off the floor and picking bits of face out of it between the protective bars. "I really do, Daniel. There are big pieces left, and we have photographs."

The lean young man began to cool off, the scarlet fading from his skin. "I'd be very grateful, Wendy. All right, I'm over the horror.

Sure you didn't touch it, Laurel? Even a slight rocking on its heels might have made this rotten lumber, ah, dissolve into its elements."

"No, neither of us touched it at all. Nor did the dog," I said. I put my hand in the pocket of my slacks and felt the bit of thread I'd jerked from the helmet bar. "Coincidence," I said, "that's all it was."

"The figures all occupy the identical places they've held for years," said Sibella, that great viola voice taking the floor away from us all. "Someone deliberately exchanged two of the black platforms, aware that the armored figure would eventually crush this one. Laurel stood before it, and it suddenly fell. Two concurrent events, remarkable for their utter lack of causative connection." She looked thoughtfully at each of us in turn. "In a pig's eye," she said.

"But how—"

"One of us knows," she said, "and one of us won't tell."

"The only one who's above suspicion is Laurel herself," said Sherry.

Wendy said, "She was closest to it, wasn't she?"

"I was looking at her when it happened. I shouted at her when I saw it teeter."

"Or I'd have been bashed," I said. "That's true. I never thanked you for it. Thanks."

"Well," said Sibella abruptly, "someone clean up the mess and put this seventeenth-century paraphernalia where it will be safe until we have another stand and a face and two good hands for it."

"It's the old man," said Belle suddenly, with an air of standing for no more nonsense. "I hear him behind the walls in the evenings, when you all gone to bed and I'm washin' up. He comes back, don't like what he finds, shoves stuff around. I hear him. I'm not the only one, and you *know* it."

"It's true," said Wendy casually. "The dogs hear him, and Felicity saw him more than once."

"My late sister," said Sibella hoarsely, "would say anything whatever if it brought her someone's attention. She no more saw a ghost—any ghost—than she ever saw a unicorn."

"I think she did," said Daniel. "I really believe she saw Great-grandfather, because I've come close to a glimpse now and then too. I swear it, dear," he said earnestly to Sibella. "I've almost seen his coattails whipping around a bend in front of me, if I'd been an instant sooner I *would* have. You can't mistake the feeling. And I smell his cigar smoke, sometimes, in the passages."

"Angels defend us," cried Sibella, throwing up her arms. "Now we're haunted by the ghosts of cheroots! Daniel, you're a splendid boy, but you have no inherent right to act fey. There isn't a drop of Celtic blood in the whole of the known Sablecroft ancestry. We are Saxon from the word go, and Saxons don't see spirits, they drink 'em."

"Belle isn't Saxon," said Wendy seriously.

Belle McNabb chortled. "She's got you there, Sibby," she said to the grande dame.

Sibella put her hands fondly on the little old woman's thin shoulders and they laughed together. I thought, they must have known each other as children, they're much of an age and there's an easiness between them that I haven't seen Sibella exhibit with anyone else. Belle must have come down from the North with the family.

"Go on, Belle, see your ghosts," she said. "Everyone knows you're a voodoo queen, so you have the right."

"I'm a damn good Baptist," said Mrs. McNabb. "But I know what I know. The old man's behind it all."

"Ghosts don't switch the bases of statues," said Sherry.

"Little boys don't know everything," snapped Belle, looking mystic and belligerent.

"I'll take this to the playroom now," said Wendy, who had collected all the plaster pieces that were as large as splinters and crumbs and held them carefully in two handkerchiefs. "It shouldn't take more than a few weeks to repair it, Daniel, really. Don't feel too bad. You'll never know it was broken."

"You're a good sort of girl," said Daniel. "I'll help in any way I can."

"No thanks," said Wendy, looking rather vacant, evidently planning the restoration. "You'd be nearly as much use as Camberwell there," she said, nodding at one of the Great Danes.

I gazed thoughtfully at the animal, a harlequin, whose coat was a beautiful light creamy white with large irregular patches of black. I had seen him before, because I recollected a splotch on his right side that was shaped (to my Wonderland-conditioned eyes) like a teapot with a small dormouse beside it. I believed that this was the first harlequin I'd met on my arrival. He certainly hadn't been addressed as "Camberwell" then. And harlequin Danes are like fingerprints—no two are ever alike.

Gradually the congregation split up, Wendy to the playroom, wherever that was, Belle to the kitchen, the others back toward the library. I went up to my bedroom, where I was welcomed for the first time since we'd left Connecticut by a loving, lonesome white cat.

I poured him out some dry food and sat on the edge of his chair. "Micajah," I said, "somebody tried to scare us away again." I fished out the thread and examined it: magician's thread, almost as tough as wire and less visible. I squinted hard at the ends, as Micajah forsook his meal and came to investigate. I told him what it was, and he, like any genuinely intelligent cat, objected with a squeak to the word that he hadn't heard before. He didn't want polysyllabic nonsense, he wanted to know what it *was*. "Okay," I said, "toy." Then he sat down on one of my feet and waited patiently for it.

One end of the meager shadow of stuff had a tiny, tiny flat surface; perhaps a quarter of the tip had been carefully sliced, while the rest was frayed where it had been pulled apart. The other end was all shredded, and this was probably the result of my own yanking at the fragment to loose it from the helmet. I noticed that my right hand was scored pink across the inside of the fingers. I was lucky I hadn't cut myself deep enough to bleed.

Dangling the thing for Micajah to bat and nibble, I said, "You see, buddy, they tied this to the lobster-tail pot, and from there it went straight over our heads and was attached to the railing of the balcony, or else back across the helmet and into one of their lookout portals in the west wall. If the first is true, then it was Sherry who stood up there and pulled the thread, rocking the soldier on his toes and heels until the wood gave way under the moving weight. The front of the platform was the most eaten away, so when a vibration was set up, that was the part that collapsed. See?"

Micajah indicated with a switch of his tail that I was talking twaddle.

"Toy," I said, and held the thread over his head and moved it away from me. He followed it back, sitting on his haunches and slapping at it, until he lost his balance and fell over. I did not laugh. Micajah was not one to suffer amusement at his own expense, and his fangs were those of an old alley fighter.

"If the thread was drawn back to the wall, then someone else did the tugging. Either way the trick would work, because I definitely saw the beastly doll teetering back and forth before he came down at me."

Micajah abandoned the thread and leaped into my lap. He curled up, his heavy body supported by my hand because he was really not a lap-sized cat at all.

"If it was Sherry, that explains almost everything. He jerks the thread sharply when he sees the soldier start to fall, it snaps off at the cut, and he reels it in as he dashes down the stairs shouting. After all, he left me standing in precisely the right spot." I tickled the cat's chin and he set up his famous rumbling purr, approximately on the decibel level of a truck idling. I said, thinking aloud, "He's rude, overbearing, threatening, and resentful of me—by his own word. He drinks too much, I think; his face is pudgy, and he slouches, and he's sarcastic. Snap judgment. More likely it's him than Pierce, who seems too distracted to be effective, or Daniel, who's mostly nice. I guess I'd rather it was Wendy. Because I envy those lavender-blue eyes? Because basically I don't like her, and she surely doesn't like me?"

Micajah lashed his tail. An agreement.

"Someone in the passages behind the statue? Mechanically it would work just as well. But *that* presupposes someone waiting for me to be right in front of the old Cromwellian, which was one chance in hundreds!"

I gazed down at the big white cat, aware of my skin creeping with the fear that I was so constantly suppressing, and I said, "Sherry, huh? Best bet. But he only wanted to frighten me, don't you see? Not to hurt me. He did yell." The huge golden eyes looked up at me from beneath the long fringes of fur that Micajah called his eyelashes. "You aren't agreeing with me," I told him. He sustained his contemplation. "Sherry shouted *as* it fell, not before, right? Oh, what am I doing! Talking to a cat who wasn't even there."

And possibly to someone else? occurred to me with a jolt. The walls had tongues; they'd had an eye; might they not also have ears? Nothing could be more likely.

"You know what Sablecroft Hall is?" I said to the cat loudly. "It's an overgrown fun house from an amusement park, and it's full of small boys and girls who never intend to grow up. Mischievous, nasty, callous kids! Wendy said there's a playroom. The whole place is a playroom! Stocked with cap pistols, menacing hounds, hidden aisles, long-gone voices, strange things that can hurt you and maybe kill you, the works. And three of them claim to believe in Gilbert's ghost! Can you imagine what it would be like without Mrs. Callingwood's restraining hand?"

I shut up. I had meant only to insult anyone who might be listening. But Sibella had said that someone meant to kill her out of hatred. If it was the same person who was terrorizing me, I musn't plant the idea that Sibella's death would send me packing. That could conceivably speed up the danger to her.

I was really floundering in the dark.

"Well, Micajah," I said, "we'll make the best of it. With a family to support, I need the job." I hugged him. "And my ruff goes up when I'm picked on," I said, "so let 'em mind their step!"

I had no firm insight into my own strengths, because nothing like this situation had ever confronted me before. I was a pretty good literary detective, but practically speaking I had no experience whatever. I knew only one thing: I am stubborn, so stubborn that Grandfather and Dad had both been driven to shout now and then that I was an obstinate, hard-bitten mule who was likely to get herself killed some day with her infernal stickling and pestering.

Be that as it may, I am never so mulish as when I'm being bullied and menaced.

Micajah and I were here to stay.

On that thought, the door opened and Wendy walked in. She was wearing an artist's smock and in her right hand she held a long, keen-edged, silvery knife like nothing I'd ever seen—except, perhaps, in old Asian paintings of strange gods and goddesses at their peculiar activities. The blade was steel with odd projections, some curled, some straight or hooked; almost as though several blades had been forged sleekly into one. She had her customary blank expression.

"Most people have been taught to knock," I said, balling the piece of thread into my palm.

"Don't get smart with me," she said. "I was just working down in the playroom," I noticed an emphasis on the last word, and knew she'd heard my speech to Micajah, "and thinking about you. You're the first stranger who's ever come here to stay. I don't like the feeling." She waved her hand as if to grope for words, the dreadful-looking knife slicing the air near my face. Micajah shot off my lap and under the bed.

"Watch that stupid thing," I said sharply, and with an effort, didn't duck, which she plainly meant me to do.

"I don't like the feeling," she repeated, focusing just over my head. "It's a little like being raped must be. I don't like you much." She *had* been listening for a while. "When are you going to cut and run?" she asked, resting the flat of the knife on the top of the fancy chair's back.

"I don't like you at all, kid," I said angrily. "And if you slice that fabric, it's not me that'll take the blame. I don't know what your point is, but I'll go straight to Mrs. Callingwood if you don't lift that object carefully and carry it away."

"I'll say you lie."

"Somehow I don't think you'll solve your problem that way. Not after that soldier fell at me. She hired me and surely won't tolerate my being annoyed."

"I'm not annoying you," she said, on the defensive now, but still holding the knife near me.

I stood, had the urge to walk away, took hold of my courage and instead stepped up toe to toe with the girl. "You annoy me when you walk in here uninvited. You irritate me with that silly weapon. If you get out now, I won't report this, but if you hang around saying stupid things in that belligerent tone, I'll go find my employer this minute." I scowled, to conceal a little twitch of panic that had started to pull at the outer corner of one eyelid. "Out, Abbott."

She backed a step. I thought she was not really as daring as she'd wanted to seem. "It's not a weapon, it's only a sculpting knife. I'm good at carving. Wax," she added, after an obvious pause. She kept retreating slowly. "Stay away from my man," she whispered. Now I believed in the possibility of her doing me harm, if she could do it in the dark or from behind or when I was helpless. I lifted my left eyebrow as high as it would reach, which is a respectable distance under my bangs.

"You invade this room again, sister, and you'll go out on your ear, and I hope your man, whoever he is, likes cauliflower," I said as nastily as I could with my heart thudding. She turned and disappeared without a word.

I collapsed on the chair and said, "Well!" and breathed deeply to ease my tension. Forget it, I told myself, she's just a dumb—and for some reason jealous—basic coward.

Micajah and I were *still* here to stay.

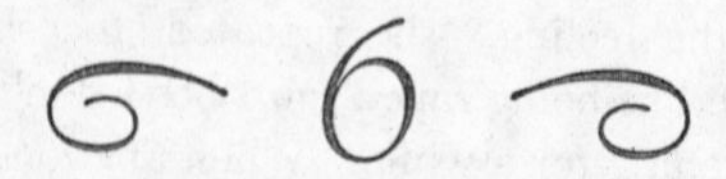

DANIEL CAVANAUGH SAID TO ME, "I THINK WE SHOULD BRING IN someone to investigate this business. It was no more an accident or coincidence than Sibella's near fall."

"What happened to her?" I asked. We were sitting in the great hall finishing our tea, which we'd brought with us from the dining room. I hadn't mentioned Wendy to him, nor would I for now, not unless she continued to be obnoxious.

"There was a balcony in the library. Quite a small one, with an old ice-cream-parlor chair on it, and a narrow catwalk with a railing leading from the balcony to a door in the corner tower. One went into the passage behind the west bookshelves and up a flight to reach it. Sibella was fond of sitting there. It dated from the building of the house and her father used to play royalty on it, looking out over the room with a book in his hand, my grandmother told me. Sibella appropriated the post after his death.

"She was going across the catwalk toward it—this was a month or more ago—when the whole thing started to shiver and tilt out from the wall. Sibella simply turned around and walked slowly back to the doorway, where she stood watching; and the balcony and walk came out away from the paneling and hung there above the floor looking like something from a Laurel-and-Hardy flick, you know, that Stan would be clinging to and crying weakly, plucking at his hair. It honestly didn't look like anything out of *life* at all, it was too good, even the precarious angle was photogenic."

"You saw it?"

"Wendy and Pierce and I. We'd all begun shouting and waving our arms futilely at the first awful creaking noise. I doubt if Sibella even noticed us. She was as cool as a fish. When she saw that it wasn't going to crash all the way, she came downstairs and stood right under it, gazing up and swearing."

He packed a pipe thoughtfully. "We had a man in, of course, a termite inspector. He said it wasn't insect damage, simply age. Seems the braces had weakened, the hardware had loosened in its sockets, all that sort of decrepitude. Said there were other parts of the house that had one foot in the grave, stricken in years. He knew a man, just happened it was his brother-in-law, specialized in old houses, and if we were wise we'd have him go over the Hall and put things right. The man himself wanted to inspect the whole place for termites and related joys. Sibella went into a towering rage and said that Gilbert had built the place to last and by heaven it was going to last long after the lot of us had gone to dust."

"What happened to the balcony?" I asked.

"We took it down piecemeal and erected a few more bookshelves to hide the scars and the tower door, replaced a panel or two . . . Sibella said she wouldn't have it put up again, people would only worry about it. 'Accidents will happen,' she said. But some of us think it may have been engineered to fall under her."

"Certainly the statue was meant to fall," I said.

He looked at me. We were sitting at opposite ends of the big leather sofa with our feet on hassocks. He got his pipe going. The tobacco was fragrant. "Yes, no doubt of that whatever," he said. "Sure you wouldn't rather leave Florida, Laurel? We may have a maniac running loose. Family pride notwithstanding, someone in this house lacks a few staves of being exactly round."

"Since I can't afford to quit, I'll stick it out awhile. And I want to find out what's going on," I said, with a lightness I didn't feel. "After all, the odds are against this accident having been aimed at me, after what you've said about the balcony."

"Yes," he said, frowning, "it would seem so—except that it was you standing there, and you're awfully cool about it." He laughed. "If anything ever dropped on me, they'd hear me bellow all the way to Clearwater! So far as I'm concerned, the strong silent type went out with the coming of sound. I'd demand detectives and bloodhounds. Even Gable would have known enough to yell if he'd stepped into quicksand."

"Yes, pride can be carried too far, and usually is. But I can't imagine why anyone would have it in for me, or what a detective could find out about the Cromwell soldier. Every one of us handled the platform, so fingerprints are out. Nobody was keeping track of anybody."

"I suppose you're right. Then just be wary, Laurel. Or—"

"Or?"

"Give up the job and go away. I could lend you some money. A bold resolution to see things through can easily become a sulky *idée fixe,* which might get you hurt."

"Daniel," I said, leaning toward him and trying to choose my words with precision, "there are some of us who—who are stuck with having to know. We may be as cowardly as the next lion, we may be certain that the only sensible act is to run, but we're rooted to the floor because we *must* know."

"You mean the other side of the hill?"

"Not quite that general, just the truth about what touches me personally. If someone shoves a plaster dummy over at me, I can't move to the next town and forget it. I don't feel that I've ever done anything bad enough to deserve being hurt."

"I see that, yes." He smiled wryly. "The elephant's child, was it, who *had* to know? Someone in Kipling, anyhow, who had a 'satiable curiosity. Girl, I tell you again, go. It's a mad house, it has killed and tried to kill, and I like you too well to see you hurt by it."

"That's a very vague warning."

"If I knew the whole truth, Laurel, I'd tell you! Look here," he said, rubbing his jaw, the splendid blue-enamel eyes brilliant with a sudden idea, "suppose you take a leave of absence? Sibella knows perfectly well that she'll never find another librarian to match you in this our life—I mean, in this our beloved subject. Go and frisk on the beaches and live in a motel until whatever has been building up in Sablecroft Hall expends its energy, destroys what it intends to destroy, or is dissipated itself. Then I'll call you back, and you can do your job in serenity instead of having to leap at every squeal in the woodwork."

"You mean, when Sibella's finally killed?"

"Certainly not!" He appeared shocked beyond words, waving his slim powerful hands melodramatically. Then he said, "Both Pierce and I are keeping a steady eye on Sibella, no fear. But whatever's prowling the Hall has to be nailed into its coffin before we can protect everyone, even outsiders, adequately. So remove yourself for the good of everyone! I believe that's what the cap pistols and voices and falling statuary are saying to you. Don't interfere."

"What if I'm needed?"

"Are you Gregory Peck or Charlton Heston? Why you?"

"Because I'm so obviously a thorn in someone's side. Perhaps I'll be the one to prevent catastrophe, and he, or she, knows it."

"That's rot!"

"And that's MGM circa nineteen thirty-five!" I said.

He blinked. "What is?"

"The exclamation, 'That's rot!'"

Daniel had to laugh. "At least I don't slap my thigh with a riding crop and bawl 'Sink me!'"

"You wouldn't astound me if you did."

He looked at me for a long time without changing expression. Then he said, "My best advice is to decamp, vamoose, get out! Or strap on a gun and a rearview mirror. But you won't take it. I agree with that suit of armor that told you the first night you were a silly little girl. But I admit I'd miss you, Laurel. You and your wide hazel eyes and your devouring need to know . . . very well. But don't think you won't be worrying me to the brim of my dubious sanity." He looked pensively at a Great Dane who was lying at full length on the cool terrazzo near us. "I wonder if I could train one of them to stick with you. Sherry could probably do it better than I could, he's the drillmaster. They've never been specifically taught to guard anyone, just to be watchdogs in general."

"I'll be all right, Daniel. I truly can't take money from you, and I'd hate going on welfare. Besides, Micajah will be coming out tomorrow, and he's tough as teak."

He got to his feet. "Dogged perseverance! A girl and her guardian cat. Go seek your truth, Laurel. I won't interfere. Screech if you want anything." He walked away.

"Come here, Palmerston," I said to the Dane, who was a dark golden brindle with black cross-stripes. He unclosed an eye and regarded me, an aristocratic sneer curling his lip. "Palmerston," I said, very firm of voice, pointing to the floor in front of me. "Come here, Palmerston."

He rose with a deep sigh, stood staring at me, then approached at an elegant sideways gait. I reached out to pat him, but he shied away. "Come here, Palmerston!" Unwilling, he gazed at me, whined in his throat, pawed the floor. "If I'm not scared," I said, "you certainly shouldn't be. Here!"

He stood before me, head rather higher than ordinary.

I smoothed my fingers down over his shoulder. Twice, and again. He turned the great beautiful head and sniffed at my hand. "Good dog," I said, thinking how easily he could remove that hand at the wrist. He had an enormous mouthful of teeth. "Good old Palmerston." He sat, looked at me from a distance of a foot; his tail began to thump slowly on the hard floor.

I went to the wall below the balcony, where the figure of the English Civil War man had been deposited, minus head and hands, to await his destiny. The dog paced beside me; I felt like a cave girl who'd domesticated a mammoth. I knelt on one knee, turning the helmet so that its face bars were up. The stub of thread that had been tied around the center bar was gone. I was not surprised.

"Let's go peek into books," I said to the brindle. He was agreeable, and so we put in the time together until I went up to dress for dinner. When I came down again, he was waiting for me at the foot of the staircase, and followed me into the dining room. Everyone noticed him, but no one said anything until Pierce Poole, turning from the hot cart, exclaimed, "You've made friends with Falkenstein!"

"No," I said, "I've made friends with Palmerston."

"And ferreted out the unholy secret of the phantom army of canines," he said instantly.

"It was easy enough after I counted the stone dinner bowls. If they're fed once a day, as my Irish setters used to be, they must each have a personal bowl. But it seems a joke without a purpose."

"It was never meant to be a joke," said Sibella. "It's only an old custom in the family."

"Everyone made a mystery of it when I asked, as if to frighten me."

"You were told they wouldn't harm you," said Sherry, across the vast table from me. "If you chose to believe they were dangerous and enigmatical creatures, that was your lookout."

"So what's the big secret?" Wendy asked.

I ticked off fingers. "There are the brindle here, the black, the harlequin, the blue with the pale eyes, and the fawn-colored dog with the black mask. Five—and they have no names."

"Certainly they have," said Daniel, "scores of names."

"You," I said to him, "told me there were 'an insane number' of them."

"Aren't *five* whole Great Danes an insane number?" he grinned.

"They haven't any real names of their own." Try as I would, I couldn't keep the reproach out of my voice. "Hasn't anyone ever seen the—the degradation of not having a name of one's own? It's disgusting. I'm sorry, but it is. You make a *thing* out of a tame animal if you don't allow it a name of its own."

"You're being anthropomorphic, Laurel," said Sibella quietly, "ascribing human feelings to dogs."

"I don't believe that. When animals live with human beings, they do take on certain human traits—"

"Or failings," said Sherry. "There's degradation for you."

"Yes, that can be true, but a cat or dog may also be, well, lifted above its common potential when it's treated as an equal by imaginative animals," I said intensely, "meaning people. You can call it humanizing them, but I think it's only helping them to use more of their minds. And how must it feel to be addressed by *any* three-syllable word, accented on the primary, with the voice raised slightly, and know that you're being spoken to? The dogs know *your* names; I've heard one of you say, 'Go to Daniel,' and the dog knows whom you're talking about. But to be called by a hundred different names and have to respond, that's unfair. It's a vile custom."

"La-di-da," Wendy said under her breath.

There was a silence, during which I suddenly wondered whether I'd just involuntarily resigned my position. Then Pierce turned and said solemnly, "She's perfectly right, we've done it so long that we never consider how humiliating it may be to the poor brutes. I remember when I was growing up there was a man who had a dog and a cat whose names were Dog and Cat; and I could cheerfully have throttled the lout every time I heard him call them, it seemed such an inglorious, beggarly thing to me. I never addressed that man except as 'Man.' Strange how I'd forgotten that. We are no better than he when we call our faithful friends by any miscellaneous three-syllable noise. Shame, shame to all of us," he finished, stirring his hot dish violently.

"They're only dogs," said Wendy.

"We're only people," said Sibella. She looked at the brindle thoughtfully. "The Apollo of dogs, someone called the Dane. Perhaps we do depersonalize the poor souls. It's a practice that's so old in the family, we've just gone along with it. It may have begun with 'Sablecroft'—that's a thought. *Duh*-duh-duh. *Ren*ardyne, *Well*ington, *Vol*marstein, *Tanq*ueray." She motioned to Daniel to open the champagne. "Laurel, you may be a soft-headed dreamer, but again you may be right. I'm not sure which. Here, Palmerston!" The brindle got up and padded to her. She felt in the depths of her purse, brought out a piece of dog candy, and gave it to him. "Palmerston," she repeated. "Good dog."

"Sentimental," said Sherry to me, with an expression I could not read. It might have been scorn or grudging approval.

Pierce, beginning to serve up fragrant sweetbreads cooked with morels, said, "The word, I fancy, should be 'decent,'" and gave him a severe look.

"Anyone have any further notions on the fallen warrior?" asked Daniel. Several theories were offered, to none of which I paid much attention, knowing what I did of the magician's thread. "That statue—" Daniel began earnestly.

Then from the wall behind me Colin Clive, in a bit from the only picture in which I had ever found his brand of nerve-ridden overacting acceptable, *Frankenstein,* shouted, "It's alive! It's moving—it's alive! Oh, ho ho, it's alive, it's alive, it's alive!"

"Pass the Taittinger's," said Sibella coolly. And Basil Rathbone shouted in his turn, "It's alive!" and, to cap the whole performance and turn it into delectable flummery, Jerry Colonna screamed, *"It's alive!"* Even Sherry and Sibella laughed as Daniel bowed modestly.

And at that instant—for no reason, it seemed to me—the whole room went sliding into a fast, oblique madness, and I saw all of them with their mouths open howling like lunatics, like the animated mannequins and fun-house figures in *Sleuth,* mankind in grotesque and crude imitations of wood and metal shrieking at me in nightmare; so that what had been only a neat little pleasantry on Daniel's part became as ominous as a door suddenly opening to insanity. I had been startled often and really scared a couple of times here, but when the whole clan Sablecroft laughed together on the heels of those tense taped voices, somehow it flayed my nerves to blood-red rawness. The effect came and went in a flash, but it left me shattered. I think I am one of the least fragile of women, but now I felt like a May fly in a cathedral, tiny and horribly vulnerable to an errant breeze or questing child's hand.

I believe that was one of the worst moments of my life. And for less reason than a bad dream would have given me. Only a few taut electronically reproduced voices and some quiet laughter—for it was quiet. I knew that even as I was recovering and shoving my hands under the table to hide their trembling. Just ordinary laughter at a mild joke, not the cackling hysteria I'd imagined. I'd had an overreaction to continuously hard-held control over my fear.

My third dinner here, and already I was a candidate for a vacation. Daniel had said I should take one. For safety.

But that was asinine! Irrational! I was able to take care of myself. This was no more than a castle crammed with celluloid dreams. The only manifestations of hostility were puerile jokes . . . still, my subconscious knew them for what they were, little windows to the darkness behind this life, this place, this family.

I wished I might leave and never hear of any of them again.

And this too passed, and shortly we were all waiting for dessert and speaking of the soldier and how quaint and curious it was that I'd been standing there when he fell.

Sidney Toler intoned, "Coincidence like ancient egg—leave unpleasant odor."

I saw Sibella's hand appear from below the table. She wasn't above playing a trick or two herself. "I agree with Inspector Chan," she said calmly, just as though he'd been another living person seated with us in the room. Maybe to her he almost was.

Striving to change subjects, and get down to earth, I asked Pierce how he'd come to leave England and settle here in Florida. "Why, Sibella wrote to me. That was in nineteen sixty. She'd heard that Father had died, and I was the last of our branch of the family. She *collected* me, rather. Expecting me to marry some nice American girl and carry on the sacred Sablecroft line. I disappointed her, though, preferring the intellectual joys. By the way, we're showing a film tonight, aren't we? What is it?"

"Mata Hari," said Sibella.

So we ate dessert, coconut ice cream with rum sauce, and then trooped through the silver-studded door into Sibella's private quarters, which—at first glance—were nearly as large as the great hall.

They took up the entire southwest quarter of the house, and were laid out in an approximate L-shape, the lower bar of the L being shortened by an interior wall with another door in it, which led, I was told, to the mistress' bedroom. All the rest of this vast space was enclosed by thickly carpeted floor, the eternal wood paneling, and a pale violet plaster ceiling from which hung the largest chandelier I had ever encountered, now unlit.

The top serif of the L, which lay at the front of the house, at the far end of this immense room, was a very exotic-looking court right out of the Valentino period, lit by dim, swathed pastel bulbs, so that I couldn't distinguish many of its details except for the gigantic green fronds of some tropical plants or trees and the sparkling mist of a playing fountain.

Because there was so much less furniture in here—and no wax figures or armor—the room gave the impression of empty distances, and unless it was fully illuminated always had a rather foggy look to it, I would find out in times to come, as though a perpetual summer haze lay between the door and the Moorish court.

Half a dozen comfortable theater-style chairs were wheeled into place ten yards from a screen, and Pierce began fiddling knowledgeably with a projector and reels of film on a balcony behind us, humming to himself. The screen was permanently mounted on the wall separating Sibella's bedroom from this chamber. It would have been remarkable if Sablecroft Hall hadn't contained its own moving-picture palace. Yet it occupied no more than a quarter of the great open area. "What's the rest of the room for?" I whispered to Daniel.

"Foot races and javelin tossing," answered Sibella, "so Father used to say." I smiled weakly. She had incredible hearing. "Like myself, he appreciated large spaces scantily furnished," she went on, sitting down in the center of the row of chairs. "The room isn't Japanese, but it has the same purpose. It offers me my own brand of serenity. Sit here by me, Laurel," she said, waving away Daniel, exercising her tribal dominance. Again I recognized the possibility that one of these people was actually intending to kill her. Given the fact of Sablecroft Hall being the only refuge any of them knew, except conceivably Sherry Todd, it might well be that Sibella's matriarchal authority was driving somebody over the brink.

One by one the lights went down as Pierce turned three or four dimmers, until they were all pale white glowworms except the nebulous pastels of the Moorish court far away on our left.

It began with a Fox Movietown News, Roosevelt campaigning, Russia enduring a famine, the Nazis electing a couple of hundred Reichstag members, George Bernard Shaw telling off the U.S.A., and other segments. How odd it seemed that this was history—black-and-white, grainy flickerings of history on a par with Jesse James and Abraham Lincoln and Queen Elizabeth I—to four of us; dimmest memory to Pierce; and a well-recalled chunk of her past, indeed, she'd likely consider it her recent past, to Sibella. Then came a Disney print of *Trader Mickey,* and a vintage Edgar Kennedy, *Giggle Water.*

I could have guessed, even if I hadn't noted the copyright dates, that everything had been filmed in 1932, and that the whole program might have been seen, just as it was presented here in this preposterous house, some forty-eight years ago in any theater in the land.

Consistency! Emerson, Thoreau, Hawthorne, one of that group . . . "A foolish consistency is the hobgoblin of little minds." My attention was wandering from Mr. Kennedy and his family, who were building a boat solely in order to christen it with a bottle of champagne they had found. The thought processes of the Sablecrofts seemed to me just as inscrutable as the Kennedys'.

All the dishes in a meal named after actors who'd played together in one film, all these short subjects of the same date as the feature, the screen of a loudspeaker painted to resemble books—was it foolish consistency? Was there any *point* to it? Daniel had said that I, as a librarian, must be as methodical as they were. Was I? Only in things that really mattered, I said to myself righteously. Yet what mattered to them but the movies?

Mr. Kennedy, predictably, did a slow burn.

A low table was set between Sibella and me, and champagne uncorked. "About time," growled the old girl, "that blasted bottle of theirs is driving me to drink." Pierce poured, the others came to get the wine, a shadowy crowd milling nearby. A glass was handed to Sibella, who never took her eyes from the screen.

Consistency—methodical finickiness—whatever they called it—*were their lives as empty as that?*

But emptiness breeds a slow and lusterless eye, a sluggishness of body. And they were all quick movers, except Sherry at times, and their eyes sparkled with life.

Mata Hari began.

We had warped back to the Great Depression, to what was amusing then, to sentimental manna for millions of souls who were gone now. I sat in the atmosphere breathed by my grandfather Alfred Vane in his fifty-fifth year. Time had become confused within the double walls of Sablecroft Hall. So had we all, perhaps. I did not actually wonder whether Mr. Roosevelt would be elected President, but I think I *nearly* did so. . . .

Pierce recharged his glass and changed reels while everyone stretched and came over in the gloom and poured more champagne. The screen turned black, gray, silver again.

"Pierce!" shouted Sibella above the murmurings of Ramon Novarro. Her voice was hoarse and angry. "Pierce! Turn it off!"

He did, so quickly that the figures froze ludicrously above us for a moment before the lamp behind the film went dead. The lights of the little theater eased up to full power, Pierce looking over his shoulder inquiringly. Everyone else turned to gaze toward her. She held out her champagne glass, the thin old hand as stationary as steel.

"Laurel, smell this."

As she didn't offer to move it toward me, I leaned as far as I could, which wasn't quite far enough. So I stood up and went to her, which I think she'd meant me to do in the first place. I sniffed at the glass.

"Nutty," I said. "Like very dry wild nuts of some kind—"

"Try the well-worn phrase," said Sibella icily. "Try 'the odor of bitter almonds.' "

Daniel swore, leaping to his feet, and Pierce came rolling down the steps. Wendy said, voice rising, "Bitter almonds? That's cyanide."

"Prussic acid," corrected the mistress of Sablecroft. "Who the devil's been pouring prussic acid into my champagne?"

"One drop results in death," said Pierce Poole, hushed, moon face pale in the white light. "Don't keep smelling it, Laurel, for God's sake, even the vapor is poisonous! Who—who could—"

I backed up in alarm, my nose tingling at the suggestion. Sibella husked out, "What else do you know about it, Pierce?"

"Nothing, I'm afraid, my dear. I've simply seen it a hundred times on the films."

"It mixes very readily with alcohol," said Sherry into the hush.

That hush deepened into silence, which I fancied might never be broken at all. There was no movement, no word; and then across silence I felt, as tangible as the almond scent lingering in my nostrils, a great thick black wave of hate come washing through the room, and knew that it was not imagination.

Hate is surely the most revolting emotion in the world, when it's strong enough to give off an aura as palpable as an aroma, or as the touch of fingers on your skin. Steve had once written me from Viet Nam that he had discovered this in the middle of a fight with guerillas. I thought of his words: "It smells like blood, but it isn't a smell." I knew now what he'd meant. I suppose Sibella would have said it was the Celtic inheritance, for my father had married an Irish girl. The Celts and the gypsies are sensitive to these things, say what you like.

Sherry walked across. "May I?" he said, and took the glass from her and sniffed it, then touched his tongue to the liquid as everyone gasped or cried out. "Well," he said curtly, "it spoilt the champagne, but it wouldn't have hurt you. It's nothing but almond extract out of the kitchen."

"How the hell did you know that?" snarled Sibella.

"I'm fairly sure that prussic acid wouldn't have turned the wine that brownish color. I think that it's clear."

"You *think?* You took a chance on dying," Pierce burst out at him, with horror and a kind of anger on Sherry's behalf, as one is angry with a child who's put its life in danger, "because you were *fairly* sure?"

"Hydrocyanic acid, or prussic acid, is made, I seem to remember, from bitter almonds, hence the smell. Almond extract that's used for flavoring may come from bitter or sweet almonds, I don't know which; but if it's sweet, it would have been easy to add a touch of Angostura bitters to a little of the extract. I'm guessing on that, I haven't actually tasted almond extract. There never seemed to be any necessity to taste it," said Sherry, sounding no more than half serious.

"Then the business is just a vicious joke," said Sibella. "But you had no right to take such a chance, Sheridan."

"Why not?"

"You're my only grandson, damn it!" she shouted.

He shrugged. "It wasn't all that risky. I'm no lame-brained hero. I simply doubt there's prussic acid in this house in any form, the acid or its salts. It can be used to spray citrus trees, but we don't keep it. We use other things. And since I'm the only person who ever leaves the grounds, and Belle takes in deliveries and checks them at once, it's pretty farfetched to believe that someone else managed to acquire so deadly a poison. Who'd dare order it through the mail? Also," he said, holding up a hand like a Great Detective cinching the case, "we all know that you don't just slug down your champagne, Grandmother—you sit and sniff each glass with appreciation, even when you've had four or five of 'em. There was no way you were going to drink that glass, with such a reek coming from it."

"Oh, *very* good," said Pierce.

"How do you know all that about cyanide?" Wendy asked.

"I read now and then."

"All right," Sibella said, "movie's over. All of you leave. Except Laurel." She looked round at them. "One of you is a marvelous faker," she said without rancor. "I shall find out who, presently."

When they'd gone and the big door was shut, she sighed and relaxed. "Anyone could have done it. They were all back there in the gloom, pouring their wine, fumbling around. And I don't know which one."

"I can't see the point of such a stupid joke," I said. Privately I was thinking of Gilbert Sablecroft and the house he'd built, and how much it itself was a huge practical joke as well as a scene for so many more. A practical joker (the lowest form of human life, save criminals) doesn't need a reason.

"I told you someone is trying to kill me," she said. "Slowly, with some cunning, with a lot of hatred. They think they'll give me a heart attack, I suppose. They're wrong. I have the toughest old ticker in St. Petersburg. Felicity was different. She didn't."

"What do you mean?"

"Nothing. I'll tell you some day. Get me a clean glass, Laurel."

"The champagne's gone."

"Then forget it. Sit down." She stared into space. "Odd, wasn't it, Sherry knowing all about prussic acid?"

"I thought so, yes," I said reluctantly. "It's not your ordinary subject. Is he interested in poisons? Does he read a lot of detective stories?"

"Not as far as I know. Ah," she said, sweeping her hand around disdainfully, "he's out of it, he'd never have volunteered that information, or tasted the stuff, if he'd been the jester!"

I thought privately that it was exactly what a clever man might have done. I said nothing.

"Except that nobody's really out of it," she went on. "There's evil here. Have you felt it?"

"Yes, but I thought of it as hate," I said. "A few minutes ago. Before you mentioned hatred yourself."

"Real pure hate is evil. Not that I can't be a trying, domineering, annoying old biddy when it suits me!" she barked, "but this sort of reaction to it, that's evil. Agree?"

"I don't know. I don't know the reason for the hate."

"I may and I may not. Nothing comes clear so far, I've no proof that I'm right in what I suspect. But if it's only that someone is vexed with my personality, or my tyranny, or whatever they call it —then they're mad as well as bad, and deserve what they get."

I received the distinct impression that Sibella was not entrusting to me the foremost reason for somebody hating her.

"Nobody's above suspicion but you," she said, "and that's because you came after events had been put in motion. I'm glad you did, it's good to have a confidante."

Very well, I thought, let's see if you'll confide in me. "You mentioned Felicity," I said. "How did she die?"

"She was startled to death."

"Frightened?"

"No, I think not. I choose my words carefully, Laurel. She was startled, and her heart died. Coronary occlusion. They did an autopsy."

"And as you were twins, someone thinks you can be shocked to death too," I said.

"Either that, or they want me to live scared for a while before one of these tricks proves serious. How little they know me," said Sibella, with profound contempt. "You've seen something of this house, of how they all dote on surprises and the unexpected. Can you imagine me so astonished by anything that my old pump would stop? Absurd!"

"What sort of thing caught Felicity so unawares that it killed her? How do you know it was just a—a surprise?"

"How do I know? *I saw her die,*" said Sibella, sitting up straighter than usual. "And it was nothing any worse than you've been put through yourself already! My heart's sound because I haven't spent a lifetime gnawing away at it, as she did. . . . Everyone assumes that a girl of twenty-five has a strong heart. You do, don't you? I never asked about your health."

"I'm very lucky, I hardly even catch colds. My heart's fine."

"And in the right place, I trust." She got out of the chair and stalked around aimlessly. Then she said, "You haven't seen our films and tapes. Look here," and going to the east wall, to the right of the projection balcony, slid a huge part of the paneling aside. It was thin and light and set on oiled rollers. Behind it were a series of identical tall white refrigerators. "Naturally they aren't kept at the freezing point or anywhere near it," she said, opening one. "None of our films are of the old nitrate stock. You know how many hundreds, thousands of motion pictures have been lost because the studios and owners simply allowed them to crumble?"

I nodded. "Most of those from the twenties and before," I said.

"And some fine ones from the thirties! At any rate, I keep our films, which aren't particularly rare, any of them, a few degrees below the house temperature; it's good for them. The tapes, too."

"I take it the tapes are only sound, not viewing tapes or whatever the term is."

"Yes, they're audio. If you've seen a movie very often, the sound track's enough to make you see it all over again in imagination. We record 'em from television, or sometimes from rented films. You're to catalogue all these too, you know," she said, indicating stacks of labeled reel tins. "I suppose it will take a year or more, the whole business."

"At least."

She pointed toward the Moorish court, pale pink and blue and violet under its lights. "All the way to that, the fridges run—more than fifty feet of them. Then the papers, the diaries and scripts and letters, they're locked up behind the opposite wall. This is really a far larger room than it looks." Which was something like saying that Carnegie Hall wasn't so tiny as it seemed. "Laurel," she continued, pensive, "I've been thinking. It could have been Sherry. He did stick his tongue into that muck awfully fast. No, I can't eliminate him for sentimental reasons, can I?" She looked at me, closing the refrigerator door. "Laurel, go to bed."

"All right," I said blankly.

"I'm not angry with you, child! I'm working up a dreadful rage against parties unknown, and when I'm at the peak of it I'm going to scream bloody hell! And there's no occasion for you to be exposed to that, so run!"

I told her good night and walked briskly to the door, leaving her pacing the floor and growling to herself like one of the Great Danes of Sablecroft Hall.

After I'd gotten ready for bed I stood at my window looking out over the grounds toward the palm grove, which was bright with moonglow. I wasn't sleepy at all. There was too much to think over. Some night bird came swooping out of the shadow of the trees. Then I noticed movement on the ground, and squinted, but couldn't make it out; so I turned off my lamps and waited till my eyes had adjusted to the outdoors. Then I saw that it was a man, digging a hole in the earth between two enormous palms. I glanced at my watch: past eleven.

That was queer.

I stayed where I was, standing partly hidden by the curtains, watching him. I couldn't tell who he was. He took up a package and dropped it into the hole he'd made. It looked about as big as my head. He filled the hole, and pulling out a handkerchief, almost paper-white under the moon, mopped his face. Then he came toward the house, swinging his spade.

When he'd almost reached the garage, he looked up, and I saw that it was Sheridan Todd. Though he couldn't have made me out, I shrank back till he was gone.

I sighted in on the two palm trees and memorized the spot. Then I went to bed and read myself to sleep. Occasionally the print would blur, and a ripple of fear would run up my spine.

7

DURING THE NEXT WEEK, THE LUMBER FOR THE NEW SHELVES came, and the men, having inspected it carefully and approved of it, went into a tornado of activity, sorting, sawing, planing, sand-papering, varnishing, all in one large corner of the library, so that that part of the house always smelled of fresh-cut wood, a lovely sharp scent that brought ghosts of great forests into the cold Hall. The library was laid with heavy dropcloths and scrupulously cleaned every evening before dinner. Seeing them manhandling the enormously long boards, toiling without letup, I realized again how strong all three of them were. Wendy vacuumed and dusted or listened to tapes with earphones, and I began my real work, which was first of all to bring some general order to the chaos of books.

I would sort a hundred or so on the floor of the great hall, carry them to their various destinations at the north wall of the library and stack them neatly within, I hoped, a dozen feet of where they'd ultimately go. The arrangement would be intricate, but for now I was using a rough order based on subject and alphabetical sequence. It was the most maddening yet agreeable job I'd ever started.

Micajah came out of seclusion that week, and preceded me at a suspicious creeping mince down the corridor to the balcony, where he crouched at the edge, glaring out over the great hall with his eyes popped, for an hour, after which he shot back into the bedroom. The next morning he inched his vigilant way down the staircase, encountered one of the dogs, and hit it on the nose. The Dane yelped and retreated. Micajah took over the great hall and patroled it for some hours, not bothering to notice me at my silly activities with the books. He hissed at Sherry, who wisely made no move to be friendly; put his ears down at Wendy; and rubbed a big splotch of loose white fur onto Daniel's trouser legs. In a few more days he was lying in the exact center of the library, on a chair and two pillows, keeping an eye on the men at their lumber work and looking as if he were bossing the job.

The dogs left him alone all week, but stared askance whenever they happened to see him. Possibly the one who'd been batted on the nose had passed the word.

On my tenth day in residence, I found him lying all over Pierce Poole's lap, purring and kneading the fat man's vest with both forepaws. Pierce beamed. "He knows I'm English. All cats recognize the superior felinophilia of the English. To us, the cat stands in our esteem just a shade below the garden and a little above the umbrella."

That afternoon the brindle Dane, whom I consistently called Palmerston now, was lying in that alert, ears-up, legs-straight-forward pose that makes you believe that they know how noble they look. And Micajah, after eyeing him from behind a hassock for some time, walked over to him and lay down with a sigh between the dog's legs, snuggled against the broad, deep chest, and went to sleep.

The dog peered down at him, head cocked sideways and an amazed expression on his face. Then he looked helplessly at me, as if asking, "What on earth should I do about *this?*" Ultimately, he sat without moving until Micajah had had his nap and decided to move off and wash. The dog rose stiffly, shook himself, and walked out of the room, a portrait of bewilderment. He was a real gentleman. I believe he'd have lain there until nightfall rather than disturb the cat's rest.

The next time Micajah met him, he hissed at him; but no one had ever told my cat that consistency was a virtue, for he wasn't a Sablecroft.

Sometimes I'd glimpse Belle McNabb, serving meals when Pierce had been too busy to prepare them, or watching me from the kitchen door or some shadowed corner. She seemed fascinated by me, but never initiated a conversation, and when I said anything she would make a cryptic utterance and disappear into her own realm. I learned absolutely nothing about her for a long time.

Gradually I'd been emptying the bookcases in the great hall. One day I found that Pierce had carried one of the heavy things upstairs and set it directly before the sealed spy hole, relocating my two-way vanity. I'm ashamed to admit that I wedged my head in between case and wall to see whether there were any tiny gaps in the wood . . . plainly Pierce had put the case there so I wouldn't worry about the mirror, but I had grown used to questioning everything. And now I'd come to the point of distrusting kindly actions from Pierce!

Why didn't I pack and leave this lunatic asylum, taking Daniel up on his offer? It was all very well to be persistent in search of the truth, to want the job desperately, to be ashamed to accept unearned money, to be afraid for the old woman of whom I was fond and who'd be at the mercy of five possible killers if I abandoned her. But if the almond extract had been prussic acid and the glass mine, I'd be *dead,* because I didn't sniff my wine appreciatively. The armor, had it fallen on my head, might have cracked my skull. And I didn't want to be dead for a long while yet. . . .

Sherry in these ten days had changed remarkably. Not for the better or for the worse; only changed. At first he'd been forbidding, almost abusive. After that, evidently resigned to putting up with me, he'd turned sarcastic and scornful. But for several days now he'd been purely a bad-tempered man, alternately ignoring me and snapping my head off over trifles. He looked profoundly unhappy when he thought he wasn't watched, and glowered if he caught me looking at him. He no longer warned me to go away, nor did he sneer if I gave an opinion that ran counter to his. He simply treated me like a silverfish he'd discovered in the binding of a book. I'd have thought that he loathed me, but he acted much the same with everyone else except Sibella. To her he was almost too polite, as if making a strong effort, and I wondered if she'd been right when she'd claimed that all of them were basically afraid of her.

Anyway, I wanted to solve the problem of Sheridan Todd, because despite his present evil disposition I had the impression that his true nature was something quite different. There was always an air about him—I don't know that I can make this clear—of not being himself, as there is with a person who is sick . . . though Sherry was plainly as healthy as one of the Danes.

And there was the matter of his burying a parcel on the fringe of the palm grove. True, he had every right to bury anything from a gnat to an elephant in Sablecroft ground, and *I* had no business to question it. But the furtive dead-of-night interment piqued my curiosity. When I got up the nerve, the unforgivable brashness, to abuse my position in this house, I knew that I was going to snoop into it.

Busybodybusybodybusybody—

"I guess so, Grandfather," I said wearily to the well-remembered voice in my head. "But you'd have done precisely what I'm going to do. If not much worse!" There might be all sorts of idiosyncrasies running in the Sablecroft blood, but there was defiance in the Vane line, an impertinent, audacious strain that wouldn't refuse a dare or ignore a challenge. Not a lovable trait, true, but it would never have surfaced if they hadn't thrown all those tricks and menaces at me.

Then I went on, inevitably, to contemplate Daniel. He too had warned me off, but more mildly, and otherwise his conduct seemed all of a piece. He was a kind of light comedian, a Dick Van Dyke character, here and there and everywhere. Compared with Sherry, he *was* something of an idler, but he could, when the mood held him, work on the new bookshelves as long and arduously as either of the other men, and all in all, I liked him quite well. So, it was plain, did Wendy, when she wasn't engaged in liking Sherry; and she didn't care for me any more than I did for her. Yet both of them seemed to be wholly themselves, as did Pierce when he wasn't abstracted, and certainly as did Sibella Callingwood. Only Sherry was a complete puzzlement.

Well, I could start on him tonight with the one lead I knew I had. It was time to be brash. So I retired when the rest of them did, waited an hour, and dressed in dark shirt and slacks, went down through the ghostly big rooms lit here and there by the glowworm nightlights and out the back way past the magnificent old Cord dreaming in its solitude.

Walking through the tangible wet woolen blanket that is Florida's summer night, carrying a spade from the garage, I reached the trees and took a sight on the part of the Hall's eastern face where my room lay. Here was the place I'd marked in memory, noting the slant of each of two-hundred-foot Washingtonia palms. Directly between them Sherry had dug his pit and buried his package, a bundle the size of a human head. There was no grass here to displace, no sod to lift carefully away and stamp down when the job was done. By the light of a quarter-moon I got to work with the spade.

Any act done furtively *had* to be investigated. Who knew what was important in this farrago of grotesqueries?

We were having a premature taste of the rainy season, and storms had been blowing in across the land from the Gulf, or out of Tampa Bay; one had hit us late this afternoon and the ground was sodden. My blade brought up enormous jagged chunks of sandy soil, dripping with water, which I heaped on one side. About two feet down, I hit something that wasn't dirt. I bent to stare into the black hole.

"Should have brought a flashlight," I grunted, straining my eyes, aware with half my mind that I was washed with the sweat of exertion. Instantly a stream of white radiance literally blasted over my bowed shoulder and hit the excavation. It was such a shock to my nervous system that I think my heart missed a couple of beats. I hoped that Belle had come out of her house to see what I was doing, but I feared that it would be himself; and it was.

"Well and truly dug," said Sherry. "That's it. That muck on top was once newspaper. Pull it aside, Miss Pry."

Not glancing behind, I shoved gingerly at the wad of pulp with the edge of the spade, trying to calm my ragged breathing.

"Afraid to soil those dainty hands?" he asked cheerfully. "Your dedicated detective wades in right up to her elbows."

"At least," I snarled, "I'm doing something! I'm doing my best to explain all the suspicious goings-on that keep cropping up in this madhouse. I haven't noticed anyone else trying to solve anything."

"Quite right you are too, lass," he said, closer to my ear than was comfortable, in a spurious British accent. "*Hell*-lo! Something's in that newspaper, isn't it? Seems to be alive, what?"

"Inspector Lestrade," I said, now nearly as angry as I was frightened, since we were quite alone in the thick, greasy night, "cut out the funny stuff. I warn you, I can slam your shins with this shovel before you strangle me." And I held it ready.

"Dear brave Mrs. Warrick, I'm here to help! This may be a significant find. A clue, a clue! I'll bet you never thought to bring a specimen jar, though." An empty can that had once held Micajah's favorite goodies came thumping into the hole. "Love a duck, lass, you have to go out prepared for anything. Go on, scoop some up."

"Some what?" I snapped. "For all I know, this may be a head down here."

"Then you remove some of the putrefying flesh—"

"No need to be disgusting."

"And take it in for scientific examination," he finished.

"Stop that!" I shouted, my voice weirdly muffled in the soggy air. "You know it can't be a head. No one's missing."

"True, unless there *was* someone living in the passages, whom I beheaded with a cleaver and dismembered—"

"Sherry, please! I'm only trying to find out the truth," I said, close to crying between fear and rage. "You're scaring me."

"I mean to," he said cruelly. "You little fool, how invulnerable do you think you are? If I'd been a person bent on murder, I could have come silently over—"

"You did!"

"—and walloped you with a hatchet, buried you, and after one more storm, who'd ever know where you'd gone? Now take a sample."

"You mean you're terrifying me out of my wits just to teach me to take better care of myself?" I said, and sniffled, embarrassing myself horribly. I *hated* to let him know how he was frightening me.

"Absolutely. And," he said, lower and more wickedly, "because I'm as angry as a wet wasp. Who are you, you little bookworm, to poke into whatever I care to do?"

"A woman who doesn't want anyone else to die," I got out somehow.

"Admirable," he said flatly. "Who's already croaked?"

"Felicity."

"I see."

I pushed away a big piece of the ruined newspaper. A squirming mass of wriggling, ugly, living things, maggots or larvae or whatever they were, lay exposed to his flashlight's glare. I could smell nothing in that gummy atmosphere, but I could fairly feel the awful putrescence. I gagged.

"Snoops ought to have strong stomachs. You didn't even bring a utensil for handling rotten objects," he said, "but I did." A hand came over my shoulder; in it was a teaspoon.

"Sherry!"

"You've come this far, you must go all the way. Scratch off the gooey creatures and take a sample. Have it analyzed for poison. I promise you, when you see what it is—if you can tell, after all these days in tropical ground—the thought will occur to you."

"What is it?"

"Food."

"What!"

"Food. Do as I tell you at once. You've meddled in things that woman was meant to leave alone," he said, calling up the ghosts of Dr. Frankenstein and the invisible man and Lord knows how many other mad scientists, but there was no bantering in his voice; he did it out of the unquenchable cinematic instincts of his clan.

"When in doubt, quote a flick," I growled. "Give me the blamed spoon."

I knelt on one knee, muddying my slacks, and took the can and flipped away the layer of crawling horrors with its edge. A brownish, lumpy material appeared. I pried out a piece, which was hideously sticky, and knocked it into the can, shuddering.

"There are two more unpleasant substances there. You must have some of each. Down this way a few inches, I think."

I'd never have believed I could do it without vomiting, but with spade and can and finally the ridiculous teaspoon, I did it. The last stuff was pale and mottled and so solid that I bent the handle. But I got it. I stood up. "Satisfied?"

"Are you?"

"Don't think I *won't* find out what this is, Sherry."

"I hope you do." His voice was cold and formal. "You've shamed me. I don't take kindly to that. Yet you must go all the way."

"But how have I shamed you? By suspecting you equally with Daniel, Pierce, Wendy, and Belle? If I alone had seen *them* burying something in the middle of the night, would you want me to ignore it?"

"Oh, stop quibbling," he said. "I'll fill that in for you."

"I can do it."

"Doubtless. But I will." He did so, levelling it with the surrounding earth. We went back together, mute. I wondered why *I*—even though I was an outsider—should feel humiliated under the circumstances. It had been his furtive act, the burial, not mine. I left the dirty spade in the garage, not even saying good night.

I found a heavy plastic bag in the kitchen and wrapped the dreadful can in it, tied the neck securely, shivering with disgust, trotted up to my room, slung the bag into the empty bookcase, had a brisk shower and washed my hair in case the foul miasma had clung to it, put on pajamas and got into my bed, after first looking under it.

The next day, after a fruitless search, I asked Pierce if there was a phone book in the house. It seemed to me that the fat man, with his mind so often appearing to wander from the here-and-now, would be the least likely to grill me about my purpose.

"I have one upstairs," he said. We went to his room and he took it from a shelf. "The Yellow Pages are handy for looking up what one needs from Out There. Then one goes to the phone downstairs and has it sent in. We each have a copy."

"Nothing's listed under the category I want," I said, flipping back and forth in it.

"Perhaps I can help."

I thought carefully. No harm in the general fact. "I want something analyzed. I thought Analytical Chemists, or Chemical Laboratories. . . ."

"Why, that's the last thing *I* had to find! There's a most discreet firm I can put you on to. I, ah, utilized their services for the contents of Sibella's wineglass. Couldn't let it pass without checking, eh? Results, champagne, aromatic bitters, and a dollop of almond extract, as Sherry hypothesized." He turned a few pages and pointed. "That one. Ask for Mr. Alfinbaugh. He'll come here at any time you request, and have the analysis back twenty-four hours later. Be at the door at the exact time, and you'll preserve your secret."

"A private detective?"

"A staunch old firm of much prudence."

I thanked Pierce, noted the number, and after wrapping my nauseating mess in newspaper, phoned, and waited till 2:00 P.M., when I walked to the front door. I went out through a slight drizzle to where a nondescript man in a gray shirt and brown trousers stood waiting. I handed the package over the tall gate, he took it and said, "Right. Same time tomorrow." He evaporated down the street, and I returned to work. If that man had come into the library five minutes later, I don't believe I'd have recognized him. He'd chosen his trade well. He could have shadowed a bloodhound unnoticed.

At two minutes before two the next day, I sloshed through the shallow puddles of the last rain to the blue double gate, where a man, who might have been yesterday's messenger or another, slipped an envelope through a hole of the paisley pattern. "Bill's attached," he murmured to a passing lizard. "Just mail it in, miss."

He dissolved, and I flew to my room to discover what Sherry had sunk into the sandy earth below the palms.

The very reasonable bill was attached by a black paper clip to an extensive analysis. My eyes skipped down the long page.

"Samples submitted contained numerous scavenger insects . . . Largest portion of material consisted of many layers of phyllo-dough, originally paper-thin but now deteriorated into a pasty mass. These layers had been spread with pistachio nuts and saturated with honey. . . .

"Second substance, also much disintegrated by action of scavengers and water-soaked soil, was concoction of sugar, pounded almonds, whites of eggs, minor ingredients such as liquid glucose, artificial color . . . Third substance, crushed sesame seeds, sugar, and negligible additives. . . ."

There was more, but the last paragraph was the heart of the matter.

"The three particular components of the totality submitted for analysis are, in order as above, the exotic sweetmeats *Baklava* (likely made in Tarpon Springs, Florida), *Marzipan* (likely imported from Denmark), and *Halvah* (likely imported in cans from Greece). No trace of any poison is present beyond the offensive animal life."

Baklava, marzipan, halvah, and no poison. Just candy and bugs.

I'd invaded someone's privacy for the first time in my life, and was a prize specimen of "offensive animal life" myself. I knew all about a very personal aspect of Sherry Todd now, and I was ashamed and remorseful. I should apologize. But that might be worse than holding my peace, and embarrass him even more deeply. No grown man wants it known that he's a candy addict trying to quit. I must pretend, if the matter came up, that I'd thrown the disinterred muck in the garbage.

A FEW MORE DAYS WENT BY, AND THEN DANIEL CAME TO ME IN the great hall where I was stacking books on the floor. "Laurel!" he shouted, waking Palmerston and Micajah who'd been drowsing in a white-and-brindle heap. "I've just had the most glorious idea!"

I straightened painfully, for I'd been lifting and putting down books for about six hours. "What?" I laughed, it was impossible not to treat this man as an enthused small boy. "Are we going on a picnic?" For the hot sunny days had returned to the Suncoast.

"Outside? You jest. Look here, you're a librarian!"

"That *is* a glorious idea."

"Don't be ironic at me. I'm going to give you the plans of the Hall, and you're to find the hidden room! You have a logical, orderly way of attacking problems. It's been walloped into you."

"What hidden room?" I asked, to hear Daniel's version as well as Sherry's.

"The one Gilbert had made but kept off the charts, that I've been looking for all my life, in which lie inestimable treasures, of course!" he told me, and flung down on a tile table an immense roll of contractor's plans, blueprinted on manila paper and grown brittle at the edges. He spread them out and weighted the sides with books snatched from one of my careful stacks. "Look these over and tell me where the most obvious place would be. We'll eliminate possibilities till—"

"Daniel," I said, glancing at the thick mass and then at his flushed, joyful face, "I can read plans and maps by common sense and a little knowledge, but I'm no expert."

"More so than me by a damn sight. Go on, try it."

"Are you sure that room's existence isn't another of Gilbert's farces?"

"Absolutely. Too many things are missing that we know were once here. I feel mortally certain you can locate it."

"*I* don't. There must be fifty plans here. And I'd need photographs of the outside," I said, thinking, "and I'd have to study these carefully, tour the passages again—"

"I'll guide you! When?"

I laughed, realizing on the faintest rim of consciousness that I'd laughed more with Daniel in my time at Sablecroft Hall than in the two years before. "As soon as I can! First I have to put in my six hours per, after all."

"Sibella wouldn't mind if you slacked off on the cataloguing, Laurel love. She thinks you work too hard anyhow."

"I would mind. But there's plenty of extra time for this. I won't promise you a thing, though," I said seriously. "I'm *not* an adept."

"You're too modest. We'll locate the blasted place now, I know we will!"

I had never seen him so excited. "We'll give it a hard try at least," I said. "Can you find me a lot of photos?"

"By dinnertime. Matter how old they are?"

"Not a bit. Oh, Sherry told me there are passages not shown on the plans."

"Don't worry. I penciled them in as we discovered 'em. Everything we know about is here." He tapped the sheaf of aged blueprints with his knuckles.

"Have you ever gone over the place with a tape measure and these plans? A room must have, well, *room* enough, it takes up space wherever it is."

He grinned. "I honestly haven't the patience. I can crawl around with a flashlight all day, tapping walls and testing floors and ceilings, but grinding away at a mountain of architectural details and making mathematical calculations, I grow faint and my mind strays. It ain't my style," he said, looking like Huck Finn admitting that he hadn't done his homework.

"I, being a librarian, just *love* to grind," I said. "To drudge, to swot, to plunge myself into monotony, what glee! Thanks, Daniel."

"I didn't mean that." He was now aggrieved. "It's only that you have the discipline and a good base of knowledge."

"A *little* knowledge, I said—"

"On the backs of a couple of the last plans, which deal with the passageways, you'll find all sorts of scribbles; I did take a slew of measurements before I realized it was entirely beyond me."

"It isn't, really. I'll show you how to calculate such things. Naturally, you have to know which portions of a building like this must be solid, and which can be hollow."

"And you know things like that?" he said, all eagerness.

"I know some things like that, from grinding, and I can find out more at the public library."

"You shame me."

"I mean to! You could have been reading up the subject for what, twenty years? How old are you, anyway?"

"Twenty-eight."

"Then you ought to be crestfallen."

"I grovel at your feet in disgrace, princess," he said, doing nothing of the kind. "But you will help?"

"Of course I will. I might even teach you to read."

"Like Irene Dunne with the Siamese children. You're a saint. I'll marry you when I get around to it. Shall we have another look at the secret places tomorrow?"

"Whenever I've studied these," I said firmly. "Now put those books back where they came from and I'll go on with my work."

His wide lips formed the word "grind," and he laughed as he did what I'd ordered. "Anything you want toted?"

"As long as you're going into the library, yes, all these."

I dawdled behind him, looking at the architect's drawings. At last I sat down and flipped through them. The game was afoot, against my sensible wishes: The notion of a secret room was entrancing. It had been lurking at the back of my brain, I suppose, ever since Sherry had mentioned the old story. Now here were the plans, and Daniel's enthusiasm was more infectious than Sherry's casual reference.

Where would it be? Off one of the main rooms, behind the paneling of the vestibule, tucked away next to a contortion of the labyrinth, over a bedroom, in a tower? I'd have to take the outside dimensions. One thing I knew, there was a definite limit to how far we could trust these layouts. Gilbert Sablecroft wouldn't have given away any secrets. I imagined that he'd paid plenty, on top of the fortune that the Hall had cost him, to keep various builders' mouths shut.

What fun it could be to seek, to measure and estimate and probe, to plot things on graph paper and narrow the possibilities until—

"In my spare time," I said firmly and loudly. Micajah mewed a question and I said, "Nothing, nothing, big fella," and went to arrange more books in the library.

I retired to my bedroom after dinner, taking the plans and a bundle of old photographs with me. I got ready for bed and spread them across the counterpane to study them. After several attempts by Micajah to turn the pictures into toys, I'd filed them with some guesses at which tower belonged on which corner, that I would confirm the next day. Then I went seriously into the blueprints. It was a fascinating chore. I got a pad to make notes on, and turned out all the lights but that at the head of the bed. I suppose two or three hours passed.

I heard a low noise in the next room. Not Pierce's, behind me, for there were two bathrooms between that one and mine; the room through the opposite wall. Felicity's room.

I glanced at the clock. It *was* late, after midnight. What would anyone be doing in there at this hour? I listened so intensely that I could hear the tiny sighing squeak that was Micajah's snoring. Perhaps I'd been wrong. No, there it was again, a tapping.

A wall in that deserted room was being quietly sounded, I thought the far wall. What was beyond it? A corridor giving at one end onto the hall and at the other into the ambulatory encircling the house.

I padded over in bare feet and put my ear to the wall. Tap. Pause. Tap. Using an old trick, I fetched a water glass from the bathroom and cupped my ear to that, holding it on the wall like a doctor's stethoscope to some flat plaster chest. Thud, thud, knuckles careful not to bang too loudly as the unknown made his—her?—*its*—way along to the front of the room, hesitated, went back, probably on a different level.

I couldn't go open the door and say cheerily, "What are you doing?" because it was none of my business if a Sablecroft, even Gilbert, wanted to investigate the dead woman's room, was it? They thought me asleep, I supposed, or else were relying on the excellent soundproofing of these private rooms.

The rapping stopped, and I distinctly heard a chair or table dragged along the floor. No carpets in there? That would be strange indeed for this house of wealth. Perhaps a big central rug and bare wood around its edges. Something creaked—springs long unoiled? Small noises came that I couldn't identify. Then a long silence. I returned to bed, and instantly a muffled thump and a very low voice, unintelligible, sounded. I sat there staring. The voice was a man's.

Not Wendy, then, or Sibella. Or Belle. Or Felicity. I smiled, convincing myself that I'd never believed it to be a ghost. Micajah opened one eye (he was lying on the other) and looked at me with wicked amusement. He knew that alone in a still-unfamiliar place, I tended to be superstitious.

"You think you know so much," I whispered at him. *Knowing* that he knew, he closed the eye.

I rolled up the plans and put them on my dresser. Whoever was in the uninhabited room moved another piece of furniture. It wasn't my affair. I turned out the light and snuggled down under the sheet. After a while I heard a door open and close quietly.

Ghosts don't have to open doors. I fell asleep.

The next day Micajah disappeared.

I'd let him out as usual when I'd gone down to my job a little before 8:30, and at teatime realized that I hadn't seen him since. I toured the house, though not Sibella's rooms—she'd have told me if he'd gone in there, because they hadn't made friends yet—and I didn't find him. I ventured into the kitchen to ask Belle whether he'd come through on his inquisitive way outside.

"Haven't seen him," she said, staring at me with her unreadable expression. "That cat never gives me the time of day anyhow."

"He's like that," I said helplessly.

"He comes through, I'll send you word," she said, grudging it, managing to give the promise a sinister overtone. I retreated.

All the men seemed concerned, and someone suggested a hunting party armed with delicacies and squeaker toys. "He must be in the house," said Daniel, "there's no way—"

"The dog door," said Pierce fretfully. "He's strong enough to press through that!" So the four of us went into the dining room and opened it—a flexible, circular thing somewhat like the lens of a camera—and I peered through at the sunny chain-fenced run.

"He could take that fence like a staircase," I said gloomily.

"Oh dear," said Pierce, "he may be on his way back to Connecticut."

"He's attached to me, not to any place in particular. I don't care *what* you read about cats."

"You're certain?" That was Sherry. "Would he prowl and then come home?" He rubbed his bandit's mustache till it bristled. "The beast will pick up ticks and fleas if he's out. They're thick in these latitudes. And earmites, probably."

"Out There," said Pierce in a tremulous voice. "Out There with all the stray dogs and stray people, and the bayou to fall into with its sharks and eels, and poisonous berries of every description—better *me* than the poor cat!" he exclaimed, fear and bravery mingled in his rich voice. "We must all go after him."

"He's not exactly helpless," I said, patting his arm.

"Neither was your Mr. Lincoln," said Pierce severely. "Nor any number of large and splendid dogs, but the outside world finished them off thoroughly, you know." I didn't think it would be kind to point out that Lincoln was shot in a theater. Pierce was too wrought up.

"Let's check the house again first," said Daniel, "calling at intervals."

"If he's under a table, mad, he won't come out till he's good and ready," I said.

Nevertheless, we tried it, and after a while Sherry got onto the intercom and said, his voice booming through the house, "Laurel, your cat's behind the paneling in the library." We hurried to congregate there. Micajah let out a muffled howl of indignation.

"He's in the lower passage," said Daniel. "How? Was anyone in there today?"

Evidently no one had been in the labyrinth. I went into it through the tower door, using the false-book opener, and walked toward the place where we'd heard him, calling his name in a mollifying tone. I couldn't find him and began to be afraid, irrationally touched with terror. Then I heard a violent burst of feline irascibility quite close, but couldn't locate it. I'd turned on all the lights in that corridor: Nothing in the way of a white cat appeared.

The next resentful scream came from above me. He must be on the second floor! Thinking that this might be the only house in America where the walls had more levels than the rooms, I climbed the tower stairs and headed west again, lighting the overhead bulbs. No Micajah. But the racket! Like a mountain lion with its tail in a vise. I wondered what Sibella was thinking of my silent, introspective cat by now. I tried to zero in on the yowl, but it kept moving.

I thought of the architect's drawings. There *was* a space between the levels of this wall, like a double flooring. But how to get into it? I seemed to recall that it was eight inches high. Oh, *dear*. I opened the spy hole overlooking the library and called anxiously down to Daniel, who claimed to know these passages best.

"The ladder," he said, neck craned. "Ten feet to your left. Pull it out from the wall and shove it down and the trap will open. Then go down a few steps and you'll see the opening."

"There's a ladder right behind me."

"That's to the roof. Stop being overwrought and dense, and rescue your cat," said Sherry Todd irritably.

Micajah agreed with him in a sepulchral blast that seemed to come from just under my feet, like the ghost of Hamlet's father. "'Rest, rest, perturbed spirit,'" I said to him, closing the port. I found the next ladder and followed orders, and a hatchway opened which was, indeed, about a foot thick, with a vacant place in the middle. Standing on the ladder, I called Micajah, wishing I had a flashlight. The space between the second-level flooring and the lower-level ceiling was dark and cobwebby.

"Come on, old boy," I said gently. "Shut your mouth and come to mama." Micajah, unseen but heard to great advantage in the long little echo chamber, swore at me savagely. "Come here, you damned albino," I yelled, and with that, a term that Micajah always took badly, he edged forward into view, his tidy whiskers dripping gray spiderweb and his eyes glowing like hellfire coals. "Come *on,* idiot," I said, balancing myself and holding out both hands. He stretched his neck forward but refused to move anything else, so I caught him by the ruff and the loose chest hide and pulled him out, together with a shower of dust and ancient nails and Lord knows what tiny dead creatures of the darkness who had flourished in that secret place for half a century.

Why we didn't both fall off the ladder is a mystery. A tough seven-year-old, eighteen-pound cat trying to get out of your grasp in midair is an appallingly difficult object to hold when you're standing on a rung of a perfectly vertical ladder. It would, I suppose, have made a marvelously humorous scene in some alas-never-to-be-made Cary Grant-Katharine Hepburn film, one of them dealing frantically with the cat while the other shouted lunatic advice and encouragement; but all alone a dozen feet or more above a concrete floor, I didn't find it funny at the time. I managed to get the beast tucked under one arm, gave him a smart tap on the snoot with my fingertips to convince him I wasn't playing, and went down as fast as I was able, while he twisted himself in all the directions he could and made hideous threats at the top of his lung power. Then I stepped off and sent the ladder shooting upward, and the hatchway closed and I held Micajah by his immense rib cage and shook him and screamed "Shut up!" and for a wonder, I guess because he'd been truly scared, he subsided. I carried him out into the library and asked Daniel to turn off the passage lights for me.

Pierce shook his head. "As messy a cat as I've seen."

"He's a perfect offense!" I said.

"Mew?" said Micajah in a repressed whisper.

"Poor old fellow," said Pierce. I wished he'd seen the poor old fellow trying to tear my arm to ribbons. "Where would he have found an entrance to that narrow prison?"

"I'll investigate that later," I said. "Now I have to brush him, and he'll give himself a bath when he's calmed down, and spit up a dustball. Then he can stay in his room and mull over his sins."

Daniel came back and would have stroked the dirty brute, but Micajah swatted at him angrily. "You *are* in a state," said Daniel. "This is your pal, remember? How and why did you sneak into that place?" But he only hissed malevolently at his friend as I carried him away.

That night we all adjourned after dinner to the great hall, where Sibella sat in state and directed us through an investigation of the black platforms that supported the throng of figures. One or two of us would lift and hold a statue while another would turn the base over, examine it painstakingly, thump it, then set it down again. No insect damage was found, and Sibella said that the collapse of the Cromwellian soldier must have been pure accident.

"Sure," said Sherry to me, voice sour with irony.

Pierce brought in a new platform he'd made, identical with the others. He set it on the terrazzo where the first had been and atop it arranged the headless, handless dummy in armor.

"Good," said Sibella, who was dressed in her black silk caftan with liberal broad splashes of gold, and looked more regal than ever. "Now we shall all—" But what we were all to do next remained unspoken forever, because she was interrupted by the coiled-steel voice of Basil Rathbone, surrounding us with a sudden smooth thunder of sound as every speaker in the enormous room went on.

"We have put her living in the tomb! . . . I tell you that she now stands without the door!"

I was conscious of Sherry, who was beside me, turning his head swiftly to look toward the arch of the dining room; but I think that most of us stared at the closed door nearest to us, which led from beneath the balcony into the kitchen. That door seemed to loom larger and more portentous than it ever had before, due, undoubtedly, to the commanding magic of the old actor's voice. I saw it begin to swing slowly open. My breath caught painfully in my throat.

"It was the work of the rushing gust," the loudspeakers pealed, "but then without those doors there *did* stand the lofty and enshrouded figure of the lady—"

All sound stopped. I think no one moved a finger. The door went full open and Sibella stood up from her chair and said huskily, "Oh dear *God!*" into the horrible silence.

I thought it was a *doppelgänger,* a grotesque counterpart of the mistress of Sablecroft Hall. Clad in a white shroud smeared with gouts of red, it stood there staring at us with eyes of unearthly brilliant blue, with the same skullcap of chestnut hair, the same sharply carved nose, the same erect lean frame under its winding-sheet. Then it swayed and fell forward, as Wendy and I screamed, stiff as a log, onto its face; and I was aware of gratitude that those enormous awful eyes were hidden.

Several of us surged forward as the spectral voice lapped over us again from every direction. *"From that chamber and from that mansion I fled aghast!"*

Pierce and Daniel reached the thing and lifted it together. "Bring that object to me," said Sibella loudly, sitting down. They carried it between them and held it up, an excellent example of painted papier-mâché work. The bed-sheet shroud had been disarranged and showed beneath it a simple, rather slapdash framework of twisted metal clothes hangers. The dummy had been constructed not to stand on a pedestal and be admired, but solely to make that one spectacular entrance.

I realized now that the eyes were wrong. Sibella's were definitely gray, while these were like the bright enameled-looking eyes of Daniel. In all other ways, it resembled Mrs. Callingwood, as interpreted by Ivan Albright.

"Well, well," said Sibella, breathing hard, her brows contracted in fury, "if it isn't sister Felicity! Struggled back out of the tomb at vast expense of gore and sweat, I see. Whose damnable work can *this* be?"

Daniel said hoarsely, "Not mine, obviously. You all know I don't have the skill . . . and I wouldn't have violated her memory."

"Wait," I put in, my voice shaking. "Who opened the door?"

"More of your blasted electronics?" Sibella demanded of the quartet, as I went to that door and inspected it for fragments of magician's thread, but found none. I pulled the edge of it experimentally, and after a slight hesitation it came swinging open again; then, a few seconds later, it closed sluggishly.

"There's a light beam in the kitchen that opens the door, Laurel," Pierce said. "It's handy when you're wheeling out the hot cart, or carrying trays of food, so long as you've remembered to turn it on beforehand. And the door closes, as you see, by itself."

"Belle?" said Sibella uneasily. "Oh, no! But see if you can find her, Laurel." I knew in that instant that she did trust only me, and that however grisly and minatory this place became, I could not abandon the proud old woman, no matter how bleak my own future came to look. I went into the tidy kitchen and turned on the light, proceeded to the garage, found other switches that illuminated that oversize concrete cavern and sent the door rattling upward. Then I put my head out of doors, to be met with blackness and the hot, sultry night air of Florida. Nothing moved between house and palm grove. I could see two lights in the windows of Mrs. McNabb's house. I shut the garage and returned to the great hall, the kitchen door opening before me, and I reported to Sibella.

"Felicity didn't open that portal herself," said she in a cutting voice. She picked up a phone and dialed. "Belle? When did you leave the house, dear? Thank you. No, everything's fine. Just checking something. Good night." She hung up, frowning.

Daniel said, "I won't forgive this. The blood on the sheet is going too far, much too far." His jaunty tone had vanished. I wondered what he meant about the blood.

"If the misled joker would confess, we could forget the whole ridiculous affair," said Sibella, prodding the dummy on the floor with one slipper. "But that won't happen. Laurel, see if you can find anything that will help."

"Such as?"

"An electrical device of some kind. In this room, near the place where *somebody* stood. Look under rugs, tables, everywhere."

Sherry lifted his hand. "Wait. This terrazzo is—how thick? Several inches? And under it is the massive concrete slab that was poured before they built the house. No room for subterranean electrical connections, so there'd have to be an exposed wire running to the door, or another beam of light out here which someone broke by a sideways step or an arm movement over the head. Right, Daniel?"

"Right. Or a remote-control switch."

"Well, as the rugs don't overlap and no wire's in evidence on the terrazzo between them, I wouldn't bother lifting rugs, Laurel."

I returned to the kitchen door and checked for wiring. I wasn't an expert, but it did seem to be an innocuous entryway. Daniel, who'd gone to the area where he'd been standing at first, said,

"Here's a subminiature remote switch. Shall I try it?"

"Did you press it before?" Sibella asked him fiercely.

"No, dear, though I knew it was here. It activates only one speaker, unless it's been readjusted since I used it on Pierce a few months ago." He put his hand on the frock-coated waist of a fine wax effigy of George Arliss as Disraeli. There were two or three seconds of silence, and then from high on the western wall the voice of Guinness' Fagin lisped huskily, "Such a pleasant piece of work."

"In dreadful taste now," said Daniel apologetically, "but at the time, extremely funny."

"Really not bad at all," murmured Pierce.

I tried to recall exactly where everybody had been: Pierce by the headless soldier, Daniel somewhere near Mr. Arliss, Sherry beside me on my right, Wendy a little to the left of Sibella, who had been sitting upright with her forearms flat on the arms of her chair. None of us had moved after the roaring and sinister quotations from *The Fall of the House of Usher* had begun—no, that was wrong, we'd all turned to look at the kitchen door, except Sherry. Why had we done that? Simply, I supposed, because it was the only *door* any of us could see from here; the front door was hidden at the end of the vestibule.

"I tell you that she now stands without the door!" Yes, logical enough. We'd all moved a little, swinging round toward it. All but Sherry. Had he actually been staring at the arch to the dining room, or at Daniel? There was no way of knowing unless I asked him, and I wouldn't do that now. It was his own business, and I'd pried enough into that.

Sibella suddenly let fly a string of mild curses at no one in particular. She pointed at the figure of her twin sister. "Take that hideous caricature away and go to bed, the lot of you. Laurel, stay."

They said their good nights almost meekly, and left at once, Sherry carrying the Felicity model into the kitchen and, I imagined, putting it in the garage. When he'd come back and gone upstairs, Sibella said, "Belle went to her house at six o'clock and has been there ever since. That leaves anyone else, to balance that fool article against the door in the few minutes after Pierce took his hot cart into the dining room and before the gong went."

"How would they come back in here?"

"Through the passages, unless it was leaned on the door from this side. Too neat a balancing trick, maybe, but it might have been managed. The dummy of my late lamented sister," she said thoughtfully. "It makes me think our unknown is growing a little frantic. *How* to scare this old woman into a fit? Eh? Damn and blast his hide," she burst out, "when I know for sure who he is, I'll banish the lout! I'll see him thrown on the tender mercies of that world out there without a cent to his wretched name!" She rose, slowly and with hands that trembled. "He needn't think I'll die before him. Or before I know who he is, at any rate. I hope he lives a long time, and suffers abominably, and never sees another movie that was made before nineteen sixty! By the eternal, I do!"

She looked at me and smiled crookedly. "That was Father's most powerful oath. 'By the eternal!' he'd shout when he was irked. I haven't thought of that in years." She put her arm across my shoulders; she was at least three inches taller than I. "See me home to bed, Laurel. I'm shakier than I'd admit to any of them."

When I'd walked to her quarters with her—she told me good night curtly at her door—I hurried back to the great hall and sat, after making certain that I was alone, in her chair. I felt along both arms, above and beneath, for anything movable. I inspected the straight back, the cushion, and even the legs for some camouflaged button. It seemed a blameless chair.

Did I consider Sibella Callingwood a possible suspect, playing games for unfathomable reasons? Not really, and still I couldn't wash her out for good. It was likely because everything she did and said smacked of theatricality, and I could never be sure when she was playing a part and when she was entirely herself. Even her rage—especially her rage—was melodramatic. That came from her lifelong preoccupation with the movies, of course. It was probably unconscious. Much has been written of actors being always "on"—what about perpetual viewers? Daniel was the same, and Pierce too. Wendy was too characterless to be playing . . . or was her lack of personality itself an act? And if Sherry was masquerading, I couldn't conceive who the model was. Maybe a young Lionel Barrymore with a stomachache.

I found where each person had stood and waved my arms over my head, though I couldn't believe anyone had broken a photoelectric beam that way without being noticed; then knelt and inspected the floor and rugs for several feet around. I examined the figure that Pierce had mounted on the new platform, finding nothing. I checked George Arliss extensively—where there was one switch there could be two. I made sure to push or try to slide everything that might be a button in disguise.

The medium-sized Persian carpet on which Sibella's chair sat was my last hope. It was quite thick and I crept over it on knees and elbows, searching for lumps. At last, feeling futile but valiant, I took one corner and hauled it back for about half its length, exposing the terrazzo flooring. Wendy had been here, some eighteen inches from the chair. I turned on another lamp and crawled over the polished mosaic carefully. At the same time I reproached myself for singling out the girl so especially. I *wanted* it to be her, which was vindictive.

I found myself staring at a square of the marble, about one inch to a side. It was the only geometrically regular scrap I had seen, and the surrounding mortar did not quite touch it, so that there was a narrow pencil-line of space framing it. I put out my fingers toward it.

"Where's Sibby?"

I twitched with the shock. Belle McNabb stood just behind me, glaring, her dark eyes snapping sparks in the gray old face. "She's gone to bed," I said, sitting on my heels.

"I come over to find out why she asked me that question. What you got there?"

"I was looking for something."

"Can see that! What? Why you mislaying my rugs?"

"I'm trying to find a switch," I said. Then, before she could grill me further, "Someone played a cruel joke tonight, and Mrs. Callingwood wanted to find out how long the kitchen had been empty. That's why she called."

"No switches under the rugs," Belle said, voice all spiky with scorn. "How're you going to put a wire into solid cement?" She shook her head and turned and went away before I could think of an answer.

The marble square *had* to be what I was hunting. I slid my fingernails down on either side of it and gripped and pulled upward. Easily, with a distinct click, the square came up out of the floor about a quarter of an inch and stayed there. I pressed it experimentally. I couldn't depress it. I stood, faced the kitchen door, and stepped on the tiny block with all my weight. It slid down to floor level again. Slowly, as though the energy I had released were barely enough to move it, the door swung open at me.

So much for Sherry and Belle's denial of any possible electric wiring beneath the terrazzo.

Could it have been Wendy and he who'd done it? Was he her man, whom I was to avoid? *Were they in league to frighten Sibella to death?*

Or had Wendy done it alone? She could have made the Felicity figure, too. And taped Basil Rathbone's voice from a record—it had been a record, not a movie this time; I knew because I owned the record.

Replacing the rug, after taking a rough measurement with my forearm, I found that the movable square lay below the center of a dark blue flower. Easily located when needed.

Felicity may have made that figure of herself, or of Sibella, long ago. It was in a sense ageless, as my employer herself was. Sibella could have hidden it, then resurrected it, clothed it in a sheet smeared with red paint, recoloring the eyes if necessary.

It made better sense to believe that Wendy had done it.

In the course of this thought, I glanced up at the balcony in time to see someone draw quickly back behind the wall. The glimpse was too brief to tell me anything—male, female, dark, mustached, plump, fat, thin. It had been down at the far left, almost opposite my bedroom. Only Pierce Poole's room lay beyond. Oh, and an entrance, inevitably, to the passages. No use chasing that phantom.

I felt suddenly cold and alone and afraid. I fled to the warmth and equivocal shelter of my own quarters.

"Do you find the days at Sablecroft passing slowly?"

"No, very quickly indeed," I said. "I barely begin a job and it's time for tea."

"That's the stuff!" said Sibella archaically. "But do you know that you haven't been out of the house for a solid month today, excepting a few minutes with Sherry?"

I stared, thinking *Not in the daytime*. "No, I hadn't realized."

"But you can't be used to such a perpetually indoor mode of life?"

I smiled. "Guess I've grown used to it. A gulp of the humid air and a squint at that homicidal sun does me for a week. And I've puttered in the greenhouse with Pierce a few times."

"You'll be a Sablecroft yet," said Wendy, making it sound like an insult.

"There's something to that," Sibella mused. "I myself have never liked Florida, always preferred the cold climates. But once the Hall was built, I could never leave it behind, could I?"

"Why not?"

She looked as though I'd asked her why she wore clothing and ate food. "But everything I want in life is here! What does it matter to me that out there it's stifling and damp, and gulls shriek and red ants sting and mildew corrupts and beetles go flying through the miasma?"

Sipping tea, I thought for the first time in ages that I really should go outside occasionally. I much preferred to work, but for the good of my soul, or at least my lungs and heart, I ought to leave this permanent 72° once in a while. It was perhaps a specious argument. I wasn't aware that anyone had ever proved the old statement that living constantly in an air-conditioned atmosphere is bad for you. I just felt guilty about sticking indoors like a Sablecroft.

"Is there anything I could do outside to help you?" I asked Sherry.

"What are you good at?"

"I'm pretty useful at unskilled manual labor."

"You'd only turn white and woozy again," he said briefly.

"There must be a way to protect myself from the sun?"

"Yes. Stay indoors."

"Sheridan Todd," growled Sibella, "don't be any nastier than you must. Laurel's was a thoughtful and amiable offer."

He stared at me. "I'm sorry, was I rude? Wasn't thinking. Of course you ought to go out once in a while. I'll show you what to do."

"Now? For an hour or so?"

"Not that long the first time. You're too susceptible to the heat." He stood. "There's a straw bonnet of Belle's in the garage, I think. Come along, Palmerston," he said to the brindle.

"Do be careful outside," said Pierce to me in something like agony. "One *never* knows."

Daniel watched us leave with an unreadable expression on his narrow, handsome face. I thought it might be jealousy.

We went out through kitchen and garage, Belle observing me silently with a ladle like a scepter in her hand. There was a pitiful breeze going, but at least it relieved the dead wet quality of the air to which I objected so intensely. I had Belle's old straw hat perched forward on my head to shade my eyes. Sherry handed me a pair of gardening gloves and long pruning shears with short hooked blades. "There are half a dozen Senegal date palms that need pruning. I'll show you how. You must be careful of the thorns." We went toward the grove. "What you'll cut out are suckers. You want to achieve, for each palm clump, half a dozen good trunks, with the fronds cut away so that the lowest droop about as high as your head. How tall are you, anyway?"

"Five-six."

"Approximate it on this tree," he said, stopping beside a kind of Vesuvius fountain of bright green leaf fronds. "Locate the trunks and cut away the suckers from around them. Take care not to let the dog go nosing into the clump, or he'll spike his nose. Lie down, Gilderoy. That is, lie down, Palmerston," he said, smiling.

"You have a nice smile," I said on impulse. "I wish you'd use it oftener."

"Why?"

His voice was edgy. I said, pulling on the thick gloves, "Because otherwise you're not especially amiable to have around, if you don't realize it."

"I'd think Daniel was genial enough for any one household."

"Oh, don't go somber on me!"

"The help one hires nowadays is a far cry from the silent, respectful servant of Victoria's golden era." He stared at me. "Apologies. Really. That was stupid. You have a right to talk up to me or anyone. If you were the cringing, mute type I'd despise you. I—I haven't been quite myself lately. I suffer a fair amount of insomnia. It makes me as thorny as one of these date palms. I needn't grant you the right to snap at me whenever you feel I need it, do I? You'd snap anyway. Laurel Vane," he said. "The valiant Miss Laurel Vane."

"Mrs. Warrick."

"Did you love your husband deeply?"

"Yes."

"Do you still?"

"Yes, differently. As the best and closest person in my life."

"That's good," he said quietly. "I think you are a good woman, despite your inquisitive digging . . . I wish you'd gone back home when I told you to, but sometimes I'm glad you're here to cleanse the atmosphere. That makes no sense at all. Give me a shout if you run into trouble; I'll be cutting spikes off that grugru." He frowned. "What are you smirking at?"

"It seems so exotic to be pruning a Senegal date palm while you unspike a grugru! I'm a long way from Connecticut."

He smiled again under that curtain of mustache. "Remember, sweeping up maple leaves and fertilizing a walnut would be just as exotic to me. I've lived all my life here."

"Where did you go to college?"

"A few miles away. I used to imagine what it must be like in other places. Shoveling snow. Driving the Cord on icy roads. Even walking up and down hills! Strange."

"You might enjoy it."

"Yes." He looked vaguely unhappy. "We aren't a traveling family. Lie *down,* Palmerston." He went off.

I found three shaggy trunks, not too thick, and began to clip off the fronds that hid them and the thinner suckers growing nearby. It was very agreeable to work just with my hands for a change. I was soon covered with a film of perspiration, in which small flying creatures got themselves stuck. A red-and-black ant ran up my arm and I flicked him away. A dragonfly came past, lilting in flight, harmless and fantastic. I pricked myself on a thorn.

I felt ridiculously cheerful. I was too busy to wonder why.

And then I backed off and looked up, just to breathe for a moment I suppose, and found Sherry was standing a few paces away watching me. He said quietly, "Do you know who you are?"

"What an odd question. Certainly—Laurel Warrick."

"A name is just words. Do you know in whose veins your blood once flowed? Whose eyes and knuckles and voices came down to you over the unimaginable years? Where you acquired your belligerent passion for facts, as well as for truth? Have you a better idea of the answers, perhaps, than you care to confide in us? Why are you such a mystery? I can't read beyond the surface of your eyes—and I want to."

"I'm the least mysterious soul in the house," I said, taken aback at the depth of this personality probing, for the man was without warning casting a kind of net of energy over me—I don't know how to put it save in hackneyed terms—like a snake hypnotizing a rabbit, so strong was the force, the intensity of his presence. I realized that this was almost the first time anyone in Sablecroft Hall had said anything to me that they couldn't have said as easily to the mailman.

"No, only superficially. With your wide and sensual mouth speaking primly of rare editions, your great hazel eyes smiling at Daniel and frowning at Wendy, your master's degree embroidered neatly on your shatterproof invisible librarian's armor so that he who rides may read, your quite individualistic cat, and your completely commonplace air of being nobody in particular . . . there's a facade to you that's all sterilized hogwash and a lie. No," he said, as I opened my mouth, stung, to contradict him, "you aren't a liar, I didn't mean that. But you project a girl who isn't yourself at all. It's not from fear, Lord knows—I don't believe you're afraid of me or

Sibella or the devil—I think you're as rugged as Micajah, and as tough-minded. It certainly isn't from meanness or a taste for deceit. It may be unconscious, though I doubt that. Caution? Politeness? I don't know."

"What do you want to know about me?" I asked, my voice coming out so small that I instantly felt embarrassed. And he picked that up.

"You sound like Dorothy talking to the great and powerful Oz. Where's Laurel under that meek little query? Standing back watching herself, and holding her tongue so she won't cry, 'What in hell do you want to know, you fat prying green-eyed bully?' But you're too nice to do it. What do I want to know? Who you are! Have you got the guts to tell me, or don't you really know?"

I looked into his eyes for what seemed a long time. Then I said, "Daniel asked me if I were a private detective—"

"Aah! You're a cataloguer of rare and fascinating lore, a superior file clerk, a bookworm. That's as helpful as saying your name's Laurel Warrick, and you know it's a mile from what I asked." He shook his head. "Not ready to tell me, are you? Never mind, you will be one day, and I'll listen. That, if you view it properly, is a kind of compliment from a two-dimensional Sablecroft who's done most of his living on a big silvered screen, in empathy with the dark and the glittering shadows. Go on with your palm pruning. You're doing it beautifully." He turned on his heel and went back to the grugru.

Palmerston gazed up at me dumbly, and I looked down at him, and I knew now why I'd been cheerful, and it frightened me so much that I went in from the tropical heat to the artificial cold, and didn't notice until I was sitting in the great hall with the dog at my feet that I still wore the heavy gloves and carried the pruning shears.

I felt intensely afraid, both psychically and physically.

Sherry was either mad or so coldly sane that he could see right through me to the thoughts in my head and the heart in my breast. Though it wasn't clear what he meant by asking who I was, I could sense some dim peculiar intent behind the query, as well as some frail near-perception of his allusion just beyond the bounds of my own cognition.

At that instant of time, I thought they should have christened this place Marienbad.

Later, leaving the dog asleep beside the chair, I went back outside and finished the job on the date palm. I would rather be categorized as Dorothy than as the Cowardly Lion.

In the next few days the new bookshelves had all been installed; the men had done a fine job of carpentry in an exceptionally short time. Now Pierce and Daniel had returned to their normal occupations, cooking, repairing machinery, greenhouse gardening, and screening movies or editing tapes. Wendy had repaired the smashed plaster head and hands—reconstructed them, in fact—and attached them to the Cromwellian figure. Sherry had gone back permanently to his fresh-air labor, deepening his tan further as the summer heightened.

Every day Daniel would ask me how I was coming with the architectural search. Although it seemed to me that I'd made considerable progress, it was never fast enough for him. He didn't badger me, but I sensed the impatience, the eagerness for the hunt to start afresh, bubbling in him. He even ventured outside with me once, carrying my clipboard and surveying tape, to marvel at how clever it was of me to compute the height of certain walls and towers by measuring their shadows and my own and calculating from this. He admitted that he was a mathematical moron; indeed, he bragged about it. He was astounded when I said that the northeast tower was forty-eight and a half feet tall because my shadow measured three feet four.

I had marked up the old plans with my own reckonings, noted many discrepancies, and formed an estimate of several possible sites for secret rooms or even passages of which he claimed to know nothing.

One Saturday night we had a long chat about it, sitting on a library sofa with the old layouts while the others watched a double bill from 1925 which I wanted to see but feared that Daniel would soon begin to twitch and gibber if I didn't show him what I'd discovered.

"At least eighty per cent of the original measurements on these plans are wrong," I told him. "Sometimes by an inch, often by several feet, and occasionally by more than ten feet."

"Was the architect or contractor so incompetent?"

"I'd guess he was amazingly capable. He made angles that weren't quite true, but that look true, and sacrificed nothing by way of strength or appearance. The dining room is square, with the northeast corner being the arc of a circle, isn't it?" I found that sheet and pointed it out. "Externally it *is,* to match the curve of the tower closest to it; but inside it's really the arc of an ellipse, and at its midpoint there's about ten feet of thickness unaccounted for."

"Laurel," he said, short of breath, gripping my hand, "you mean you've discovered the old man's hidey-hole?"

"It's possible that there's a closet in there, and if the walls are bowed like a crescent moon, it may be seven feet deep in the middle and taper out to a foot or so at the ends."

"Laurel, you're a genius!"

"Not at all. You could have done it if you'd used a tape measure." I flipped the big pages and showed him where sixty-one inches were missing at the southern end of the bedroom corridor, and other discrepancies. "I need to consult a book or two at the library, but—"

"Can't we go investigate that crescent tonight?"

"I suppose we could. All I need to learn at the library is something of load-bearing walls and—"

"Don't tell me, the brilliance is wasted. Sherry will take you there whenever you like. You're the only organized mind to hit this place since Gilbert died," he said, admiring me up and down as though I'd thought the problems out with my body.

"No," I said, freeing the hand that he'd grasped again, and trying not to blush, "Sibella has a razor for a mind. She just wasn't interested enough to bother with the mythical room."

He cocked one brow. "She's intelligent enough—I'd say we're all fairly intelligent—but in a purely intellectual way, not in the line of regimenting numbers and data and all that. You're entranced by her, aren't you? The way you watch her!"

I was faintly surprised at Daniel's perception. "I believe I am. She survives, and with flair. But she's not intrigued by treasure houses and priests' holes and such. Having grown up in little plain houses, I am. I'm sure I've discovered that there's some kind of cellar, too," I told him triumphantly.

"Oh, come on, Laurel, this is Florida!" He laughed, and managed to be holding my hand again as though he'd never let go. "We do everything above ground level except skin dive."

"Well, there's at least a gap below the flooring. It may be only a very shallow space, or one or more finger-thick troughs, but it's not the simple solid concrete slab you all say it is."

He bent forward. "That would mean that some droll experiences we've endured, like Grandmother's image, can be explained easily," he said. "Pierce and I couldn't solve the mechanics; Lord knows we tried. But if there's a hollow, say under the terrazzo in the great hall or the parquetry here," he thumped the floor with a heel, "even tiny open channels in the slab, then wires could be fed from place to place, and *anything* accomplished." His eyes sparkled, and the lean fingers gripped mine tight. "Why wouldn't a movie fanatic and an old stage man like Gilbert have installed a trapdoor, too, with a pit of poured concrete, down which to vanish in spurts of blue and crimson smoke? More? More, love?"

"Someone believes Felicity's old room has something hidden," I said, and he sat up, agog. "He or she or *it* thumps and scrapes and mutters in the night."

"Gilbert! Giving us a clue. Is it possible there's another vault, closet, pigeonhole, built into that room?"

"I haven't measured any of the bedrooms but the spare at the far end. I didn't want to do it alone—pry, you know."

"Nonsense, anything unlocked is available to all of us."

"You'll have to go with me. You live here. And I haven't measured Sibella's quarters, except outside the house. You said those passages would be sealed off?"

"We'll beg permission and check it. But since we have so much—and you've done more in a few weeks than I have in twenty-eight years—we'll look into what we know about first. The best bet is—?"

"A guess: The crescent in the dining-room wall."

"I'll snag a trouble light," he said, bounding up. "Brighter than a flash and more professional. Meet you by the passage door—the front door, in the vestibule." He ran off.

I strolled toward the door, and Micajah, who'd been obsessed with his new friend the Great Dane lately, chose to follow me for a change, in cat's fashion choosing the one time I didn't want him along. We waited for Daniel for a minute or two, and then he turned up, grinning, and opened the closet. "Are we to be blessed with company?"

"No," I said, and then as only a determined cat can, Micajah avoided my foot and flew into the unlit corridor ahead of me. But after a touch of solitary prowling he came and found us, to pad along at our heels. He'd probably remembered his earlier sojourn in the miserable dark spidery gap above this ceiling.

Daniel flashed on the lights as we progressed. "Ground level first?"

"I think so. There might even be two rooms, come to think of it. One on each floor of the passages."

He looked as transported as a hungry faun who'd stumbled on a cache of black truffles. That's what he reminded me of—a domesticated faun! If you could imagine a faun living indoors and being afraid of meadows and forests. The wicked yet charming grin, the almost artificial-looking eyes, the very long and flexible hands, and sometimes a sort of caper in his walk. All he needed was a pair of small horns poking through his curly black hair. Not a leprechaun at all, a Pan-descended faun. The thought made him even more desirable for a friend, oddly—or something beyond that. Was I falling for Daniel? There was a fascination there . . . and he did seem a better choice than the irritable Sheridan Todd, if it came to a choice.

We reached the curving corner where the wooden wall hid a largish quantum of undisclosed space. We stood together at the beginning of the turn, which was twenty feet long and lit only by the reflected shimmer of a ceiling light well behind us. Daniel plugged in the long cord and swung the 200-watt bulb in its aluminum cage carelessly in his hand.

I estimated ten feet from the start of the curve. "About here," I said, pointing inward toward the dining room, "there are seven feet of mysterious depth. This is the center span or axis of the possible crescent-shaped room."

"The absolutely definite crescent-shaped room, dear—think positively." He slung the hook of the trouble light over a rusty old staple in the wall behind us. "I've never done much along this wall but rap my knuckles bloody and push everything that sticks out. But I can safely say, Laurel, there's not an inch that sounds hollow. You take it from there."

I stared for several minutes, during which the eerie silence became acute and Micajah huddled down at my feet. Often in the passages you could hear faint gull screams, like old women being throttled, from various minor openings to the outside, and even muted voices that crept in from the rooms of the Hall around the loudspeakers or the spy holes. But now there was no sound except our breathing; the gulls had gone to bed. At last I said, "Try the two-by-fours."

"How?"

I pointed to a great X made by two beams just short of the center of the arc. "Lift up and sideways, as though it were an enormous lever. Then try it downward."

"But you can see it's a load-bearing structure."

"No, it needn't be. The wall itself is, probably, and some of the X's, but I see no reason why they'd all be necessary."

Obedient, he thrust his shoulder under the nearest beam and strained upward. After some groans and grunts he stepped back and said accusingly, "A man could sprain his back! The thing's anchored fast."

"Try the other, then, and haul down too."

With a martyr's sigh, he did. "Ugh! Ugh! You want to put me in the hospital so you can have my scones at tea. These are spiked to the wall and the floor."

"There's another X down there." I unhooked the light, went a little way around the bend, and hung it again. "Try the same thing."

"I don't suppose you'd care to? No, I guess not. Fragile female and all."

"Don't imagine I can't see through that flimsy putdown! I only thought you'd want to carry your share of the load; *I* did the brainwork." I pushed under the two-by-four, which was unpainted and splintery, and heaved. And the silly object began to move. I was delighted. "Don't you feel a fool?" I grunted, taxing my strength to its limit so the beam would shift as quickly as possible, to make Daniel suffer shame. But he only laughed and clapped his hands.

"You never needed to let me in on this at all, Laurel! You could have looted the place and vanished into the night, never to be heard from till you surfaced in the South Seas! You're a dream. Push it up some more, there's a good girl. You've sent half this wall out of sight already."

Wondering what that meant, I put both hands under the displaced beam and shoved up. The timber went to its limit, having swiveled on the spike that appeared to hold the two arms of the X together, but was actually a fulcrum for the great lever. Then I stepped back, wiped the salt out of my burning eyes—it was hot in that passageway, and after the eternal sweet coolness of the house it felt airless as well—pushed a sweaty hand through my damp bangs, and looked. A section of the rough wall had disappeared, and another one was there, a finished, flat, painted, sea-green wall, with a big dial set in its middle.

"Judas Priest!" said Daniel.

"Wow!" I agreed.

We stood gazing at it, even Micajah. Daniel motioned with his lithe body as if to go forward, but his feet stayed where they were. He actually swayed back and forth, and said finally, "Laurel, I can't budge," and emitted a laugh like an embarrassed giggle. "Why does it frighten me?" he asked in a child's voice, thin and wary and puzzled.

"Because you've been waiting all your life to find it." My voice wasn't a noticeable improvement on his. "And now you have, and you don't know what it is. . . ."

"Or how we get in."

"What happened?"

He said, "The old timber wall went sliding up into nowhere, into the ceiling; you can see the bottom of it up there. And this was behind it. Is it some kind of *safe?*"

"That's as good a guess as I can make," I said, leaning to pet Micajah, whose fur was on end. He slithered away, saying *kkkkkkk* under his breath.

"We riddle out the combination, the great door swings wide, the golden coins come spilling out." He stepped across the aisle and went to one knee on the stained old carpet before the green wall, stark in the hot white glare of our portable lamp, looking at the dial narrowly. "No numbers," he said, surprised. "Letters."

"Not the whole alphabet!" I nudged down beside him. "Oh, thank goodness." I counted. "Ten letters and a blank space. But that still leaves us more than a thousand combinations."

"Look," he said, "my dearest astute and clear-headed lovely, solving the combination should be no task at all for your mother wit."

"Daniel!" Exasperation overcame me. "You've been here all your life longing to find this, and now that I've started you off, you expect to sit back and have the rest done for you too! Aren't you ashamed?" I glared at him and added, unkindly, "You sat around looking at movies when you might have been working on this, and you're too clever and capable to have thrown all that time away in front of a screen. I'm scolding you for your own good," I ended lamely, "which is a venomous thing to tell anyone, and I'm sorry. But why *didn't* you discover such a primitive mechanism?"

"I always looked for things like the closet hook to turn, little knobs to twist or panels to push, and I thumped for hollowness till I hadn't any skin on my knuckles. It never dawned on me that one immense two-by-four leg of a crossbuck might be a lever."

"It was the only possibility in sight."

"But I wasn't aware of the crescent space hidden away! You're intelligently devoted to detail, as Great-grandfather was, and I can't ever seem to organize my wits except to memorize things. I go all scattery. Just *look* at this jumble," he exclaimed, rapping the dial.

"I'll try to teach you systematic thinking," I said, very much the little missionary out of the northland, spreading knowledge. Then I was suddenly conscious of his breathing close by my cheek as we stared at the polished two-foot-wide steel dial projecting from its green wall, and grew less certain of my motives. I stood up. "Look at it yourself, Daniel. Don't simply see a nonsense word and give up —it's there to be read."

He frowned. "Taking the blank segment as the start, it spells *Abceflorst*. Sounds Scandinavian."

"Look at it again. It's a scrambled name. See it as a whole—"

"Eureka! *Sablecroft!*" he shouted.

"Right. That's likely too easy . . . however, why don't you try it?" as his face fell. "Start with the blank—see the painted pointer on the wall—and try left-right-left."

He did, but nothing happened, and we heard only the ratchety little noise of the wheel turning. "Nary a tumbler clicked that I could tell," he said.

"You're not supposed to hear them unless you're a cracksman, silly. Try it right-left." He did. "Not that either. You'll have to figure out all the sequences possible. This must be an expensive lock—I think you might try two letters in one direction with a pause at the first, then two the opposite way, and so on."

"And so on," he repeated unhappily, "and on."

"Yes! Then there'll be shorter words hidden in the ten-letter name, *croft* and *sable* for a start, and *frost* and *slate;* maybe the combination is in them. Use anagram letters if you have them, or make a set of cardboards, mess 'em around on a table, write down all the words of three letters and over that you find."

"Like a contest. And names, old movie names. Look, I already see *Boles* and *Rose,* that's Blanche Rose, she played in Charles Ray silents . . . marvelous! Laurel, thanks."

He patted my shoulder a couple of times, and I knew that if I hadn't bent to pick up Micajah just then, he'd have turned me around and kissed me. One doesn't mistake that all-but-embraced feeling. Whether it would have been from gratitude or passion, I couldn't tell; such nuances are hard to distinguish when you have your back to a man and are perspiring violently.

"Can we close it up?" I said quickly. "We discovered it, so it seems only fair that we have our chance to solve the puzzle before the others can. They've lived here a long time too, after all."

"I didn't want to suggest that we exclude them," he said, much relieved, "but since you have, yes! I feel a proprietary emotion. Look at the cat. You don't suppose they're back there somewhere, listening to us?"

"Wendy, maybe?" I asked.

"She'd come right down and ask what we'd found. So would Pierce, probably. Sherry, well, I don't know. Sibella . . . the everlasting enigma," said he slowly, watching Micajah, who was straining in the direction of the nearest entrance, eyes exorbitantly bugged. "Shall we put back the what's-it, the screening wall?"

"Yes, pull down that beam, I want to watch the apparatus this time." The old rough timber wall came sliding down out of nowhere to cover our find. It was marvelously made, and after all these decades fitted as flawlessly as when it was built.

Daniel wiped his hands on his handkerchief and gave it to me to brush the grime from my own. "Let's go to the great hall, stake out a corner, and celebrate quietly," he said, bouncing on his heels. "I intuit chests of doubloons and a pirate's ghost waiting for us behind these wooden curtains!"

"More likely mummified bats festooned on a statue of Theda Bara," I said. "Seriously, what do you believe *is* in there?"

Micajah escaped from my grip and huddled at my feet, glaring into the murk beyond, watching ghosts. I felt a light shudder just skim over my body.

"Almost anything. Diaries—our family's kept them compulsively for centuries, and some are missing: not destroyed, which to a Sablecroft is unthinkable, but hidden. Manuscripts. Information."

"Daniel, do you hear something?" I asked, bending to stroke the bristling Micajah.

"A quiet sort of rushing noise? That's rain. You can always hear it in here if it's hard enough, and this is our regular, seasonal, persistent, belligerent downpour. A little like background music, isn't it?" He took my arm and after unplugging the light's cord, we walked toward the exit panel that led to the library. "Tell me, Laurel—you've had almost as total an immersion in movies as I have—don't you honestly expect life to furnish background music? I do. Back there, when I nearly kissed you, and would have if we hadn't both been so damp and dusty, I *know* I anticipated a dreamy waltz, plenty of violins followed by a symbolic crash of cymbals—"

There was a low, muted roll of thunder, and we both laughed. "Cecil B. is watching over this scene!" cried Daniel, and we emerged hilariously into the library, Micajah scrambling out beside us. We went to the great hall and collapsed side by side on a sofa. "Champagne?"

"I'd like a very cold cola."

"Your wish, et cetera, et cetera." He vanished and was back before the count of ten with two colas and a damp cloth, which we took turns using on our faces and hands. And suddenly I found myself being kissed. It was a good, intense, expert kiss, and I kissed him back, all the loneliness in my soul and body rushing to my lips. Our arms tightened around each other. "Wanted to do that for weeks," he mumbled against my cheek. "You know I'm somewhat in love with you, right? Do you honestly feel anything in return?"

He kissed me tenderly, then ferociously. After a while I said, "I think I may, Daniel. Don't rush me. Please? It's been so long, there's so much going on—"

"Yes. I might, I admit, be a candidate for Raving Mad Fiend of Sablecroft Hall. So long as you know I mean it, dear."

"I think I do, yes. One more—"

We engaged in one more. Then Micajah jumped up between us, where there wasn't room for him, and began to turn round and round to make a nest; and we laughed, and Wendy came in, looking angry, to plunk down in a chair with a book.

"Good night, Daniel," I whispered.

"Sleep well," he said, "and don't dream."

It was odd, his saying that, because when I'd gone to bed and fallen asleep, I had a nightmare of the Felicity figure with its terrible painted eyes turned into deep sockets from which someone peered malignantly at me and its craggy, empty features mowing at me in grotesque threat. It fell toward me endlessly out of some unimaginably vast doorway, hurtling, rushing, crashing down, and never quite touching me, till I half-woke, whimpering and almost recollecting whose eyes had stared at me from the dead sockets. But whether they were the blue of Daniel's or the green of Sheridan Todd's, Wendy's lavender orbs or Pierce's pale bulging Ping-Pong balls or Belle's blazing jet jewels, I could not be certain. At last I sank far enough into sleep to stop dreaming, or at least to forget what else I'd dreamed by the time the morning came.

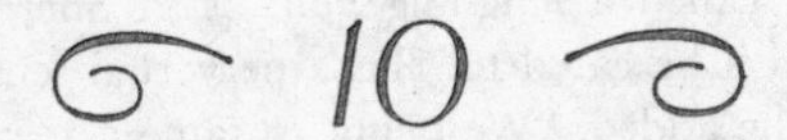

TWO DAYS LATER I WALKED INTO THE GREAT HALL, WHERE UNDER the soft glow of one of the big table lamps Daniel hunched over a notebook, writing furiously for perhaps the first time since he'd left school. Sherry Todd sat, if one could call it sitting when all his weight rested on the back of his neck, opposite his cousin. They both said, "Hello, there," in abstracted voices.

"I'd like to go to the library. I haven't taken any time off and—"

"I'll drive you," said Sherry. "If you want to bring books home, I have a card." Daniel glanced at him as though a library card were the last item he'd have expected to find here. "Meet me in the garage in ten minutes," said Sherry, and trudged out, looking weary and listless.

"How are you coming with the combinations?" I asked Daniel.

His eyes lit joyously. "Damn fine! I've found some more old actors whose names can be formed with our ten letters, as well as words Gilbert might have used. Must have nearly a hundred—I'll try them while you're gone."

"Remember, right and left, then left and right for every one, and so on—"

"I adore you."

"You ain't so bad yourself," I said, and left my cat humming away happily on his knees.

We were quiet, Sherry and I, as the Cord passed the rows of stuccoed and tiled masonry houses, with here and there a more sprawling, fancy bungalow and once an old two-story that put me in mind of a cheap imitation of Sablecroft Hall.

There were a great many birds to see, gulls of all sorts, big pelicans sitting on posts like demons wrapped in the wrinkled shawls of their wings, man-o'-war birds seven feet across, some herons, and, floating serenely on the waters of the frequent bayou canals, tiny fleets of black-headed scaup ducks. A brown pelican sailing almost over the car with a flopping fish in his bill suddenly veered off as a gray-and-white gull came tearing at him screaming harshly. The gull caught the fish and jerked it away; the pelican floundered in the air and looked terribly embarrassed.

"That's what's called a laughing gull," said Sherry. "He could catch his own fish if he cared to. Has a perverted sense of humor." After a moment he added, "We ought to tame a few for the Hall. Fit in nicely. Play mean little tricks with a coarse splutter of mirth. Damn!"

"Damn?"

"Very much damn. I'm thinking of that Cromwellian soldier. I believed I knew who'd toppled him, Laurel, but after the Felicity figure and the pseudo-poisoned wine, I'm not so certain. Maybe we have more than one jester. More than one fidgeting, would-be killer. What did you do with the thread you snapped off the helmet? Send it to Scotland Yard, St. Pete branch? Examine it under a microscope?"

"You saw me, then."

"Of course. I removed the rest of it. And saved it, in case of possible identification, which I haven't managed." He turned his head my way for an instant, his bloodshot green eyes piercing. "You thought I'd tilted the thing over at you. Do you still?"

"I really don't know," I said lamely. "Sometimes I believe I do. It's so hard to imagine anyone else engineering it."

"You're right, I can't believe it either. So pat, so incredibly neat. I leave you in its shadow and it topples. Someone in the walls might have had to wait seven years for you to stand just there. It must have been me. No defense. I throw myself on the mercy of the court. *But it was not I.*" He reached to pat my bare arm. "If I can prove that, I shall. Lord knows how. Are you falling in love with Daniel?"

I couldn't follow his changes of subject without blinking and starting and feeling like a fool. I laughed uncertainly. "I don't know, Sherry."

"You kiss him easily . . . and yet I think you're a girl who never kisses lightly and casually. An old-fashioned girl. Why? I read you that way. I've been wrong in my life once or twice, though."

"Do you spy on us?" I asked angrily.

"No."

"A fortuitous accident. You came innocently around the corner and there I was, crawling all over Daniel."

"No," he said, and that was all.

"What, then?"

"I was—nearby. I was a little disturbed about you. That sounds like jealousy. Take it as you will."

"You were spying."

"As you will," he repeated. "You never had children, Laurel?"

"No."

"Strange, you seem a motherly type when you're off your guard."

"Oh, the instinct's there all right. But I worry about the population growth, crowding the world unnecessarily. I might adopt a child some day. I haven't made up my mind."

"You mean if you married again."

"Yes, or maybe if I don't."

"Here we are," he said.

The library was faced with charcoal-colored Mexican beach pebbles on concrete panels, had solar-glazed windows, and looked modern and inviting. Sherry told me as we parked and went in where to find what I wanted. We walked back through comfortably air-conditioned rooms, the walls paneled in antique cherry (was *all* of Florida paneled?), the colors of everything charcoal, orange, and tan, the furniture and the stacks sleekly new. Sherry forgotten, I searched till I found four texts to borrow. Then I looked and saw him, slouched half hidden behind a pile of thick old tomes, watching me.

And I was out of Sablecroft Hall in the ordinary world, my own world of stacks and quiet people and trillions of words about everything that man knows or believes he knows, waiting to be consulted; and I realized that I didn't want to go back to that mad, inexplicable family.

Daniel so resembling a faun that he might be full of wicked mischief. Wendy a malicious little self-centered witch. Belle truly sinister, as had been jokingly said. Pierce with his curious inconsistencies of behavior, sometimes with us keen and friendly, sometimes far away sporting a glazed unseeing eye, definitely not reassuring. But of them all, only Sherry to openly dismay and intimidate me.

Why should I be so disturbed by a hollow-eyed, languid-energetic, bullying-apathetic, plump young man who . . . who apparently observed me in my every indiscreet moment? I was frankly staring at him now, and he gazed back without so much as a twitched eyebrow or a ripple of the heavy mustache.

This was ridiculous. I gestured at the door and smiled. He arose with his peculiar weary undulation and ambled toward me. I realized that he was really a good deal thinner; he could not be called lean, but neither could he any longer be branded as fattish. Could simply cutting out candy have done this in a month or so? I wondered soberly if he had some wasting illness. He'd be the last to admit it if he had. He was the sort who'd keep his health problems to himself, I thought, and when the time came, crawl off to die alone in a bramble thicket, like some old wolf.

As a matter of fact, he was looking more and more like Daniel, except that there was no touch of the woodland godling in his manner. "Finished?" he asked, blinking sleepily. I nodded. He took my books, glancing at the titles. "Going gung-ho for the secret room, I see." I followed him to the charge desk, and waited while the cards were photographed, picking up a green pamphlet on the library from professional curiosity.

It was pouring rain now, and in Florida that is not just an old cliché, but a clinically precise description. I waited under the shelter of the big concrete hood as Sherry dashed out to bring the white car to me. I got in, and we drove through an imitation of Niagara Falls, taking three times as long to get home as we had reaching the library. We didn't talk, for he seemed to concentrate entirely on the road. Yet the only bird I saw was a soppy gray-and-black creature sitting forlorn on a telephone wire. "Loggerhead shrike," grunted Sherry.

"You have remarkable vision."

"The better to see you necking with, my dear," he growled. Then we both shut up till we reached the bayou and eventually the Hall.

"Home and dry," Sherry said, "you silly child."

"Why 'silly'?" I demanded. "For that matter, why 'necking'?"

"Silly for not running when you're warned!" he blazed at me, back on his hobbyhorse. "Digging in your heels and balking at the only good advice you're ever likely to get here! Playing with razor blades and ground glass! And what in hell do you know about Daniel?"

"More than I know about you!"

He grinned fiercely under the bush of mustache. "Do you really?" he drawled, and turned on his heel and went off into the kitchen, leaving me to close the garage door in a perfect rage and go to my bedroom to lie in the gloom, the rain smashing on the panes, and sulk.

"Necking" indeed. Next he'd be accusing me of "making out." Or, considering the isolation of Sablecroft Hall from almost all things modern, of "spooning and sparking."

Men! And, as long as I was mad, this *place!*

Did I have to stay on? Was I endangering myself in more ways than one? Was the atmosphere not osmosing into my blood? How often these days did I think of anything beyond the limits of the everlasting silver screen? Was it worth it to me to stay? Sibella had been paying my salary into a savings account every week by mail, and I had enough by this time to get out of Florida—but to where, and what, and whom?

I thought hard and long, skipping tea, getting up once at a wood-splintering scratch to let in Micajah.

What had I done when I was independent? I'd worked all day and read all night. I'd gone skiing—alone—and sometimes to a good restaurant, with "the girls"—and . . .

I had led a lonesome, faintly unhappy existence, that's what I'd done. I'd mourned my dead, and when that was over I had stagnated.

No cause for me to bad-mouth Sablecroft Hall. It was full of eccentrics, but also of enthralling facts and intriguing mysteries, the finest collection extant of my own best-loved subject, hidden rooms to riddle open, bright inquiring minds which, if somewhat limited in breadth, were deep enough to make for lively conversation almost every night. And I wasn't to be here forever.

"Blast the man!" I snapped at my cat, who had lain down on my stomach to have his jowls rubbed. "Let him do and say his living worst. Let him throw statues at me and pour almond extract in all my drinks, and do tricks with string and switches and—and all the other stupid stuff!" I sat up, dislodging Micajah, who batted me with claws half unsheathed. "Just let the bush-faced pink-eyed humbug try to chase me home!" I said, and to the devil with any hidden mikes in the walls, bugs in the furniture, two-way mirrors or peepholes.

I bathed and dressed for dinner in my best, just for spite. Then, it being only a little after six, I went looking for Daniel, one of the library books in my fist. Micajah, sensing a certain irritation in me, decided to stay put in our room and chew on one of his toys, solitary grandeur incarnate. I shut him in with some sort of extravagant notion that I was emerging into dangerous territory.

Daniel was asleep below. I woke him with a tap on the nose. "You're goofing."

"I was awake half the night thinking," he protested amiably. "And while you were gone, I knelt for hours on the passage floor, trying every word and name on a list of thousands."

"Let's see it," I said.

He grinned. "Well, dozens, then, but with all the sequences!"

I sat beside him and glanced down his list. "You've missed *labor* and *stable* and *blots* and *clear* that I can see offhand," I said severely.

"I am a slow-witted pupil, dear. Sorry. May I kiss you?"

"No. Here's a treatise on house-building. I want you to learn everything in it about load-bearing walls."

"If I must. Why can't I kiss you? We're alone."

"Because you asked, you coward. And you've been slapdash in your job. And I'm in a rotten mood."

"Sherry insult you?"

"Sherry always insults me."

He frowned at the book. "How would Gilbert have imagined we would ever find out about load-bearing walls, of all things?"

I had to smile. "He assumed, I suppose, that some day one of you would go to a library. A Carnegie was established here in nineteen fifteen."

"How'd you know that?" His mien was that of one questioning a certified sorcerer.

"I brought home a pamphlet that gives the history of the various branches, in addition to a splendid description of the main building from five-foot crawlspace to nine-foot mezzanine stacks above. For pity's sake, Daniel dear, you can discover almost anything through the printed word!"

"I begin to sense that, yes," he said, and after glancing around the great hall, drew me to him and kissed me hard. Then, "I kiss your feet," he said formally.

"You have a rotten sense of direction," I said, a little gaspy. "Try again."

He did so. I had not realized that I was so lonely for the touch of lips on mine. At last I said, "What about Wendy?"

"Wendy? Wendy? What's Wendy got to do with us or safe combinations or kissing or anything whatever?"

"I had the idea that you and she, well, that she anyway—"

He laughed outright. "Laurel, what are you implying?"

"That if there was some understanding between you before I came," I said too primly, "I would not want to interfere."

He took my hand. "Laurel, Laurel! What on earth could there be between me and the girl who married Sherry Todd?"

"What?"

"They were married years ago. I thought surely you knew that. Oh, there was a divorce, but I suspect there's a spark still there that one, t'other, or both are fanning. I have no designs on Mrs. Wendy

Abbott Todd, even if she does go around calling herself Miss Abbott again." He rose, lifted me to my feet, and tucked my unresisting arm over his. "You don't seem to have heard the gong, but it went," he said. "And Pierce is cooking tonight. I wonder what there will be?"

With an emotion shaking me so that I felt, and must have looked, as if I'd contracted an ague, I went in to dinner. I tried to tell myself that now I knew who'd collaborated with the dark-haired girl on the night of Felicity's dummy, and that I was disappointed, and that that was all. But somehow I didn't believe it was all. Not all by any means.

I had never felt less like eating a plate of rich, fragrant, marvelous food in my life.

ALTHOUGH I LONGED TO GET AWAY, TO GO TO MY ROOM AND SORT out my sentiments, to consider in solitude where my sympathies and desires lay and why, I was not allowed to do so. Sibella wanted to talk about the catalogue I'd be making her, and yarned on in that usually appealing deep voice until I wanted to snap, "Oh, do shut up! Can't you see I'm in trouble?"

Of course I didn't. I admired the grand old character, and she was my employer. So I sat at the table till several people had put their heads in and said good night, and still Sibella drank champagne and talked. "What?" I said, as a silence grew. "I'm sorry."

"Are you brooding over something?"

"I guess so." I took the plunge, too tired to control my tongue. "What's happening about all the 'accidents'? Are we merely waiting for the next attack?"

"What's it to you?"

"For God's sake," I said loudly. "I'm involved, I'm here, I'm fond of some of you, I don't want to be mangled by another falling statue or lose my job because everyone procrastinated!"

"Fond of some of us. Which, I wonder?"

"Oh, what's it matter?"

"It ought to matter—Daniel? Pierce? Sherry?"

"I like Daniel, with a few reservations, very much; I would dote on Pierce, but he often has a certain incoherency of manner that worries me; I'm actually a little afraid of Belle; I like and admire you; and I understand that Sherry doesn't need my affection because he has his former wife living here waiting to marry him again," I blurted.

"Ah, *that's* it. Have you only heard it today? That accounts for the pallor and unfocused eyes," she said calmly.

"What sort of family *is* this? Where a couple are divorced and keep on living under the same roof, spending most of their time in each other's company?"

"They're both born Sablecrofts," she said in the reasonable tone you take with a fractious four-year-old. "They belong here."

"It's . . . it's honestly crazy."

"Not at all. They were incompatible, they grew apart, they didn't want to be married any longer. Was that a reason for one to be turned out? They don't hate each other, you know."

I drew a long breath, clenching my hands. "It may not be an absolute rule of conduct that you go away and never see your divorced husband again, but if Wendy had any pride—"

"She has pride. She's a Sablecroft."

Blast the Sablecrofts and their high-handed above-the-common-herd outlook. "I was told they may marry again. It startled me. But the other thing, the tries at giving you a heart attack or whatever they hope to accomplish—"

"Are you in love with Sherry, Laurel?"

"No!"

"Too fast, too loud, too defensive," she murmured.

"Well then, I don't *know!* I'm beginning to feel strange about both of them," I admitted. I had to confide in her, I did admire her, and I wanted advice I knew nobody could give me, and still I had to say it. "When I'm with Sherry, he's so often grouchy and makes me feel disliked and afraid; then for a moment he's tender or concerned, and I realize I'm ambivalent past belief over him! And Daniel, most of the time I can't take him seriously as more than a tall kid playing with his films and tapes, and then—"

"He kisses you and you're as confused as though you were sixteen again." She poured champagne and offered it to me. I shook my head. "Everyone knows he's kissed you. Wendy saw you."

"And was jealous?"

"Who knows? She simply told everybody. Never been known to keep her mouth shut about anything, not since she came here at fourteen, orphaned. I never did see what Sherry found so fascinating about her—though she is very pretty, and has a certain cold sexiness, and a quite adequate mind when she chooses to employ it, plus those exquisite legs—but eventually he married her. She was then eighteen, and it lasted three years."

"And she's lived here for the three years or so since?"

"Naturally."

"*Does* she want to marry him again?"

Sibella considered. "No one ever has known exactly what Wendy wants," she said at last. "My guess would be Daniel." She laughed her pronounced, descending *ha, ha, ha.* "Don't let that bug you, as the children say. You can give her a mile start and beat her to the finish."

"Why do you say that?"

"Because you're warm in the heart, and she's ice. You have depths of love, bottled up for quite a time, yes, but down in that slim and handsome frame there's certified emotional lava. It's on the point of boiling over, Laurel, and I can't tell you in which directions to channel it. Nobody can. But with three choices in this house, I predict you won't wait to meet other men; you'll make your choice here. Don't turn all pink and take offense, child, it's a fact of nature."

She sipped her bubbly wine. "So be patient. And to reassure you on what you asked, two reels back, I'm doing something about the shocking, stupid stunts. People are being watched. Even you."

"Me?" I said, honestly shaken.

"I didn't necessarily mean watched with suspicion," she said mildly. "Watched for your own good."

"By whom, when everyone's a suspect? By Wendy?"

"Don't try the heavy irony on me, girl. I could have insulted you into the ground when I was nine."

I shrugged impatiently. "'Watching' us all is impossible! You couldn't keep tabs on any three people in this crazy labyrinth of a mansion all day and night with a squad of detectives. And speaking of that—and, Daniel agrees with me—what *I'd* have done after that wretched dummy of your sister fell in on us would have been to call the police, have everything fingerprinted, check where we all stood for some of those abominable switches and wires, told the cops everything, and let them solve it that night!"

"Zeal," she muttered. "An excess of zeal. My dear young woman, have some mother wit! A houseful of people reared on the flicks isn't likely to contain a madman who forgets to wipe his fingerprints off anything he touched when preparing his crime. Nor was it a crime, but, to the outside world which believes we're a sack of nuts in this place anyway, a practical joke. So was the almond gunk in the drink. The balcony sagged out because it was old and put up with faulty nails or rivets or whatever they put balconies up with. The soldier pitched over because his armor was too heavy for a bug-infested platform. End of official report."

"And Felicity's death?"

"She was startled and fell, I told you. The police *were* here for that. Anyone can be startled—by a flying roach, an errant bat, a sudden noise, or a misstep in the gloom."

She leaned forward. "Laurel," she said, with a quick flash of laughter in those gray eyes, "getting down to basics, I want to warn you against falling in love out of simple old-maid's desperation—"

"See here!" I yelped.

"Don't contradict, I don't suffer it gladly. You're a woman who ought to be married. You've too much natural affection to give, too deep a desire to care for some fool man who can't take care of himself properly. Men can't, you know. Men are great bumbling braggarts who think they can manage anything, but don't in reality have the least notion what's best for 'em. You could make a man succeed without his realizing that you'd had a thing to do with it. I see it in your eyes now and then when you look at Daniel or Sherry or, yes, Pierce Poole: that marvelous softness, that damned motherly instinct at work. I neither have it nor want it, but you do and it's fine."

I kept blinking at her to keep tears away, and I wasn't sure why I wanted to cry, but there it was.

"You must wait, Laurel. Weeks, months if you have to. Don't give way to that instinct, not yet. We're dealing with a shadow in the dark. We don't know who it is. Don't throw yourself at part of a man. Wait to see all of him."

"It's good advice, Mrs. Callingwood, if I can take it."

"I know that youth must have its romance, Laurel." She laughed.

"And one must take human nature as one finds it, a fact that's been a thorn in my side all my life."

I yawned without warning. "Sorry, I'm very tired."

"And you've sat up to pamper my whim. You're a sweet child, no matter how irritable your chief librarian claimed you were. I find your temper equable enough, if I don't cross you." She smiled again. "Go to bed! A trip outside always wears one down. I hope you won't do it again soon. Sherry spends altogether too much time out of the house. One of these days he'll break down, or contract a skin disease from the sun . . . bed!"

I picked up my discarded shoes and trailed along to the darkened great hall. I knew it by heart, and could avoid bumping into statues and cabinets with very little light—tonight, what filtered down off the balcony from the line of small corridor lamps on the second floor. I trudged through, between Lillian Gish and H. B. Warner, past a menacing blackness that was Cagney in his *Public Enemy* role, up the staircase, into my room.

"Hello, scourge," I said to Micajah, who'd scratched back the sheets and made himself a nest under my pillow. He opened an eye, nodded curtly, and went back to sleep. I bolted my door, as always now, and got ready for bed. It came to my mind that I hadn't checked the spy hole for weeks; not, in fact, since Pierce had moved the big bookcase in front of it. I edged into the space between the case and wall to look, and the strips of cream-colored paper were gone.

I turned on the lights and inspected the rug, even moving the bed. Not a sign of them. Belle may have picked them up in cleaning. Or they'd been lifted by whoever pried open the hatch.

The carpet was wall-to-wall, but not nailed down. I tugged it up at the edge of the outside wall, and there were two of the paper bits, wadded as if they'd been chewed. Beneath the rug by the door I found the third strip, torn to bits and carefully shoved out of sight, and in the fourth corner, the last of them. Micajah, discovering them on the floor, and shut in and bored, had disposed of them for me. In no way could he have extracted them from around the peephole. It was too high. They'd fallen out, as I'd intended they should, when someone reopened that sealed hatch; then the cat had taken them over. Maybe weeks ago, maybe tonight.

I turned off all the room lights and with the aid of my pencil flash and a nail file, tried to open the "secret" door. I found the file unnecessary, for the thing swung away from me, and it had not been bolted. Someone's second mistake, the first being to imagine that I wouldn't set the most elementary of traps for him, the strips of stationery.

Who? Who? Who?

Robed, I unbolted my door and went out, easing it shut behind me. I was fully as enraged now as I'd been glum and tired half an hour before.

Entering the passage behind the painting, I proceeded to the outer wall, my path lit by the pencil flash; crept under the windows of Felicity's room, then mine, and straightened to glare at the spying port. Daniel's two metal straps were still in place. I pulled the door all the way open and saw that the nails meant to hold them tight had been hacksawed off short. When the door was shut, they barely pushed into the deep holes he'd drilled for them.

"All for a practical joke," I hissed aloud. "All to put a rubber snake into my room. Sure!"

Unwillingly I then thought of such absurdities, for it was an absurd house, as poison gas, venomous reptiles and vampire bats, blowguns with darts dipped in exotic South American poisons. Nowhere else in the world would I have ever thought in such terms. Maybe I *would* hand in my notice.

I shut it quietly and crept back under my window block. Standing, I breathed deeply of the hot, humid air to calm myself. On a hunch I shone the thin beam of the flash across the inner wall here. Sure enough, Felicity's room had a hatch too. I slipped back the bolt, which was oiled and noiseless. I drew the square of wood outward.

A streak of brilliant white shone directly into my face.

My hand froze. I jerked my head to one side. Dear God! I'd expected darkness and silence, and there'd come light and the whisper of voices. Or at least of one voice.

The hair sat up on my nape, and I began to shiver, the sweat running down my forehead. Taking my hand off the hatch with great caution, I listened, but could distinguish no words. It was a ghostly sound, but I doubted that ghosts turn on lamps.

Then, plucking up my courage from where it groveled on the

floor of my heart, I pulled the port another inch toward me and looked in.

Wendy stood there, sidelong to me, listening to the whisperer. Her small mouth, clean for once of its glossy lipstick, was pouted peevishly, and her lavender-blue eyes stared down at the man, whoever he might be. The indistinct words ceased, and she tossed her head and said loudly, "I don't care how you insist, you damn devil, I won't!"

"I think you will," came the whisper. My ears strained but I couldn't tell who it was, only that it was a man, I thought. "And keep your voice down—Laurel will hear you."

"I don't care. Why shouldn't she? Who's *she* to say where I can go, how loud I have to talk! Ever since she came you've been gaping at her. It's been Laurel this and Laurel that till I want to screech! If it was Laurel you were talking about, I'd say yes, I'd be glad to help. But you can't ask any more of me now, no, not even you."

"I can and I will ask more of you," said the relentless wheezing voice. "And if you keep shouting, you stupid wench, I'll choke you down to a faint rustle, I promise you." *Was* it a man? I gritted my teeth in frustration.

Wendy said more quietly, "I won't help you murder anyone. Unless it's Laurel, and no, no, not even her. Drive her away, yes, but don't hurt her. I *can't* hurt anyone."

"Noble young Wendy." If there can be sarcasm in a whisper, it was there. "Draws the line at killing. Frighten someone to death, sure, but touch them, oh no."

Wendy scowled ferociously. If only I could see the other, I had the whole answer to everything right under my nose. I dared to pull the door slightly farther toward me, but the second person was out of sight, evidently sitting against the wall that separated Felicity's room from mine.

The silence stretched out, agonizingly unbroken by a word. Then the sibilation came. "Has that stood open all this time?"

Instinctively I fled. Perhaps one more second would have shown me the face, the sighing, hissing, wicked face. But I was incapable of waiting. I feared that one as I had never feared anything or anyone before. I crawled clumsily under the obstruction that cased my bedroom windows, bumping painfully against it, clicked on my minuscule flashlight and dodged and crept beneath more blocks and went forward at a run, around the curved tower wall, down straight short passages and around bends, gulping deep hot breaths and fleeing like a ham-strung gazelle, limping from a crack on the ankle somewhere back there, the thread of light leaping wildly before me as my arm shook with terror, imagining that I heard the thud of pursuing footfalls echo in the narrow coffin-space of the labyrinth.

Maybe the steady pursuit wasn't my imagination.

I raced down the length of the dining room, turned left, and went on till I found one of the movable ladders and, thankful I'd studied the architectural plans, whipped it out from the wall and jammed it downward so that the floor moved and there was a hole to drop through, my clumsy bare feet hitting every second step on the way to the bottom. I shoved the ladder violently up and the flooring slid into place above me. A few steps farther, I dropped the flash in my robe pocket and opened the door to the dining room.

Sibella had gone, but the light was still on and the table hadn't been cleared. I sat down in my usual chair, pulled the last champagne bottle toward me, poured half a glassful, and leaned back, waiting. Eventually I stopped panting and was able to breathe normally. I didn't think of anything I'd heard or done. I drank the flat champagne and sloshed out some more.

Sherry Todd came in from the great hall. "I thought you'd gone to bed." He was still fully dressed, and looked more awake than ordinarily.

"I had, but I couldn't sleep."

"Something on your mind?" He sat opposite.

"No. Oh, yes—not that it kept me awake, but why didn't you ever tell me you'd been married to Wendy?"

"Didn't realize you weren't aware of it. Why, what's it matter to you? I think that under those bangs, you're frowning at me."

"My bangs and your mustache. Disguises," I said at random.

"I like a mustache."

"I don't, much." I remembered, like a sudden unwilled flashback, what I'd heard in Felicity's room. Sherry whispering must sound almost exactly like Daniel whispering—they had similar baritone voices, and phrased things in much the same way. Pierce, for that matter, too . . . having lived here for two decades, might he drop his English accent when he liked? The whispering unknown might have been any one of them. Even Sibella, with her big dark voice. They all talked alike.

"What did you say?" I asked, emerging from the fog.

"I said, I'll shave it if you like."

I stared at him. "How silly to cut it off for some nobody out of Connecticut!"

"Not permanently. Just so you can see I have a stiff upper lip and a full set of my own teeth."

"Why should I care?"

He said, "I don't suppose you should," and stood up. "I'll see you to your room."

"I'll go up in a while."

"You'll go now, Laurel." I widened my eyes at him. Slowly he nodded. "Sing loudly all the way; then if I bury an axe in your head, someone will notice the abrupt hush and come running. I'm not kidding, I am escorting you to bed."

"Well of all the—" I began, voice squeaky.

"Perhaps I don't like the feel of the place tonight—too many footsteps pounding through the walls. Perhaps I'm the guardian Sibella mentioned this evening."

I said, "You listen at doors."

"I put my head in to say good night and you two were talking earnestly about people watching people. Lord, Lord! I'm being watched myself. It's hardly a secret."

"You don't listen at doors?"

"Only by accident. Nothing one could hear would be worth the loss of self-respect. It's a selfish kind of honor, but valid. Come to bed."

I stood. "Sherry, I'm glad you don't listen at doors. I'd be disappointed. I was, for a minute. Sorry."

"Yet you're pretty sure I'm trying to frighten my own grandmother to death," he said, smiling.

"That's—I don't know—"

"A less *low* crime? A more dignified sin than snoopery? Murder is an enormous outrage, but spying is cheap and feeble. I see the point. I'd rather know a murderer than a blackmailer, and an eavesdropper's nearly as despicable." He took my hand. "But to scare an old woman half to death—and Sibella's frightened, don't let her pride fool you on that—well, damn it, there's nothing of the noble, violent savage in that, is there? No grandeur as of a peasant pulling down a great queen? Surely playing mean tricks on someone is as bad as skulking furtively?"

"Yes, when you spell it out. I'm just glad you don't snoop," I told him stubbornly. "No need to compare it with killing."

"Right. Come on," he said, and I began to walk beside him. "Remember, though, sometimes one *must* listen—when there's murder in the air."

"Yes," I agreed. "And obviously you wouldn't suspect Sibella and me of plotting *that*."

"Correct. Hush up and walk, lean on me if you like. You ought to sleep in tomorrow. You've been either working or worrying too hard."

We crossed the great hall. I was exhausted, probably the aftermath of being frightened so badly. Sherry helped me up the stairs and waited till I locked my door. Shoving the heavy bookcase slam against the wall over the falsely bolted hatchway, I fell into bed, and Micajah landed with a thump on my abdomen, uttering a small *urk* of welcome.

All that about tawdry, despicable eavesdropping . . . had Sherry been the whisperer next door? Had he seen me flying down the corridor, or come straight to my room to find me absent? Was he mocking me when he balanced murder against meddling?

How could I tell? Who, at this stage of weariness and the night, gave a whoop?

I slept like the dead, right through the alarm, and never woke until noon.

12

THE INTERCOM ANNOUNCED HOLLOWLY THAT MRS. CALLINGWOOD wished to see Laurel in her private chambers at once. Luckily I'd finished dressing. With Micajah romping ahead—for all he considered himself so old and wise and dignified, he was forced by a good night's sleep to frisk and caracole, kitten-fashion—I ran down the stairs and was shortly knocking at her silver-studded door. Belle McNabb opened it.

"She's in bed, you go on in," said the tiny gray wisp of vigor, glaring at me.

"Is she ill?"

"Sibby's never ill. Everybody knows that."

The mistress of Sablecroft sat up against an amassment of gaudy pillows in a bed the size of a handball court. I hadn't seen the bedroom before, but was given no chance to admire it. Dressed in a housecoat of gold-laced royal blue, she swung over the edge and beckoned me to follow her out, where she pointed dramatically to the gigantic chandelier. It was the most fantastic one of its kind I had ever seen, much farther from the ordinary than even the great hall's giant Tiffany. Formed of at least thirty immense branches of blown glass, the whole affair was spotted thickly with enamel ornaments, streaks of gold and silver, and rococo designs in brilliant colors. Basically clear crystal beneath its blobs and splashes of gilt, maroon, crimson, yellow, vivid blues, and startling pinks, each of its branches was tipped with three transparent glass candles, in which the scarlet glass flames gave the only hue. It was so ornate, so thickly tangled in its swirling stems and surprising bursts of curious colors both mellow and garish, so dazzlingly eighteenth century, that I stared up at it for several minutes. Belle went out and closed the door. Then Sibella said, "You're taken with my great jewel."

"I never saw it in daylight before. Where did it come from? How on earth do you light it?"

"Venice, of course. It's one of Briatti's masterpieces. Father bought it for my thirtieth birthday. We don't light it. It was made for candles, and thank God it was never electrified! If you look closely at the flower bunches and the swags of lace glass, you'll see the candleholders. Its probable date is the seventeen forties."

"It's—incredible."

"Have you a good head for heights?" she asked suddenly.

"Yes."

"That's fine. Then get up there and examine the fastenings of the thing, at the ceiling and on the fixture. Please," she added as an uncommon afterthought.

"How do I get there?"

"Ladder down yonder. Come along." We walked the fifty feet or so to the Moorish court, which was lit now with the sunshine from a broad skylight in the roof. Sibella pointed to one end of the blue-tiled court. "Behind that curtain. Pull the cord on your left." I did, and the hangings swept aside—they were floor-to-ceiling drapes, nearly thirty feet high—to reveal the biggest stepladder I had ever seen. "Specially made," grumbled Sibella, "and no way to disguise it unless I hide it there. A stepladder isn't the most aesthetic object in creation. Roll it out. It moves easily." I shoved the towering silver-colored brute, which was permanently in an open position, across the tiles and onto the carpet. "Don't hit the lamp, for the love of heaven!" she shouted hoarsely.

"I won't." Cautiously I maneuvered the ladder up beside her chandelier and anchored its feet with heavy weights that slid down either side of all four legs. I clambered up until the stupendous fixture was below me. The ladder quivered but did not sway, to my relief. I stared down at the writhing mass of crystal and rainbow and saw where the heavy chain went into the midst of it. "There isn't anything to see but chain and glass," I called.

"No sign of tampering?"

"No. There's nothing to tamper with." Compulsively I started to count the candleholders.

"Check the ceiling, then," Sibella ordered.

I crept up a few more steps, trying to remember my good head for heights and to forget that I was almost two stories high on a ridiculous aluminum stepladder, leaned out and prodded the gilt cap that covered the hole in the ceiling where the chain disappeared. It was solid enough. I tested the screws that held the cap, and they were all right too. I went down to the floor, breathing faster than usual. "It's in perfect shape as far as I can tell."

Her voice had an anxious ring that I'd never heard there before. "Do you think we ought to unscrew the plate and check on the—oh, I suppose not. Except, damn it, that I don't *know.*"

"Don't know?" I repeated stupidly.

"Don't know what attics or crawlspaces there are beyond this ceiling."

"I've studied the plans; there's a low attic." I looked at her closely, she was for the moment so unlike herself. "Why, Mrs. Callingwood?"

"I don't want anything to happen to my great jewel," she said. Then she blinked and came alive, as it were, and didn't look eighty any longer, but ageless. "I'm not in the least *afraid* to die, Laurel, but I don't *want* to die, and I don't *mean* to die."

"I really don't understand."

"Put that fool ladder away and shroud it again, and I'll explain." I did so, and she drew two chairs together under the great antique. "Sit, Laurel. You recollect the theater chandelier falling in *Phantom of the Opera*. Lovely gruesome scene. I was thinking of it this morning, after hearing certain sounds up there. I entered my quarters at a time when I'm usually back in the kitchen talking with Belle, and heard a metallic hammering that seemed to come from just above the chandelier. I waited quite silently and after a minute the clatter stopped." She paused. "And before you ask—I'd seen no one, so no one's in the clear. Belle hadn't come over, and the others weren't in evidence. I then heard nothing more for some time, after which there was the unmistakable sound of a door closing high up within that western wall. It occurred to me that when the prankster grows tired of trying to bedevil me into a coronary, it's possible he'll rig that monster to fall." She jerked a thumb upward. "It would fit the pattern of the house, wouldn't it? A really spectacular murder right out of the cinema. If it pops into my head, it can as easily have popped into his."

"Why in *hell* are we sitting under it, then?" I demanded.

"Oh, long habit. And defiance."

"That's dumb."

"Right." We wheeled the chairs away. The mighty chandelier hung there looking festive and ominous.

She said, looking at me, "How old were you when your grandfather, Alfred Vane, died? About eighteen, wasn't it? Do you know you're the image of him? Not physically, except at a certain angle with your head turned slightly away, but in gesture and attitude you could be him all over again, especially when you're impatient with someone, as you are now. If you could have known him in his prime! A splendid, strong man. He always talked to me as though I were an ignorant brat, and made me like it. And me thirty-three at the time."

"How long did you know him?"

"He was here some months—three, and a few days over. He followed the old precept: Treat the duchesses like charwomen, the charwomen like duchesses. What the devil was I saying? Oh, above, there, you say there's a low attic. Big enough for some damn monkey to crawl around loosening bolts and snipping wires in comfort?"

"Yes. Do you want me to investigate it?"

"Now?" She was asking, not ordering.

"As soon as I change into old clothes. It's probably filthy. I'll need keys to the doors of the passages that circle these private rooms."

She went into the bedroom and brought me a huge ring with twenty-odd keys. "They're in this lot somewhere. Leave your cat behind," she said, smiling. "He has the honest feline urge to pry. I hate to think of that glossy pure coat full of cobwebs again."

"He doesn't like the passages now unless he can stick close to me. He thinks they're haunted—or hears people nearby that he doesn't care for."

"Who would that be? I know he dotes on Daniel and Pierce, and I caught him eating shrimp from Belle's hand the other day. Ready? You can locate the chandelier with no trouble?"

"It's marked on the plans."

"Good. Come back when you're done. I'll stay here till tea. I'm in a foul humor with all of them, and want to think. Scoot!"

I went to my room, annexing an apple on the way, and got into jeans and an old linen shirt. I found the attic on the architect's drawing and memorized what I'd need. Into a big denim shoulder bag I put a three-cell flashlight and a small crowbar from the garage, the key ring, Scotch tape of the nearly invisible kind, a reel of surveyor's tape, and a spool of black thread. By way of the northwest tower entrance, ignoring everyone in the library, I went into the hot corridors and up to the second story, where I walked toward the front of the house, using my flash rather than bothering with the lights. Where the library ended and Sibella's chambers began, I found a door, and in a moment the key that opened it. I pushed through, locked it behind me, and ran the beam of the flash across the floor. It was filthy indeed. There were a multitude of dead insects in various stages of mummification, a lot of plain dirt, at least one terribly old bat carcass, and spider webs that might have come straight from Dracula's castle. No compulsively tidy Belle or drudging Wendy had cleaned here in decades, and the outer walls must have had more chinks than one would have thought. . . .

I knelt to examine the floor. Someone had walked here, scuffing the dirt aside carelessly, confident that no one would ever follow, and left a sort of central rut with no plainly marked prints, for a hot, sticky breeze blew from somewhere, and on really windy days the dust would be stirred and mixed so as to blur outlines. I proceeded down the aisle, uncomfortably aware that another presence accompanied me, a shadow among the shadows thrown by the flash —a thin and obscure shade of someone, dead or living, human or elemental, such as I had not felt in the clean, often-used parts of this ambulatory. It seemed not to menace me, but to be *aware*. To watch, perhaps amused, as I strode onward.

Gilbert or Felicity, Sherry or Daniel or Wendy, or even—my granddad? He'd lived here three months, Gilbert would have showed off his toy palace, his semimedieval hidden places; after, that is, using them to startle his friend Vane.

"I am not afraid of ghosts," I said aloud, and my echo mocked me. I assured myself I was sweating from excitement and temperature, not from fear.

Another door, locked. I found its key and went on.

A third door, this without lock or bolt. I was at the corner, and turned left, went on twenty feet or so in the direction of the great antique chandelier in Sibella's room. I moved slower here, aiming the torch up and to the sides of the narrow high-roofed gut of the passage. I saw one of the ladders just ahead, stopped and examined the dirty floor. Yes, the intruder had been here too, and it had been a male; these were large, masculine shoe prints, overlapped and scuffed together by more than one trip. I pulled the ladder so that it swung, creaking and stiff, away from the wall and at last flat opposite to me. I shoved it up; it resisted. I played the light on the ceiling, and among the thick masses of long-gone spiders' making, saw the square hatchway. I smashed upward with all my might, both hands gripping the near sidepiece. The ladder moved, the hatch opened slowly above me, showering my upturned face with old filth that made me shudder and almost cry out in disgust.

The ladder reached its limit and stuck, its movable hooks caught where they were meant to catch. I adjusted my bulky shoulder bag and shook my face free of most of the dirt, spat out some debris whose nature I refused to think about, and ascended rung by rung.

At the top, with my head in the attic blackness, I stopped to examine the last rung on which a climber had to step. Its dust was smudged. With the powerful beam of light shifting all around, I went on, stopped before I could hit my head on the concrete ceiling, stooped and came off the ladder sideways to stand all bent and streaming with perspiration in the place I'd come to find.

The long white ray glanced here and there, and it was only any big building's old attic, stretching out to north and east interminably and full of nothing but dust-moted space, wiring, ancient stale air, an occasional pillar of cement. The place was four feet high and what seemed miles broad. There was not nearly so much dirt up here. Roof and walls were solid, the towers unconnected to the interior by any doors or vents or fenestrations, the whole enclosed by steel-reinforced concrete without a break. I didn't even spot a dead lizard.

I moved to my right at a crouch, found a corner that led me right again. Here I began to measure with my tape, ten feet to the south, then eighteen feet directly out from the wall, going over Sibella's huge room to where the chandelier must be anchored.

I'd hit it on the dot! A low framework of steel crisscrossed here to form an enormous anchor that would have held up half the house. I inspected it on my knees, and found eight or ten bolts with stains around them. Feeling below the bars into which they were set, noting the little short bright lines of dented metal here and there where a hammer had left its scars, I found the nuts all tightened. With a finger I smeared some of the dark stain-stuff off the metal, and smelled it. Not oil, but a substance to loosen corroded or badly rusted parts and unfreeze the metal—one of those liquid-wrench preparations that are better than oil.

The blood *can* run cold. They realized this sort of thing in past times. Before it became a meaningless phrase, it was a plain fact. I could feel my flesh chilling from the inside outward.

Sibella had been right in her wild cinematic hunch. The chandelier was meant to fall. A day or two from now, when the liquid had had time to work on the bolts, all it would need would be ten minutes labor and—Lord, what a crash!

I wiped my finger carefully on the tail of my shirt, thus preserving the greasy evidence, which was fresh because there was no dust on the smears. There was plenty of dust on the floor and parts of the steel framework. I looked at the motes hanging in the flashlit air and guessed that the goop had been applied today.

There were more scuffed, overlaid footprints around the anchoring apparatus which I had not made. A man's again. I found a good clear one that might have told a detective a lot about the wearer, but I wasn't even on a par with Dr. Watson. I knew that ichnology, the study of fossil and modern footprints, was a precise science, but beyond the two kinds of tracks, *punched* and *pressed,* I remembered little of it. I looked closely for patterns of wear on sole and heel, maker's trademarks, and ridges of dust around the perimeter, but found nothing usable. The dry dust was not a prime material for retention of small details. However, I measured the impression from toe to heel and across the widest part of the sole, which was all I could think to do; having forgotten my notebook, I wrote the figures in smeary ballpoint on my tattered sleeve.

This amount of investigation seemed inadequate, but there wasn't anything further to do. Nowhere was there a distinguishable set of prints to tell me the length of stride. I retraced my steps, noting how his multiple path had paralleled my own single one, and found the ladder; descended and pulled the old rope that unlatched the hooks, thus bringing it down and closing the trapdoor.

Grubbing in my bag, I found thread and Scotch tape, and holding them in my left hand and the flash in my right, returned to the corner where the last door, the one with no lock, stood closed as I'd left it. I went through and shut it again, turned to go on, and—merciful heaven!—saw in the ray of my flashlight, facing me at a distance of a dozen feet, the immense black Great Dane, his scarlet tongue lolling. I stopped instantly, swept by all the centuries upon centuries of unreasoning terror that coal-black dogs have inspired in the human heart: the symbol of death in many lands, Satan in earthly form, the witches' familiar, the plague, the famine, the Celtic pooka, even the Hound of the Baskervilles. . . .

How had this hobgoblin passed through two solid doors—no, counting the climb from the library, *four?*

I tried to speak, failed lamentably, cleared my throat, smirked, and said, falsetto, "Hi, Marmaduke. There's a good boy, Falconlair. Nice doggie."

He closed his mouth, the fangs and tongue disappearing so that all I could see was the sheen of black hair and the uncanny glow of his eyes, and he growled at me. I wished I'd brought Micajah, he'd have flown screeching and fearless at the creature's head. Dropping tape and thread into my bag, I groped in its depths till my fingers closed over the crowbar. I'd brought it with me in case any doors had been barred by boards or metal straps that would have to be pried free. Now it was the only weapon I had, and too light and short for comfort. That beast could tear out my throat.

He snarled, opening his mouth again so that he seemed to slaver. I felt blindly, caught the knob, turned it, moved to the rear slowly. The growl was louder. He came at me, stiff-legged, deliberate, head turned a little to one side in that awful forbidding attitude that an angry dog takes when he starts into battle. I jumped backward and slammed the door in his face. There was nothing with which to prop it, so I ran, my breath cold in my mouth in this close and sweltering air. Here was the ladder. I jerked it out from the wall and jammed it down. Nothing happened except that my hands hurt from the shock. There was no trapdoor under the layer of dirt beneath my feet. Quickly I moved the ladder, slithered round it, pulled it into place to block the narrow way.

A dog that had come through four closed doors wouldn't mind another door and a ladder in his path. I took two steps and turned right with the passage.

I fled him for what seemed a long way, hearing nothing but the hacking breath in my gorge, seeing only two confining walls dwindling ahead in the jittering, bounding beam of the flash. An end wall approached as though it were moving rather than I. Then I realized that I'd just gone by a door on the left. It took all the courage I had, but I whipped around and went back. It was locked. Feverish, quaking with panic, I scrabbled in my shoulder bag till I found the ring of keys. First one and then the next, for God's sake try to keep them separate—

I risked an instant to throw the light back along the corridor, and here came the black brute, eyes gleaming in the sudden stream of brightness, long legs moving slowly as he padded forward.

Key after key and never the right one, and the dog came on, tongue like a red flame hanging over his white teeth between the fangs. A key went in easily, but wouldn't turn. Try the next. I was nearly at the end of them. Perhaps this door had no key. Perhaps this was where I was to die.

I beamed the flash down the aisle again, the dog was walking slower now, terribly close, sure of me, and behind him nothing, no one urging him on, only the narrowing walls.

A key went in to the hilt. I turned it left, then right, and it moved around a half circle. I shoved on it, sobbing, sick with a mortal funk of the creature behind me. The door did not move.

I heard him growl, as close to me as heat to fire, and his jaws snapped together with a grinding click. I would not have been so afraid of a coiled rattlesnake.

I tore at the heavy door, hauling it inward, and it came with such a crash that it struck me in the face. For some peculiar reason I seemed to think that I had to take the keys with me, and stood there half in and half out, jerking at the ring. The key came loose and I whirled roundabout and tugged the door shut. I found the key again—it was hanging separately from the rest—and locked the beast into its haunted alley.

Then I leaned against the door and burst into tears. I had not cried for a long time, and the sobs hurt my ribs and racked my already parched throat. Stinging tears mingled with the sweat in my eyes. At last I put the flashlight and crowbar in my bag, and the key ring, and found a handkerchief and blew my nose and wiped off my face in a haphazard way, and looked behind me. I stood on a tiny platform, with a thin wrought-iron railing, from which steps descended into Sibella's huge chamber. Holding the rail I went down slowly, staring at the chandelier and wondering if it had been worth it.

I recall looking over my shoulder once with a sudden start, imagining that the black Dane had come through his sixth barrier too and was following behind me; but his supernatural powers evidently did not extend to a well-lighted place.

Sibella, in one of the castered easy chairs out of range of any falling crystal mass, watched me as I came down. I collapsed helplessly on the carpet at her feet. "The dog," I said, my voice unrecognizable to me, "the black dog, chased me, came through five closed doors and a ladder and ran after me, snarled, it meant to kill me."

She handed me a handkerchief, made chiefly of fine lace and air. I shook my head, tugged out my own again. "Nonsense," she said. "None of our dogs ever hurt anyone, except the harlequin who stepped on my sister's foot and broke her damned dainty toe. You've imagined things, Laurel."

"I don't imagine dogs in passages where they can't possibly be!" I shouted. "He was as near to me as you are. He slavered and growled. And there was *nobody* there, only me and the dog."

"We'll see about that. They can't get into the secret places alone," she said. "What did you manage to discover? Anything? Or did the dog interrupt you?"

I told her about the metal framework, the tracks in the dust, the bolts that had been lubricated to loosen them. She stood up. "Go into my bathroom—on the left as you enter the bedroom—and wash. You're an unholy mess, and have dead things in your hair. Your forehead and nose are growing extraordinarily pink under the dirt, too."

"I pulled the door against my face." I went and did what she'd ordered, and returned. "They've had time now to get the ghastly brute out of there, of course, " I said, "but if we can find it quick enough, it should be dirty on the paws. If you don't believe me."

"You're calm enough now, my dear, and you don't look like a gypsy who's been without water for a month. I believe you." She went to her intercom station on the west wall, clicked it on, and in a drill sergeant's tone said, "Now hear this, you lot! Everyone within sound of my voice go at once, *at once,* to the great hall. Jump!"

She straightened my shirt a little and fluffed my bangs into place. "It's refreshing to know that you *can* look a fright. You've been almost too neat to bear." This, from a woman who'd never had a hair out of kilter in her life. "We'll have a court of inquiry. It's long past time I squelched this maniac, whoever it may be. Oh!" She moved to the intercom and shouted into it, "One of you bring the black Dane, you hear me?" Then, smiling ruefully, "Should have said that at first. But if they haven't cleaned him up yet, they won't have time now. Come along. It's very dirty up there, eh?"

"Filthy. No one's been there for years, except one man."

"Take my arm, Laurel," she commanded. I thought that the shock of finding her suspicions confirmed had made the old woman wobbly, but it was she who supported me as we passed through library and dining room. I did need it, I was like a rotten reed in a wind. She talked to me quickly and forcefully until we'd come into earshot of the family.

She lowered herself into one of her thrones and pointed out a chair nearby for me. The others were sitting in a rough semicircle waiting for us, all but Sherry, who came in now with the black dog at his side. I looked at it, and I know the terror sprang up again in my eyes, if not my whole face. It stared at me and gave a tentative gurgle of menace.

"Challenger!" cried Sibella, pointing to her feet. It came slouching over, eyes showing the whites. "No! No!" She bent and gave it a sharp but not cruel slap across the side of the nose. "No! Who in hell's name's been teaching you to growl at people?" She gazed up at us as the dog cowered. "Well? Who?"

"He wasn't growling," said Wendy vaguely. "He was saying hello."

"The bloody blue blazes he was!" roared Sibella, making them all blink. "He attacked Laurel just now in the passages."

"What!" said Sherry, and scowled heavily at me. "Impossible."

"He didn't touch me, but he chased me and growled and—looked sinister. Threatening. I ran and he chased me—"

"Naturally he chased you, he wanted to play," said Pierce, eminently reasonable and wrong.

"No he did *not* want to play! I met him, he snarled, offered to bite me, and came after me—" I stopped short of saying "through several closed doors." That would have branded me a mental defective. "I know a threatening dog when I see one."

Daniel said, "I'm inclined to agree with Laurel. She's not a girl who imagines such things. Maybe the poor pup's coming down with rabies, or going mad, if it's not the same thing."

Sherry picked up the great head and looked into the eyes. Challenger—as I would always thereafter think of him, in memory of Wally Beery and Claude Rains who had both played the irascible, brilliant professor, George Edward Challenger—gazed sadly up at him. "He's all right, but someone's taught him a trick he'll have to unlearn. Come here, sir!" He led the dog to me. I shrank. "Give her your paw." The dog made small motions at me with a foot whose sleek shiny blackness was clotted and powdered with dirt. I took it, still afraid of the animal, and murmured forgiveness that as yet I couldn't feel. Sherry said, "Look at that paw. He was in the passages all right, those that aren't cleaned. That's not outside-run dirt. Sorry I doubted you, Laurel."

"How'd you happen to be there?" asked Daniel, face fighting a grin. He plainly believed I'd been hunting more secret rooms.

"I was investigating them for Mrs. Callingwood." I dropped the dog's paw and studied his mournful long face. You cannot blame an animal for being trained to do things that are immoral from a human standpoint. "Good old boy," I said. "You never meant it."

Whining, he gave me his paw again. There was no doubt that he was not in the least angry at me. No, someone had led him up the stairs, opened the doors for him, and vanished behind the last of them after ordering him to terrify me. "Sic 'em," or whatever it had been. Poor dog! I smoothed his permanently furrowed brow. Then Sherry had him go and lie down in the shadow of the figure of the Bride of Frankenstein.

"Very well," said Sibella coldly, and when that voice went chilly, your skin crawled. "I didn't assemble you to do jury duty on a dog. This is a court of inquiry. This is the dock. This is the delivery of an ultimatum. I am sick to death—" she paused, cocking an eyebrow; they all had that trick except Wendy. "Unfortunate choice of words. I've come to the end of my patience, then. Let me recapitulate the recent occurrences. When I was on the catwalk leading to our former balcony in the library, several months ago, it began to shake. I went back, and the entire structure sagged out from the wall, so that had I still been on it, my weight would have brought it down. Laurel arrived, to find taped messages of warning and intimidation and a ridiculous cap-gun rig with a photo of herself set up on her bed. Shortly afterward one of the heavier figures in here nearly knocked her flat."

I was watching Sherry and Daniel alternately. They looked a little bored, both of them. Now I glanced at Wendy, who projected stupidity with her half-open mouth. She must have been sure that I hadn't told Sibella about her visit to my room with the knife; she'd have heard about that before.

"My wine was then 'poisoned' with some ludicrous combination of kitchen stuff. Micajah, the cat, was cruelly put into the space between floor and ceiling in the passages."

That startled me. I'd assumed he'd wormed himself into it; but now as she talked I began to see that due to the construction of the silly ambulatory, he couldn't have done it alone. There were no entrances except when the ladders were down and the trapdoors open. He must have had help. Who would want to scare a cat?

"Some miserable fool made a figure of my late sister and put on a grisly rigadoon with it and the tapes. I considered then, in a rage, that I might call in the *gendarmerie;* but it was Sablecroft business, and we're accustomed to deal with our own here. So I set you to watch one another."

She gestured, and Pierce handed her a glass of ice water which he'd poured from a thermos pitcher on the nearest table. She drank slowly and with relish. The time was coming—on the way here she'd given me my instructions. I glued my eyes on Sherry, who was watching his grandmother closely.

"I was in error," she said, even more bleak than before. "I placed mercy and family pride before justice. Always a stupid action. The needs of justice transcend blood ties and old affection. I was dead wrong. I admit it. I was in danger and so was Laurel, an innocent woman only lately come to live here. So I have grown tired of mercy. Whoever has been doing these little jobs, putting on these sick performances, deserves no compassion from me." She smiled, a grimace as cold as her voice. "The slides used to say, in the good old times, 'Came the dawn of a new day.' "

"You're calling in the cops?" asked Wendy, and I speculated whether it was my imagination that she'd gone pale around the mouth and eyes.

"Don't interrupt me. Just because I haven't donned a full-bottomed wig doesn't mean I'm not running this court, Wendy. No, I haven't yet called the police. I am delivering the ultimatum of which I spoke. You will all listen carefully. You'll take what I say with the gravest seriousness. You will not—Wendy! Daniel!—let your minds stray to any possible similar situation you've seen in a motion picture. *You will listen.* Do you understand me?"

She had them all now, no doubt of it: They nodded like puppets on a single string. During the brief silence I found my eyes shifting from Sherry Todd to a couple of the statues, who seemed also to be listening to the queen of the Hall. And Micajah had come out of somewhere, perhaps at the sound of his name, and sat on Fred Astaire's waxen foot with his golden eyes perfectly round. Even black Challenger was watching her alertly. The woman radiated power and a kind of monarchial fury.

"Today I had Laurel examine the locked corridors that surround my quarters. She found that someone has a duplicate set of keys, and has been in there recently. That is bad enough, but there is worse. Someone, doubtless the same someone, forced the dog to all but attack her."

She drew a long breath. I watched Sherry.

"But before Laurel was so cruelly frightened, and pursued into my room, she discovered what I'd begun to suspect. The miscreant is planning, has indeed prepared, to drop my Italian chandelier and kill me stone dead."

Sherry gave a distinct jump in his chair, a convulsive twitch of his whole body, and instantly recovered and stared blankly at her. As ordered, I then turned my gaze to Wendy, and saw that she had gone white—no doubt of it this time—and sat back in her chair like a girl who wanted to disappear into the upholstery.

Sibella had said she'd watch Pierce and Daniel, but I spared the latter a glance, and he was shaking his head slowly, blinking. He was the first to speak. "Sibella, dear Sibella, are you *sure?* No error? I mean, everything to now could have been harmless practical jokes. . . ."

"Nothing of the sort. They were meant to give me a heart attack or a stroke, or whatever the doctors call it today when one drops dead. Or else to make me cringe and walk in fear until the time came to pitch or squash me into an early grave. They were also calculated to injure Laurel or drive her away, or even to kill her. Never before have the traditional jokes of Sablecroft Hall been heartless, witless, meant for anything stronger than amusement. If you think that spoilt wine and broken balconies are amusing, then, Daniel, you're a consummate ass."

"Hear hear," said Pierce.

"I didn't imply they weren't a collection of mean-spirited stupidities. But I always thought somebody had slipped a cog and was, well, just four-flushing you, to get a good rise out of you," said Daniel.

"Laurel found that a preparation has been used on the bolts that hold the lamp up, an oil or something that dissolves rust. Plainly, they intended to remove those bolts and let the chandelier fall. That would be an appalling calamity, the act of the ultimate vandal. Because it is the single most valuable object in this house."

Pierce Poole nodded vigorously. Nobody said anything. Sibella went on. "You've likely forgotten the history of the chandelier, which was made by a famous Italian glassblower in the eighteenth century and is virtually unique. To call it a museum piece is to downgrade it. Its perfection has never been marred—by the most incredible luck, it's exactly as it was in seventeen forty. I will not see it harmed. The nihilist who planned to destroy it, along with me, will never venture into those attics again."

They all watched her, waiting. Wendy was still quite pale.

"To this end," she said, allowing her face to assume what the old novels always called a wintry smile, "and to stop the rash of vicious idiocies, I have prepared and had witnessed, and sent off to my attornies, a new will."

Something between a gasp and the ghost of a sigh came from one of the people sitting around us, but I could not tell the source.

"I don't appeal to pride, to decency, to any finer feeling. Beyond question the culprit has none. I appeal to greed. If I am killed accidentally—and it doesn't matter if every last one of you is a hundred miles away at the time—every cent, and the house and contents, goes to charity. The books will be sent to The Motion Picture Academy Library, the relics as well as the films and tapes to various respositories such as the Museum of Modern Art Film Library and the George Eastman House. The furnishings will be donated to a prominent museum. The estate will be sold, and that money as well as my personal fortune will be divided among several worthy retired-actors' homes and the like. Perhaps a scholarship will be set up for a few promising young people in the cinema."

"What about Belle?" asked Pierce.

"I've already settled enough on Belle to last her into her hundreds, and I believe that in addition she's saved most of her salary for the past seventy years."

"Where is she, anyway?" asked Wendy, a little revived. "She ought to be in on this. It isn't just us six who have the run of the house."

"Never you mind about Belle. Think of yourself. Think of all of yourselves. You haven't got a blessed fifty-dollar bill among you! Every nickel in the family is in my hands and utterly at my disposal. If I want to hand it over to charity tomorrow, or leave it to a home for indigent armadillos, I can legally and morally do so. My lawyers assure me that this new will cannot be broken."

"Your sanity might be questioned," murmured Sherry.

"By you?"

"You know better than that. You're in total control of your faculties, and we all realize there's good reason for you to protect yourself this way. I simply wondered if you'd had time to think everything out."

"Look, boy," she said harshly, "besides Laurel and Belle, there are four of you. At least two—I hope three—are innocent of anything worse than perennial fascination with movies. Wouldn't they all tell the truth if I were shoved off a tower or died in my sleep with the stench of arsenic on my lips? Wouldn't they proclaim my rationality and swear I'd never commit suicide? I put it to you that the guilty one wouldn't have a chance. He might not be caught—I suppose he or she is clever enough to get away with it, you're all smarter than you look—but he'd be flat broke for the rest of his rotten life! What could any of *you* do to earn a living? The days of the servants' hall are over. Pierce could be a restaurant cook, Sherry a gardener, Daniel an electrical repairman. Wendy could do housework. Is whatever you hate me for," and her glance swept the row of them, "you who want me dead, is it so unbearable that you'll throw away your comfort and pleasure and luxury forever to satisfy it? No more security *ever?* I beg leave to doubt it. Milords and ladies, I rest my case. You are warned. And remember this: Whatever I die of, when I do die, *if* I die before the lot of you, there's going to be the most thoroughgoing postmortem examination that's ever been seen in Florida!"

"And if you die of natural causes?" asked Wendy.

"For God's sake, shut up," said Sherry with disgust.

"Then naturally the former testament remains in force. And none of you knows what's in *it,* either." She stood. "Laurel, come to my rooms. This meeting with all its friendship and jollity is adjourned." Regal, arrogant, and splendid, she strode off, the black dog following her as though instinct told him she'd had the last word and was still the boss.

"Mesdames et messieurs, rien ne va plus," said Sherry, grinning. *"Plus rien.* I think that's that. Laurel, you've been writing things on your blouse."

"Gosh, so I have," I said. "Excuse me." I hurried after Sibella.

I heard Pierce say heavily behind me, "For the love of God, whoever you are, take her warning to heart. If we should lose the Hall—" The rest of his speech, which I knew might have been clever camouflage, was lost as I passed through the archway and turned toward Sibella's quarters.

"Come in, my dear." She was standing in her doorway. Carefully she closed us in and led me to her bedroom, where she made me sit in the almost bottomless depths of a gigantic feather-stuffed chair. "There are no microphones here, so far as I know, but we'll speak softly nevertheless." She hauled up another vast backbreaker of a seat next to me. "How did I do? Spot anyone writhing in guilt?"

Reluctantly I told her the truth. "Sherry started violently when you first mentioned the chandelier falling, and Wendy went fish-belly white, but it may have been from simple horror at the whole idea."

"Hmm. Daniel dropped his jaw and opened his eyes as if he'd been shot in the middle. Pierce imitated a gaffed porpoise. Nothing to go on, then, unless they're all in it together for the money, and I won't credit that. This vendetta isn't for gain, it's for hate; but maybe the abrupt loss of everything they've been used to all their lives will end the affair. Certainly Daniel's nearly as terrified of Out There as Pierce is. We'll see."

"The change of will was clever," I said.

"Also highly untrue, but I'm going to do it now. I'll write it out in longhand—I'm certain it will hold up, and my handwriting, as you know, is inimitable. But I'll phone my lawyer that I've done it, and you can mail it across the street. Call Belle and get her here in half an hour. You and she can witness my signature."

"Where is she?"

"At home, cleaning. With your clever eyes sharpened by all this hugger-mugger," she said, chortling quietly, "you may notice, if you haven't already, that Belle McNabb wears shoes as large as a man's. They are, in fact, men's shoes. Don't jump to the notion that she's been prowling up yonder. Belle gains nothing by my death, and loses her last close friend from childhood. Okay?"

"Okay," I said, thinking that it was just as possible for an old friend to go insane as it was for a relative.

"Don't fret about your job. I know you need the money badly, and I've already deposited two years' salary for you in a special account, in addition to what's going into your regular one every week. Just in case."

"No, that's unnecessary."

"Don't you presume to tell me what's necessary! I'm a long way from my dotage, girl."

"Thirty years, I'd guess."

"At least." And suddenly, for no more than a couple of seconds, her face crumpled and her voice went gray. "Laurel, Laurel, those were Sablecrofts I had to threaten out there, and so few of us are left." She shook herself, and recovered. "To work now." She heaved out of the sagging chair's suction and went to a giant sycamore desk, English Victorian like most of her bedroom furniture, to find paper and a fountain pen. Naturally, Sibella would loathe ballpoints. I do myself.

I phoned Belle, and then sat down to watch the black dog. He lay at ease, looking at me and then at Sibella, squinting and wrinkling his brow, trying to decide what was going on in this bewildering house.

In half an hour Belle knocked and came in, and we both signed our names at the bottom of each of three pages after Sibella had done so. She folded them and put them in an envelope. "You know where the mailbox is, Laurel? Across the street and to the left?"

"I can mail that, Sibby," Belle objected.

"You work too hard, Belle. We can't have you running errands too."

The old woman glinted those dark eyes at me. "Never get used to gentry doing their own runnin' around, Sibby."

I laughed. "I'm not gentry, Mrs. McNabb. I'm hired help."

"Hmmph," she said, enigmatic as a Grecian priestess speaking with the voice of a god, "hmmph!"

Sibella, having addressed and stamped the envelope, stared at me. "What do you *have* in that bag, thirty pounds of avocados?"

"Stuff I needed upstairs. By the way, nobody's likely to hand over the set of duped keys, so I'm going up again to lock the doors and set detective seals."

"What are they?"

I hesitated, reluctant to tell in the servant's presence, she being a suspect in my eyes if not in Sibella's. "You know," I said finally, "when the private eye leaves his crummy hotel room, he wedges a scrap of paper in the door which everyone sees but the burglars. Or he glues a hair across a drawer, so he'll know if it's been opened."

"Smart girl. But I don't think our unknown skunk," she said, emphasizing the term so that it sounded venomous, "will go back there."

"That depends on how much you're hated and for what," I said. "And how sane the mind at work is."

"Do it, then. If you aren't afraid of the corridors."

"I don't *think* I'm afraid," I said, and took the letter and went out. The air was as hot as a curtain of sparks when I walked into it, and by the time I'd reached the mailbox, about a hundred feet from the gate, I was ready for another cool wet washcloth. I dropped the envelope in and immediately felt better. At last Sibella had done something to protect herself. I trotted back to the house, putting up the big bar after I'd come through the double gate, and bolting the Hall's door from what was rapidly becoming force of habit. The black dog had come out and was sitting in the dining room as though he imagined it was time for tea. He got up when he saw me and stood, irresolute.

There were two things in Sablecroft Hall that I feared—one was the man or woman who was trying to hurt me and kill Sibella, and the other was this dog. I stared back at him. Hardly an hour ago he'd been baring fangs and lolling tongue at me, as hateful an enemy as you'd care to meet. Later, with everyone around us, I'd felt sorry for him. Alone together, I was a rabbit again, eyeing the fox.

"Oh, thunder!" I said loudly. "Come here, Challenger." He came obediently. "Heel." I walked through the library, ignoring Wendy who sat on the floor gazing into a volume of film criticism that I'm sure she didn't see. I opened the tower door by means of the steel book. "In," I told him, "go in, Challenger." He knew the word, and stalked in. "Up," I said, pointing. He preceded me up the winding tower stair. We were alone in the passage once more.

The three-cell flashlight showed our way. I went south between the encaging walls, the dog walking ahead, and came to the fourth door on that level, the one that had no lock. It was open, as the other three had been. I shot the beam down the next aisle and saw that the ladder had been pushed against the wall.

The great black head turned round to me. "All right, old fellow, we'll go downstairs now." I reached out a hand that shivered a little, patted his shoulder. He leaned his head toward my arm. "It's all over, then. You aren't the wicked spirit of old earth, are you? You're only a poor obedient dog. Challenger. Stout lad, Challenger, no pooka thou. Come on." I went back through the door, shut it, and with my invisible tape stuck a short length of black thread to door and lintel, the light pouncing wildly here and there as I held the big torch under one arm. Then I did the same with the next three doors, locking each of them afterward. I couldn't even see the thread myself unless I turned the light directly on it.

I laid my hand on the jet-dark head. "Finished. Down now." We went back to the library.

Wendy turned her face up from the book. She still looked wan and frightened. I wished that I'd heard the whole conversation last night; if she hadn't wanted to harm anyone then, how must she feel now? I couldn't imagine Wendy cast on the world without a penny. She'd panic and marry the first well-to-do oaf who looked at her.

"You went up there again," she said. "With the dog. You're crazy."

"Nothing to fear unless someone orders him to attack, is there?" I said lightly.

"What if it wasn't someone?" she said, achieving no more than a whisper. "What about *something?* Gilbert? Felicity?"

I said a really rude word. "Do you believe in ghosts?"

"I don't know. I don't know anything." I'd guessed true—all the courage and disdainful aloofness had drained out of her. "*I* wouldn't go up there. You're crazy."

"I'm not the only one. There's another crazy."

"Not crazy. Mean, just dirt mean."

"Who?"

She stared at me, and a wisp of her intelligence revived and looked out at me from those stunning lavender eyes. "I don't know what you're talking about," she said.

"Come on, Challenger," I said, full of bravado, and the dog and I went to my bedroom. He lay down on the rug and allowed Micajah, who'd followed us, to sit on his back and play with one of his ears while I tidied his paws with a clean cloth. I took a quick shower and washed my hair, dried it with my blower, and dressed for tea. That was no more than five minutes away, and everything had happened in a matter of a few hours, although it felt like a week.

I looked at the two animals, the ornery cat and the noble dog. "Micajah, I'll leave you here. Challenger, come."

He observed me with what I interpreted as affection. Rising to his great height, he gave Micajah one friendly lick with his tongue that would have crushed a lesser cat's skull, and padded to the door. Micajah went to drink his fresh water. The dog and I walked down the stairs side by side, as once Palmerston the golden brindle and I had done.

It occurred to me that I'd have to copy those numbers I'd inked on my shirt, and then sneak about measuring people's shoes. Why sneak? I'd ask—*demand.* I represented Sibella in this, didn't I?

Daniel appeared from behind a plaster dummy and said, "Laurel!" and I, not quite on an even keel yet, gasped.

"You startled me!"

"You startled me, strolling with that hound. What if he *is* developing rabies?"

"Daniel, rabid dogs don't open doors to chase their victims."

The gong sounded, and Daniel said, "Opened doors, did he? Sounds as if he had a companion for sure. Sherry's right, he'll have to be debriefed. What a loathsome way to scare someone, teaching a fine dog to feign attack! It's a wonder they didn't paint his dewlaps with phosphorescence." He took my arm in a proprietary manner, possibly, I thought, to impress his cousin with our intimacy. I gently disengaged it. "Imagine conquering your terror of a dog by taking it back to the place where it threatened you!" he said, and replaced my arm.

Oh, well. I left it tucked into his.

"I am so proud of you," said Daniel. "Can I pick 'em? What a woman you are!"

As we were finishing tea, I announced my intention of examining the shoes of all three men, and was stared at blankly. "Shoes?" repeated Pierce.

Sibella picked up on it at once. "Laurel found some clear footprints in the attic. You'll do as she says. Go inspect their closets, dear, and I'll keep an eye on 'em till you're through." They each looked momentarily as though they'd object, then composed their faces . . . or my imagination was working overtime. I went to get the surveyor's tape and the jotted measurements, and began with Sherry's footwear. His work shoes and moccasins were out of the question—wrong configuration—but all his others were much alike, and any of them could have made those almost featureless prints. The same was true of Daniel's and, surprisingly enough, of Pierce's; somehow I'd expected the huge man to have larger feet than his cousins.

I returned to the dining room and glumly drank a glass of Perrier water.

"We could have told you," said Daniel, grinning, "that against all odds, we three wear the same size."

"I found that out." I was going to hint at worn spots or trademark patterns, but stopped short. That could put me in danger, while being of no use at all. "And all your heels are that anonymous rubber sort that leaves no individual cast in very dry dust stirred by the breeze of your passing."

"And we throw our shoes away when the bottoms are damaged," muttered Sherry, "for the purpose of going anywhere without being identified."

I glared at him. "I wouldn't be surprised at *all,*" I said.

WE WERE DRINKING BREAKFAST COFFEE IN THE LIBRARY, JUST two of us, and Wendy said abruptly, "It was you night before last in the walls, because I looked in your room and you were out but the lights were on."

I said, "The lights weren't on." Wendy smirked, and I'd been trapped through overconfidence. Hadn't I been warned not to sell her short?

"You were flying down some tunnel, scared sick, with him at your heels. But you didn't tell the old lady, and I *know* you heard me. Why?"

"Why should I?" I hedged. "I never mentioned you coming in with that stupid knife, either, or you'd have been dressed down for it."

"That's true. But how about him? Why didn't you tell Sibella—

oh! You couldn't *see* that part of the room! That explains it. You still don't know who he is."

I nodded reluctantly. No use to lie.

"I still don't understand why you didn't tell Sibella on me. I'd have thought you'd sneak right off and—"

"I don't sneak," I said, hard and cold with anger, "and if you insult me again, you dizzy long-legged icicle, I'll thin out that dyed mop with my fingernails, get me?"

I was ready to explicate further, resurrecting some of the picturesque things that Dad's Hollywood friends used to call one another, but Wendy backed off. I realized that she was truly afraid, and trying to cover the fact. "You wouldn't tell Sibella?"

"Not if you stay out of my way and stop insulting me. Don't give me that purple-eyed innocent gape, you're three times as smart as you look. I *would* have told Sibella, except that I heard you claim you wouldn't hurt anyone, even me, no matter what he did. That's all that saved you."

"That was weird," she said. "I didn't even know until I said it that I'm not up to doing real harm. Funny thing to find out about yourself when you're almost twenty-five, isn't it? I just started saying it and realized it was the truth."

"You pushed the floor button that opens the kitchen door," I said.

"Sure. And he made the dummy. But it was only a gag. *I* never thought of her dying of fright."

"And the balcony collapsing?"

"That was before I was roped in. I think it was accidental," she said, uncertain, wanting to believe it.

"What were you refusing to do?"

"I was supposed to, you know, get her to sit under the big lamp, which would have been easy because she does it often. That's out now, that bit. It has to be *all* over. She sent out the fear of God yesterday." She picked at her fingers. "Crazy, no," she mumbled. "Mean, yes." She stood up. "Here comes that black dog. I can't *look* at him any more. He makes my skin creep. I don't know how you can bear to touch him."

"Challenger's a good old boy," I said, snapping my fingers for him.

She edged away as the Dane approached. "Laurel, you won't

think this is sincere, but you're the only one of this whole menagerie worth saving. Maybe I knew that before, and that's why I didn't tell him that you were out of your room. Thanks for what *you* didn't do. I am grateful. I really am." She went away, her head down.

"Wonders never cease," said Sherry. I was not surprised that he was there. "You may be the first soul to whom she's ever said she was grateful. What brought that on, or isn't it any of my business?"

"It isn't. I'm sure you listened to the whole conversation anyway."

He gave me a gimlet gaze for a few seconds, then opened Sibella's door and called, "Grandmother, will you tell Laurel how long ago I left you?"

The great hoarse voice answered from far within. "No more than a quarter of a minute. Is she checking up on you?"

"She always does." He shut the door. "Satisfied? I heard Wendy thank you and say she was grateful for something you didn't do. That's all." As I put on my abashed face, he said, "Did you sleep well? You look fresh and bright."

"And you look like the wrath of the devil. Is there no way you can sleep long enough to wash the crimson out of your eyes, Sherry?"

"No. I don't go drowsy till 4 A.M. And one can't lie abed all day and miss the sunshine, the flowers, the palm-tree trimming, the fertilizing and weeding, and everything else that earns one the right to watch movies in the evening, now can one?"

"One," I said, "has fallen out of the right side of the bed for a change."

"One isn't always the ultimate grouch. If you'd like to prune more palms this afternoon, it won't rain till four or five."

"I think I will."

"Come out when you like, I'll have the tools. Oh, I forgot—do keep more of an eye on Micajah. I try, but he slithers into nowhere with alarming frequency."

"Why the cat in particular? I'd think Sibella needed watching most."

"That business of shoving him under the passage floor was a savage act. Haven't you felt that? He was terrified, as well he should have been, even though no harm was done. Now Sibella," he said slowly, "I can see a few reasons why she was, or is, a candidate for death, and at least one motive for snuffing you, but it's no use my snarling about that again. The cat, though. Why the cat? I worry. We have no animal haters here."

"Wendy doesn't give a damn about animals."

"True, but she'd never frighten one or injure it. She's simply oblivious to animals. She wouldn't have shut Micajah in. I can't see why anyone would. It's senseless, and that worries me. So take good care of him."

"You don't tie Micajah to a post or lead him about on a string or tell him to heel. But I'm bothered too," I admitted. "If anything happens to him, I swear I'll kill somebody!"

"Me too. Him, or her. Nobody's really out of it, not even me. Or are you thinking, me in particular?"

"Why should I?"

"You're avoiding a straight answer. And yet I'm not the one you must suspect. Ah, I'd naturally say that! Put it this way: Don't trust anyone but Sibella."

"I've done all right so far," I said stubbornly.

"You've done miserably. You've almost caught it three times. Not that I believe the black dog would really have hurt you—his instincts are stronger than any training could be, at his age. What was I saying?"

"How poorly I'd protected self and cat."

"No, the cat episode couldn't have been predicted. You, though, you incredible lovely idiot, you go charging through the world like Nora Charles on a case! Don't you realize that even a pretty child can die? Or a neat, clever, self-assured widow? Damn, damn, I wasn't to roar at you."

"If you keep it up, I won't garden with you."

"Not another word. Promise." He tousled my hair playfully, a most unSherrylike gesture, and went out.

That afternoon in borrowed hat and gloves I weeded a border of crown-of-thorns plants. I learned after several sharp jabs that this curious bushlet can jump at you when you're not looking, and worked as deliberately as I could. In half an hour Sherry lounged over, plastered with dirt and bark. "Good work! Watch your wrists, those spines are wicked."

I showed him a hole oozing blood. "Too late. I'm going to do that strip next. What are they?"

"Transvaal daisies. Handsome. I like the violet blooms best, but this batch runs to pink and salmon. They came from South Africa."

"I used to date a South African. His name was Floris, which means 'flower.' "

"Did you like him excruciatingly?" He knelt beside me to tug up a noxious weed.

"He was too prejudiced for words, and he couldn't stand roller coasters. I dropped him gently by telling him that my grandmother was black as ebony."

"I dislike everyone you ever dated," said Sherry, not looking at me. "Everyone you ever kissed, everyone you had a crush on in grade school. Barring, of course, your husband. I like him."

"Why?"

"He treated you well and cherished you." He pulled another weed. "You're wholly aware that I'm in love with you."

"I'm nothing of the sort!" I gasped. "That's why you keep harping on the wish that I'd leave and never come back?"

"If you left, I'd follow you. Daniel wouldn't, because he's psychologically unfit to live away from Sablecroft, but I'm not. See, I'm undermining his charm for you. It isn't his fault that he's nailed to the Hall, any more than it's Sibella's or Pierce's—all three of them for different reasons, but equally nailed down here. So are Belle and Wendy. I'm not, and that's simple fact."

"You'd hate being kicked out if Sibella were killed," I hazarded.

"Oh, yes. Aside from the fact that she's my grandmother and I'm fond of her. The disgrace of being suspected would be equalled by the loss of that fantastic library, built up by four generations of flicker fanatics. But I could survive. And if you left, I'd come after you."

"What about all that money salted away by your ancestors?"

"Hell!" he said. "Is that how you see me?"

"I don't see you at all."

"You mean through the clouds of suspicion."

"No. I mean I can't understand you. What you are, who you are, what you think and dream, what on earth you're going to say next, the whole bit."

"I'm not that complex," he said, sitting down abruptly with a long-rooted weed in his hand. "Daniel's harder to figure than I am, don't you think?"

"Not at all. I can almost predict his next remark."

"Are you in love with him?"

"Who says I'm in love with anyone? Sherry," I blurted, "why are you the only one who makes me afraid?"

"I don't mean to. Maybe I did when I bellowed in your face the first day, but no more, no more. Am I so forbidding?"

"Sometimes. But," I said, barely conscious that I was thinking aloud in his company, "if it were Daniel who frightened me, I think I'd leave in a hurry. I wonder why."

"Daniel's hardly a forbidding personality, is he? The jolly satyr, sprinkling cinema quotations as he leaps from behind a tree." He pulled out a half-smoked pipe and lit its dregs.

"Not satyr, faun. I am drawn to him." I admitted.

"And not to me."

"I didn't say that! You're a dreadfully attractive man, especially since you lost all that weight. Sherry, why do you frighten me?" I asked again. "What's behind the happy-sad, kind-and-curt, love-you-hate-you exterior? I don't understand you, or what I feel about you, for two seconds running. You never let me in behind the mustache. Oh," I said, "I didn't mean—"

"That I never let you kiss me," he said, mocking. "I know what you meant. I can't explain why I'm an enigma to you, Laurel. I try to be simply myself with you. Always."

"Then you're incredibly complex."

"Isn't every human being? Even Wendy's complex."

"She hates me."

"Certainly she does. She knows Daniel and I are both in love with you. But she managed to say this morning that she was grateful to you for something."

"Does she want both of you to herself?"

"She might," he said pensively. "It would fit her greed, the longing to be the only woman in a world of men. But I think she really wants only one of us."

"Which?"

"You grill a poor soul worse than Sam Spade!"

"Don't you love her at all any more?"

"I'm not sure I ever did. Or that she loved me when we were

married. I told you, she's complex too—probably more so than I." He saw me shake my head. "Not in your book, eh? Have you been thinking it's surely me that wants Grandmother dead?" he asked abruptly. "Could that be why you're leery of me?"

"No, for it might be Daniel or Pierce or even Belle."

"It's among the four of us, then? How do you know it's not Wendy?"

"I know it's not Wendy, and that's all I'll say."

"Well, don't waste your time suspecting Belle."

"You love her very much?"

"I love her very much. How can you tell?"

"The way you look at her, the sound of your voice on her name."

"Belle McNabb," he said slowly, "has been as kind to me as anyone in my life. My mother died when I was born. Belle was a mother when Sibella couldn't be bothered with the prattle of shrill tiny voices. Dad was helpful, but a kid wants a woman to patch his pants and wipe his bloody nose. Belle was always here. Sometimes I believe that she'll be here forever. At least I can't imagine the Hall without her."

"Yet you'd leave her to fly after me if I left?"

"I would. I said I love you, and I meant it. Now try to forget it," he said, rising. "You have enough on your mind for now. Wait, and perhaps I'll grow on you. Wait. The watchword of the Sablecrofts. Wait, and everything will be the same or go away. It ought to be engraved on our escutcheon, just beside the blot."

"Wendy," I said thoughtfully.

"Why should you consider her a blot on—"

"No, no, *no!*" I shouted. "I was going to ask impertinently why you fell in love with her. Because if it was plain and simple propinquity, then why isn't it only that with me? I may be nothing to you but the first new face in years!"

"So, if you don't love back, what's it matter?" He sat on his heels. "Why did I marry Wendy? . . . I think that's an easy one. I was far too young—as, of course, was she. But even then there was the quick, surprising intelligence in certain sharply defined fields. She held up her end of a discussion, from a different point of view than mine, without lapsing into argument—always a rare quality. She didn't get angry very often, in a house where there used to be a lot of anger. And with those qualities, there were the physical—eyes like drowned lilac petals, half-open mouth presumptive of contained passion, great legs, and—which I must have known but ignored in the heart of adoration—a heart like a snowball soaked in ice water."

"That's not nice of you."

"My dear scrupulous fair-minded female, do you think I'd say it to anyone who didn't already know it? Wendy's aware of the failing herself. Sometimes you can actually see her struggling to feel a warmth that simply isn't there. She's not to blame, she was *born* with the lack. And so after a time, we decided we didn't want to be married any longer, and that was all there was to it. No broken hearts, no recriminations and smoldering hates, just a mutual agreement. We're friends, we enjoy our conversations as much as ever. We have, in short, that rare thing—an amicable divorced state. If this answers your impertinent curiosity, I'll be getting back to my feather palm, which has alarming symptoms of manganese deficiency."

Our teatime was horrid with tension, little spurts of conversation starting up and dying, everyone looking at the plates or the dogs but Sibella, who watched us all with a half-amused curl of her lip. I was glad to escape to my job in the library. Pierce billowed in after me.

"Laurel, Laurel," he said, big moon-face woeful, "whatever must you think of us? When I welcomed you with the information that we weren't the most everyday lot of people in the world, I'd no idea it would be proved in this fashion. Are you worried? I mean, do you want to leave? It would sadden us, since you've brought such a flood of sunshine with your superb cat and your delightful self. Sunshine, dreary word. I'll think of a nicer term presently." He sat down beside my desk. "Yet perhaps you should—it seems you are inexplicably in danger here. I'm mortally sure that nothing further will happen, after Sibella's impersonation of Vengeance—but what if it *should?* The black-dog episode is disturbing, most deeply disturbing."

"I stayed at first because I was very poor," I told him, "but I'm staying now for Sibella. I couldn't leave her alone, no matter what. How could I live with myself?"

"She has me," he said, then, shaking his head, added, "and much good I've been to her!" He patted my arm and stood up again. "Take care of yourself. I have every faith that it's all over, but Lord! who can tell for certain?" He departed, looking perfectly miserable. I could read his up-and-down shifts of mood no better than I could Sherry's.

With various companions now and then—Micajah, a subdued Challenger, and Daniel to announce that he'd tried sixty more combinations of words and sequences without success—I worked until nearly eight. Then I went and prepared for dinner.

Sibella had the first word as Pierce cooked succulent beef in oyster sauce. "What the blazes happened to you, Sherry? Your face!"

"I accidentally trimmed my mustache."

I stared at him, as everyone did. He now wore what used to be called a military toothbrush, in the fashion of Colman, Gilbert, and the Dougs Senior and Junior. "Oh," I said without thinking, "I like it!"

"How long will it take to grow in?" asked Wendy irritably.

"I won't let it bush again. It was interfering with my soup. Have you ever tried to comb noodles out of a Yorkshire terrier?"

"Bravo," said Pierce. "I like it too. You could play Bulldog Drummond. Less sinister than before, if I may say so, old fellow."

Sherry smiled ever so slightly, a manifestation that would have been entirely hidden under his former batch of bristles.

"And easier to kiss people?" prodded Wendy.

"Haven't tried that yet, but I imagine so." He beamed at her. I told myself that I knew now of whom she was jealous; I'd been thinking that because of our rather careless kissing Daniel was the object of her heartburn. Sherry . . . well . . . oh, maybe he was right, and it was both of them.

Sibella introduced the topic of the gangster cycle in the movies, which now lasted us through dessert—mangoes on snow ice—after which she suggested that we have a showing of *Little Caesar,* and Daniel irrepressibly said "Yeah, sure" through his nose, and we trooped into her quarters where Pierce got out the film cans and brought down the screen.

I always enjoy *Little Caesar*. Despite everything, I did this evening too. "Compare that with *Rififi,*" said Sibella as the lights went up. "Compare it with any overpraised foreign film on the subject.

They can't touch Hollywood! When there *was* a Hollywood," she added bitterly. "Why'd they have to kill it? With their damned wide screens and method actors and bland faces you only see once, with their frantic pursuit of new plots that are only loose snarls and barren silences and lack of endings!"

Pierce said, looking down on us like an obese Olympian, "The good old fellows who loved the movies died off, retired, went broke, grew senile. The great actors from the stage became old, as did the comedians who'd learned their trade in vaudeville and burlesque. The training grounds vanished overnight."

"And the character actors," put in Sherry. "Where are they to come from today? How often do you recognize any except the very-old-timers?"

Daniel stood up and pointed at the blank screen. "That's the real world up there," he said tautly. "That's your family and your closest friends, your kids, your bosses, even the gods that run the universe. Compare *that* with what's out there!" he cried suddenly, gesturing toward the wall beyond the Moorish court. "Did you ever have a friend like Cooper, who'd go through fire for you? Did you ever woo a woman as fascinating as Colbert or Vivien Leigh or either of the Hepburns? Take your troubles to anyone as kind and wise as Travers or Kellaway or Davenport—look up to anyone as you could to Tracy, Gable, Hawkins, Mason, four-score others? You're damn right you didn't! The people in the movies never failed you, never let you down. As *nobody* does in what's called 'real' life, they acted faithfully, nobly, skillfully, entertainingly. . . ."

"But Daniel," I objected, "they were *actors*. They played parts in a great big dream world."

"Exactly my point. Theirs is a dream world; but it ought to be—for me, for all of us here and millions who went before us, it is—*the real world*. The world as it should have been made."

"A lot of people used to feel like that about books before there were movies," I said gently. "Thousands of girls married glum and moody men under the impression they were snaring Mr. Rochester."

Sibella said, "Thank God I lived when I did! What I'd have missed—even a decade later!" She meant only the movies, not the fascinating progress of mankind, and for that I felt sorry for her. But I couldn't point it out, for you don't waken a dreamer . . . and I recognized that I was paraphrasing a line from *Sunset Boulevard,* and it wasn't my place to sneer or correct when I was really one of their own breed.

"Coop was a lot of man," said Sherry, "but I doubt he'd actually have gone through fire for anyone. Or stood up against a whole town with one sixgun and a badge."

"That doesn't matter. It's a world where good is brave and decent and—and empathetic." Daniel flung his arms wide. "A skipper after a battle takes off his cap and feels rotten about his dead seamen, and one's heart is wrenched. Would he really? I don't know. But he should, and if life isn't like that, it ought to be."

"And when they told the leader of the expedition, 'Your companions will be the celebrated scientist Professor X and his assistant Dr. Y,' you could bet Dr. Y was going to be a great-looking dame with four degrees, age twenty-three, and wearing false eyelashes. That's how it ought to be," said Sherry. "Right." Did he mock Daniel? I thought not.

"On the nose, Sherry lad! What is life without imagination? Drab, stale, flat."

I nearly said, "But this is other people's imaginations you're feeding from!" but I didn't.

"I want to go home!" It was Pierce with a line of the Cowardly Lion's, delivered in the true accents of that most American of men, Bert Lahr. Pierce might indeed have been the person who whispered in Felicity's room, that sexless, American sibilance. "We all yearn for the Emerald City," he said, "and in our films we find it again and again."

"And as for evil?" asked Sibella casually, bending forward, watching them all.

Daniel said promptly, "It's horrible, filthy, it spoils the green earth—but up *there,* it's flamboyant, bold, fascinating, imaginative, and it loses out comfortingly in the end. I ask you, could there be a finer way to order the universe?"

"How better could you spend your leisure time," said Sibella, "than with a collection, say, of the Warner Brothers stock company, or this pack of First National people we've just seen?"

"Even Caesar Enrico Bandello?" I asked.

"Especially Little Caesar," she said, and rose. "I'll say good night, family. It's been an enjoyable eighty minutes."

I stood too, with a powerful urge to get away from the escape of motion pictures if only for a brief unpleasant chore. I walked back to the kitchen; peering out the window, I saw lights shining beyond the palms. I took the surveyor's tape from the garage, went into the hot humidity, through the grove to Belle's place, and rang the bell.

Her small gray face peered out with no faith that it might be someone she wished to see. "Oh, it's you. What you want?"

"May I talk with you, Mrs. McNabb?"

She opened the door grudgingly. "Right in the middle of my best TV program, but come on in."

"No, I won't interrupt. I'll come back tomorrow."

"Come on in, girl. TV don't make that much difference to me. Sit down there." She closed out the hot night. A large new-looking air-conditioner worked away full blast in one window. She saw me glance at it. "You get used to the Hall, so you don't like the heat anymore. When I was younger, up in New Jersey, I liked it, and down here too. This contraption's unnatural, but you get used to a thing and you got to give in to it." She sat opposite, turning off the television volume. "What you want with old Belle?"

"Did Mrs. Callingwood tell you about the chandelier?"

"No, what about it? Which one?"

"The big crystal job in her room."

"No," said Belle, watching me from behind the impenetrable mask of so many years of wrinkles and experience.

"Uh," I said, floundering and wishing I'd thought out what I was going to say, "someone oiled the bolts on its brace, up in the attic. I wondered if somebody had asked you to go up there and do that."

"Why'd anybody do that?"

"I think they'd have lied to you about the reason."

"I wouldn't do any such a thing without askin' Sibby first. What's that?" she asked, indicating my surveyor's tape.

"I've measured everyone's shoes with it. There are some tracks in the attic dust, and Mrs. Callingwood—"

"How come you call her that? Everyone here calls her Sibella, and me, I call her Sibby."

"That's what she told me to call her," I said helplessly.

"So you want to measure my shoes," said Belle, eyes flashing. "You think I'd do a dumb thing like go up in the attic without she asked me to?" Belle laughed, not the cackle of an aged woman, but a full-throated sound of merriment. "Here, girl," she thrust out her foot, "measure away! You got no reason to figure me for the only one of the bunch that don't tell lies. I wear a man's shoe," said Belle, settling back at her ease. "I was born with big feet and walkin' on them all this time ain't shrunk 'em so you could notice."

"I think you must work harder than anyone I ever knew," I said, verifying my eerie suspicion that they'd be the same size as everyone else's. "It's wonderful at your—"

"My age. Huh! Sibby could do it same as me. We're tough old buzzards."

"Was Felicity as tough?" I asked on impulse.

"Fee-liss-eye-tee," contemptuous. "Mrs. Queen Felicity Ryder! She wouldn't dirty her hands if she was to starve waitin' for something to be done for her. She was a pickety-snickety, hateful woman, that Felicity, and God smited her for it. You hear me? It didn't turn one hair of my head when she dropped down them stairs, dead as last year's lettuce. And that's the plain truth, and I'd tell it to anybody!"

"She fell down the stairs?"

"Died on her feet, smited dead, and naturally she fell down! You think she was gonna stand there dead?"

"I never heard how she died before, exactly."

"Sibby likely tell you in her own time. Sibby likes you," said Belle. It sounded like an accusation, as if I'd wormed my way into Sibella's affections dishonestly. I told myself that it was only Belle's way of speech. "Lady Jane Felicity, she's dead. T'hell with her."

I stood. "Thank you for giving up your program for me, Belle. You understand, this is for Sibella."

"You're scared for her," she said keenly.

"Yes."

"Me too." She regarded me with what seemed dislike, but said, "Keep your eye open, girl. There's something bad up at that house these days, and it sure isn't the old man hauntin' the passages! *He* got no grudge at anybody! Watch out you bar the door at night, hear?"

"I do. I try to look after Sibella, too."

She gripped my upper arm with astonishing power; everyone in Sablecroft Hall seemed to be stronger than I, except Wendy. The ancient face came up toward mine. "If Sibby gets hurt, I'll put their lights out! I'll *kill* 'em!" She released me. "Good night, child."

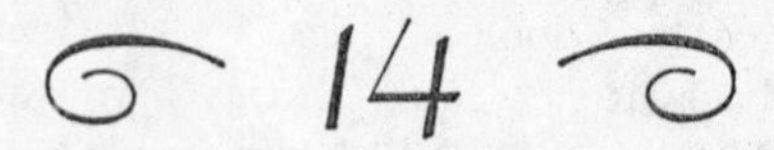

AT TEATIME NEXT DAY DANIEL BROUGHT ME A PLATE OF VARIED goodies and a cup of black tea, and sat beside me on the floor. "Have you thought of anything new?" he demanded.

"No. I've been catching up on my own work."

"Are you avoiding me?"

I took his hand. "Daniel, early this week we were in the passages together, yesterday we ate dinner and saw a movie together. I have to work! I'm not avoiding you." I plowed into the caviar bread and smoked salmon. "Keep digging for possible words and names," I said, encouraging. "Remember the combination might be two short words, like *soft crab* or *blasé rot*."

"Or *stab force,* I see." He determined that we were alone, and kissed me. "Thanks, Laurel. What did I do before you were brought to us from the far icy reaches of the north?"

"Not nearly enough!" I said, laughing, and kissed him in return. Daniel's physical presence, the touch of him, always gave me the heart to hang on—and whether I should bless him or curse him for that, I couldn't decide. He wasn't your standard tower of strength, but with his unabashed affection and sparkling animation he often lent me by his very human lightness the nerve and stamina to remain here, where everything else was unbelievable. In particular, I thought, as he left me to try his lettered disk once more, my staying under this roof another hour was unbelievable.

His kisses did not last today, and by teatime, having thought of the others and their mysteries and menacings to the detriment of my work, I had little appetite; nor did I eat dinner with any gusto. We watched *The Public Enemy* and the rest of them discussed it vigorously, and we broke up and headed for our rooms. I began to trudge up the stairs; and Pierce Poole was leaning on the railing of the balcony above me, a monstrous mountain of a man looming formidably in the half-lit dusk as if photographed from a low angle to exaggerate his bulk. The shadows made his face cold and intimidating. I was still periodically afraid of everyone but Sibella. Why? The consensus was that the danger was over. Pierce said good night gently, and I squeaked something back. I went to bed with a glass of water and a couple of aspirin, and a shadow crept in beside me that wasn't Micajah: an unseen, unfelt shadow that was nonetheless there. It was made of poisonous suspicion and terror of the sunless danger without a name, of a growing involvement that I'd done my best to smother, of the multitudes of the flamboyant dead who lived on forever in Sablecroft Hall repeating their actions and speeches of long ago. The shadow questioned me silently, remorselessly, atrociously, in the thin whispery voice of the single-minded lunatic who'd founded and branded this family and erected this monument to the beloved undead and their all-but-vanished glory.

Biting my lips, I wondered whether, having stayed here through some of the maddest events I'd ever heard of, I was now about to have a whole-hog nervous breakdown as payment for my stupidity. If only I could be sure of nights without dreams! The dark world crept through the cracks of my unconscious when I slept. . . .

Micajah snuggled in, warming my ribs and elbow. I slumbered, leaden with mental fatigue, and dreamed that Dad was breathing in gouts of crimson flame and I couldn't find any water. I woke screaming and the cat leaped wide of my thrashing arms, and I dozed and thought I was with Steve in a decrepit barn of a hospital when Belle appeared and dragged me away through miles of thorned brush, cannon fire all around us—which was the night storms of Florida sweeping over the land from Tampa Bay—and I cried for my husband and all the scenes faded to pastels and then a bright white void, in which Micajah and I rested on the invisible hand of God and were afraid of nothing anymore.

In the morning I went down to eat breakfast with a set of normal people who happened to have a thing about the movies, my cat strolling sedately beside me. The five dogs came in to beg, dear uncomplicated Daniel poured a cup of coffee and set it before me, Sibella asked Pierce if he'd let me help in the greenhouse lately, Wendy gave me a magnificent purple-lipped orchid she'd brought from there for the table, and the rain slashed the Hall but we were bathed in the soft dry radiance of many lamps, and I knew that sometimes for a day, and more often for a night, we can all be very foolish. And Sherry looked attractive and dashing in his new mustache.

Later I found him going through my typed master cards with a frown. "Anything the matter?" I asked.

"No, why should there be?"

"You're making faces at my work."

"Concentration and eyestrain," he said. "Laurel, have you begun to realize that I love you?"

"Oh," I said helplessly. "Oh, Sherry!"

"Yes?"

"You mustn't keep saying that. It's coals of fire."

"Why?"

"For having that gunk analyzed. You insisted I should, and yes, I pried."

"Never pay attention to what a man says when he's foaming with righteous bile. So you know. I've always been a secret eater," he said quietly, looking off into past times that I could not see. "My sweet tooth would unsalt the seven seas. When I was a kid, I spent my whole allowance on candy bars, unless I was saving up for a book. The habit carried over into adult life. You know the old line."

" 'It's easy to quit. I've done it hundreds of times.' "

"But it never lasted. I crave sugar, honey, caramels, chocolate as the penniless drunkard yearns for canned heat or rubbing alcohol filtered through a loaf of bread. Thank God there's no history of diabetes in the family!"

"I was like that with cigarettes," I said. "I've thrown a hundred half-smoked packs into trash cans. But I never quit until—"

After a moment he prompted, "You fell in love?"

"No. Steve used to worry about it. I inhaled every drag, had a nasty cough . . . but I couldn't manage it. Then he died. And I quit cold and haven't touched tobacco since."

"Yes. Takes some wrenching, overwhelming emotion, doesn't it? With me," Sherry said softly, "it was meeting you. Right between the eyes, *crack!* So I gave my last hoard a decent burial, but the resurrection man came, the grave robber with the long damp nose and lust to know—"

"No! A woman who thought you'd buried something that would incriminate you."

"And so I had. Nobody ever knew before you. They used to fret about my weight, suggest that my metabolism was disarranged and a doctor was indicated. I ate less regular food than they, never raided the fridge, seldom had seconds at tea unless there was imported honey or a batch of sweet rolls that I couldn't resist, and yet I was tubby! It was an advantage to my Mr. Hyde aspect, being the only one who went outside where the gourmet shops are."

He began to pack a pipe with aromatic tobacco. "Between eleven and one every night I have a small taste of unadulterated hell even yet. But it's easing up. I begin to think that down there," he patted his flat abdomen, "the ugly craving is withering away. I'm proud to have accomplished something just this side of parting the Red Sea, so please stop looking so unpardonable! You were right, it could have been someone's head in that newspaper."

"Naturally I won't tell anyone—"

"I know that!" he exploded. And he shoved out of the chair and walked away, calling the brindle dog. An unpredictable and difficult young man. I wished I knew whether I was growing to love him. My mind was almost inoperative on that subject, except when it was asking me caustically why I should keep on kissing Daniel if it was Sherry I wanted.

There was at the least an intense fascination. . . .

I glanced at the back of my arm and saw that the skin, nicely tanned now from my hours of weeding and pruning, was prickled into gooseflesh. My fascination was tenuous, an evanescent emotion. It could not be held long in the mind or written down for analysis. But Sherry had slowly begun to govern my thoughts, and either I was in love with him, or aware that he was a definite force for evil in this place. In other words, Alpha or Omega, nothing between.

I realized that there was no joy in my attraction to him, and I had had that especial joy once and would have recognized a trace of it again. When he'd said that he loved me, my heart hadn't leaped up with a gladsome shout, or given any of the traditional responses. If anything, it had contracted briefly with an unspecified *fear*.

Then a perfectly appalling thought struck me, one that would recur to me at intervals for weeks to come, and plunge me into fevers of uncertainty. Wendy had said that "he" had made the Felicity dummy. I believed this because she'd been so unstrung and accessible at the time that she wasn't up to lying, not till she'd taken a grip on her nerves and just balked at saying more. Now Pierce was a carpenter and Sibella didn't bother with making things, and it wasn't Belle's style (as I read her) to concoct papier-mâché atrocities. Which left Daniel and Sherry as the prime suspects for that extremely good grotesquerie in the fashion of the eccentric painter Albright. And it was a recognized fact in Sablecroft Hall that of all of them, only Daniel lacked any creative ability, while Sherry, as his waxworks proved, was a fine artisan at such things.

Oh, *hell!*

And now life began to go on as usual in Sablecroft Hall. The taped quotations were brought out again, they bellowed or hissed at us from the walls. They'd been abandoned for a while, when we'd all been waiting to see what new atrocity the secret mountebank would concoct, but when Sibella's threat of a new will had evidently worked, and nothing happened for a week, one or another of the family started a tentative campaign of movie bits, and soon it was in full swing. The jesters had returned to their play, the cap and bells had been taken out of the trunk.

Sometimes this sort of thing was pungent and funny, and sometimes a pain in the neck, as on the day when the first version of *King Kong,* probably the noisiest movie ever made, crashed out at me in super-quadrophonic sound and made me spoil a sheet of intricate inventory work on which I'd been typing for half an hour. No one ever admitted to this sort of joke; Wendy was my candidate. On days when it was too frequent I worked in my room, having discovered that no sound however stentorian originating in the library carried as far as our bedrooms, which were catercorner across the immense width of the house and well soundproofed to boot. This I did so as not to give myself the reputation of a chronic complainer.

Daniel continued to kiss me now and then, and I to kiss him back, wondering which of the men I might eventually fall in love with, and feeling, as Sherry for some reason hardly spoke to me these days, that sheer proximity and desire unslaked would probably make it Daniel. Sherry's avoidance of me was bewildering. He hadn't touched me or said he loved me in weeks. And Daniel had, and I liked Daniel immensely.

And I knew now that I trusted Daniel a shade farther than I did his cousin, if a trifle less than I did Pierce Poole, who was not so abstracted these days and more *with* us. Further, I had begun to realize that after so long, I needed to be in love with someone who would love me back, for life at its core was empty now that it wasn't cold with terror anymore.

But Sherry was quiet and withdrawn, often invisible, though several times I felt him watching me; my skin would prickle, or a dog would look up sharply from its doze, and I would know.

One dog or another, and when I could find him the white cat, sometimes went with Daniel and me to the sealed crescent room to fiddle with the endless permutations of the dial. The Dane would sit alertly watching us while Micajah watched for ghosts, at which he occasionally ruffled his fur. I remember that one night Daniel admitted to sensing the presence of something besides the four of us. "Gilbert," he said matter-of-factly. "Whatever they say, he walks these corridors."

"Daniel believes in gho-osts," I chanted.

He broke into laughter and hauling me to my feet, embraced me. "Right enough! Oh, Challenger, you've seen me do this a dozen times," he said, as the black dog growled. "Does he snarl when Cousin Todd puts his arms around you?"

"Sherry doesn't."

"Surprising—he never takes his eyes off you."

"I don't read Sherry very well," I admitted.

Daniel shook his head. "I used to believe I knew him better than anyone. Now I don't. Maybe I don't really know anyone, except you." He kissed me gently, and we walked to the great hall, hand in hand, the dog and cat following.

One day Sibella sent me into the passages again, the dirty unused ones, because again she'd heard a door close on the second story. I discovered that someone had passed through all the doors, but hadn't gone into the attic.

"Blast their guts!" she shouted. "What colossal nerve! I suppose we'll eventually find out the reason, and meanwhile no one's going to kill the goose that's sitting on the golden eggs, not when it'd mean the end of the world for them. Go along, child, and wash your hands for tea."

"Yes, ma'am," I said, curtsying, and left her laughing her hoarse, amused *ha, ha, ha.*

Our teas were growing more lavish and tempting even as Sherry underwent his withdrawal symptoms from a lifelong diet of sweets —the reason, I finally settled on, for his avoiding me, and for his gloomy appearance when I did see him. He would often skip tea-time entirely. Along with the rosé, cream sherry, and Perrier water, we had delicious imported cordials and almond marsala; and besides the constant scones, which everyone adored, there were always finger sandwiches, cakes, English biscuits in profusion, lovely fresh tomato sandwiches, and half a dozen honeys and jams. There would be hot dishes too, and caviar on tiny crackers, and smoked Nova Scotia salmon. No wonder our dinners were limited to one gorgeous dish and dessert! I could have existed nicely on our teas.

I looked at the calendar one morning and discovered that this was my seventieth day at Sablecroft Hall. Micajah was under the impression that we'd lived here forever, and I'd begun to feel the same way.

Nowadays I would listen to movie tapes myself, wearing a set of lightweight earphones with soft cushions full of liquid which enclosed my ears and shut off all sound save that from my borrowed player, a successful attempt at privacy. During certain phases of my job, when I only sporadically had to think of what I was doing, I'd put on the sound track of a favorite film and entertain myself while mechanically copying data. Hearing it was almost as pleasurable as watching it. I'd always considered cinema as primarily a treat for the eyes; like old radio, it was an astonishing feast for the ears too. Eventually I took a couple of machines and a stack of tapes to my bedroom, where I'd let a love story or even a Western put me to sleep.

Today I spent some time in my room, arrived in the library about ten, had a cup of strong rich Ceylon tea, and plowed into my job. I ate our afternoon meal absent-mindedly and worked on, and then it was time to go and dress for dinner.

I was on the point of leaving the bedroom, arrayed in my best cocoa-toned dress, when the speaker on my wall blatted at me. "Kid, this ain't your night . . . this ain't your *night!*" roared Brando angrily, and Margaret Hamilton's wonderful cackle followed with, "I'll get you, my pretty—and your little dog, too!" and,

"You do well to be afraid," said Wendy Hiller, in what had once been a murmur but came out through overamplification as a hissing bellow.

Startled, I leaped back and trod on Micajah's tail, so that the word *afraid* was blended with the cat's hideous screech of astonishment and rage and my own yelp. Then there were runs in my pantyhose and bloody holes in my leg, and I had to use bandages (Micajah had really been annoyed, maybe because he'd been referred to as my little dog) and put on fresh hose, and so went downstairs in a high temper.

For reasons of my own, I reached the dining room via one of the passages, but no one seemed to notice that I came out of one of the so-called secret doors.

We'd begun on the evening's sliced tenderloin sautéed with water chestnuts and snow peas when Sibella asked me how the work was going. I said hotly, "When the interruptions allow me, I'm working well!"

"You never shout at meals," she said. "Has some oaf been annoying you?"

"I don't appreciate people bawling loudly in my bedroom. They frighten my cat, and they don't make *my* life any easier."

"On the intercom?" Her gray eyes burned like cold sparks in the lean handsome face. "If it happens again, I'll have every electrical gadget in the place removed, and you'll all have to go back to playing with rubber balls and jacks! I won't even *ask* who did it. Just stop it."

"I don't want to cause trouble," I grumbled, "but I don't see why an employee has to put up with dismal practical jokes as if—"

"As if she were the owner of Sablecroft Hall," finished Sibella.

"'You do well to be afraid,'" said Sherry thoughtfully.

I stared at him. "Your work?"

"No, no," he snapped. "I was on the stairs, and it boomed out of your room like thunder. Everyone on the second floor must have heard it."

Pierce rolled up his eyes in their sockets of fat. "From Conrad's *An Outcast of the Islands*. A beautiful picture. But of what are you afraid these days, Laurel?"

"I'm not," I said, which wasn't exactly true, but I didn't want to get into that subject just then.

Sibella said acutely, "Unhappy, then?"

"No. I've always been happy in theaters, and that's what we're living in, isn't it? Sometimes we watch a two-dimensional drama, and sometimes we change our seats and watch, or act in, a three-dimensional farce. This is a one-topic, one-obsession, one-environmental place. The Hall is theatrical, we are theatrical—"

"How could it be otherwise?" she demanded. "Our life is the art of the motion picture. Consequently, we've acquired habits, gestures and catchwords, movements, ways of thought, from it. So have you."

"To some extent, but my whole life doesn't consist of watching!"

"Nor does ours," said Sherry, closing his eyes as if he were either bone-tired or bored stiff. "Behind our film jokes, our trivia, our obsession, we're actual people doing concrete tasks. You've confused us with the characters in our films. You hear little else but flicker jargon, quotations, and technicalities. You should have expected that, when you came here to catalogue many thousands of books on the subject."

"Good point," said Pierce, putting down his fork. "Inevitable, wasn't it? You discover what looks like a motion-picture set on some fancy back lot in early Hollywood. A balcony has lately torn loose from a wall—obviously a jerry-built set of painted plasterboard. The voices of actors cry out from the walls, from armor and portraits, from the ambient air. A pack of enormous dogs prowl at large, some rooms tower two stories above your head, the temperature is that of a picture palace in midsummer. You're shown through a mile or more of hidden corridors and told of secret rooms. There's a Valentino setting, a real Hispano-Moorish court.

"But, of course, you could hardly have anticipated the so-called practical jokes or the danger, and so you must fit them desperately into a mad movie, everything else being so cinematic. A drink is doped with false poison—well, they wouldn't hand the star *real* cyanide. *The Fall of the House of Usher* is re-enacted with an ugly dummy resembling your hostess: a Halloween house party turned cruel. You discover that a priceless chandelier has been prepared to fall and crush the dowager who rules the roost—pure nineteen twenties corn. The inhabitants are cryptic, even sinister at times, and Lord knows what things they say to you of which I'm unaware."

Pierce sipped wine. Everyone watched him, mute. When he was determined to hold the stage, he did it with the best.

"So it's most natural for you to generate the belief that we're not real people, but composite characters without blood or original thoughts. That we are, *en effet,* false, flat, histrionic . . . scarcely more than marionettes, pulling our own strings in some phantasmagoria with little or no point."

His finger shot out at me. "Am I in essence right, my dear?"

"Yes," I said. "Will you deny that that's your own general impression at this period in your residence, Pierce? That the whole thing is one big gag without tangible sense, a movie scripted by an idiot, full of sounds of audio tape, signifying God knows what?"

"I will indeed deny it! You've been here how long now?"

"Seventy days," I said promptly.

"During which you've never seen any of us at our normal best, but have been a part-time actor in a hell's broth concocted by one of us who has flipped his wig, flown out of his tree, and all the modern expressions for the grand old 'gone crackers'! At any other stage of our lives here you'd have found us—eccentric, yes; out of the common run, assuredly; but mad flatlanders hurling ourselves across this great screen of ours, absolutely not! We are *real,* we accomplish real things, as Sheridan points out."

"When you do anything but *watch,*" I said. "This house is inhabited by spectators, living vicariously all your lives long." I could feel my job wobbling badly under me. "A group of onlookers sitting forever in the theater that's your world, not contributing anything—spending time instead of using it—wasting intelligence and artistic talent and your *lives,* all the precious years, in watching!"

"Now just a damnation minute," began Sibella, setting down her glass with a thump.

"It's true!" I was shouting again, but I was mad. They were so blind and innocent about their existence, they had no conception that they owed it to the world and themselves to do something beyond lounging in the gallery. So far as humanity benefited from the Sablecrofts' existence, they might as well be wax figures in the great hall. And if the same could be said of many people who worked very hard to earn a living, it seemed to me that great wealth and superior intellects carried a moral responsibility that they ignored.

Even if that duty were all in my own head, derived from my personal morality, even if they owed no debt to anyone else, as a den of foxes or a nest of falcons surely owes nothing to the world, they had no right to sit here feeling smug about themselves. Which they did! Or so it seemed to me.

I wheezed in a breath through a throat engorged with righteous anger. "It's such a waste of brains and money and life," I began, and gave them a censored, capsule version of what I'd just been thinking.

Pierce interrupted, implacable. "That's your impression of us because of what's been taking place. You're tarring us all with the brush that's blackened a single warped soul. Suppose we were composed of a plumber, a clerk, a lawyer, a model, and a baseball umpire. Suppose you'd come to catalogue our collection of bubble-gum cards. If attempts to drive one of us to suicide or heart failure had erupted in such a family, would you feel that we weren't real, but dullards who lived in Never-Never Land? You confuse the reality of our household with the fantasy that is our hobby. You see us as through a television screen darkly. I swear, Laurel, we've never mistaken ourselves for actors in any bloody 'B' flick."

"You deny that you live an illusory existence?"

"Not illusory," said Sherry, who had finally opened his eyes. "Ideal for our temperaments, a little too involved with make-believe, but we share that with your average movie buff, artist, writer. Yes, and your scholar, historian, archaeologist, palaeontologist . . . all dedicated to research into one narrow aspect of life, in most cases past life, that won't improve mankind's lot or the average fellow's knowledge, morale, or standard of living by a millimeter."

"But they *do* something!" I cried. "They don't passively *view*, they actively *do!*"

Sibella said between clenched teeth, her dinner growing cold before her, "And just who in creation ever laid down the law that I was born to improve the lot of mankind? How many folk manage that?"

"How many are born with the money and the time to do what you all might be doing to help others?" I shot back. Good-bye Florida; good-bye, job. Micajah and I would be cast on the mercies of Out There!

"Laurel," said Daniel, louder than his wont, to get Sibella's attention, "is irritated at the constriction of our life. The emotion isn't foreign to us, either. Sherry went verbally berserk on the topic a year or two back. I remember you yourself, Aunt, as recently as last Christmastime, forbidding the mention of motion pictures for a solid week because you were feeling the pressure of a single subject for three meals a day. And Pierce once said that he sometimes felt he'd strayed into *Sunset Boulevard* and might never find his way out again."

"It's not uncommon to grow weary of one's favorite things occasionally," said Sibella. "But it doesn't last with us. And I will not be told that I should be tramping from door to door in the poorer districts, distributing hot soup and kind words to the indigent. I live as I please and no one may criticize me—not even a child whom I have grown to like and admire."

From the wall across from me, in a big rumbling complaint of a voice, Orson Welles growled, "I am not fond of the prattle of children. . . . In this house, the only alternative is the prattle of a simple-minded old lady; it's nearly as bad."

Daniel laughed helplessly. Pierce informed his plate that it was from *Jane Eyre,* 1944, and a magnificent performance. Sherry widened his eyes and Wendy made an O of her mouth. Sibella in her iciest voice, which would have frozen alcohol, asked, "What simple-minded old lady had Mr. Welles in mind?" but there was no response. "Our *dulce domum's* lost its balance," she said. "Where in hell's name is the dessert?"

Pierce sprang to his feet with that graceful strength that always surprised me. "Strawberry cheesecake, instantly."

"You were saying," Sherry informed me, "that we don't do anything, yet you know better. You're talking from a false premise. Very well, we have money, inherited money amplified by sound investments. We spend a great deal of it—"

"You certainly do," I said, reckless now, my bridges in ashes behind me. "I'd love to see your electric bill."

"Do not be vulgar and rude," said Sibella.

"And don't break in with flippant cracks when I'm explaining something," said Sherry testily. "We don't hoard it, we let it go out and circulate and give work to many people. This system is known as 'capitalism.' "

"But—"

"But me no buts. That, by the way, is from Fielding, and not any movie that I'm aware of. I read a little. What in sanity's name was I saying?" he snarled, so loudly and viciously that the resident dog stirred and lifted his head. "Beyond keeping cash at work out there, which helps the economy, we do perform certain tasks that you're well aware of. Yet the fact that they don't bring us more money is evidently bothering you. What under the sun would we do with more money?"

"I didn't mean that," I said.

"The devil you didn't. Deep in that respectable bourgeois mind you believe we ought to climb out of bed at seven, dash off to some job at eight, take an hour for lunch—wearing ties and jackets—trail home exhausted at half past five, change into soiled undershirts, break out the cans of beer, and flop before our TV sets."

"Oh now really—" I exploded.

"Shut up! What's so natural and heaven-ordained about emerging beyond the boundaries of one's own domain to work five or six days a week at something that one knows is of little or no consequence to one's own happiness?" He paused. "Cuss you, Pierce, you have me slipping into that 'one' routine and I get slued up in it. Who says that 'doing something' has to mean in an office, a truck, or a field? If I don't need the salary, why should *I* take it rather than some poor guy who must have it to exist? If my life, our lives, center on this house, who the blazes are you to raise objections?"

The wall said, in the voice of Franchot Tone, "There's a great deal of speaking of minds here tonight."

"Not me," said Daniel, grinning, as several of them looked at him. "Wish I could claim it, but no, not my work!"

"I don't say that you all ought to be running offices or whatever," I said, "but only that you should never have let yourselves be mired in this universe of nostalgia and secondhand emotions. You used the term 'movie buff'—well, your lives are an extreme exaggeration of the life of any serious movie buff, extravagantly overdone. You were born into a house that encloses that atmosphere, but you've given way to it shamefully. The worlds of nature, of intricate relationships among many people, are shut out. This is more of a desert island, isolated by its walls upon walls, than any island could be."

"Don't you like us?" asked Daniel wistfully.

"Good merciful God, certainly I like you! I'd never bother being angry if I didn't!" I shouted. "I simply can't bear the waste of such talents and brains—"

Humphrey Bogart said very loudly and flatly, "Shut up, lady."

Wendy whistled. "Somebody's doing a terrific job with the tapes tonight."

"That was from *Petrified Forest,*" Daniel noted, mainly to me. "Well done, whoever you are," to the table at large.

"We do not live on nostalgia," said Sibella, her cello-range voice rising mightily over us all. "The appreciation of any art is not nostalgia, girl. I suppose you'll admit that cinema is an art, since you've devoted most of your own life to the study of it?"

"I do admit that. My family was as involved in it as yours, Dad and Granddad worked in it. I'm not putting down the movies, only the continual immersion in them."

"What's so odd and unique about that?" she asked, snorting through that magnificent nose. "Look at your notable art collectors—do they create? They appreciate, they collect, they may even advance the cause of painting and sculpture by their enthusiasm, but principally they enjoy. They have the means to surround themselves with what they love. So do we. So I really don't see why all the fuss."

"Because," I said quietly, "I've been thinking that all the stupid, evil things that happened here were the direct result of living in the movies. Some of you, at least one for sure, has no conception of the realities of life because he was born in the middle of ten thousand films—some masterpieces, some very jolly, some intellectually stimulating, but many, many of them presenting a world that's false, based on false values, idealized notions of human nature, sentimental slush, and immoral glorifications of the bravery, nobility, and all-around superiority of the criminal mind. And that—"

"We see through you," said Sherry. "You're a pedantic lecturer, out to do good."

"Little friend of all the world," nodded Sibella, restored to high humor. "Granted, Laurel, some of the tricks with which our villain tried to scare you off and me to death came straight from the movies; but the sick hatred behind the attempts comes from a soul warped by its own poison, not from some innocent piece of celluloid."

"But you have such creativity in your blood, and you throw it away on watching dead actors mouth dead writers' words."

"Laurel," said Daniel, having already inhaled his dessert, "you've idealized our artistic abilities. None of us are that terrific. We've talked it over among ourselves many a time. Sherry and Wendy have enough skill to please and satisfy our tastes, but not enough to contribute marvelous things to the world. Pierce has an English genius for growing things. It's no sin to confine that talent to a greenhouse rather than, as Sherry says, taking some other poor chap's job away by hiring out as a gardener. Same for Sherry. The Hall's our work, we're a family of carpenters, electricians, workers in stucco, landscapers, and we act as our own servants. You talk as though we sat on our broad rumps all day and night gaping at a screen, but be truthful now, you know how hard we work!"

"Well, yes."

"You've never seen a repairman come from outside, have you? We do everything, which in a fifty-six-year-old castle is a fair amount. All the time you're typing your little cards, we're sweating at some frightful task. I recall that very early in your residence you were told we work a six-hour day. What you're criticizing is our recreation."

"Had you arrived a year ago, you'd have seen us more clearly," said Sibella. "You'd hardly have objected to the fact that we have somewhat more leisure time than most, although," she said, and halted a second, irresolute, reluctant to admit even this much, "I suppose we might have struck you as single-minded, yes."

Pierce said, "We've never considered it polite to bombard one another with our individual hobbies. We do share a pleasure in our family history, but I think we've not pushed that down your throat. Our separate passions are our own affairs, not to be used as boring monologue material."

"There's so much going on Out There," I said. "Did any of you even watch the first broadcast from the moon?"

"Outrageous!" cried Sibella. "A profanation! While I'm alive, by thunder, the moon remains a marvelous white jewel in the sky, not a piece of dead rock with acne."

" 'The moon,' " Pierce murmured, " 'kingdom of dream, province of illusion.' "

"I saw the landing," drawled Sherry. "Interesting. But I can't feel it improved my mind or made me a better human being. You remind me of a man."

"What man?"

"Man who used to teach us social studies. Completely hipped on keeping abreast of current events, but could never explain precisely *why.* 'Watch the eleven o'clock news and go to bed!' he used to order us. Once I asked him why, and he spluttered and said, 'You have to know what's going on in the world!' and I asked why, and he gave me a D for the course because he was stuck for an answer. There is no answer. If some people believe that gulping down every scrap of factual matter on train wrecks and murders, political battles and celebrity divorces, will educate them and improve their personalities, let 'em think so. Yet if I'd never heard of the Bomb or the Pill or Idi Amin, would I be any the worse for it, when my major interest in life is the development of the motion picture?"

Before I could answer, Sibella growled out, "You defied my wishes and watched that foul intrusion on lunar privacy?"

Sherry said, "Yes, I did. It was my decision and could harm nobody."

"I'd expressly forbidden it!"

"And I couldn't see any reason to obey such a ridiculous demand."

"While you're under my roof, you'll do as I say. Where'd you get a television set?"

"I went out to a bar!" Sherry yelled. They glared at each other with an approach to hatred. "Since the only TV was and is in your room, I went to a saloon and drank scotch and watched a man step onto the moon!"

She looked ready to send him to bed without his untouched dessert. But she merely shouted, and he shouted back, and Wendy said drearily, "Let's not argue," while Pierce studied the champagne label and Daniel looked quizzically at me. After a few minutes they calmed down and Sibella said breathlessly, "I forbid you ever to do such a thing again."

"Go into a bar or watch a moonwalk?"

"Go sneaking off behind my back."

"Grandmother," he said wearily, "I am thirty years old, and the civilization beyond these walls is not really that vile, hateful, obscene, and dangerous."

Before she could answer, Cary Grant said from the wall, "It's a pig's world."

They goggled, all of them, even Sherry the imperturbable. "This becomes eerie," said Daniel slowly.

"Do you know that the world is a foul sty?" asked Joseph Cotten, his splendid voice tuned low and tense and insane. "Do you know if you ripped the fronts off houses you'd find swine?"

"Sylvia Scarlett," I said as nonchalantly as possible, "and *Shadow of a Doubt."*

"Ye gods of vengeance," said Daniel weakly, "the biters bit. Do you know who's been steering this whole conversation, and set up just one single tape with all those quotations dubbed neatly on it?"

"Pierce is the only one who could do it," said Wendy.

Daniel corrected her. "No, pretty—it was Laurel, *and* with both hands on the table. She's learned how to press the button with her knee. I wondered about that pair of recorders you lugged upstairs! So winsome and innocent . . . how did you know in what order we'd say everything?"

"It was easy. I knew what I wanted to say, and once or twice I got lucky."

Sibella began to chuckle. "Pierce, make us some hot buttered rum for a toast! Laurel, you're one of us now!"

"But you're a pack of nuts," I said. "Don't you realize that I was deadly serious about this? That I worry for you because of what's happened to someone's mind, at least in part because of the constant atmosphere of unreality?" Pierce Poole had already vanished toward the kitchen; I hoped that what I had to say wasn't aimed at him. "Someone's confounded the real world—as Daniel calls the screen—with the actual world, where people who are killed don't bleed catsup and stand up and go home. It's an awful state of mind to let grow on you, and I believe it's what's happened in Sablecroft Hall. This is a sick house."

"Agreed," said Sherry, "but it wasn't sick before. He's made it that way."

"When you say 'he,' cousin, do you mean me or Pierce? For that's all there are, except you and the dogs and the females."

"I can hardly say 'it,' can I?"

"You see," I said earnestly to Sibella. "We *have* to find out, even if your new will has ensured that there'll never be another nasty joke."

She looked tired half to death. "I admit it. Somewhere in the Hall there's a worm eating away at its own guts and exuding hate like a horrible dew, perhaps still thinking only of vengeance . . . in return for what was no more than an accident." She stared into space, no one else spoke, and she said, "A slow, repulsive green worm in the guise of a human being. In our home! It doesn't bear thinking of."

She roused herself, brought that steel backbone up straight, eternally proud Victorian. "Father knew there was a world outside, none better! His friends poured in to enjoy his dream castle with him. Have we told you who used to come here? Sennett, Keaton, Griffith, George Arliss once, a gentle kindly man—but mainly the clowns: Lloyd, the Conklins, Ford Sterling, Turpin, Stan Laurel once for a whole wonderful week. I wonder if you were named for him?"

"Grandfather swore I was; Dad said no."

"I like to think you were. He was my favorite. That Mack Sennett used to chew tobacco *any*where. . . . Good Lord, the old days! They were sweet enchantment, with some exceptions." She laughed to herself. "And Alfred Vane, as natural a clown when he chose as any of the actors. Was he like that when he was older?"

"Sometimes." I wondered where this digression was leading.

"I remember him sitting exactly where you are," she said. "I wish he might have known that one day his granddaughter would be living under this roof. You always wish such things for friends after they're dead.

"Well, Father designed the Hall for a silly, jolly, comfortable home where a person could do what he liked. He wasn't the monomaniacal monster you've conjured up, Laurel. He knew the unimportance of what he enjoyed, in relation to the fate of nations and the hard grind of life. But he also knew the importance of having all the fun he could manage. He'd paid his dues, as they say nowadays.

"And he was a lecturer, as you are." All vigor restored, she threw back her head and laughed the dying-fall merriment that was her most individual expression. "He used to tell the pair of us, 'You girls have money, you can do what you like. But do it well and thoroughly and to some purpose, even if it's no more than to make yourselves a happy life.' Poor Felicity didn't listen, or couldn't follow his advice. I was lucky, I could."

Pierce brought in a tray on which six double-walled blue mugs steamed, throwing off a thick fragrance of rum and butter. He handed them round and the company drank to me as promised. I took a cautious sip and found it delicious and boiling hot.

Sibella drained half of hers, the liquor nearly incandescent, without visible effect. "The result of Father's other purpose is all around us. He wanted to give a home to all the information on his art, which wasn't far out of its infancy in nineteen twenty-four. He was one of a very few who recognized it as an art form that early in the game. *Lost Horizon* wouldn't be written for years, but he conceived a Shangri-La, a house built to stand weather and time, to preserve the history of the medium that had been growing ever since a few men in several countries had learned how to capture forever the movements and emotions of what even *minutes* afterward would become Time Past. That's why we have so many unique scripts, manuscripts, diaries . . . he was laying them up when others were throwing them away.

"He hoped that his silly, giggly, brawling girls would feel the same one day, and I at least did. So did Daniel's mother, Gloria. So does Sherry. One in each generation. So we have the best library on cinema in the world, and we expend great quantities of energy fuels to protect it, as every such repository and museum must do, and *there's* your answer to the wisecrack about our electric bill!"

She finished her rum. "I'm off to bed. Arguments tire me. I'm not as young as I was sixty years ago. And we haven't had a real argument here since Felicity died." She glared at all of us, though I alone was to blame. "We won't have any more of them," she said, in the tone of Charlton Heston reading from a stone tablet, and swept out, her black caftan rustling majestically.

"I've never heard Sibella speak of her age in that fashion before," fretted Pierce. "This affair must be brought to a definite finish. She is, after all, eighty."

"But it's over, isn't it?" asked Wendy pathetically. "I thought it was."

"Not yet," said Daniel grimly. "Not so long as there's a question in anyone's mind, it isn't over. It's true that the Hall was a jolly laughing place, Laurel. It has to be again. We've got to cleanse it. This business isn't fair to the house or Gilbert's specter or us. We musn't relax as we have. Someone's got to find out the truth."

"Someone's trying," said Sherry, watching me.

I couldn't imagine this haunted fortress as a cozy, genial home. I had to take their word for it.

Pierce said good night, then Wendy and Daniel. Sherry and I sat on, myself rather numb, amazed that I wasn't fired. At last he said, "Think you can riddle it out?"

"I think I nearly have."

"Risky, telling *me* that."

"No, I take your word that you're in love with me."

"Men have killed their loved ones before," he said gravely, "for their own safety, for jealousy, in fits of anger—with a kiss or with a sword. The tapes tonight were nicely done."

"Would you like to hear the last quotation?" He nodded. I shoved up the button with my knee. Boris Karloff, young Baron Frankenstein's undying monster, said in a prolonged grunt, "I love dead—hate living."

"You guess what I would have said to lead into that."

"'This house hates life, it loves only the image, the shadow, the simulacrum of life.' Something like that."

He stood and came around the table and slowly, almost leisurely, tipped up my face and kissed me on the mouth. It was the first time. "You taste gorgeous," he said. "Like butter." He pulled out my chair. "Go to bed, Sherlock. I shall come behind, thinking my deep, dark thoughts. Trot briskly. Remember we're alone."

I fairly ran out of the room, hearing him laugh behind me.

15

NEXT MORNING EARLY I WENT AT SIBELLA'S ORDER TO CHECK the galleries that surrounded her quarters—not only in the eastern walls, where I again found my threads broken, but within the three walls where I'd never before ventured, and on both levels. Everywhere I discovered signs of travel, scuffed and sometimes clear footmarks in the dust and litter; and all the doors were locked. I taped up many bits of thread. Sibella told me to keep the keys and to make the same rounds every day. "I want to know why he's prowling," she said.

"I'll study the plans again, and try to find out for you, but there seems no sense at all in it. The peepholes I've found haven't been opened for years, they're all over cobwebs and dust."

"Yes, probe away. You understand," she said, her voice steady, "there is no one else I can trust to do this. If something's going on after that threat of mine, which they all took seriously, then we have a mind so mad that it won't take account of consequences. And madness can't always be recognized, can it? Why," she said, clinching the matter in the only way she could, "once George Brent turned out to be the villain, mad as a hare! If you couldn't trust George Brent, is *anyone* above suspicion?"

"But—"

"Yes, I know what you yelled at us last night, but it's a good example. George Brent was the *nicest* man in the movies, and there he was in *Spiral Staircase* killing off innocent girls. What I mean is that if a sane man slips a cog, as it might be Pierce or Sherry, but keeps his native wits about him, you can't read the blood lust in his face, can you?"

"Yet you trust me."

She smiled slowly. "You think it's because you're a stranger. You're wrong. I know considerably more about you than you imagine, Laurel. And you're sane, and you're not full of hate."

"Just like George Brent."

"Oh, my," she said.

So for three days I made the rounds of those dismal passageways, hundreds and hundreds of yards on both stories, and found sometimes one set of doors that had been used and sometimes another. But always someone had come through from north to south, or vice versa, passing between the library or the great hall and the Moorish court at the front of the house.

Then Pierce and Daniel moved into Sibella's quarters for the better part of each day, and suddenly my secret threads remained unbroken. I tried to riddle that out and failed: It may have been one of them before, or their presence may have scared the prowler away, for what they were doing was cleaning and refurbishing the Moorish court itself.

The vegetation was Pierce's task and he repotted, replaced,

cleaned leaves, nourished, and pampered everything that grew in that lush oblong space under its vast skylight of shatterproof glass that showed the pale blue of the sky crossed with the heavy clouds of summer.

Daniel's chore was to clean all the ceramic tile, which was blue for the floor of the court and a vibrant golden yellow, almost the color of Micajah's eyes, from floor to head level. The small square Italian tiles were set in pale jonquil grout, which Daniel was scrubbing with a solution of muriatic acid. Having begun in the center of the floor, he worked outward from the old drain in circles, flushing the acid down periodically. His major tool was a toothbrush dipped in the liquid. He estimated that the floor and three walls would be an eight-toothbrush job.

"Then the statues must be cleaned," he said, his supple body folded down tailor-fashion as he scoured industriously. "Lucky for me they've invented a spray mist that does a good job with marble. And *then* I paint the walls above the tile—eleven hundred fifty square feet give or take a foot—and all on the ridiculous ladder. And then clean the fountain and check all the wiring." He gazed up at me mournfully. "What were you saying about my hunting a job, Laurel?"

"Nothing. Not a word. Poor Daniel."

"It's really fun," he grinned. "I only clean it once a year, after all, and paint every four years. But imagine the discomfort it must have been before air-conditioning!"

"I won't think about it. It's so hot these days that I don't even stick my nose outside to weed."

"Sensible," said Pierce firmly. "Mad dogs and Sherry Todds go out in the midday sun, as dear Noël would have said had he known us."

In a couple of days Daniel had finished the grout, cleaned the tiles, and begun on the largest of the statues. There were two life-sized nymphs, nineteenth-century English work without distinction, though I had to admit they looked nice among the greenery; and a trio of small fauns, Italian-made of a better quality marble and with life in their blank eyes, pointed ears, and buttons of horns. I could fairly see their tiny goat tails twitch with excitement as they peeked out of fern clumps at me. They reminded me of Daniel:

mischievous without being cruel. I said so to him, for Pierce had finished his work and Daniel labored here alone.

"I'm four feet taller, and have pupils in my eyes, and hair covering my horns, but I appreciate the comparison. A faun is sprightly, full of life and laughter. I thank you, Laurel." He turned and kissed me suddenly.

"Sibella," I whispered.

"She's reading. Besides, she has to know about it when we're married."

"Oh, when's that?"

"I'm waiting for you to propose. Any day now, you will."

"How could I help it? And where will the honeymoon be?"

"In front of that dismal door, twisting the dial left and right! Now let me at this plump and pleasing lump, whose draperies are too grimy to attract even a faun." He squirted a jet of foam in the big nymph's face and attacked it vigorously with a rag.

I went into the library, past Sibella who was absorbed in a book, stiffly upright in a chair near the door with her huge round reading glasses high on the bridge of her splendid nose, and climbed one of the rolling ladders to rearrange some books that were next on my list. It was about noon then. Most of the volumes I wanted were on the highest shelves, and belonged down on the fifth level from the floor, so there was a surfeit of climbing and descending and sliding back and forth across the face of the filled wall. By two o'clock my arms were tired and my legs ached, so I took twenty minutes off for coffee and deep breathing.

Pierce, shifting books on the southern wall to conform with the cards I'd finished, was in and out constantly, and I scarcely noticed him, absorbed with what I was doing, and now and then thinking involuntarily about Sherry.

I always came back to that frightening question—was it the irresistible attraction of evil?

Why should wickedness seduce me, who prided myself on my moral values and judgments? That problem bewildered me. Maybe I was fascinated *despite* his presumptive capacity for savagery. Women in films and books were always falling for men who snarled at them, bullied them . . . I thought that was pretty sick. That was what I *would not do.*

It was flattering beyond words, of course, when a man dieted off thirty pounds or so because of me. I didn't think I was being gullible to believe that, when I remembered the burial of the candy. He had no reason to lie about that.

Still, someone in the Hall was a devout liar.

Such thoughts were getting me nowhere, bounding to and fro in a forest of contradictions and mysteries rather like those baby fauns of Sibella's, which Daniel would be cleaning now. I sighed, looked at my watch, and went back to the ladder as Pierce bustled in. "Just consulting with Belle on dinner," he said. "She'll prepare us some tinned pheasant in wine sauce, and apple charlotte, and Sibella's champagne mania to the contrary, I've ordered some fine old Beaujolais. Look here, my dear girl," he said kindly, "don't work too long on that ladder. It's bloody murder on the feet and calves."

"I don't mind," I said cheerfully, stretching the truth a little to match his own jauntiness. I went up twenty feet or so and scooted the contraption left and began to gather another armload of books.

That was at 2:20.

I went up and down and up and down, and left and right, no longer thinking of anything but the new arrangement of the volumes, and wondering vaguely how often I'd move them before everything was exactly right.

At about 2:35 I tried to remove a book that turned out to be painted on the cloth screen of a speaker. I recall the time because I glanced at my watch again in vexation, speculating whether I'd been working longer than I'd thought, whether I was really too tired to continue on this towering affair of flat steps and smooth round mahogany bars and giant casters. But it was only 2:35 and I put my error with the painted book down to eyestrain.

I shoved the ladder toward the middle of the wall, sailing along faster than usual—temper, temper, I told myself; or embarrassment at being caught by somebody's fool-the-eye coloring job. I wondered who'd done it, and supposed Wendy, who was the most skillful with a brush.

Almost as I thought of her, I passed her, staring out at me from a gap in the shelving. It was a lookout hatch that didn't have books or the images of books on the front, but when closed seemed to be simply one of the artistically placed squares of blank wall that broke the monotony of the otherwise solid mass of book spines.

I was a trifle startled, being seventeen or eighteen feet above the floor and seeing a face watching me from behind the wall. I slowed and stopped the ladder and, more sedately, rolled it back to speak to her.

If I'd noticed anything wrong with her face, that first time past, I no longer know. I may have. But I think it was only subconscious, if indeed the false note had registered at all.

It was on the left side of her forehead, a long cut from brow to hairline, which had oozed blood that was now thickened and clotted. There was an appalled expression on the girl's face, as if she had just heard something that horrified her. But Wendy hadn't heard a sound for some time, because the skin of her beautiful face was mottled with a dreadful blue, and she was dead as a spring flower in October.

She lay half-propped in the little spy hole, the weight of her body apparently taken by the wall itself, due to the angle at which she rested on it. Her lavender-blue eyes looked directly into my face, the right side of her head leaning against the upright edge of the opening. Her mouth was partly open, as in life.

Gradually I became aware that I was gripping the heavy poles of the ladder so tightly that my fingers were throbbing.

"Pierce," I said, "oh, please, Pierce." My voice didn't carry to him; my tongue was a flannel rag in a hot dry box. I tried to take hold of myself, and for a few panic-stricken seconds found that I couldn't even move my hands, to pry them loose from the mahogany. I shut my eyes and swore at myself for a coward. It wasn't as though I'd never seen death before.

But I'd never encountered it while standing on a ladder that moved sidelong under me because of the shaking of my body. The fact that I was standing precariously on the thing, some three times my own height above a hard parquet floor, turned my bones to gelatin. I tried to call Pierce Poole again and could hardly utter a sound. So, with a last look at the dead girl, a look that her glazed eyes exchanged with me fearfully, I began to descend, foot after foot groping anxiously for the next flat rung, and somehow came to the bottom without mishap. I turned toward Pierce, standing with his back to me gazing at the books on the new southern shelves, and I ran to him.

Somehow being off that abominable ladder helped me regain my common sense. I gripped his huge arm, startling him out of his revery, and said, "Oh, Pierce, Wendy's dead."

He looked at me. "What are you saying, Laurel?" He seemed shocked into incomprehension.

"Wendy's been killed," I said. I made him turn, and pointed up at her. "Please come with me," I said hoarsely, and ran for the nearest entrance to the passages, which was a hinged panel beyond the open doorway to the dining room. I heard him coming behind me. I dashed along for a short distance in the gloom, the only illumination coming from the open panel behind; then shoved on a light switch as I passed it and took the straight stairs two at a time to the second level. There were no bulbs lit in that corridor, and at the end of a long stretch of blackness I could see the thick beam from the library pouring in to glisten on the girl's white blouse and the jet black of her hair.

I dashed toward her as Pierce turned on the naked brilliant globes above and ahead of us. I came to Wendy and stopped.

"My God," whispered Pierce. "Oh my God, how can this dreadful thing have happened?"

The corpse lay at an angle against the inner wall, the feet trailed out behind, the body held up partly by its own weight leaning on the wall, partly by her shoulders which were wedged into the opening. The door of the spy hole, which was on the other side of the body from us, had been opened to its full extent and pushed against the wall.

"Lift her down," said Pierce, who could not get past me for the narrowness of the passage.

"Shouldn't we wait for the police?"

"That's only in cases of murder," he said sharply. "This has been a terrible accident. Look." I turned back to him and he nodded at the ladder that rose from floor to ceiling just across the corridor from the porthole. It was not one of those ladders that swung out in a quarter-turn and went up or down as one pushed it, but was permanently fixed below a trapdoor leading to the attic. "D'you see?"

Two of the round rungs had shattered in the center and their fragments dangled on either side. "She was going to the attic, I suppose, and they broke under her and she fell," said Pierce. His teeth were chattering slightly from shock. "Do take her out of the embrasure, Laurel. Lay her decently on the rug."

Obediently I took hold of the girl's body under the arms and lifted her free.

There is nothing in the world, I believe, that is heavier than a dead body. It would have been as easy to lift the trunk of an oak. I stepped sideways across her legs and with Pierce's help brought her in and laid her supine on the floor. Rigor had begun to set in, though not to any great extent.

In the glare of the light bulb that hung directly over us, her face was a ghastly parody of the beauty she'd been. I stood above her, still half crouched, and stared at her in dread. "Get the police," I said. "Call the police, Pierce. I'll wait with her."

"Do you think that's necessary?" I glanced up and recognized that he was more shaken than I. He had known her for many years. "Hadn't I better fetch Sibella first?"

"Oh, Pierce! Please call the police. An accident like this *has* to be reported immediately." They all thought that Sibella ran the world.

He inhaled loudly through his mouth and clenched his hands together and shook his head. "Sorry, my dear. Can you bear to be alone with—"

"Pierce! What's going to hurt me here?"

"Right," he said, and went swiftly down the passageway.

I discovered that I was crying. I let the tears run, blinking and shuddering as I knelt beside the dead girl. I touched her cooling face where the light sick blue of death had stained the lovely skin in patches. "I'm sorry, Wendy," I said. I hadn't liked her because she'd never seemed any warmer than one of her own waxworks. She'd been unable to comprehend the fact that dogs had rights as individuals. With an insensitivity like a small child's to the feelings of others, she'd fallen in with someone's practical-joking cruelty, though she'd balked at murder. At least she hadn't borne real hate, but could manage only a weak disdain and irritability.

I realized that I knew almost nothing of Wendy. I knew only the prejudices between us, some of which had been wrong. She hadn't been stupid. She'd disliked and resented me, but then I'd reciprocated. Maybe that had been no more than mutual jealousy? She'd once been Sherry's wife, she seemed interested in both Sherry and Daniel and angry that they spent so much time alone with me.

I touched her head above the ear, and it lolled awry. As I'd thought when we lifted her and laid her here, her neck was broken. The cut on her forehead looked deep enough to have finished her, too. . . .

How could she have fallen from those broken rungs and turned in midair and received that gash and broken her neck and ended wedged into the spy hole looking *outward?*

I stared up at the shattered ladder, the uncontrollable quivering of my body intensified. Why had she been climbing it? To go into the attic for more devilment? Was I excusing her of everything simply because she was dead? Had she been the culprit all along? I thought of the omnipresent tapes that could make anyone say anything to you at any time. What if this girl had been alone in Felicity's room that night, talking loudly for my benefit to one of their damned three-speed four-track solid-state audio-tape recorder-players? Perhaps she'd staged all the sick tricks herself, and now been caught by the god of poetic justice in some final bitchiness.

If that were true, I thought coldly, she was better off dead.

Of hard evidence there was little, and that confusing, to point to an accomplice, but there was a lot that said, "Wendy." I turned her face upward again, and looked into her filmed eyes.

No. No! If she'd been unfeeling, she hadn't been crazy. And the terror in her face when she'd said that someone else was not crazy, but "dirt mean," and the fear she'd had for Challenger after his mock attack on me—I didn't believe she'd had the ability to feign those.

I was going into a dull, smoldering rage on her account. I kept our gazes locked, and promised her that no matter how long it took, or what dangers would arise for me, I'd find out the truth—and if someone had callously killed her, then I'd bring them to justice. Wendy had not been lovable, but so physically vulnerable, and yes, at the end emotionally so too, that I felt I owed it to her to see the truth revealed. No doubt an excess of guilt on my part . . . but we can't always choose our motives.

I'd begun to smell murder in that narrow gut between the walls. Obviously an accident—but why had she turned in falling? There might be a simple reason, but I couldn't see it. The whole thing stank of killing. Suppose *he* had tried to enlist her in his campaign again, in spite of Sibella's warning. Or suppose he felt that she, a frightened woman, might eventually confess. He'd have shut her mouth for good. Perhaps he had.

Then I heard them coming.

Sibella led, behind her Pierce and Daniel, filling the passage with sound and bulk even though they came single file. I stepped back to allow them room. Sibella passed Wendy's body and stood beside me, looking down. "So it's true. I hardly took it in, when Pierce told me I couldn't believe it."

"Where's Sherry?"

"I called him on the intercom," said Pierce, "but he may be out of hearing. I said to come here at once." He pointed out the two broken rungs above our heads, and Daniel moved as though to climb and examine them.

"Stop!" said Sibella, quick and sharp. "Don't touch a thing, especially the ladder. You two should never have moved her."

"Why?" said Pierce blankly.

"Don't you remember when my sister died? Any fatal accident must be treated as a murder until proven otherwise. Don't touch anything."

"But you don't believe—" Pierce began.

"I believe only that Wendy is dead."

Daniel knelt beside her. "God, God," he said, his voice a raw red gash of sound. "At twenty-four!"

Then we all began, naturally I suppose, to babble; except for Sibella, who stood there watching us. At last she said, "Who will let the police in?" Pierce exclaimed guiltily and vanished. Soon we heard voices, and two officers appeared at the turn of the corridor.

They seemed to tramp toward us forever, but at last they were here. They made me feel strange, not because they were policemen, but because they were the first outsiders I'd seen in Sablecroft Hall. The larger of the two said, "I'm Sergeant Quarterstaff." It was the best name for a tall broad keeper of the law that I could have imagined. "Who discovered the body?"

"I did," I said.

"Has anyone touched anything?" His voice was low, carrying and calm. He might have been asking if we wanted a drink of water.

"Only Wendy," I said, "the dead girl," and compared with his, my voice sounded loud and unfamiliar, echoing and rattling in that cramped place until it died away over our heads.

"Will all of you please go downstairs," he said, "and I'll be there in a minute. Please don't touch anything here if you can help it." He pressed against the wall, motioning his partner to do the same, to let us pass. "Joe, Signal Seven with a possible Code Five. Notify the M.E. Secure the scene and get technicians from the R. and I." He nodded at the broken rungs. "She must have been climbing that. Miss, will you wait a second?" he asked me as I followed Sibella. "Did you just touch the body, or actually move it?"

I described how she'd been wedged into the opening, and how we'd laid her on the rug.

"You didn't know she was dead?"

"Oh yes. Cyanosis was well advanced."

He gave what I interpreted as the faintest suggestion of a skeptical blink. I said, "We shouldn't have touched her, I know, but—"

"It's a natural thing to do," said Sergeant Quarterstaff. "The gentleman who helped you can describe the original position?"

"Of course."

"All right, you go on down. Why don't you have a shot of whiskey? You're pale around the gills," he said. I liked Sergeant Quarterstaff.

"I will," I said. And when I reached the ground floor, I went into the dining room, across to the sideboard, and poured a large brandy. Then I went to sit by myself in the library.

Sherry had not appeared. "Daniel's gone for him," said Pierce across the room, as I looked around inquiringly. "He's outside, likely. Belle's at home resting, we thought there'd be no need to disturb her yet."

The two cousins came in and walked to me. Sherry, his face utterly wooden, put a hand on my forearm, as I sat on the edge of the chair trembling and clutching my knees. "What happened?" he asked.

I couldn't look into his face and tell him. I stared at his hand on my arm; it was smeared with dust, which had been clotted into lumps of dirt here and there by the sweat. I glanced at Daniel's hand as he did what Sherry had done, touched me for my comfort: there were dark stains between his fingers—yes, he'd been cleaning statues. And Belle had been, perhaps, in her little house. And Sibella reading, and Pierce here or somewhere. . . .

I said dully that I'd been on the ladder and passed her, and gone back, and all the rest of it, without mentioning what her face had looked like staring forth at me.

"You poor kid," said Daniel.

Sherry said nothing. He looked up at the open square among the books, where the naked light poured out. Against my will, my eyes went up there too. There was a small squawking noise coming from within the passage. I assumed that Joe was talking to the R. and I., and the M.E., whatever they were, with his signals and codes.

Death. Not false death on a screen. True violent death. My frame shook helplessly. I drank a little, the brandy sloshing in the big-bellied glass.

"I'm going up to see her," said Sherry, and walked off.

"They won't let him near her," Daniel muttered. "Not till they've gone over everything with . . ." His voice trailed away.

"But he was her husband, once."

"When Grandmother died, it was the same. I'd been here in the library, I never knew a thing till they'd come. They wouldn't allow me near her until they'd finished, and put her on a stretcher."

Sherry came out of the panel door, which was propped open, followed by Sergeant Quarterstaff. They walked toward us. Sibella and Pierce came over to join us. "I can't see her yet," Sherry said.

"You understand why, sir," said the officer.

"Yes, yes, certainly."

"I'd like to speak to this young lady alone," said Sergeant Quarterstaff. "If all the others will sit down at that end of the room?"

"Don't you bully her!" said Sibella, going even stiffer and taller than usual, Her Majesty of Sablecroft Hall speaking to a bailiff.

"No indeed, ma'am," he said quietly. I saw the corner of his mouth twitch. It was as good as a broad grin.

"I'll be safe with the sergeant," I said.

"No third degree," ordered Sibella, and stalked down the room, followed by the other three.

He sat down in a chair opposite me, pulling it forward till our knees almost touched, and bringing out a notebook from somewhere behind the wide black belt that carried his radio, a box of ammunition, and an enormous black-handled revolver. "May I have your name, miss?"

"Laurel Warrick. Mrs." I watched his huge hand write swiftly. "I'm Mrs. Callingwood's librarian."

"I thought you might be her nurse. Not been here long, I believe?"

"A little over two months."

"It's a queer kind of house, isn't it?"

I winked both eyes against the tears. "Is that an official question?"

"No," he said, smiling. "Personal comment."

I admitted that Sablecroft Hall was different.

"I came here once before," he said. "An old lady, I think this one's sister, fell down a long pair of steps a couple of years ago. You don't forget the place easily." He asked suddenly, "Feel better yet?"

"Yes, thank you. You're very kind."

"It must have been one hell of a shock," he said. "Tell me how and when it happened, as fully as you can, please."

I did so. At one point the doorbell rang, but he motioned Pierce back as the fat man rose to answer it. "Patrolman Maxwell's there," and dropped his voice again to say, "Go on, ma'am." I finished everything I could think of to tell him. He looked at me closely. "Do you think there's anything strange about this fall she took?"

I noticed that my hands had clenched together, and separated them and laid them on my knees. "I can't understand how she could be facing outward, away from the ladder, or how she got that cut," I said. "And her neck's broken, too."

He wrote something. "Exactly. It doesn't look right, does it? How do you know her neck was broken?"

"I touched her cheek."

"I see. That's all right, you don't have to describe what happened. Everyone else in the house, they're related, aren't they? I thought I recollected that. Even the Englishman." He sat back, eyes focused above my head. "Have you any reason to think that the deceased—that Miss Abbott might not have fallen accidentally from that ladder?"

I thought it over, perhaps too long, for I saw him bring his gaze sharply down to mine. I said, "No, I haven't. But this isn't the first time that something's crumbled in this house. There used to be a balcony on the wall down there," I nodded slightly at it, and saw the family all watching us. "Its moorings came loose and it had to be taken down. There was a statue—"

"Yes, in the other big room," he said, encouraging me as I faltered. "I remember all the wax models and statues. Like a museum."

"Yes. One of them fell because its pedestal was full of bugs. Powder-post beetles. Sometimes it's seemed to me that the Hall is caving in around us."

Quarterstaff *hmm*ed agreement. "These old Florida places are full of everything from termites to damp rot. No one else has been hurt?"

"Unless Mrs. Ryder fell when something collapsed, but I don't think so. The dead woman, my employer's sister."

"No, that was simple heart failure. There was an autopsy. She was very old."

"Was there much blood?" I asked abruptly.

"No, none that I recall. Why?"

"Someone said something once . . . I thought there'd been a lot of blood on her."

"No. I see," said Sergeant Quarterstaff calmly. I had the uncomfortable feeling that he saw more than I'd told him, though no outsider could have guessed about the bizarre, bloody dummy of Felicity. "Are you afraid, Mrs. Warrick?"

"I'm only shaken up."

"No wonder. But with all these articles dropping around you, it's enough to frighten a man."

"Let alone a woman?" I asked.

I think he murmured something about Women's Lib. "Yes, and let alone a stranger, too. Unfortunately, there's no law that says a family has to protect itself by any special means in its own house. But if *you* were hurt, you could plaster them with lawsuits."

"She was so young," I said at a tangent, thinking aloud.

"Yes. You're angry about that. Were you good friends?"

"No. I wasn't fond of her. I'm sorry now, but that doesn't help, does it?"

"It never does. But the truth helps us. What was she like?"

"A sort of cold fish," I said uneasily. "Speak no ill of the dead, I know, but, well, we had very little in common, and I have to tell you what I think."

"Did anyone hate her? In your private opinion?"

"I think they all liked her better than I did."

"Anyone benefit from her death?"

"Not that I'm aware of. Mrs. Callingwood has all the money in the family."

"I see." He wrote. Then he produced a card from his notebook, scrawled something on it quickly, and leaning forward, offered it to me. His back was to the others and they couldn't see it. "Put that somewhere safe. If anything else happens, even if nobody's hurt, will you let me know? I have an uneasy instinct about this house." He smiled faintly again. "I guess half of St. Pete has it. My dad used to tell me that if I broke one more window, he'd send me to Sablecroft Hall."

I picked up my bag, which I'd left some hours before on a nearby table—*when Wendy was alive,* I thought, and forced back a rush of tears—and dropped his card into it, aware that I was concealing it from the family as he had. "Thanks. Really, thanks."

"I'll talk to the large gentleman next," he said. "He was with you?"

"He was working in this room. We went upstairs together after I'd told him about her."

"Can you say that he was here all the time?"

"I think so," I said. "We're all in and out at random, every day. Nobody ever seems to keep track of anyone."

"But you and he alibi each other? If necessary?"

I hadn't considered it in that light. "Yes. I think so. I mean, I was aware of Pierce off and on, as he probably was of me."

"Mr. Pierce, is it?"

"Pierce Poole."

He wrote it down on a fresh page. "You go and send him to me, Mrs. Warrick, please. The C.I.D. man will ask you all these things again when he's ready. We each have to file a report. Don't be impatient with him."

"I promise. I thought the term 'C.I.D.' was strictly British."

"It's used here too—Criminal Investigation Department. You happen to read Agatha Christie?"

"I adore her books," I said, and smiled for the first time in what felt like years.

"I eat 'em up," said Sergeant Quarterstaff. He stood as I did. "Thank you for your help," he said. I went away feeling guiltily that I should have told him much more than I had, but none of it amounted to anything except practical jokes and meaningless acts. Of course, there was the oil on the chandelier bolts. Well, I could always call him if I decided that he ought to know about that.

I sent Pierce to him, and sat down a little way from the family, who were spread out across the western end of the room, none of them talking. I watched Sergeant Quarterstaff, liking him very much. He was a breath of sane *outside,* most comforting as he sat here in our sacrosanct library, large and capable and decent in his pale green shirt open at the throat, his dark green trousers and heavy black shoes, with his green mesh cap sitting on the parquetry beside him, and the butt of his gun thrust out as he wrote.

I wished that I could keep him here forever.

He was talking with Sibella when the man from the Homicide Squad came in, wearing a plain dark suit, a tie, and a bemused expression. He had a word with Sergeant Quarterstaff and began questioning us all again in the same order. Time seemed to have forgotten the Hall. The interviews went on interminably. At last we were called together, and the detective, Lieutenant Jones, spoke to us, reading periodically from his notes.

"I hope you all understand that this accident has to be treated as a homicide until verified as accidental death. I don't believe there's much doubt that it was an accident." He fished out an envelope and plucked a long sliver of wood from it with two fingers. "Dry rot," he said, "and likely in a couple more rungs, too."

"Yes," said Pierce, staring at it, "the typical red-striped appearance. The fungus Merulius. The wood fibers seem almost destroyed."

"Correct," said Lieutenant Jones, sounding testy at the interruption. "Miss Abbott was evidently coming down the ladder after storing a box in the attic. Several of you have agreed that she always came down a ladder facing away from it, due to fear of not seeing where she was stepping. That accords with the injuries and the stated position of the body, which should not have been moved." He glared at me, making me feel wormlike and criminal, although Pierce had been the one who insisted on moving her. "Her head struck the upper portion of the open window," he went on, stammering over the last word, plainly at a loss for anything else to call the thing, "at which time her neck was undoubtedly broken too. The body came to rest across the sill of the window."

I tried to remember if I'd ever seen Wendy on a ladder. I hadn't. What he'd said did explain the biggest mystery.

"Fingerprints on the ladder are those of the deceased only," said the lieutenant in that strange official jargon. "Same with the box we retrieved from the attic," he added more casually. "We'll return the box when its contents have been analyzed."

"What was in it?" demanded Sibella.

He scowled at her, decided that she represented an immense amount of money and influence, altered his face and said, "Numerous boxes of sound tape, Mrs. Callingwood. I understand that she may have been getting ready to play a joke on somebody. When the body is released by the M.E., we'll call you for instructions pertaining to crematory or funeral home." He looked around at us and turned into a human being. "I'm sorry you had to answer so many questions right after the poor kid was killed. It's part of the routine, and I know it's always hell on the survivors. If you want to see her before we put her in the ambulance, she's in the front hall. I've put in a Signal 35—I mean I've called for an ambulance."

"We will all go and say good-bye to Wendy," said Sibella. "Thank you for your courtesy, officer."

Sergeant Quarterstaff and Patrolman Maxwell had departed in their cruiser. With a faintly abandoned sensation, I trooped through the great hall in Sibella's wake, listening to the lieutenant urge her strongly to bring in a good exterminator to check all the wood in the house. She unbent enough to promise that she'd do it. "What does M.E. stand for?" she asked him.

"The Medical Examiner, ma'am," said Jones of the C.I.D.

"Ah." She reverted to the previous subject. "I've thought it over, I'll have the experts in tomorrow morning. I don't care to own a death trap, and this house grows old."

"The walls'll stand for a hundred years, but you know wood in Florida, ma'am."

"You are absolutely right," said Sibella, "and I thank you."

In the vestibule Wendy lay wrapped on a stretcher. Two men

and a young woman, all dressed in sport clothes, the girl with a camera slung round her neck, stood waiting. Jones murmured that they were technicians from R. and I.—Records and Identification. He bent and uncovered Wendy's face.

I did not look at her again. Sherry and Daniel knelt beside the stretcher, Sibella watched her for a moment and turned away.

"Damn," she said under her breath.

Then they'd taken Wendy away, and we drank strong coffee and brandy at the table, and didn't talk for a long while.

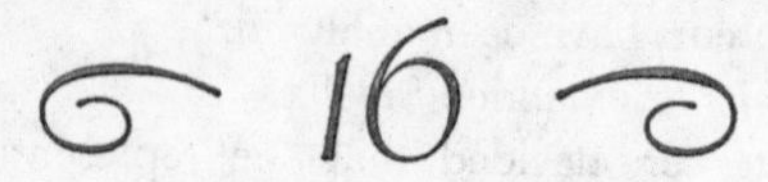

"ALL RIGHT, THAT'S DONE WITH," SAID SIBELLA, AT THE HEAD OF a table that looked more uselessly vast than ever. "They'll bring in 'accidental death.' We know more than they do, let's trot it out. Laurel, what happened?"

I repeated what I'd told Sergeant Quarterstaff and the man from Homicide.

"You were in the library and heard nothing, no thud or scream?"

"Nothing."

"Seems impossible," she said, "with the hatch open—"

"Why was it open?" asked Sherry, his words formed of lead. "Was it open all the time you were on the ladder?"

"I don't know. I only started on that level a minute or so before I saw her." My hands, traitors to my mind's determination, were shaking again. There were black chills of terror in my heart, for Sibella and for myself. It was a delayed reaction, brought on by the departure of the police. I longed to collect my cat and run away, after them, after sunshine and sanity. Yet, how could I leave the old woman alone to face the next attack?

"We know that its being open was wrong," she said. "We have a certain advantage over the police. But if we tell them everything, it will seem suspicious to them without helping them a bit. Did anyone tell them more than the essentials?"

"I mentioned the balcony, the statue, and Mrs. Ryder's fall. The sergeant had been here then, he remembered that it was heart failure."

"That's why Jones was insistent about having a bug man in," Daniel said. "Good idea too."

"I'll call tomorrow. You did well, Laurel."

I asked about Wendy's curious mode of descending ladders. They agreed that when she'd been more than two steps off the floor, she'd come down frontwards, clutching the side bars and watching her feet. "It was a phobia," said Sherry. "As a kid she'd do the same, getting out of a slanted palm tree."

"There was a dent above the spy hole," said Pierce. "The detective fellow told me. Falling from as high as she did, she must have struck it with terrific force. It accounts for everything."

"Except the open window and the box of tapes." Daniel hit the table with a fist. "What would ever possess her to hide a box of our tapes in the attic? Senseless!" He paused, and looked at Sibella and said, "*Impossible* is the word."

"That's true," she answered him. Then, coolly and with her usual delivery—if you state your opinions firmly, they will always be right—twirling a long-stemmed glass between her fingers, she went on to say that she believed, though she was sorry to tell us, that Wendy had been the vicious prankster, that she had become unhinged as it were, and that the tapes in the attic were part of some new-hatched devilment. Wendy could have worn man's shoes, made the tracks in the dirt, everything.

Pierce shook his head, causing her to raise her brows autocratically. "Why would she climb the ladder with the spy hole open, unless it was for illumination? And why wouldn't she simply have put on the passage lights? They were out, you know. No sense. No sense to it. She must have heard Laurel sliding back and forth on the library ladder and known she could be discovered at any instant." He gestured incoherently. "I grope for truth in perfect darkness."

"Dry rot," said Sherry viciously. "No one had used that ladder for years, I should think. Dry rot. Damn this vile climate! Why couldn't Gilbert have built in the English countryside?"

Belle McNabb came in, looked startled at seeing us sitting there, so against custom, and Sibella said, "Teatime. I think we'd better eat something, and no arguments. Belle, something plain and nourishing. We'll call this supper too. Wendy will not be here."

Belle peered at her and then at us all. No one spoke. "She's dead," said Belle sharply. "Little Wendy's dead."

"Yes. She had an accident."

"No accident," Belle said slowly. "She got herself killed. No surprise to me." Then she was gone.

"Voodoo?" Daniel hazarded, not trying to be funny.

"Put yourself in her place," said Sherry. "You'd know. The bunch of us sitting here like stricken images." He stared at his grimy hands. "I'll wash up. I was working in the storage rooms, rearranging stuff." He followed Belle. Daniel said that he was a mess too, and left us.

"What about alibis?" asked Sibella. "I was questioned on that twice. I was at this end of my room and Daniel was working in the court. We were each aware of the other all the time. I could hear him scrubbing away without a break, and he could see me. Sherry, poor boy, was all alone, I take it, out in the rooms beyond the garage."

"Laurel and I were in the library," said Pierce, "but I was out several times, once to have a bottle of ale, once to visit the lavatory. Either time would have allowed me just long enough to dash up to that passage, do—what was done, and return without Laurel noticing. However, she couldn't have done the same, I can say that positively, for she was too high on that ladder to manage it in such a brief interval."

I said, "I could have swung into the opening from my ladder, and done everything quicker than you could, Pierce."

Sibella snapped, "Don't quibble! We'll say that you alibi each other to a ninety-five-per-cent certainty. There are seven—oh no, no, there are *six* of us living here now," she said, "and four have alibis that should satisfy the law, if this comes to anything other than death by misadventure. Look here, you two," she leaned forward, "among ourselves only: I don't like the stench of this, I don't like it at all, and I trust the pair of you to keep your eyes wide and be frank with me. Sherry and Belle, might one of them have done it? We know nothing, we can't guess *why*, but could they?"

"I cannot believe it," said Pierce instantly.

"I don't know," I muttered, half-occupied with my struggles against revulsion and fear. I said the name, the talismanic safeguard against harm. "Sergeant Quarterstaff asked me who profited by her death, and I said no one, thinking of money. But what if by her death a secret is kept, one that would disinherit somebody?"

"Remember it was likely an accident," said Pierce.

"A damn fortuitous accident," I said, anger rising for Wendy again. "I have to tell you two this, but not the others yet." Swiftly I described the night scene in Felicity's room, and what Wendy had told me next day. "I'm like Belle. 'No accident.' "

Sibella nodded. "So there it is."

"Anyone could have entered and left the passages except you and Daniel. Oh," I cried, banging the oak with my fist as Daniel had, "if I could only get at what I know! I'm sure I know more than I can dredge out of the deep places in my mind! It's there, it's all there, and I cannot get it out."

"What do you mean?"

"Clues, statements, things I've seen, that should tell me who, and how, and maybe even why! The passages," I said, leaning back, "the passages, Sibella!"

"Sherry might have made his way through them without being seen, certainly—as could Belle."

"The passages around your rooms! I can tell if they were used. I checked them this morning! That would crack Daniel's alibi wide open."

"I admit I couldn't see him all the time," she said. "I wore my reading glasses, you know how large they are, what's three feet away is a blur unless I take them off. But I heard him scrubbing—"

"Tapes, tapes, tapes!" I shouted, and leaped up and sped to the northeast tower door, leaving them agape behind me.

The key ring was in my purse. I went down the wall corridors as fast as I could, checking my little devices with the pocket flash, not bothering to replace them as I passed through the doors, both levels. In about a quarter hour I was back in the dining room, where the two young men had joined us. "Well?" said Sibella.

I shook my head. "No one but me, not today, not this week."

"You look disappointed," she said, shrewd as ever.

"It was a good thought," I said lamely.

"Why 'tapes, tapes, tapes'?" asked Pierce.

"Any sound can be taped and run off at any time. Sablecroft Hall's taught me that."

"I see," he said. "Voices, sounds of toil . . . yes."

"What's this all about?" asked Sherry irritably.

"Nothing that's brought us to any conclusion," Sibella said.

I looked at Daniel, aware that I was wrenchingly disappointed at not having broken his alibi; feeling a traitor to him, my capering, loving faun. Knowing something else, something I didn't like—that my disappointment might indeed mean that I was in love with Sheridan Todd, who may have killed his former wife not two hours before.

I couldn't eat a bite of the food that Belle brought, but managed two glasses of milk. We separated and I went to my room, trailed by a glum Micajah, subdued by that uncanny instinct that tells an animal when the world has gone wrong. I lay down and instantly fell asleep, to waken at 8:30, numbed with lying motionless so long. I changed clothes and went downstairs, leaving the cat.

They were all in the great hall. I sat down with them. We were for the most part silent, with short bursts of erratic conversation on a dying palm in the western grove, the need for more canned goods to be laid in, the absence of Belle McNabb since she'd served us.

"I made her take the evening off," said Sibella, and called out suddenly, as if to God, "What will we do? What? Sherry, only you and Belle aren't exonerated by anyone. There's reason to believe that Wendy was in cahoots with the cowardly rascal who was after me, who likely killed her to shut her mouth. I don't suspect you for a moment—"

"Nor do I," said Pierce loyally.

"Nor I," Daniel added. "Not a whit, old lad."

"Leaving our Laurel to eye me askance alone," said Sherry. "Poor Laurel. Too bad to put you in such a fix." He did not say it banteringly, but quite frankly and somberly. "I'd clear myself if I could, but I can't."

"It was a simple, dreadful accident, nothing more," said Pierce Poole. "The police think so, and they aren't fools."

"They don't know what's gone before. We do." Sherry leaned forward and took my hand. "I did not kill her. I promise you I'm speaking the truth."

I looked into his steady eyes, and could not believe him, however I longed for the chance. "I'm not the police," I said. Inadequate! I felt his fingers flinch as he withdrew them from mine.

"We may know more when we find out what's on the tapes in that box," Pierce suggested.

"There won't be anything but movies, we all know that," Daniel said, his face desolate.

I walked across and threw back the rug and showed them the movable square in the terrazzo that I'd discovered on the night of Felicity's effigy. I pulled it up and stepped on it so that the kitchen door swung open. Now Pierce and Sibella knew just about all that I knew, and the others nearly as much. Despite my impression that I had enough data with which to solve the mystery, I began to think it was beyond my intellect, and one of them might see what I could not.

"Who stood there, that night?" asked Sherry.

"Wendy, wasn't it?" said Daniel.

"Yes," I said.

"Then there's our answer," said Sherry. "She pulled the stunts. Wendy did it all—prepared to loosen the chandelier, everything—and then Wendy had a fall. She couldn't foresee dry rot and so she died. There's only one thing wrong. Wendy wasn't capable of murder, or attempted murder, or even thoughts of murder." His voice, louder than usual, was utterly sure. "One of us is, obviously. But never Wendy."

Sibella sighed. "Laurel, dear, may I violate a confidence and tell them what you confided to me and Pierce this afternoon?"

"I will." It had better all come out. I repeated as nearly as I could recollect all that the girl had said to the whispering voice, as well as its replies. I mentioned my theory of Wendy staging that scene, talking to a tape player, and her early visit to my bedroom carrying the misshapen knife.

"I stick to my opinion," Sherry told me. "Vague streak of shabby malice, yes. Potential of spooking a girl of whom she was jealous, perhaps. Capability of killing, even hurting—*no!* Absolutely not!" He sank back on the sofa. "Having condemned himself to intensified suspicion, the fool retires into his folly."

"No, no, dear old boy," said Pierce, blustering, "we don't credit for an instant that you'd—"

"Who would? Pierce, don't play the Second Fool. One at a time was enough, even for Shakespeare."

"How do we find out?" Pierce intoned, pale and ill-looking. "When will this all be finished and done with?"

We stared at one another. The hush grew and grew until, caught by an *outré* fancy, I thought I heard old Gilbert begin to whirl in his grave . . . it was the distant air-conditioner. The statues observed us from the corner of their glass and plaster eyes. In the distance, even von Stroheim watched through his monocle. I wished I had never seen a copy of the *Library Journal,* never answered an ad, never left Connecticut, never heard the names of Todd and Cavanaugh, Poole and Abbott and Callingwood, McNabb.

"An early bed's the best idea," said Sibella out of her thoughts, breaking the silence. "Warm tub, hot milk, aspirin, and a dull book." She arose. "God rest her," she said quietly. "I don't believe that anyone's said that yet."

Pierce repeated it, and we all trailed out, turning off the lights as we passed them. I shut the bedroom door and bolted myself away from horror.

I soaked in the bath and got into bed, leaving the reading lamp on. Relaxed to some degree, I thought through the afternoon once more, and then through the time since I'd arrived here. When the clock said midnight, I slung on a robe and sidled into the hall. Tiny night lights at the base of the walls gave glow enough to show my way. Barefoot I passed Felicity's vacant room, Daniel's, Sherry's, to stop at Wendy's. I tried the door: unlocked. Turning the knob gently, I went in, eased the door shut and bolted it without noise. I groped in blackness till I found the wall switch, and turned on the ceiling light, which was pink and dim. Realizing too late that anyone staring out his window would see its reflection on the white pebbled roof of the kitchen below, I hurried to pull down the blinds, which were dark blue and nearly opaque.

I searched, ignorant of what I expected to find, working at the command of instinct. I went through both her closets, dipping into pockets, shifting the hangers, feeling along the backs of shelves and down in the corners. I carefully explored her two enormous chests of drawers, the bedside stand, the bookcases empty but for statuettes that she'd made, I presumed, when she'd been bored and had no life-size work on hand. Under the bed I went, and upward from the floor till between springs and mattress I found a little silver revolver with five bullets in the cylinder, which I dropped into my robe pocket, thinking it might come in handy. An almost characterless room, except for the clothing which was very Wendylike.

I went into the bathroom and opened the medicine cabinet. Carefully, for here I was separated from Sherry's room by only the wall, I took everything out and scrutinized it before returning it to the glass shelves. The last items were a bottle of black dye and a tube of mascara-style tint, like a thick mechanical pencil, dark as pitch, too large for lashes or brows. I stared at these for a long time. Then I replaced them, glanced around, found nothing else, and turning off the pink radiance, I left, closing in the dead girl's room with its memories and its ghost and its terrible silence, and I fled down the hall to my own place.

Next morning Sibella phoned an extermination company, and for two days Daniel guided their man around the Hall, probably amazing him with the hidden ways and spiral staircases. He did find more bad wood, due again to dry rot; no termites, luckily, but an enormous gray nest of red paper wasps in the southwest tower where they'd come in through a small lancet window and built their haven unnoticed, high under a wooden console. I have a dread of wasps, and was glad to hear he'd destroyed the nest and its inhabitants with an evil-smelling spray.

I received the impression that the exterminator was crestfallen, in such a huge old place, that he hadn't produced an infection of termites, or at least of silverfish and booklice, considering the tons of paper we were housing.

"We've secured the stable door," said Sibella to me, "but the poor mare has gone forever. Well, perhaps it *was* accidental, as the Medical Examiner has decided. His office person called me this morning. I had Wendy sent to a crematory."

"She won't be laid out?"

"Certainly not. We never are. Her ashes will be laid where Gilbert's rest, and Felicity's and Constance's and so on. There's a small mausoleum back beyond the pool."

"Is that legal?"

"How the dickens should I know? Who's going to tell me that we can't have our own tomb on our own grounds?"

"No one, I'm sure. Will there be religious ceremonies?"

"Of a sort. We'll all go down there when the ashes have come home. It's expected, though I disapprove of making a fuss over what's left when one goes on. Smacks of savagery, fear of reprisals, medieval superstition . . . you'll come too, of course."

"Yes."

"All we Sablecrofts will attend."

I didn't remind her that I was a Warrick and a Vane. She had absorbed me into her family, I thought from loneliness.

"So the M.E. judged it accidental," said Sherry at dinner that evening, his voice harsh and scornful. "Did they play the tapes yet, I wonder?"

"And returned them," said Pierce. "The verdict on *them* was 'nothing but old movies.' I'll play them myself, but . . . Sherry, you must not disdain the police, they made a thorough investigation and the pattern of an accident was clear." He looked weary and sagging. "It's only to us that the open hatch and the curious matter of the tapes in the attic would be suspicious."

"I don't disdain the police. I only hope they're right. Otherwise, we haven't come to the end of things."

I contemplated trying to explain those two points to Sergeant Quarterstaff. He had seemed a sensitive and concerned man. Now that I was over the initial shock, I might be able to make my terrors and suspicions sound sensible to him.

"What are we to do?" demanded Sibella, investing the helpless question with more power than anyone else could have managed. It was like Elizabeth I saying, "What *am* I to do with you wicked people?"

"Lie-detector tests?" I said tentatively.

"Rubbish. I've read about 'em. Inconclusive. You can outwit the things—I forget how, shamming excitement or lying consistently. Wait till Pierce audits the tapes. Maybe there's something there."

"Maybe," repeated Sherry, and it sounded like an oath.

Meanwhile, there was life to be plowed through, until the impact of the girl's death had worn off or she'd been avenged. And being tired of typing cards to which I couldn't bring enthusiasm or interest, I signaled to Daniel to wait till everyone else had left. I said then, "Got your riddle solved, Danny Boy," as lightly as I could. "Shall we go and try it?"

"What a silly question!" he retorted, bounding to his feet, the old Daniel again.

He opened the timbers with the great lever, I sat opposite with my back against the outer wall and an arm slung over the neck of the black dog, who'd come with us. The beam of the trouble light threw sharp forbidding shadows across the sea-green wall. "How did you try 'Sablecroft'—what sequences?"

"Alternate rights and lefts, alternate lefts and rights. All turns right, all turns left."

"And that's all?"

"Two rights to two lefts; two rights to one left; I have a list somewhere. . . ."

"Well, I thought of another order, by accident, some days ago," I said. "One of the movies we saw suggested it. It's left, left, left, right, left."

"What witch's ritual is that?"

"An old marching cadence they used to sing out when they were drilling recruits or whatever they did in the World War One times. Maybe they still do, I wouldn't know. But Granddad used to hum me to sleep with it. Very soporific. And when Gilbert built this monstrosity and ordered his lock made, every kid in town must have been playing war and bawling that out. It's natural."

"I know it now. From the movies," he said, looking faintly ashamed. "Sorry."

"Forgiven. Try it." I told him to start turning the big shiny steel knob left until he came to *S*, pause, then continue left, and so on. He tried it and began to giggle weakly as he blundered.

"Count cadence for me, honey."

I did so. "Left to *S*, left to *A*, left to *B*, right to *L*, left to *E* . . ."

He finished it on the *T*. He tugged with all his might on the dial, which was the only possibility for a knob, then shoved against the barrier, in the middle and on each end. "No good. I didn't hear any foul clicks, and the miserable door is still clamped as shut as a filthy oyster!"

Before I could answer, my dog turned his head and growled, and out of the dark padded the harlequin, head low. Challenger heaved to his feet, solid menace, jealous of his privileged presence here with us.

"We did close the panel behind us?" said Daniel, frowning.

"Yes. Hello," I said, and called the dog by some name or other. He sat down on the other side of me, but the black stood peering into the unlit depths of the passage. "Daniel," I said, as the steel-blue Dane came in sight to join us. "What is this?"

"Some jackass being funny. Saw us come in and rounded up the dogs to pester. The full treatment, here comes the black-faced fawn."

The fourth monster hove up from the night beyond the left-hand curve. "Daniel," I said, my flesh chilling, "what if whoever trained Challenger to threaten me has trained all these to attack? What if we're in a trap?"

"Sherry?" he asked, his voice low.

"Or Pierce or Belle! We wouldn't have a chance if it's been done. They could tear us to pieces."

"Be quiet, your voice is scared. And don't move." Walking deliberately, he went down the corridor. "Come," he ordered them, "come here!" They all followed him. Shortly I heard a door slam violently in the distance and Daniel returned, wiping his face with a handkerchief. "Wow!" he said. "I don't want to try that again. They kept leering at me, hanging back—I guess they smelled the fear on me. That's a lot of muscle and tooth."

I admitted my own quick dread.

"Devil with it, what are we to do with this pea-green incorruptible?"

"*Sea*-green incorruptible!" I laughed, a blessed relief. "Why don't we try lifting it up where the outer door went? That's the sensible direction."

He cupped both hands under the dial. Taking the trouble light from its hook, I held it so that the whole door was ablaze. Daniel heaved up, and the big green panel, moving surely on oiled ball bearings, surged aloft with a whoosh and then a subdued thunk as it hit the limit. I saw a glint of reflection from a silvery wire stretched vertically on our left. This snapped with a thin musical twang, and right in front of us the most colossal rocking horse in the world began to roll back and forth violently, its mottled enamel hide shining and its crimson mouth gaping hideously wide in a deep grin framed by broad square teeth. Somewhere in its interior a toy siren went off, rose in volume, and ran down. Gradually the giant rocking nag slowed and came to a shivering halt.

Daniel swore. "One of the old geezer's oh-so-funny amusement-park tricks! I don't mind admitting that it jolted the daylights out of me, love."

"Me too." I have never liked objects that are a great deal larger than they ought to be, and the titanic brute with its vivid, clashing colors and insane mute laugh put me off from the whole secret room for a minute. Its globular pink eyes were especially repulsive. If that outrageous creation had once been a child's toy, the poor kid must have used a ladder to mount it. Easily twice the size of a merry-go-round horse, it gave me the fidgets. Somehow it carried a psychic chokedamp of old ill memories, and the illusion of a mind worked away behind the shiny pink eyes.

"Come on, Daniel. It was only a so-called waggery," I said, taking his arm, angry that my breaths should be fast and short. We walked past the dismal being into the room shaped like a quarter moon with the tips squared off. It was some seven feet deep by ten wide; larger than I'd anticipated. Down at one end, crammed into the small space, was an old table of raw wood, and in a rickety chair before it, its back turned squarely toward us, sat a skeleton.

I held the light steadily on it, and Daniel said, "Don't be afraid, Laurel, it's just a set piece."

"Long time since a fake skeleton made me shriek," I said boldly. The ridiculous thing *had* startled me, of course, but then so would a stuffed elk or almost anything else, after the hobbyhorse. I edged in back of the horse—it nearly filled the depth of the room—and went to the small tableau. I leaned over and looked at the skeleton. Then I began to laugh.

"Don't go hysterical on me," he said, coming at once. Then he too laughed. "The old buzzard!"

Crushed against the front of the skull, where it could not be seen from the middle of the room, was an artificial custard pie. Gobs and sprays of white and yellow plaster filling dripped down the bony chin and splattered the front of the ribs.

"Straight out of the days when a fat man falling on a banana peel in a silent comedy could start a theaterful of people roaring," Daniel said. "Happy, silly nineteen twenty-three! You will admit it broke you up."

"Oh yes, but what an amount of money went into hiding this piece of schoolboy farce!" I shook my head. "In real dollars, back then, to have that dial and door mechanism installed . . . it would have kept a family of four for a year." Our multiple shadows fell weirdly across the walls as I moved the trouble light. *"Anything* for a chortle. Your great-grandfather was a sadistic fiend, if this is what you've been hunting for a lifetime."

"He had his laughs. I wonder if he's watching us now, chuckling, with the flames trickling out of his ears."

I touched the fleshless upper arm nearest me. A quill pen was glued between the fingers of the right hand, and a couple of sheets of paper lay under it. "It's real," I said. "It's a real skeleton."

Daniel pulled the paper free and read, "Boo! Congratulations. But this isn't it."

"Isn't the room you're hunting, I suppose," I said. "What's the other one say?"

"It's in some foreign lingo." He showed it to me. In the scrawl of a dying man, which had been intended, obviously, for the skeleton's, I read, *"Discite Mori."*

"What's that?"

"Latin." I shrugged. "I've forgotten a lot of mine, I can't translate it, but *mori* has something to do with death."

"Cheerful." He gazed at the walls, which were covered with framed mottos and pictures. "We'd better read everything, there may be clues. But I think the place is only a joke on us."

I looked at the skeleton again, who had sat in this black silent room down all the nights and days of half a century, symbolically blind from the Fatty Arbuckle confection spread across his ghastly chops. The "joke" was on a par with those of a legendary studio head of whom Grandfather had told me: "It was impossible to work for him and do justice to your talent and dignity," he'd said. "The man had a sense of humor composed entirely of carpet tacks, joy buzzers, and sneezing powder." Yet that crude and primitive man had pioneered in the young industry, and turned out dozens of still-famous pictures, and had retired with honor.

Hollywood had been a strange, coarse place, but now and then, as in Yeats' 1916 Dublin, a terrible beauty had been born.

Which was more than I could say, at this point, for Sablecroft Hall in St. Petersburg.

"A grisly kind of clownery," I said to Daniel. "More of a joke on this old scrag than on us. It's not pleasant. I wouldn't want *my* bones used like that. I wonder who they first belonged to? Who lived and died outside them?"

Daniel mopped his face, wet from the hot stale air, and grinned at me. "Someone who doesn't care now whether they're laid in hallowed ground or set up for a comical surprise. I'd rather my framework was used to give someone a fright now and then, than be wasted in a damp casket!"

"Not me. That Latin—" I began, dimly recalling it.

"Discite Mori," said Sherry, and we both jumped. He was leaning in the doorway, watching us. *"Learn to die.* They used to paint it in the corners of pictures a few hundred years ago. They were very hipped on ending well, and since they generally did so in their twenties, it was an admirable effort to make." He shoved himself off the jamb and came in. "There's a light in here, if the bulb's still good. Ah," he said as the room sprang into stark clarity all around us, "that's better than your burning cage, Laurel. Put it out before you broil your fingers." He lounged over. We were fairly cramped in the narrow end of the room. "Old Gilbert had depths to him," Sherry went on, as we remained dumb. "The pie in the face—not a mere gag. You must treat Old Man Death as though he worked on the Sennett lot, one of the boys; an awesome Keystone Cop. Laugh at him, at least when it's *your* turn to die. Pretty good moral. You could almost believe that our modern trickster had absorbed that lesson and got it wrong: laugh at the deaths of other people." He reached and clicked off the trouble light in my hand.

Daniel shouted, "Have you known about this place all along?"

"For a year or so."

"And you never told me? You let me waste my time—"

"I let you have the fun that I had, solving Gilbert's riddle. The sequence of rotation stumped me for a month, but I finally picked it up from a movie, Cagney I think it was. You know the Sablecroft primary directive, man! Never spoil anyone's diversion by squealing. Never tattle on anyone. If you intend to hit me, Daniel, consider that I'll then knock you through this wall into the dining room."

"You're right, but it'd almost be worth it. Are these things, the bone rack here and the horse, *all?"*

"And the framed bits of wisdom. You ought to damn well thank me for finding it first, son." He went and draped an arm over the high saddle of the monster. "He was rigged to give you a lot worse than you got. The wire that breaks when the door slides up sets him off, but before I caught it, instead of rocking and whistling at you, the broncho spat a stream of indelible ink straight out, to ruin your clothes and stain your skin for a week. I couldn't bear to replace it, so I put in the siren. I'm kindly. You ought to thank me, you ungrateful lout. That's a silk shirt you're wearing, and Laurel's dress is too fine to be ruined."

"Gilbert was of his time," I said. "Ink! Itching powder and chewing gum full of pepper. Exploding cigars."

"But nothing hurtful, except to dignity and clothing. Now study the walls, children. They'll repay the time."

"Another moral lesson from the mighty mogul?" asked Daniel, pleading with his eyes and voice. "Just that? No treasures, fabulous films, gilt-edged securities?"

"There's the hobbyhorse. An heirloom."

"That spat ink," I said.

"Yes, that's how I located this room," said Sherry. "There was a stain across the rug just outside, so I figured there'd be something *inside*. There are two now, one old and faded, the other fresher. That one was mine."

I wriggled out between them and peered at the stains. Sure enough, they'd come shooting into the corridor from within, the shape of the splashes gave that away. I felt stupid beyond redemption.

"Great-grandfather caught Felicity with it, Lord knows when, and she refilled the bulb and set the trap for an encore, which nailed me. She did that after a certain amount of adding to the decor."

"What's that mean?" asked Daniel angrily.

"The long wall was Gilbert's. The wall on our left was Felicity's. And the wall to the right is mine. I consider them all worth studying."

Gilbert's wall was neatly covered with black-framed sayings and quotations, four parallel lines of glassed cardboard, identical in size and shape. "Say them aloud," Sherry suggested, "for those who move their lips when they read."

I said, " 'Well, I got to go make faces.' Peter Lorre."

"I like that best," said Sherry, "since it was said by a splendid, dedicated actor as he was about to practice his craft before a camera. Think about it."

" 'We who play, who entertain for a few years, what can we leave that will last?' Ethel Barrymore," I read. " 'A tree is a tree, a rock is a rock—shoot it in Griffith Park.' Carl Laemmle. 'The kind of jackass who likes the movies as they are is the man who keeps them as they are.' H. L. Mencken."

I went on down the rows. Some material was serious, some flippant, some surprising when the sources were considered. " 'The public is entitled to a good show.' Errol Flynn." Then I read the last, and disagreed with Sherry. "Here's the best, here's the whole idea that Gilbert wanted to broadcast from his wall. 'Movies and the theater aren't life. They're only part of it.' "

"Who said that?" asked Daniel. "Laurel Vane?"

"Joseph Cotten. I always knew I adored him, and wasn't sure why until now." I turned to them. "Don't you see that Gilbert, who founded the clan and the way of life you've all embraced, agreed with Mr. Cotten and me wholeheartedly? Movies are pleasant, movies can be wonderful, but there's *life* beyond them! He made this wall, had these sayings printed, as clear-as-day signposts to a wisdom that he feared you didn't have. Oh, not you two, he died when you were kids; but his daughters and their daughters! I bet there are twenty other rooms snugged away in this pile, every one concocted to teach his family a lesson!"

"But is this *all?*" cried Daniel. "A lesson, a lecture?"

"Maybe it's enough," Sherry said mildly. "You'll admit, each sinks in deeper than if you'd found it written in a commonplace book. I tell you this, every time I've felt desolate about Wendy, I unwillingly remember this ridiculous room with the pie and the skull . . . don't take death too somberly. Well, I take hers seriously, but maybe the thought of him," he jerked a thumb at the skeleton, "keeps me from wallowing in regret as I might. And this collection of quotes says something that isn't as universal as the other, God knows, but it also stabs into the guts of our noble family, and I like it. I thought of it when Laurel was lecturing the other night, and half-decided she must have been in here already! Yes, I appreciate all Gilbert's work."

"I'd like to sock him in the face with a pie this minute," snapped

Daniel, and then grinned. "He'd like that reaction, too! The old cuss!"

"Felicity's wall came next. I imagine a good many years after Gilbert's death. Go and read it out, Laurel."

I walked to it. All the aphorisms here were of different sizes, colors, and mediums. One was a sampler in lovely needlework, another black ink on delicate water color, a third crocheted on burlap with bright golden thread. There was one in oils and one simply written in a spidery italic handwriting, something like Sibella's, on a sheet of very old browned parchment. They were scattered over the surface of the wall in an apparently random pattern that only a true artist could have achieved. "How do you know it was Felicity? Why not Sibella?"

"The artwork is utterly beyond Sibella. Read."

" 'I've never done a film I'm proud of.' Stewart Granger. 'There's only one thing that can kill the movies, and that's education.' Will Rogers. 'The legendary wonders of Hollywood were half mirage and half bad writing.' Ben Hecht." I looked at the men. "Her choices are rougher and less amiable about the cinema, I must say."

"I don't know why," said Daniel blankly. "She was as involved with movies as any of us."

"Her character was—different from Gilbert's," said Sherry.

" 'Acting is a neurotic, unimportant job. I'm only in it for the dough.' Marlon Brando. 'Roller skating and acting—once you learn how to do them, they're neither stimulating nor exciting.' George Sanders. 'Being head of a studio is better than being a pimp.' Harry Cohn. Oh," I said, turning from it, "I don't like this wall! It's something like Gilbert's, but it's nasty."

"Yes," said Sherry, "though I believe Felicity thought she was only carrying on what Gilbert had begun. She didn't see it as a gentle reminder that the movies are not All. She saw it as digging into the hides of her family with a harpoon. She was not the most sensitive of women. Sorry, Daniel, but it's true."

"I don't understand how she could expend so much art and energy on anything that *Cohn* said," whispered her grandson. "She wasn't like this at all."

Sherry caught my eye and nodded imperceptibly. Felicity had been like that, he seemed to say. Plainly, it was true.

"Try the third wall," he said.

Here, under the large painted heading HOWEVER, were neatly printed framed quotations arranged haphazardly around a painting of Donald Crisp as General Grant in *The Birth of a Nation,* about which portrait there was a subtle wrongness that I didn't bother with at the time. I read aloud. " 'It is a fact that good pictures are made, from Mickey Mouse to *The Informer.*' Stephen Vincent Benét. 'The cinema has an extraordinary richness, an extraordinary range and vitality. We have just begun to study it.' Peter Wollen. Oh, Sherry, marvelous!"

"Have I vindicated us a little?"

"Yes. Sometimes I've forgotten these facts," I admitted, "in the welter of trivia and taped voices. . . . 'The cinema makes it possible to experience without danger all the excitement, passion, and desire that must be suppressed in a humanitarian society.' Carl Jung. There's rebuttal of Felicity with a vengeance!" I exclaimed, forgetting that she'd been Daniel's beloved grandmother. Glancing back, I saw that he was oblivious to us, reading her choice of references again. " 'Drama is life with the dull bits left out.' Alfred Hitchcock. Bully!" I went on till I'd finished Sherry's wall, and then peered again at Crisp as Grant. I saw it this time—a bottle on the table at which he sat, its label reading "Old Panther Sweat," and Mr. Crisp's narrowed eyes ever so slightly crossed.

"Another feeble prank, like the monocle in von Stroheim's eye out there," I said, scornful.

"Don't cast stones, you whited sepulcher," said Sherry. "The eyes and bottle were Crisp's idea. Gilbert painted him on the set of the picture in nineteen fourteen. It was a serious study. Then Crisp said, 'Grant wasn't known as an abstemious man, Gil, old chap,' and Great-grandfather sketched in the bottle. That tickled Crisp so much that the eyes were unfocused to boot."

"I didn't know Gilbert painted," I said. "This really ought to be hanging out in the Hall, then."

"It was his talent that trickled down to some of us . . . the von Stroheim is his too."

"What idiot stuck the real monocle in the eye?"

"Herr von Stroheim," said Sherry.

"Oh dear," I said. "Was it?" I smiled uncertainly. "That was one of the first things that convinced me everyone in the place was loopy."

"Von Stroheim donated one of his own monocles for the painting. He thought very highly of the result."

"I'm glad." I stared at this odd room. "Could there be secret cupboards at either end?" I said. "There's room for little triangular cubbyholes. Did you check?"

"No. You might do that one of these days, Daniel. Gilbert might have hidden something of value besides ideas in the place. Come to think of it, you might look into the horse's mouth."

"Have you?"

He inclined his head. "But that hiding wasn't Gilbert's doing, it was Felicity's."

"What? What? What's in the horse's mouth?"

"Her diaries. In the open throat you'll find the end of a wire, attached to a staple behind the tongue. In the barrel, hanging at the end of the wire in an expensive silver mesh bag—Felicity stinted herself as little as her sister does—are diaries covering sixteen years."

Daniel leaped to plunge his arm into the awful maw of the wooden beast. "And this godforsaken nag's been sitting here—"

"While you tapped on walls for echoes?" said Sherry. "That's right. I imagined that it would eventually occur to you to investigate the ink stains; after which you would realize that small things can be secreted in smallish places. And the horse, which is nearly eighty years old, has a capacious belly. Surely you remember Felicity getting high on champagne and telling us how she used to clamber up into the saddle when she was a tot, and how she'd love to do it again, even at her age, if only the horse hadn't vanished when they moved to the Hall? She knew then where it was hidden, waiting . . . for me, as it turned out. With a gullet full of ink."

I said, "Things are seldom what they seem, as I was told when I arrived. A horse is a squid is a safe-deposit box."

"What are you two maundering about?" Daniel cried, reeling in the wire and staring at the long, lumpy silver-metal sack on the end of it. "Todd, you knew I wanted to read these diaries!"

"To the contrary, you never mentioned 'em."

Daniel frowned. "Yes, I think you're right, I didn't tell you, did I? Sorry, old boy."

"Quite all right, old fellow."

"Up the Empire," I said, "and form a square, the Fuzzies are coming. You sound like *Bengal Lancer*."

"Well!" said Daniel, hefting the big bag in both hands. "You two won't mind shutting your room up, will you? I want to sort these out." He disappeared into the dusk of the passage.

"So it's our room now," said Sherry. "Poor Daniel, I wonder what he expects to find. Not what he *will* find, I daresay. Shall we shut up shop?"

"May I take General Grant for exhibition to the others? No one else is going to go through what we have to get in here."

"Unless it's the next generation. Yes, take him, we'll hang him in the great hall."

"What next generation?"

"I don't know. Wendy gone . . . we have nearly reached a dead end, haven't we?"

"Was she killed, Sherry?"

"I think so. Don't you?"

"Yes." An embarrassment lay between us. "Poor Wendy. Do you feel her loss awfully?" I asked, a little timid.

"Not for myself. Pity for her. I take it you want the truth."

"Always, thanks."

"Time to go home to your cat," he said, and turned out the light. We left the room behind us, Sherry pulling down the green wall and then moving the beam that hid it behind its barricade. "A good room, that," he said. "I never really searched hard for others. I wonder how many more there are, scattered through the house? With gems of wisdom and heavy-handed lessons in them. Still, a good room, a good lecture. You want to ask if I read Felicity's diaries. I did. When a person hides that sort of intimate record where she obviously means to *leave* it, then she intends it to be read. If she'd been alive, naturally I wouldn't have done so."

"Are they valuable?"

"Only to a Sablecroft. Who came to visit, why Felicity thought them dull or stupid or high-handed or madly attractive, that breed of history. Interesting stuff on directors and actors—allowing for her biases. She was heavily prejudiced in favor of your grandfather, Alfred Vane."

"May I read them, then?"

"Ask Daniel, he's her direct descendant."

I asked him if he'd let the dogs in to annoy us, which he denied. "You or Daniel didn't close the door firmly enough, I'd say, and it was nosed open. You have a tendency to leave doors ajar." He turned harsh without warning. "When you reach your room, bolt yourself in, and don't neglect it!" he snapped, and left me gaping after him.

THREE MORE DAYS WERE GONE. I'D BARELY SEEN DANIEL, IN HIS room deciphering his grandmother's barbwire penmanship in the sixteen small pink diaries. He'd shown me one of them the first day, so excited he stammered. Sherry was constantly around, having given up his outside work to lounge aimlessly and scowl. Pierce was gloomy and withdrawn, while Sibella was outwardly herself, but in the manner of a dedicated actress grinding doggedly through a play that she'd grown sick of. And Belle was always watching from the shadows.

Whatever had been festering in this house had not healed with the killing of Wendy. The infection still hung in the air we breathed, in the coldness of our air-conditioned fortress and the stultifying hellfire breath that puffed in viciously when a door was opened, even a door to a passage. Once I toured the corridors around her apartment for Sibella, at her request, to find my warning signs unbroken; no one had been there but me since Wendy's death. I didn't check them again, because I had almost fainted this time from the stifling, sweltering air that was like tangible malevolence.

In bed with Micajah on the pillow, I made my choice. I wanted to run; no stubborn curiosity or resentment was strong enough to overcome that sensible desire. I *ought* to have run months ago. Job and pride meant nothing now that I'd looked on my dead. (Poor Wendy, how amazed she'd be to learn that I thought of her as mine!) I'd promised her to stick to it, to expose her slayer. To remain in the Hall for that was only a form of pride, and the well-remembered look of her face going blue was enough to remind me that the better part of valor was to get out. Hardly an hour passed that I did not feel that rippling shudder that's supposed to tell you something's jumped over your grave; my nervous system was in a deplorable state. To collect my wages and slip away into nowhere was the only sane answer.

Of course, I couldn't do it. Let job, money, pride, reputation, and all slide into Tampa Bay and good riddance to them, but if I left that staunch, arrogant, magnificent and vulnerable old woman to wait for her violent finish, I would never look in a mirror with any comfort again. *Vulnerable,* the last word I'd have applied to her ordinarily, but the right word. Sherry had said it: Anyone can be killed.

And Sibella was alone, barring only me. There were four others here, yet who could she choose to be at her side day and night? Belle, her ancient friend? Belle was strong, but incredibly old, and not proven innocent. Pierce, Daniel, Sherry, all tougher than I, far better protectors, but all with innocence unverified and in dispute. She had four unknown quantities and one scared librarian.

How could any decent human being put her own safety above that of a threatened octogenarian?

And if I were attacked, I could fight in more ways than the murderer would imagine, and if I lifted my voice to its best shriek, two or three of the others should come running.

I made my choice, therefore, and then plan after plan until my restless tossing chased the cat off the bed to a calmer spot. I wished I had enough evidence to call my Sergeant Quarterstaff, but I didn't. It was up to me. I grew so cold thinking of that, I went and turned my thermostat up another notch.

Eventually I concocted a kind of sacrificial-goat scheme, the best I could contrive. If it didn't work, well, we were in one of those classic ridiculous situations where everyone knows that the killer will strike again, so at bedtime they go off to separate rooms. I would simply have to convince Sibella that I was going to share her bedroom, and stay beside her through each day, and wait.

However, I thought the idea would succeed. I had, after all, been the victim myself of several verbal and physical attacks. The house had menaced me since my arrival.

Somehow I managed to work through the following day, and although the great plan looked suicidal by daylight, I refined it and practiced my lines and took black Challenger for a walk around the house—inside, that is, and avoiding the passages—and finally dressed for dinner. Belle was serving it, as Pierce was too distracted these days to cook properly, so we were all in the dining room when I cleared my throat and said, louder than I'd intended, "We're in a screaming blizzard of nerves, and nobody dares to mention it nowadays, but I must. We hope that everything evil in this house ended with Wendy's death. But we remember that we hoped it would happen when Mrs. Callingwood changed her will, and it didn't. We all recognize, admit it or not, the atmosphere of hate and rage and doom. Even if no other cold-blooded act is done as long as we—as you—live here, the horror will never be expelled till the truth is known . . . who, why, everything."

"True," said Pierce heavily. "There's a spiritual miasma which cannot long support life as we know it. But if Wendy was the culprit and died by mischance—"

"No!" I shouted. "Every damn soul of us knows that's hogwash!"

Sibella, who I thought might be angered, said, "I agree," very strongly. "Pierce, did you listen to the tapes from the attic box?"

"Nothing in them but a random selection of movies."

Sherry watched me. "Does anyone have a clue to the answer? Do you? You seem so sure—"

"So am I," barked Sibella.

"We ought to share our ideas on this," nodded Pierce. "Laurel, have you any solid reason for denying Wendy's guilt?"

I looked slightly flustered. "Only what I told you all about hearing her talk to someone in Felicity's room, someone with"—I dropped my voice and threw the phrase away—"with dirty hands."

"Then I'm damned if I see how we can sleuth out the culprit," Daniel mused into the silence. "But you're right, the waiting is intolerable."

"Yet what can we *do?*" asked Pierce plaintively.

Belle, like a tiny statue against the far wall, her eyes glittering, said, "You can think!" She shrugged. "And that's about all, bar you call back all those cops."

"That's about it," I said. And I stood and walked out, forgetting to say good night to anyone.

I found Micajah asleep on the softest chair in the great hall, scooped him up, and carried him to the bedroom.

Within two or three minutes Sibella burst in, breathing rather hard, whether from emotion or the unaccustomed stairs I don't know. "You've done it now! Get your things together."

"Firing me without notice, Mrs. Callingwood?"

"Don't be thick. You'll have to sleep in my room, don't you see that?"

"After tonight I will."

"If *I* caught the dirty-hands reference, so did he. You've let it be known that you've narrowed it to Sherry and Daniel, haven't you? On purpose?"

"Yes. Unless I was speaking metaphorically."

"You weren't, and he'll know it. God," she said, "and I alibi Daniel. So you think it's definitely Sherry."

"I think nobody really alibis anybody. Don't worry, I'm ready for a confrontation with come-who-may."

"You? You're only a girl," she whispered, scornful. "How are you to protect yourself?"

"What would *you* do if you were told you're 'only a woman'? Raise the roof! The days of 'only a woman' are over for me, too. This is nineteen eighty."

"You woolly bleating lamb!" she exclaimed, lifting one eyebrow to its maximum. "Equality of the sexes doesn't automatically make you as sturdy and ruthless as a man!"

"Ssh, the walls have—"

"Yes, yes," testily. "Answer me, Laurel."

Recollecting that a low mumble does not carry as far or as clearly as a whisper, I mumbled. "Dad was a stunt man, he taught me a lot of tricks that I'll bet nobody else in this house can manage."

"That jujitsu or king foof or whatever they call the balderdash?"

"Not that intricate. Just where to hit and how to move if I'm attacked."

"And if he has a gun?"

"Then I have a gun."

"What?" She was really startled. "You never!"

"It was Wendy's. I found it in her room."

"Lord! Loaded?"

"Oh yes, but I won't kill anyone."

"I realize that, I'm aware of your character. You'd likely aim for a leg and shoot off his ear. Well, if you're grim set on going through with it, I may's well save my breath."

"That's right."

"You're a fool. Bless you, you buckra gal," she said. I hadn't heard that old word since Granddad left me. "You honestly think you know who it is?"

I shook my head. "If I did, I wouldn't go through this, I'd call Sergeant Quarterstaff. The 'dirty hand' reference was a shot in the dark. It eliminates Pierce and Belle, so if it *was* one of them, nothing will happen, they'll take it as a figure of speech. Otherwise," I muttered, "either Sherry or Daniel has to shut my mouth."

"And if Wendy's death was not arranged?"

"It was."

"You're so certain. Damn it! I'll stay with you."

"No."

She observed me, lynx-eyed, angry. "I don't take orders in my own domain, girl."

"Oh, Mrs. Callingwood, go to bed! I don't want you in any more danger than you have been," I said, my temper shortening to match hers. "This is a thing I must do, for you, yes, but for Wendy too."

"She was no friend of yours."

"She was a human being! Good night," I said irritably.

"Hang the brat! Good night. If poison gas is pumped into your room through a vent, or the ceiling drops on your face, don't come whining that nobody warned you," she said, and went out, slamming the door.

I went into the bathroom, had a quick shower, put on my dark blue Chinese pajamas, brushed my hair, wished for the first time in ages that I had a cigarette, and went back into the bedroom. The cat was staring at the bookcase. I saw that the tall, volume-weighted rack had been moved out catercornered from the wall. I slid Wendy's miniature silver revolver from where I'd hidden it between springs and mattress, checked on the cartridges again, aiming the gun at the floor and looking at the dull metal bases in the cylinder, and went to investigate. The spy-hole door was slightly ajar. I jerked it closed—the echoes must have scurried up and down the passage outside—and set myself to heave the unwieldy barrier back into place.

I knew instantly how it had been prodded away from the wall: Someone, during the past weeks, had sneaked in and fitted the bookcase with oiled casters. I could move it back and forth with one hand, even across the thick rug.

I refused to give anyone the satisfaction of listening to me search the room—I felt sure a mike had been planted, masquerading as a picture, knob, or book—so I ignored the possibility that something had been introduced through the hatch. I didn't really believe in hooded cobras, fragile glass pellets of deadly vapor, tarantulas or any of those Fu Manchu trappings, even in this madhouse, and Micajah would have found them anyway. I manhandled the dressing table over and smacked it against the bookcase, pinning it to the wall. There were no wheels on the table. The wicket was shut for the night.

Rain began to splatter on my windows. I pulled down the blinds, hearing a long low roll of thunder far away to the southwest. We were in for another summer storm.

I sat on the bed waiting. After a while I picked up the revolver and dropped it into the pocket of my pajamas. Lying down, I pushed two pillows together behind my head and stared into space until from sheer sorrow I closed my eyes and fell fast asleep.

Some time later I awoke, got up and turned off the lights, and slid under the sheet and went dead off again, though I hadn't meant to.

I was running through a labyrinth, the walls of thickly tangled yew trees, going left or right without volition at that strange, infinitely slow pace of a runner in dreams. I heard Micajah calling for me, and I could not find him, and I was crying, crying, because he was all the family I had in this world.

Then I came awake in the darkness and heard him mew, his "why doesn't someone help a poor cat in distress" call, faint and miserable with a question mark at the end of the sound.

I spoke his name; he might be having a nightmare himself. The thunder was cannonading outside, the rain tattooing on the glass. "It's all right," I said, groping for the lamp switch, "it's all right, Micajah." I clicked the switch, and it was not all right at all—the electricity had failed.

My white cat mewed again.

"Coming!" I said, untangling myself from a sheet that was alive and malignant, as though this were an M. R. James ghost story. "The lights will come on in a minute, they always do," I reassured him, trying not to think of Sibella's warning, back when the rainy season started, that sometimes the power was off for hours. I blundered my way to the door and found the main switch and shoved it on, which left me still in the dark. Then I had the happy thought of hurrying to the windows, bruising myself on a chair and a small table as I went, and yanking the three blinds so that they flew up rattling on their rollers, admitting the eerie illumination of the lightning. The sky was totally black—if there was a moon, it would do me as much good as a rubber ball beyond that overcast—but the lightning was frequent and gloriously white.

"Mmrrowrr?" weakly.

"Micajah!" I shouted. "Where are you?" I thought of my little flashlight, jerked open the drawer of the nightstand, groped in the odds and ends, paused, scrabbled more frantically; it was gone. I knew I'd put it in there. I turned the drawer upside-down on the bed. Lightning's blaze showed me no flashlight. It had been stolen. I stood quite still and thought; stumbled to the dresser and searched its top, then the left drawer, the only one in which I might have dropped it. Nothing.

I went marginally crazy, and hurtled around my room like an axed chicken, fumbling in pockets, the depths of chair cushions, anywhere that a pencil flash could have slid from sight, all the time knowing quite well that it had been in the nightstand and that my bold and silly plan was now shot to blazes. Then, standing by the door, I dropped to my knees and listened. The next mew came on the heels of a great bell-peal of thunder.

"Oh, you dumb cat!" I said. Somehow while I was asleep he'd escaped from the room and slunk off, and was now back, cowed by darkness and the resounding anger of the local storm gods, begging to be let in with me.

I put my hand on the doorknob to turn it, remembering that the lock and bolt had not been set.

The knob was already turning as I touched it.

I don't know whether I crawled or rolled away, or somersaulted backward. All I'm sure of is that I wound up in a shuddering heap against the foot of the bed, and had to force myself with what little brain I had left not to creep under it like a child.

The door opened and there was a scuffling noise and then a slam. I pawed wildly for the gun in my pajama pocket and it wasn't there. I could see nothing. Someone or something was breathing nearby with a thin wheezy sound. Not Micajah, thrust kindly in by a friend. He didn't whiffle like that.

Faintly I heard his mew—still in the hall—and scrambled to my feet, determined to hit with the edge of a stiffened hand anything that touched me. Or bring up my knee, and claw for the eyes.

At that instant everything froze into a tableau that would have appealed to old Gilbert himself: in the prolonged light of a multiple burst of bolts, great thick brilliant shafts blasting straight down at the earth outside, I saw my room as clearly and yet weirdly as by the repeated vibrations of a strobe light, and in its center the enormous dog, staring right at me with ears pricked forward and powerful body tensed. I didn't know which it was, the black or the blue. I have never been so terrorized by anything else in my life. I'd become used to the black beast. Had I been sure it was he I think I might have handled the fear to some degree, but the blue was not a friend—hardly an acquaintance—and the black *had* once pursued me. . . .

It was as though the malignant spirit of this house had transported me to the waste of the Grimpen Mire, where the spectral hound with its "flaming jaws and blazing eyes" stood waiting for me as for a Baskerville. The lights on the great head were only the vagaries of the reflections on his flat, short-haired coat, and I suppose that my own eyes must have glowed horridly too in that protracted vast flickering from beyond the windows; but it was no moment for rational thought.

He took a step toward me, whining.

"Stay," I husked out. "Stay, good boy." I edged sideways, saw my little revolver on the rug where I'd lost it, darted to pick it up and run my thumb over the back of the cylinder and feel the cartridges still there. The animal took another slow step in my direction.

"Stay!" I cried, babbling by now. "Sit, stop, no, no!"

Then I leaped past him, pulled the door open and whirled myself into the hall, fumbling out the big key as I went, closed it behind me and locked it. I leaned against the wall, aware of my whole body dank with sweat, shaking and whimpering like an unsophisticated, credulous savage in some primitive grotto with the sabertooth tigers prowling beyond.

It was dreadfully black here, for even the double row of tiny night lights had gone out and the hallway was without windows. I'd thought that Micajah's shining white coat would be visible, but nothing broke the coal-cellar dark. Fighting the panic, I took as deep a breath as I could, dropped the gun into my pocket and the key beside it. I had the urge to hold the weapon free in my hand, but it was a deadly thing, a last resort, and I was so charged with adrenalin that I'd be a raging lunatic if someone touched me. Even with the fear upon me I shrank from shooting an innocent person.

Micajah uttered his sorrowful call again, down the hall near the head of the balcony stairs.

"Come here, you blithering numbskull," I called. The thunder was just as terrible out here away from the external walls, particularly one mighty roll that began like the approach of tumbrels far down in the east and went surging from horizon to horizon above my head, exactly the sound of vast lumpy wheels of wood and iron crushing cobblestones. "They're fetching the king," I said half-aloud, "to bring him to Madame La Guillotine." I wondered where the *tricoteuses* sat, who knitted and counted the falling heads. Above the low-hung clouds over Sablecroft Hall?

Oh, it was a jolly night, full of cheerful pictures, from *The Hound of the Baskervilles* to *A Tale of Two Cities*.

Mew? . . .

Oh, my poor terrified cat! I set off down the corridor with left hand brushing the wall to guide me and right extended with clawed fingers ready. The place was like a tarn full of ink. You could almost taste the blackness. I must be close to the steps by now. I waited, looking out toward the great hall. Firmly—if that word can be applied to me at that moment—I endeavored to concentrate on the architecture of the place. I'd lived here long enough, I ought to know where the windows were.

There weren't any in the great hall. Or were there? Of course not. I was giving way to hysteria. I must not. I'd set a trap for a killer, playing the bait myself, but he wasn't a celestial murderer who could arrange to come for me with lightning in his hand and a vast cloak of night to cast over the house. He'd spirited Micajah out of the room to entice me into the hall, shoved the dog in to terrify me, but he was only a human being. No reason to be dismayed by thunder and darkness. I was tougher than he could know.

There were *no* windows in the great hall, of course. I'd noticed that on the first day, a hundred years ago. There were four tall windows in the dining room, north wall, opposite the arch that led from the great hall. Lightning should throw some glow or flash as far as the collection of statuary below me. I waited, watching darkness, my long-nailed fingers held out like talons.

The glare came soon again, and I saw as though in an impressionist painting the vast room spread out below me. I hurried over while the light lasted and gripped the balcony rail in a clutch like a closing trap, leaning over it and calling into the sudden return of night, "Micajah? Come puss, puss!"

The whining cry came from below. All cats are maniacs, they run from help and complain about it, I said to myself bitterly. Oriented now, I crept along the rail to its end, dabbed down timidly with one foot, found a step, got myself half-turned and headed properly, and went down to the museum-and-waxworks combination that was our great hall.

So used to that staircase had I become that I managed it in little more time than it would have taken in the broad artificial daylight of the two big chandeliers and myriad table lamps, though there wasn't even a glowworm of phosphorescence to show the way. I stood at the bottom, attempting now a different sort of orientation: I had a deep desire not to walk into a wax figure or a plaster dummy in heavy armor. It would have been nearly as bad as bumping against a living person or a corpse.

I started out confidently from the foot of the staircase and bashed into an object all flimsy and fluttery, which swayed alarmingly until I grabbed it and held it steady. It was the Nazimova doll, ethereal in light but ghostly in the dark. Heart pounding, I made sure it wouldn't fall off its pedestal, and let it go and stepped back. Where the dickens was I?

Lightning blazed, and its dispersed reflex lit for a moment all the stiff figures surrounding me. I saw no flicker of bright white fur. I called his name softly, and before the thunder I heard him say, querying, "Mmrrowrr?"

There was something wrong, wrong above and beyond the ordinary orneriness of a cat flitting away from rescue in accord with its basic cussed nature. I didn't know what it was, but it *was*, and as wrong as it could be.

I had no time to stand pondering that ambiguous notion. First, I had to find Micajah as quickly as possible, and then, I had to decide where to go with him for sanctuary. If I fled to Sibella, my trap would have been useless, the killer could pick his time tomorrow, and besides I'd be putting her in real danger now that I was the prime target.

There came a fantastically vivid flash almost concurrent with its thunder, and I got my bearings and moved ahead to stand beside the Arliss-as-Disraeli sculpture while the great hall reverberated horribly to the clangor just above our roof.

"Micajah!" I heard his pale answering whimper in the echoes that rolled around me. I looked up at Mr. Arliss, who showed as a black shadow in the obscurity as an explosion of distant lightning—it was a broad storm, it must have covered several square miles—gave me enough thin radiation to barely tell space from solid. Mr. Arliss lent me an illusion of company, of protection. I put my arm around his waist, the stiff old fabric of the frock coat reminding me of all things Victorian, safe, stuffy, sane, consolingly pompous.

I had long since forgotten the subminiature remote switch that Daniel had shown us the night of the dead Felicity farce. I was gazing about, squinting at the throng of silent presences, trying to find a hint of crouching cat, when from the high wall toward the front of the house, Akim Tamiroff in an oily voice blared out, "Salaam, salaam! My poor hovel is yours, everything here is—" Thunder blotted up the last of the speech, but I knew it: *"everything here is for your pleasure."*

I snatched my hand from the miserable button on Disraeli's waxen carcass as if it had been a white-hot piece of steel. What a fool! What a careless, unthinkable fool! At a time when every movement that I made should be considered, I must embrace a false body as though it were a living friend!

If the treacherous voice had alerted the man who must kill me or face trial and prison, it would be only what I deserved. I wasn't smart enough to live.

I moved away, passing between a menacing Cagney and an unheeding Gish, wondering if that amplified quotation would wake anyone who'd slept through this booming giant of a storm. But our bedrooms were nearly soundproof; in mine I'd never heard the tapes unless they'd been piped directly in. I chose a wide vacant space ringed by the shapes of dead actors, and posed there stiffly, watching by the dim bursts of faraway electricity a large cluster of the models, where anyone coming after me might be likely to stand and watch. In the next flash, a real explosion of pure white like that of a photographic bulb, the bolt striking ground somewhere near the arm of the bayou out there, I peered hard at the mob of images.

They *all* looked unfamiliar, and grim, and just on the verge of moving toward me. Four, five, half a dozen pairs of glass eyes stared at me out of pallid grimacing faces. Were the eyes all glass?

Everything here is for your pleasure.

Dear God!

The faces glimmered into darkness again, no lightning came to help me, and half-hypnotized by the counterfeit people, I began to imagine them all alive, their wax turned flesh, the glass eyes glittering into animation, the stiff hands uncramping and reaching out. The black dark is the ultimate trickster, you need nerves of leather to hold your imagination in check for long.

I heard Micajah's call from behind me, not far off. Whirling toward it, I lost my bearings and dared not move until I could see something again.

I'd listened to that piteous cry for help and solace a good many times now; what was it that rang false? I'd have known Micajah's voice among those of a hundred cats, and this was it. Why did I persist, standing in the middle of imagined and real dangers, in feeling that something was wrong with a simple, familiar meow?

And knowledge came over me like a bucketful of ice water. It was *too* familiar, it was all the *same* meow. It wasn't my dear old boy crying out to me in the night; he would not by any means, he could not if he tried, repeat precisely the same *mmrrowrr,* with the little question mark at the finish, and never vary it, never let loose one of his irritable howls, or his friendly hello-there-Mama urks, or his patented personal what-the-hell's-wrong screams of wrath.

I realized instantly what had been done. The enemy had taped some of Micajah's yammerings, chosen this one as most likely to lure me from my bedroom, and retaped it onto one of those loops that I'd encountered the first night I'd lived here. An unending circle of tape like the one in the armor's helmet, which had repeated Claude Rains' warning each time I'd passed the starter beam. Then he'd slid it into one of those little players you could carry in your hand or clip on your belt, and beginning at my door, pushed the "play" bar at intervals as he drew me into the hall, down the steps, and among this forest of statues, where he could hide simply by remaining motionless whenever the lightning flashed.

But where was Micajah? Under my bed asleep, like as not, shut in with that dreadful dog.

The storm was incidental, a help to whoever was terrorizing me, no more. If you've lived in a house all your life, it's as easy as parting your hair to go down to the fuse box, throw the main switch or maybe just one or two that would black out part of the place, find your way back and move all around your victim in the dark, knowing precisely how many steps are on the staircase, how many yards separate one dummy from another . . . you wouldn't need a torch, particularly if, in preparing for the charade, you'd carefully paced off and memorized all the necessary distances a day or two before.

But having lured me down here, what was he going to do? Why this flitting about with the false mew?

Lightning, nearby again, with its instantaneous crash of awful sound. I was looking in the general direction of the front of the house, for the huge crystal chandelier caught the white beam from the windows behind me and turned it into a thousand points of scintillation. I was only aware of that extravagant glory on the upper edge of my vision, however, for I was staring between a couple of waxworks at a figure that *moved*.

It was twenty feet, perhaps, from me. There was nothing to reflect the light about it, no pale oval of a face, no hands showing faint against darkness. He must be all in black, with a ski mask or false face over his head, gloves, deerskin moccasins to make no sound. But I could see he was tall and lean as he stepped lithely into the shelter of the Cromwellian soldier.

Not Pierce or Belle then. Something definitely proved, if I lived to pass it along.

Realizing that I faced no innocent person, I dragged out the little gun and stood shaking, a weed in a high wind; aimed it where I'd seen him disappear, holding it close to my waist to steady it as Alan Ladd used to do. "Come out," I called. "I want to talk. I see you." A palpable lie, for neither of us could see in this raven midnight. I must not lose control of my deteriorating nerves. I tried to calm my breath, without success.

"Mmrrowrr?" He'd turned the volume up, the cry resounded

among the exhibits of the great hall, louder than a puma's squall. He was laughing at me.

Instinctively I changed my position, my icy bare feet as silent as his soft-shod ones. Not knowing where he might be now, I eased to my right, in the direction of the glass-front cases that held the memorabilia, and as I did, it came to me that the cases were not wired into the main electrical system, but had individual batteries. Pierce had showed me when we were browsing among the collection, weeks past. There were no unsightly wires to dangle, and the cases could be moved anywhere—

Light! It would make a difference, for I was armed and he might not be, since in the dark he needed only his powerful hands.

I kept edging sideways, all my senses alert, watching nothing and hearing the indistinct ratatat of rain and the minute creakings and cracklings that rose around me. It couldn't be the ordinary noises of an old house at night, because nothing expands or contracts when the temperature holds steady twenty-four hours a day. With pulse slamming in my ears and limbs quivering in terror of the silent waiting death, I found myself considering that, forming mad theories about the statues breathing, shifting position, even simply growing old and squeaky in the joints as they stood waiting for the golden age to return from the past.

If I'm an example, then dreadful fear does not drive out useless, idle notions, but brings them in shoals to clutter up the mind and hamper sensible thought.

I bumped into something, gave a horrified gasp, realized then that it was one of the taller cabinets. I went to a knee, felt beneath it, found a switch. Holding the gun ready, I clicked the switch, and a moonbeam of cool white light sprang into being, shooting out above my head, doubtless illuminating me, and radiating far enough into the blackness to show the center half of the hall, fading away to tunnels of dark at either end.

The lightning, after the long interval, began again with renewed violence, and staring down the hall toward the south wall, I saw that the front door was standing open.

Crabwise I scuttled along the row of cases and cabinets, finding the switches, turning on light after light, bringing the great hall to life and making the hateful, erratic lightning superfluous.

Had he gone outside? Why? Was it a trap?

I rose, turning my head constantly, and I walked down the hall to the short vestibule, at the end of which the heavy door swung wide on a flickering, flashing vista of soaking muddy lawn and pale blue gates in a blue wall. An invitation to run?

A change came in the cold light that threw the hall into such odd relief behind me. I glanced back, but couldn't see what it had been. Then, as I turned to move toward the door again, another small change occurred. I whipped round, thrusting out my weapon in panic. I could see no movement, no black slim figure anywhere, but the farthest two cases had gone dark.

He wanted me to go outside.

You don't belong here . . . Sherry's voice in my head, repeating that angrily.

Mean, dirt mean . . . Wendy's.

He wanted me to go blind with panic at this rigamarole of taped meowings and turned-off lights, to run, run, run, out into the night and rain. Why?

Another "accident" waiting to happen? Or a simple disappearance, perhaps with some of my clothes missing so they'd believe I'd lost my courage and retreated after all. Then a call, faked when the rest of them were elsewhere—"Laurel says she's sorry but it was too much for her, and will we mail her things to Connecticut?"

Holes, it was full of holes. Yet wasn't it just simple enough to work? And if the soil was deep enough to bury pounds and pounds of exotic candy, it was deep enough to hide a dismembered corpse.

Looking back, I saw him out in the open area of the great hall now, scrambling along clicking off the cabinet lights from a squat—an all-black figure, only the eyes catching a reflection now and then, mere sparks with no clue to their color. He moved so easily, so swiftly, there were only two lights to go.

I stepped into the doorway and waited, watching him. Whether there might have been safety for me out in the grounds, I'll never know, for I didn't go outside, but stood there deliberately silhouetted athwart the alternate glare and afterglow, watching him, striving to see some familiar, characteristic motion that would identify him as he came down the line of cases like a huge, sable spider. One light left. The great hall ready to fade into Stygian mystery once more.

As he turned it off, I reached forward, caught the sliding bar with one hand, and brought the enormous door back into place with a crash. Then I turned to my left, found the handle of the closet, pulled it open—blessing Daniel's constant oiling of all entrances to the hidden passageways—and slipping in among coats and sweaters and umbrellas, pulled it shut behind me. I floundered my way through the hanging garments till I came to the back wall, groped for the hook and got it on the third try, turned it downward, and felt the rear panel of the cubicle slide away to the side. As I went through, I recollected that these levers worked electrically. That meant that only part of the house's power was off. I shut the panel with the inside hook and felt for the mercury switch that would light my path down the narrow corridor.

Two possibilities: If he'd missed seeing what I'd done, and assumed that I'd bolted outside, he'd hasten out in the rain to catch me where no screams would do me any good; or, if the sudden darkness hadn't confused his vision for a split second as I'd hoped, and he'd seen me stay indoors, then he'd be bare seconds behind me.

The big naked bulbs went on in the tunnel. I laid a course with my eyes, straight north in the direction I'd come from for some long steps, then a right turn and eastward. I allowed an extra breath of time to memorize this first span, then pressed the switch down and in the coffined dark ran forward, left hand stretched before me, right still clutching the pistol.

If he was following me, if he would plainly catch me, then I'd shoot. Trying for only his legs, yes, but I *would* shoot.

I slowed, touched wood, turned right and went on, without pausing to flash on the next overhead lamps. I knew approximately how far I had to run here, and if I could find what I wanted, I might be safe in a matter of six or eight seconds.

The thunder was louder than ever, seeming to originate between the concrete walls on my right and the wooden partitions on my left, rolling down toward me, over me, shaking the foundations of the house, of the very world. Surely I had come far enough. I stopped, felt blindly along the wall and touched the cold roughness of cement. I'd either overshot or halted too soon. Frantic, I groped forward some yards, searching for wood. Then, unable to visualize how far I'd come, or even where the door that I wanted had been placed along this alley, I started back, trailing my fingers at shoulder height on the wall.

I found a line of switches, five or six of them. One would light this section of passage, the others . . . Lord knew *what* they'd do. I sucked in a desperate lungful of warm brackish air, slapped my palm across all of them, and shoved up.

A blaze of light showed me the door, only two feet from where I stood.

And *noise!* Merciful powers, the noise! From speakers above me, to rear and front of me, the hateful tapes blasted out all at once; it was horrible enough here in the passageway, and what it must have sounded like in the library and the great hall beyond was inconceivable. Some of them must have been old reels, not yet removed after puerile jokes or surprises. Others may have been lying in wait for someone to be indiscreet in word or subject. I couldn't distinguish much in my dismay and abject cowardice, but I did hear Laughton say something to Mr. Christian concerning cheese.

Those tapes would locate me for the hunter. Well, if I were going to die in Sablecroft Hall, then I'd do it in the traditional Sablecroft manner, to the tune of a pack of dead actors going about their jobs with loud relish.

But I *wouldn't* die here! I riveted my gaze on the lock of the door, and slammed off the switches, plunging myself into silence and darkness. I moved, reached out, touched the latch.

Around the bend, twenty feet or so back, that first bend I'd taken almost at a run in the terrible night-dark of the passage, I saw the glow of an unseen bulb flash on, casting its reflection around the corner. He had come through the closet and was almost upon me. I tore open the door and went through it, praying for a bolt on the other side. There was none.

He would, if my luck held, just be rounding the corner, and wouldn't have seen the closing door. The next turn of the passage was no more than ten feet past it, so he might believe I'd gone on that way, making for the kitchen. I'd never been through this door, but remembered from the plans that I stood now in the base of a three-story tower, at the foot of a winding stair that went up and up to the top, fifty feet above ground. There were three doors above me, two on the second story and one on the top. Stark sightless as one of those poor pale fish who live out their generations in cave water deep in the earth, and with an inkling of what blindness really meant, I began to grope for the staircase. The thunder growled without, dying away at last in the west.

I barked my shin painfully on the bottom riser, put the sweat-slippery gun back in my pocket, bungled awkwardly for a rail, found it, then located the second step and went up as fast as I could, keeping to the railed side and turning, turning, a mad creature in an upright tube without end, panting, sobbing, and feeling decidedly sorry for myself. I missed the second story by stupidly clinging to the blasted railing. Up and up I went till I came full tilt against another rail that drove the breath out of my body with an excruciating *whoosh.*

My overactive imagination flashed a picture before my mind's eye: a small boy tramping up an interminable winding stone staircase in a near-dark castle tower illumined by lightning . . . bats sweeping round his head . . . wicked Uncle Ebenezer crying out from far below, "To the very top, mind ye, and then to the right!" and the boy—Freddie Bartholomew—treading on the final step to nowhere, a long block of stone which teeters and crashes down the immense center well to the distant floor as the lad staggers back, barely saving himself. *Kidnapped,* yes, and the scene all shot from above, horrifyingly real and exacerbating my already mortal funk as luridly as any tangible mass of cobwebs or stack of pallid bones.

Think, think! I opened the door I found on my left, flung it as wide as I could, my face lashed with a rainy wind, and did not go out, but started down the inside of the tower again, hands patting and clutching at the wall this time. The descent was far worse than the ascent; one false step and I'd go straight to the bottom, smashing every rib and limb I owned.

No light appeared below, and nothing but a filtering of wan, colorless motes of dimness, which couldn't be called "light," from above. I put my faith in a providence that must not let him open that bottom door till I'd found my exit. And in what could have been only a few seconds, my palms did slap on wood. I found the latch and swung the door inward. It was the wrong door: it opened on the passages of the second story, where I'd be back in the foul labyrinth again. I closed that one—he *must* believe, if he came this way, that I was on the tower roof, which was flat with a crenellated wall like the watchtower of an Algerian fort—and after a quarter of a turn down, came to the door I wanted. This opened to an outside wooden platform. I stumbled into the rain and pushed the door tight shut behind me.

Then, miraculously, I could *see*. Oh, the blessed relief of that! It was terribly dim and gloomy, the whole sky still overcast with a bank of thick cloud and the rain coming slantwise in vicious sheets, but after the absolute dark in the hall and tower, this was as good as a rosy dawn. I put both hands on a rough board rail, flat and splintery and sopping with water, and stared out over the blue wall and deserted street to where a light or two showed, shimmering in the rain, and beyond them to a car moving slowly along on some late errand. I was out!

I leaned there far too long, with a random hash of notions filling my head. He was searching the passages one after another, perhaps now with a dog or two to help him—where were the Great Danes, anyway? He'd trailed me to the top of the tower and even now was looking down on me, bending out through a crenellation. Giving up the chase at the thought of the countless places where I could lie concealed, he was back in his own room, stripping off the black disguise.

I should have assumed that he was only a moment behind me, I should have fled on. Yet I stood there, looking through the night toward sanity, panting and feeling my long hair cling dankly to my cheeks and neck.

Finally I shoved off the railing and turned to my left, with a catwalk stretched before me that ended at a door, black with long rain, which led into the southern end of the bedroom hall that overlooked the immense room of the waxworks. Twenty steps, no more, to that dark, dry balcony above the great hall, where I could go on to my own place and chance the dog who waited there.

I had a horror of entering Sablecroft Hall again, that was certain. But this small platform and the catwalk were no sanctuary, despite the distant normal lights, fresh cool wet air, and momentary solitude. I had to go on, to go in.

I moved a grudging step, and then I heard the door creak in the tower beside me. I made a lunge, panic-stricken, and a hand came down on my forearm and tightened relentlessly, with all the menace and cruelty of that pitiless night in the savage grip of the fingers.

18

UTTERING THE SCREAM OF A LIFETIME, I TORE MYSELF WITH A quick twist out of that terrible grasp and ran forward along the soaking, slippery planks of the catwalk.

Thunder drumfired across the flat underside of the cloud mass, simultaneously with a bolt of lightning so vivid that it hurt my eyes. I must have sheered involuntarily, because I crashed against the railing and fell asprawl, rolling away from the edge and onto my back. The dark figure loomed above me, looking frozen in midstep. I clawed at my pajama pocket, wrenched out the gun, fumbling it into position with both hands now, shouting the whole time that he must get back, get away from me, that I was armed, that I'd shoot; I, who had never fired so much as a cap pistol in my life.

He brought down his foot beside my leg, took another short step and stood looking directly down at me, straddling my body like a nightmare colossus. Lightning slashed again, bringing him from a raven-dark silhouette into full definition. He was a goggling, glaring bogle, an apparition of hideous fantasy. Entirely clad in dull black, he showed above me as a slim man with the head of a gargoyle. The face was like a Tibetan devil mask, multi-ringed eyes and an open mouth from ear to ear, all black and shining wet, a laughing, odious distortion of a face, a thing to shock the Gorgons. His hands were reaching for me, curled into talons.

I aimed the little silver gun straight into that abominable face and fired, and fired again, went on pulling the trigger until the hammer had clicked more than once on empty chambers.

He took every shot in the cylinder—five or six there must have been—full in the face, point blank, and grunted as they struck, and then flung up his snout to glare at the heavens, lit by the white branching bolts of the rekindling storm, and staggered backward, pawing at air, the fixed open grin leaking a long gurgling moan, and swayed sideways and fell to his knees and then went over like an unholy black beast pierced with silver arrows, slamming down against the posts of the timber rail and rolling off them onto his back on the catwalk to lie still, his deformed face to the sky.

There is a horror beyond terror that is literally unspeakable.

Creeping on all fours, I left him there with the rain splashing off him to creep my way, shuddering, weeping, vomiting, on all fours, to the door in the stuccoed wall. There I found that I could not get to my feet. I floundered and clawed at the wood of a railing support, driving splinters under my nails, calling out for help in a voice that would scarcely have pierced paper. I stared up at the dark belly of the cloud mass. Forgive me, please forgive me . . . I never meant to kill, even to hurt, anything, ever. I was only so afraid, mad with fear, because he'd killed Wendy and meant to kill me. He'd have thrown me off this thing, to the ground below, to break my neck as he'd broken hers.

And remembering Wendy, I felt suddenly that I was forgiven, and a kind of watery strength came to my body and I stood up. The rain had thickened once more, I was soaked to my skin and my pajamas were being cleansed as I wavered there on the threshold of safety. For a while I stayed as I was, then fumbled with the latch and opened the door.

The darkness inside was not as deep as I'd expected. Brushing the rain from my eyes, peering in, I saw the tiny night lights glowing again. I made myself look back at the thing on the sodden planks. It lay in a grotesque crumple. As I watched, lightning brought the mask alive for a moment. I felt I should go pull off that mask, make certain who it was, but I was unable. Not to dispel the shadow over Sablecroft Hall, not to learn what I'd believed I must know or die, could I travel those ten feet, as limitless as a parsec, and touch that ghastly being, even now that my panic was fading and I knew in my heart that it was no more than a dead man in an ugly disguise. Besides, all those bullets at point-blank range would have destroyed his face, crushed it into an unspeakable welter of anonymous blood and bone.

And I was starting into the house, moving with a ragged lack of co-ordination that was the beginning, I suppose, of collapse at the scarcely formed knowledge that I wasn't going to be murdered—dimly aware that the worst of the trial, at least the physical threat to my life, was ended and I might relax—when I glanced briefly back at the pool of ink that was the dead adversary and saw by a great bolt and its afterglow that *Oh God in heaven he was rising from the catwalk. . . .*

He came up like the lissome feral creature he was, gathering his arms and legs under him and leaping to a bunched posture rising spiderlike from fingertips and toes, holding thus a moment, then advancing on me with splayed-out fingers ready to grip and hold.

I swung to my left and felt the top crosspiece of the railing against the small of my back. It gave a little as my weight hit it. I convulsively turned a bit farther and snatched at the flat thin narrow board with both hands, wrenched it toward me as I braced myself on icy numbing feet, felt it tear loose with a twisting protest of rusty nails and rotten timber. It was a flimsy imitation of a weapon perhaps a yard long. My palms ground into its soggy, prickly old surface as I flung it up into a guarding position.

The sheer incredibility of the business must have washed the concepts of terror and awe right out of my head. I remember every move that I made; each least action came instinctively, out of nearly forgotten corners of my adolescence when Dad had taught me the mechanics of defense. It was the triumph at last of the sensible body over the dithery and overactive imagination.

And so, I attacked the corpse that was attacking me.

He came with his arms outstretched and high, as though to throttle me. I dropped my right hand down beside my hip, holding the stick in it. He was lit by a blast of lightning from the horizon behind him; hardly more than arm's length away by now and coming stupidly slow. With a quick underhand swing I drove the end of my stick into the center of his abdomen, shifting my right foot forward at him as I did so. His arms were lowering as he began to bend with the pain; I swung my left up and gripped his right wrist, jabbing again with my rotten old piece of board, which skinned off his rib cage as he twisted.

Yanking him toward me by his right arm, I backhanded the short end of the stick straight into his gut and stepped to my right, whipping his arm across between us as I did so, and backing out of reach and letting him go as he dropped to his knees and then down on the wet timber in a curled-shrimp position. I held my club at the ready, but he was whooping and gagging for air behind the mask and quite helpless.

Reeling, I got into the corridor and shut the night out. Muted thunder swelled and died, a requiem for an undead monster. I must rouse the house and warn them.

I went downstairs, still carrying the erstwhile railing. No lights here, but I found a switch and flooded the place with multitinted resplendence from the huge Tiffany. Walking across to the intercom station beside the arch, I picked up the mike and after a few false passes at the wrong buttons, brought it to life.

"Oh," I croaked, "oh please, somebody, everybody, please come to the great hall. I'm sorry to bother you," I said, with a childish embarrassment at waking them when I didn't even know what time it was, "so sorry, but it's important. Please come here, I need you."

The door to the kitchen instantly swung open, and I was so shattered, so crawling with nerves and fear and relief all at once, that I actually for the mad space of one missed heartbeat *saw* the dummy of Felicity fall crashing out on its bloody chest. But it was Belle McNabb, her little gray face pinched with sleep, scowling down the room and then running toward me.

"Honey!" she cried, holding me by the waist and staring up at me, "Laurel baby, what is it? He hurt you? Did he do you harm?" And all those ancient folds writhed into a fierce scowl. "I'll fix him good, did he do it!" she rasped.

I put my wet arms around her and hugged tight, this good soul of whom I used to be afraid. "I'm fine," I said, teeth chattering to make a liar of me. "I'm all right, Belle, oh dear Belle, I'm all right now, but I may have killed him."

"That's fine!" She embraced me in turn with the amazing power of her thin arms. "You did just right, lamb. He deserved it. Did he try for you like he did Wendy?"

"Yes, like Wendy."

"You sit and breathe yourself steady, baby girl." She led me to a chair and eased me into it, as if it were 1850 and she my very own mammy all my life. "Just breathe. Don't you talk yet. You're white as skim milk."

Then Pierce was beside us, anxiety written large on his moon face, his bulk swathed in a splendid iridescent green dressing gown. "I woke a few minutes ago to find my light gone, and went to check the fuses, half a dozen of them were thrown, I suppose by the storm—" He stopped, said "Babble!" severely to himself, and asked what had happened to me.

Holding Belle's hand, feeling incredible comfort flow from that little woman, I said, "He put the lights out. He lured me out with a tape of my cat—where's Micajah?"

Pierce pointed, and I saw the white beast sitting bolt upright on the shoulder of Anna May Wong, head cocked at me. I smiled feebly. "The man had a tape of a mew, and I came to find Micajah, and he chased me through the dark, and I went into the passages and turned on a lot of tapes—you never heard them?"

"I heard only thunder, and ignored that," said Pierce, lowering himself to a hassock beside me. "This *is* the lightning capital of the world, you know. . . . Go on."

"Then I made it outside, but he came after me, there was a mask over his head and I was scared and I killed him," I rattled, the words gall in my mouth. "I shot him in the face and he groaned and fell down. Then he stood up and came at me again and I hit him in the stomach with a board, and oh God but that stopped him deader than the bullets."

"But who *was* it?" asked Pierce.

I gave a dry sob, completely cried out. "I don't know."

"Don't matter," said Belle. "It's best he's dead and gone. Never touch my lamb again." I squeezed her fingers.

Into the great hall swept Sibella, every hair in place and a silken Chinese robe that had been woven for a mandarin sheathing her tough old stick of a body. "What happened? I was blasted awake ten minutes ago by a lot of tapes going off in the library—"

"Ten minutes?" I repeated. I'd have guessed half an hour.

"Yes. I went in there, but found no one."

Pierce repeated what he thought I'd said, and I added a detail or two, and we heard someone coming down the staircase and all turned to look, and it was Daniel, his hair tousled and pajama legs flopping below a bathrobe, blinking and staring. And that was that. I began to cry without tears, huddling into myself, and Sibella gave an all-over jolt and said, "It's only Daniel, dear, you mustn't be afraid."

"But where did you find a *gun?*" asked Pierce, trying to put my story together.

"I found it under Wendy's mattress. That's why I offered myself as b-bait, I was so sure I could manage him."

The fat man objected. "Wendy was terrified of firearms."

"Not so much but that she kept a revolver."

"Where is it now?"

"I don't know. Out there beside *him,* I guess," I snuffled.

"And how can a man be shot in the head and still rise and walk?" he persisted.

"I don't know, I don't understand anything!"

Daniel asked, yawning, "What about a gun?"

"Later," said Sibella, "later. The girl's ready to faint. Put your head between your knees, Laurel."

"I'm not going to faint."

Oh, Sherry! I'd killed the only man I'd loved in all these lonely years, shot him in the face and smashed in his middle, too—I almost wished I had let him fling me off the catwalk into night and death. Whatever he'd done. At that moment I'd rather I had died than Sherry.

"What the hell's going on down here?" demanded Sherry irritably.

I mouthed and gestured, but my voice wasn't there any more. I jumped and began to stand up, and collapsed into Belle's arms, and was sitting down again. "What *is* it?" Sherry said. "What's the matter with you all? Laurel, you're wringing wet."

Pierce said severely that Sherry ought to realize that Laurel was quite aware she was wet, bloody fool that Sherry was. By turns they told one another what had happened to me, insofar as they knew it.

Sherry said, "I can't fathom some of this at all, but I gather that ultimately you shot and *then* knocked down whoever was chasing you. Making allowances for everything else, but only for the moment," he said, "who the blazes did you shoot? Who's missing? Have I forgotten someone else who lives here?"

Even Sibella's eyes rounded with dismay. "But we're all here!"

I howled. *"I've shot a ghost!"*

"No such thing," said Belle, gentling me with her hands as if I were a hysterical filly. Sherry came forward and she slapped his hand away, saying, "Don't you touch my little girl! She's had all the pawing she's gonna take! You be useful, go up and find that gun and see who's a corpse outside."

"Yes, Belle," said Sherry, turning away. It was only then that I realized he was fully dressed in the slacks and shirt he'd worn at dinner. And the right side of his face was red and looked dented, as though he'd been struck a number of times by small round objects.

If the mask had been bulletproof, if that were a possible thing, the slugs might have pressed it in and bruised the flesh. It didn't matter. He was alive. I thought I understood love for the first time, and it was not a desirable sentiment to leave me feeling this way, but I was saddled with it. Had I known for certain who the man in the fiend's mask had been, I'd have gone to my own death out there in the rain, grieving but of my free will.

Numbly—sitting with my cold, dirty feet tucked under me in the big chair, dripping dismally—I answered more questions as he went upstairs, and eventually gave them a fairly complete if impossible picture of what I'd done.

Sibella looked baffled, and whispered, "Who could it have been? Or *what?*"

"No ghost grabs you by the arm," said Mrs. McNabb. "It's some man we don't know about. Maybe been sleeping in the passages this long time back. How's anybody to tell if he's in there? Plenty of places to hide when we go past him, plenty of food to steal at night. Laurel," she told me, "I can move my folding bunk up to your room. I was sleeping on it in the kitchen tonight, but you shouldn't be on your lonesome." I smiled at her gratefully.

Daniel, who evidently woke rather slowly when he hadn't had his sleep out, said, "Look, no common burglar or tramp who's taken refuge in the warren of Sablecroft Hall is going to tape a cat's mew, dress in a Tibetan mask, flit around turning off lights, and chase a girl outdoors in a storm! This is insane."

Then Sherry called from the balcony, "Here's your room key, but there's no gun. Nor is there any corpse—or any gun—or anything whatever, on the catwalk, because I turned on the outside floods and looked."

"Don't you call my baby a liar," said Belle.

I said flatly, "I can't imagine how, but I must have missed him."

"A girl might miss, even point blank, I suppose," said Pierce, "if she were unused to weapons."

Daniel said to his cousin, "What have you been doing to your face?" And everyone suddenly looked at Sherry, noticing then what I'd seen before—the slightly pitted redness of the right cheek and temple.

Sherry glanced into a mirror. "Must have been where the wads hit me," he said, poker-faced. "You know, blanks aren't exactly harmless. The wads come out with high velocity, and when you're wearing a thin rubber mask—"

"Oh, Sherry!" I wailed.

"Oh, Laurel! Don't be absurd," he said, gentler now, "I wasn't your man in black. I was typing in my room, too tired to work, but wouldn't admit it, and I had one ear cocked for noises I obviously couldn't hear over the thunder . . . and I fell asleep with my stupid face on the typewriter keys. If you count the pockmarks, there must be more than any six-chambered revolver could have made."

Daniel leaned over, hand on Sherry's shoulder, and did it. "True! I can't actually distinguish the letters, but you have ten or twelve big dimples there. How can you sleep on a typewriter?"

"You try getting four hours sleep for a few months and see how soft a bed of nails can be, let alone a nice comfy keyboard."

"What about our midnight prowler?" said Pierce. "Who's gone away with bullets in his head? Ideas?"

"Sherry's got it," Daniel said, "blanks. We know Wendy was as scared of firearms as of ladders. If she had a gun, which beats me in the first place, we can be sure it didn't hold live ammo."

"Then why didn't he just laugh and throw me over the railing, instead of moaning and falling down? Why a mockery of dying?"

"Yes, he'd pursued you keenly enough," said Pierce, "why let a few harmless explosions stop him?"

"He *groaned?*" said Sherry to me, and I said yes. "My sainted love, a man shot repeatedly in the face doesn't groan! He's *dead*. He flies backward and his head comes to pieces and—oh, never mind, but he can't groan!"

"How would I know that?"

"Movies," said Sherry, withering me. "They *were* blanks, then, and the mask heavy enough to protect him from hurtling wax or packed cotton or whatever they use. May I suggest the sleeping arrangements? Pierce, since he's in the clear, can bolt himself into his room, which with its Fox lock is the most impregnable in the house."

"It is," said Pierce wryly. "I own up to my phobia, Sheridan."

"Daniel and I can sleep in my room, and if one of us is dead by morning, t'other's the guilty party." Daniel nodded. "Instead of moving your bed into Laurel's room, Belle, you and she go sleep in Sibella's. Take Micajah with you."

"Some rationality in the family at last," said Pierce.

"Anyway," I said wearily, "since I'm the prime target now, and can't stand having everyone on tenterhooks with the strain of waiting to see me drowned in the cesspool or crushed by a falling tower, I'll leave tomorrow."

"No!" shouted Pierce, billowing up to his fullest size. "Better you tell us all you know, Laurel, than that we lose you."

"You can't leave," said Sibella, "you belong here."

"I do?" was all I could think to say.

"This is the last stronghold of the Sablecrofts, this will be their home."

"And you are a Sablecroft, honey," said Belle, her eyes bright, I think with tears.

"That's true," said Daniel.

I looked at them one by one. "It's very generous of you to say so—but I've done nothing worthy of adoption into the tribe."

Sherry grinned. "Come on, don't play at being the second Mrs. De Winter, too innocent to exist! I told you weeks ago that everyone knew it. Even if we hadn't been aware of it to begin with, your nose gives you away: It crops up in the family like the Hapsburg lip and the red hair of the Elphbergs. Why d'you think we all assured you that you're beautiful? It's because you look like *us,* you foolish girl."

"What?" I squeaked. "You mean you're talking literally?"

"And you cock one eyebrow clear up to your hair," said Pierce as though I hadn't spoken, "which is an inherited or acquired trick that we've all had, except for Wendy."

"Yours is the family mouth, broad but firm," said Sibella. "In short, Laurel, you're so obviously a Sablecroft that even that large policeman asked me if you weren't related to us."

I sat back, shocked numb. I had to accept their statements, they were all so sure, and it explained so much of my background that had been unknown, but—"How long have you known of my existence?" I asked her.

"Belle and I since your mother was pregnant. Pierce since he came here twenty years ago."

Mrs. McNabb crackled out a peal of laughter. "I know I scared you some," she said, "just trying to watch over you, baby. Once I let the dogs in behind the walls when you were there, to keep you from harm if they could."

"Why?"

"You are Alfred Vane's granddaughter," she said, and closed her lips firmly and stared upward, seeing visions from an unimaginable past.

"I am, but *Gilbert's* great-granddaughter too?"

"Oh, come off it," Sherry snapped angrily. I ignored him; let him believe what he liked.

"Belle and your grandfather were close friends," said Sibella. "Sherry, when did you pick up on Laurel?"

"I read Felicity's diaries a year or so back. When I heard Alfred Vane's son's daughter was coming, I put it together. Daniel, who told you?"

"No one! I was left in the cold and never knew till yesterday, when I came to the nineteen thirty-three diary of my grandmother." He gave me a leer from the corners of his enamel-blue eyes and said, " 'Hail, cousin,' as the Egyptian said in you-know-which flick."

" 'Hail, mortal,' " I answered automatically, mind awhirl.

"If that's true," said Sherry slowly, "then you, Daniel, should be in the clear on previous attempts to scare the liver out of our mousey librarian. Did you really *not* know she was a Sablecroft? Didn't that nose give her away the moment she came through our door?"

"I only thought she was extraordinarily lovely," said Daniel. "Never occurred to me to wonder why I thought so . . . which doesn't seem odd or suspicious to me, I must say."

"Bed!" said Sibella, rising and taking Belle's arm. "Laurel, bring the cat."

"I'll just get his box and some pajamas, after I shower," I said. I went upstairs beside Pierce, silent and bone-weary, with things meshing in my memory that had been there all the time but had never fitted together till now. I stopped, two steps from the top, exclaiming aloud. My companion asked if I were all right.

"Dear Pierce, how could I not have seen the truth before?"

"You mean you honestly didn't know you were one of us?"

I glanced down at Sherry and Daniel, saw them in conversation out of earshot of us, and whispered, "No, I didn't, whatever the others think! It's a total surprise to me. But I'm talking about the man we've been trying to identify . . . the trickster."

"And how have you come to the truth of that?" he whispered back, looking frightened of whatever knowledge I had.

"Something I read, and something I found in Wendy's room. There isn't any doubt, I know the murderer."

"Might it be a stranger?" he husked, still hopeful.

"No, it's one of us. It's a Sablecroft. There's no mysterious outlander in the rain with a devil mask and merciless hands. There's only us, and he's one of us." My voice was so thick and sad, I could hardly say it. "I'll tell you all tomorrow, when I've rested and come to grips with—everything." And I went to my bedroom to release the puzzled, whimpering, harmless Dane.

19

"SHE'S ALWAYS LOVED YOU," SAID SIBELLA, EATING THE LAST OF her shirred eggs, "since you were born. I didn't realize she scared you. I suppose it takes long acquaintance to read her face. Belle is, after all, a very old woman—much older than I. She worried about you from the day I told her you were coming here. You see, Laurel, she was the only one besides Pierce who took that balcony collapse seriously. The rest of us wanted to believe it was only decrepitude that broke it when I walked on it."

"I think now it was very silly, but I'd find her staring at me and assume that for some reason she resented me, as Wendy did."

"She was fretting. She thought all the Sablecrofts but one were slated for death."

"I presume," I said carefully, buttering a scone, "that you had some communication with my grandfather, or my father? I mean, to know when I was born."

"Detectives. Shoddy, but we had to keep in touch somehow. By 'we' I mean myself and my sister, and for twenty years now Pierce, who's always had my complete confidence."

She took a scone herself. We were having a full breakfast at the big table, she and I. It was late morning and we were both famished. Pierce was off searching for the boys. "Belle was devoted to Alfred Vane. The only white man, she once told me, she'd ever have married if he'd asked her."

"You realize I know *nothing* of my history? The Sablecroft half, anyway."

"I had no notion of that. There are things detectives can't learn. What *do* you know, or what have you guessed?"

"I knew that Grandfather spent several months here, and now I see that under Gilbert's nose he must have had a love affair with one of the twin daughters. That there was a child, a boy called John, born long after he left—"

"Not 'long,' Laurel. Even the Sablecrofts whelp after nine months, as ordinary mortals do." She grinned. Despite royal airs and aristocratic dictation, Sibella didn't take herself half as seriously as I'd once thought. "Sherry was certain you knew that before you came."

"I was made aware of that! I had a letter from him—I told him I hadn't received it, although I had—and I *hate* to lie—but he'd written that Sablecroft Hall was a dangerous madhouse, and that I must send you my resignation and not come down at all. I couldn't accept that without seeing for myself. I once told Daniel or Sherry that I must know the truth about things that matter. It's intolerable to me—unendurable—not to know the facts. I'm driven. I'm obliged like Rikki-tikki-tavi to 'run and find out.' That's why I answered your ad, which I see now was aimed right at me, wasn't it? I needed the job, of course, but I had to learn about all of you when the opportunity came along. There was, is, so much I don't know. All I could say for sure was that the Hall had been desperately important to my grandfather, and he'd never brought himself to tell me why. In fact, he'd made a mystery of it with enough hints so that I always knew he wanted to tell me something about it and couldn't quite do it.

"The truth that touches me and mine is as vital as anything can be, but when I felt I was in danger, I nearly left," I said, feeling a deep flush come over my features. "But by then I was the only person I could trust to help you. I've come to love you."

After a long pause, she said, quietly for her, "Why, thank you, Laurel. I'm very fond of you too. But if you wanted to know something, why didn't you simply ask me?"

I looked levelly at her. "Because nothing in this house is ever what it seems. Sherry's letter was right, and it's an insane place full of secret corridors, secret rooms, secret wiring, secret people. It exudes a subtle infection to which nobody's immune, even so sane a man as Grandfather. You must all create mysteries out of the simplest matters. Sometimes you've all reminded me of Olivier in *Sleuth*. I had no reason to expect the absolute truth from any soul in the Hall until last night. Nor did I know I had any right to ask questions."

"So you stayed for me, and not for truth's sake?"

"Yes, I was so frightened that I'd have gone to Connecticut and never wondered about the place again, but I couldn't leave you, and if that sounds like I'm buttering you up, well—"

"You don't butter, girl! Don't explain it into the ground. I never knew Sherry'd written you," she said, cocking her brow. "I wonder why? The young scamp! He must have been serious when he suggested you were a fortune hunter who meant to worm your way into my good graces and cut yourself a slice of the pie. Speaking of that, I wonder if Belle has any apple pie?"

"When did he say that?" I asked, huffy.

"Oh, before you arrived! I think he's changed his mind," she touched the bell that rang in the kitchen, "I think he changed it very soon."

"He never stopped demanding that I leave!"

"Yes . . . we don't know why, do we? Well, we soon shall. Belle, is there apple pie? Good, bring the whole thing, the men will be here soon."

"Why should he consider me a fortune hunter when I was simply answering an ad?"

"He said you surely knew you were family, yet you never mentioned it in your letters, and he was suspicious. I asked him why you should speak of it—you might well be ashamed of the fact—father born on the wrong side of the blanket, no communications—"

"Sherry is a suspicious man," I said, still touchy.

"Only since the balcony fell. No, wrong," she said, thinking, "only since Felicity died. I don't know why. He was never close to his grandaunt. But he became jumpy, and often unlike himself." She poured us more tea. "Go ahead, we've sheered off the track. What else have you deduced by this morning?"

"That for some reason Alfred Vane got the child instead of its mother, although he wasn't married and was then about fifty-six years old—which is such an unlikely switch on the sordid old cliché of a story that it's no wonder I never figured it out. And then he reared John practically alone, and made a good job of it too. I suppose you know that John was married at twenty, I was born when he was twenty-one, and he was killed when I was twelve, Mother having died ten years before. I lived with Granddad until nineteen seventy-three, when he died. And that's all."

"Just how little did Alfred tell you about the Hall?" She frowned as Belle came in with the pie sliced in fifths, put one on a plate for her mistress, vanished again.

"He'd sometimes talk about his visit here, how he and Gilbert Sablecroft had the finest arguments that ever were argued. And I heard about Mack Sennett and the lion, and all the other visitors, and the passages and peepholes and library, and the beautiful twin sisters. Everything else was half-hints and abrupt silences."

"He had a cussed streak as broad as my father's. And so you don't know any details. Well!" she exclaimed, beginning heartily on her pie, "some day I'll probably tell them to you."

"Your own streak of cussedness, Mrs. Callingwood," I said, "is a yard wide."

"I'm me father's daughter, dearie, and don't you forget it." She laughed. "That's how he talked, old Gilbert, when the mood took him. He was American as hellfire till he got a notion to recall his youth. You and he would have enjoyed each other, Laurel. Pity. Where do you suppose all the men have got to?"

"I can't imagine. Why wouldn't Granddad tell me the whole truth? He wasn't cruel in the least, and it wasn't typical for him to tease a person, especially one he loved."

"And I'm sure he loved you, Laurel."

"We were always best friends."

"I'll tell you this—my father was *purple* with rage over the matter. Your grandmother said she wouldn't marry Alfred Vane, though she loved him as much as it was possible for her to love anyone. But it wasn't enough, not deep enough nor wild enough to make a good marriage. She knew herself pretty well by that time: after all, she—I should say we, Felicity and I, were thirty-three years old and both widowed. We'd already had one child apiece, and your grandmother at least had recognized that she wasn't the model mother of the world. Maybe that was her last great flash of insight. The prattle of tiny tots wasn't her favorite music, though I think perhaps she hated herself subconsciously for that.

"Gilbert swore he'd not have the nameless brat in his house. He felt betrayed by his kin and his guest. On the other hand, Alfred Vane adored children. Though he'd never been married, he'd half-reared all his nieces and nephews, always had a houseful of female relations to lend a hand with a baby—in short, Laurel, he said he wanted the child when it was born, and if she wouldn't marry him, by gad he'd have the babe at least! That being agreeable to all parties, it was so settled. Father made Alfred swear never to tell anyone who the mother had been, and evidently Alfred kept his promise, even with you.

"So when John was old enough to travel, one sister took him north to his father, and there he stayed, growing up, from all reports, into a fine, healthy, adventurous, intelligent lad. And here *we* all stayed, and eventually it was just as if Alfred Vane had never entered our door. I suppose there were papers, adoption proceedings or false birth certificates or whatever, which Father paid for and never mentioned. I think that up north it was given out that Alfred had wed John's mother, who'd died early in foreign parts. One of those complicated, horsehair-sofa-and-overstuffed-loveseat Victorian melodramas of life that were always made about four times as intricate as they needed to be. But I never heard that John Vane was any the worse for it."

"No, he was fine," I said. "He was a good guy."

"He went young," she said, "but he went tough, doing what he wanted. Isn't that so?"

"That's so."

"I'm glad," she said, and finished eating her pie.

"The only thing I don't comprehend, barring exactly who was Dad's mother and a few small things like that, is why, with detectives and all, Pierce didn't know how Dad died. You remember the first night I was here, he seemed shocked when I told him about the fire gag that killed Dad." I looked steadily at her. "And Pierce Poole doesn't lie, does he?"

"No indeed. I had never let him know."

"Why not?"

"Laurel, when you innocently spilled the beans, Pierce suffered agonies for days, thinking of that story. He is, you must recognize by now, the most empathetic of men. Knowing you, loving you as he did at once, he felt it more keenly, I'm sure. But even if I'd told him back when it happened—"

"When did you hear?"

"The day afterward. In May of nineteen sixty-seven. We sent a wreath, anonymously, to John's funeral. A hundred red roses . . . we'd heard they were his favorite flowers."

"I remember it," I said. "We thought it must have been from some friends in the business."

"Felicity and I simply told Pierce that John had died peacefully in his sleep. I'd go to any imaginable lengths to save Pierce from sorrow."

"I feel the same way."

"And Felicity could be bullied into saying anything, especially if it was a lie. She had a natural affinity for the fraudulent and insincere, not to say the sanctimonious and hypocritical."

"She was my grandmother, wasn't she?" I asked. "And that's why you're not telling me."

The fat man came in before she could answer and dropped into a chair, mopping his face. "Not a sign, a footprint, a fleck of pipe ash," he said, panting. "I even went Outside. But they're nowhere to be found."

"Never mind, they'll turn up."

"You forget we may have a masked intruder prowling the grounds," he said stiffly. "You're taking all this far too tupenny-ha'penny. I don't understand you, Sibella."

"Pierce Priam Poole," she said, "there's no masked intruder! This isn't a Republic serial! There's no Captain Mephisto, Dr. Vulcan, Crimson Ghost, or Black Hangman! There's a Sablecroft with a deck that's not quite full." She sank back, her face suddenly an old, weary mask, and said, "I'd give everything if some lunatic were found cowering in a corner, but there's no chance. You and Belle are cleared, thanks to this child's idiotic escapade, and that leaves two. I have no idea which it may be, but it is one of them."

Pierce growled out, "So Laurel told me, but I'm not convinced of that."

I cleared my throat, feeling like an intruder. "When did Wendy start to go gray?" I asked.

They made me repeat it. Sibella said, "You mean her hair? Why? Is it important?"

"No, as long as I know she did. You see, I didn't check before they took her away, but I did find tint and dye in her room."

"The world's gone mad," said Pierce. It would have been comic if it hadn't been so dreadfully pathetic.

"She was about eighteen," said Sibella, visibly controlling herself again with that iron emotional grip. "She felt it was the end of life. I was sorry for the poor thing, and bought her every preparation under the sun, and her hair, which had been halfway between brown and black, turned to jet overnight and stayed that way. Now tell me why you ask. It seems crucial."

"It's definite proof of who killed her, and given an hour or so, I can find the absolutely final confirmation, which I know exists. No, no, wait," I said, hushing them, "and when I tell them what I know, I think the guilty one will admit it. Because I don't believe he truly wanted to do it, and is finding it very hard to live with himself since it was done." I thought, and added, hesitant, "Unless I'm wrong."

"Wrong?"

"About how he feels. Sibella, you told me that Felicity was *startled* to death. How?"

"Why?"

"I wonder—don't see how I overlooked it—if the same person who startled Felicity has done all these other awful things. If that's possible, then I'm wrong about his character, but right otherwise."

She said, "You may take it as proven that it was not the same person."

Pierce said at a tangent, looking at the remote edge of bewilderment, "They wouldn't have left the grounds. Sherry, yes—though the motorcar's still here—but not Daniel, never Daniel."

"I am very tired," said Sibella. "I—"

And James Cagney in his maddest role, the insane Cody Jarrett in *White Heat,* screamed out horribly above our heads—"Made it, Ma! Top o' the world!" and the tremendous explosion of his finish rolled through Sablecroft Hall and faded away.

Pierce stood up and cried, though I think he knew the answer, "What does that mean?"

And Sibella said dully, "Don't you see? *He's killed himself.*"

I leaped from my chair and flew in to the great hall, the dog Challenger galloping at my heels. I went into the passageway through the panel, and snapping on the light, ran down to the entrance of the crescent room. The green door was shut. I heaved up on the big dial, and the room lay before me, but with a change so hideous, so expected and yet feared, that I caught the jamb in both hands and leaned there, half-standing, half-sagging, my ears filled with ringing and my sight gone all aslant. The black Dane nuzzled me, and that brought me to myself.

The skeleton that had sat for so many years at the old table was now perched jauntily on the saddle of the hobby horse. It must have been articulated with wires to begin with, so that it could be twisted into any position, and there it crouched, bent forward, fleshless hands on rotting leather reins, a jockey in death's race. The plaster pie had been removed from its face, and it regarded with immortal grinning wisdom the thing that now sat in the wooden chair.

The room's bright lamp was lit. I said to Challenger, "Lie down," and he did so, whining. I left the threshold and walked over to what waited for me. The chair, which had been set with its back to the door, was now on the opposite side of the table. In it sat the man, eyes staring, apparently, directly into mine. I leaned on the table with both hands, gazing back at him, recognizing with astonishment that he did not frighten me. All I could feel was an incredible sadness at the loss, the waste, the downfall of the human being.

I remember saying something aloud; I believe it was a prayer for the final repose of his spirit. Then I straightened, and saw the big cassette player on the table, his favorite brier pipe in an ash tray, and, lying on its side, a cracked breather glass with a puddle of amber fluid still in it.

He sat there because he was fixed there: he'd taken a memento from the great hall, the antique photographer's head clamp, and attached it to the wooden chair; then he'd wired both his legs securely to the legs of the chair, and his left arm to its arm, as well as (what a difficult task it must have been) twisting several locks of his hair around the old clamp with more of the thin, strong black wire; a coil of this, and the needle-nose pliers with which he'd done the job, lay on the floor beside him.

He had thus made certain that when he died his body would remain upright, looking out across the room instead of crumpling to the floor, whatever convulsions wracked him after he'd drunk the poison.

A Sablecroft to the last, making an effective and striking exit.

I smelled a peculiar odor, reminding me not of the classic bitter almonds, but of peach blossoms. What had he taken? It had not spoiled his lean and handsome face, there was no sign of pain, and his complexion was not the horrid blue of Wendy's, but rather redder than in life. His jaw had dropped slightly, that was all. He might almost have been alive.

Someone was approaching along the corridor, calling my name. Challenger got up, and Micajah trotted in past him, and looked at the man and instantly shot by me and jumped onto his lap. I cried out in horror, my voice weak, and the big white cat reared to put his paws on the chest and advance his head toward the dead face as if to smell the lips. At once he contracted his body, hissed, laid his ears flat, and pouncing across the table came to me and patted my shin, demanding to be picked up and comforted.

I snatched him into my arms and retreated, not from the dead man but from the lingering poison vapor. Then Pierce and Sibella appeared in the doorway and stared, appalled, saying broken words, unmoving. "He's dead," I told them unnecessarily. "He killed himself, as you said." I felt unhinged, and a little proud, and made no effort to hide my tears. "He killed Wendy, and he meant to kill me and Sibella, but by God, he went out like a Sablecroft!"

"Yes," said Pierce. He crossed to the table and leaning over it looked into the man's face. They stared fixedly at each other for a very long time, without movement or sound, and the light caught their eyes equally; but Pierce was alive and poor Daniel was dead as stone.

20

I BENT ACROSS THE TABLE, MICAJAH FIGHTING ME, AND PUSHED the first key of the cassette player. The familiar, loved baritone voice—more stilted than in life and a little uncomfortable because he was reading the words—spoke in the narrow confines of the secret room.

"My dear, dearest Laurel, for I hope that with your sharp intuition it will be you who finds me, on the other side of the reel is a message for your ears only. But I do hope you'll play this here when I can listen too, and perhaps watch you. . . ."

The others exclaimed *No, No,* at that, and I turned the machine off as Micajah scrambled free and vanished out the door, followed by the dog. I should have been patient with them, for they'd known Daniel all those years when I hadn't, but I could not, and rounded on them angrily. "Leave if you like, go if it's too hard on you, but I *will* listen to him here as he wanted!"

Sibella nodded. "Sorry, Laurel. I keep forgetting that you're as tough a Sablecroft as I am. Must be the Vane blood, too. Pierce, if you'll bring chairs, I'll listen with her."

We stood watching each other, the old lady and I. "You knew who it would be," she said.

"Yes, I know everything now. I have since last night." I rubbed my tear-wet face with both hands, and said, "In this house, where the dead speak every day out of thin air, I don't think it's so terrible to want to allow him his curtain speech in the place he chose."

"Of course it isn't. Hello, Alborak," she said to the immense wooden horse, and actually patted him on the nose. "I always wondered where you'd got to." Then this amazing woman went to the rear wall and began to read the mottos there. Whatever vulture tore at her vitals, she would preserve her personal image.

Pierce brought two chairs; I made him take one, and I stood near the table. I clicked the player on.

Daniel said, in those doubtful, stuffy accents of a man reading aloud who's not accustomed to it, that he hoped I wasn't afraid of his corpse because he loved me, and that in life he hadn't been able to hurt me (though he'd tried), and was glad of it now. He hadn't lied when he said he loved me. Wherever he was going, if there was memory there, he would always love me.

I felt a laceration in my heart like a sword's wound.

"I won't embarrass you with more, dearest Laurel. There may be others with you. But do try to forgive me."

I nodded at him, sitting there so grotesquely mounted to the old chair. "But you're only the second person I've loved in all my life, and to think that I frightened you so badly last night saddens me more than I can say," he read, and there was a small clunk on the tape as if he'd turned it off briefly to let his nerves settle.

He said then that he and his cousin had warned me away quite early, Sherry because he thought I was in danger, Daniel because he thought I was dangerous. "And we were both right." It was Daniel who'd done all the threatening tapes, and made the Felicity dummy; set up the pistols, snitched the photo from Sibella, and toppled the soldier at me. That had been chance—he'd exchanged the pedestals before, and led the line from helmet to hatchway—but when, eavesdropping, he saw me standing there, he decided to pull the thing down on me instead of Sibella, whom he'd meant to injure or kill with it. I'd been too agile for him. When he'd realized that I wouldn't be badgered away from the Hall like a sensible girl, and when the spy hole in my bedroom with its sawn-off nails had produced no fear in me, he trained Challenger to threaten on command.

"I felt rotten, making him do it, and he wouldn't have attacked, I simply taught him to growl and bare his fangs. The command word is 'marzipan' and Pierce or Sherry can easily untrain him."

Marzipan, I thought, how unwittingly appropriate.

He said that his talking with Wendy in Felicity's room hadn't been a setup, and he'd been afraid I'd seen him until next day Wendy told him it was all right. He'd taped Micajah again and again to secure a plaintive mew, till he'd finally had to imprison the poor cat and frighten him into one. It was for his final try at me, and it hadn't occurred to him yet to kill me, only to scare me into leaving. "I must have had a poor opinion of your courage. It's hard to remember that now, when I know that you're the bravest, boldest woman in the world," said Daniel.

The reason for all of it, he went on, was that he was afraid of me from the start, me and what he called my keen outer-world intelligence, which he feared more than the wits of all the family, who had lived here forever and were so used to fantastic, unorthodox things that they hardly noticed one another's eccentricities. "We've found it hard, I think, to see what the hell anyone really *means* by anything. But you wondered about everything in the Hall, and that made you a menace. Yet I was in love with you by then. Curse all emotion, it ought to be confined to the screen where it belongs!"

He said then that he'd been afraid long before I'd arrived; in fact, from the moment when he knew that he meant to kill Sibella.

I glanced at her. She was looking at his body with great pity.

He said, in that artificial voice that was so like his own yet so different, that the family would be surprised to learn he had no real self-confidence, but had been in a constant sweat for fear of being discovered. He'd tried to act as he always had, showing his emotions save for the hate and the fear. He had to kill her, he was an instrument of morality in a case where the law couldn't act. I wondered what he meant by that.

"Somewhere I read that revenge is actually an urge for power. I don't want power, I only want to live happily and decently, but no one else could touch Sibella. I was stuck with the job. If men who plan murder are insane, then I was . . . only a little, though, for I stood to gain nothing. I'd have lived as I always have. I was ready to carry the knowledge all my life that I'd killed a human being, and I saw that it was worth it."

Pierce gave an exclamation of revulsion.

But whenever he felt he'd come close to putting the fear of death into her, there I'd be, interfering, nosing, discovering items like the door-opener floor plug. Wendy had worked that, as I'd guessed, while he did the sound effects from a switch on a statue's wrist disguised as a watch, which he'd leave it to me to locate.

He admitted that Wendy was the weak point in his scheme. He should have abandoned those ideas that took two to accomplish. But she'd taken to dogging him around, whimpering, as he put it, about wanting to start all over again as a wife, a real wife this time. After I'd been here a while, she bored him stiff. "The truth is callous sometimes," he said. And she'd caught him stringing thread on the soldier, so he'd enlisted her. To her it was a game, it never occurred to her that the heart-stopping practical jokes were meant to stop Sibella's heart literally, until he decided to finish it with the chandelier. She was to maneuver the victim under it. Wendy balked, and he pretended to be fierce with her, but though she was frightened, her mind was made up. She couldn't see that justice was on his side.

And after Sibella had read them all the riot act, Wendy collapsed. Every day he trusted her a little less, she came nearer to "peaching" on him, as he put it, and finally threatened it. So she had to die.

After he'd killed her—Daniel's voice went to pieces and he shut the microphone again—then he came on, rigidly controlled, and said, "I wasn't meant to be a killer. I don't suppose I could even have survived killing Sibella, much less poor Wendy. I never realized that until I read these words I wrote. And I thought myself so intelligent! I should have written this to you months ago, and revealed me to myself. Wendy'd be alive, and so would I."

I turned off the machine. My head was starting to reel. "There are vapors here, we'd better finish this in the great hall," I said.

We closed the sea-green door all but a crack, too small for the cat to creep back through, and walked unsteadily to our big living room. Pierce set the tape player on an antique cobbler's bench. "Where can Sherry be?" he asked nobody in particular.

I said, "He had nothing to do with all this. He'll turn up." My head was better. Sibella was pale, but with the event and not the fumes, for she'd been nearer the door. Pierce looked like a man who'd been savaged by his own hound. I found Micajah on a loveseat and joined him.

Pierce turned on Daniel's tape with evident reluctance. The voice, steady and less hollow here, continued.

"I've written a letter to the police, admitting my crime and suicide. I did it last night in Sherry's room, as well as this. It should be entirely acceptable to them, they shouldn't bother you. This is a private communication which you can restrict to the family, what's left of us. I told Sherry just about all I've told you. He's going to let me come to this room, which you and I found together, my dearest Laurel, and I'll die alone—as Sherry says he'd have wanted to do had it been Sherry and not Daniel who'd been moonstruck. No one can prove that he allowed me this, not without this tape, so you must erase it. They might consider it a crime on Sherry's part, and he mustn't get in trouble for being decent to me. He's a good man, Laurel. I'm sorry that I tried to throw suspicion on him. I've been pretty sure that it was him in your eyes lately, and not me. Your instinct was right. Oh, the police letter is in my bedroom desk."

Sibella murmured, "He thought of everything, didn't he?" Her voice was not unkind.

"Read my grandmother's diaries, Laurel, those for nineteen thirty-three and thirty-four. You'll find that we had the same grandmother, making us first cousins. It was a jolt to me to learn that you're a certified Sablecroft! I once thought you were a detective hired by Sibella. If things hadn't gone out of control, we could have been married, you know—if you'd loved me and not Sherry—because it's legal between first cousins in Florida."

"Felicity!" I said, and I know disappointment rang in my voice. Sibella shrugged.

"The noises you heard next door, dear heart, were indeed me, searching for the diaries. There was so much in them I wanted to know, about her, not you. How could I dream *you* were in them?

"Regarding Felicity," and the voice darkened and some taut, savage strain entered it, "she was murdered as surely as though her sister had struck her with a lead pipe. We'd been fooling with the tapes for years, making one another jump with amazement or laughter; but by mutual unspoken consent, we never played tricks on Felicity and Sibella, because they were so old and we worried about their hearts."

"Old!" grumbled Sibella. "My land!"

"Then one day Sibella made a tape and hid it in our newest place, the armor on the balcony at the top of the stairs—which once spoke to you—a machine Felicity knew nothing about. The beam was set so that when it was interrupted, the damned armor would shriek like a lost soul. Where Sibella found that noise I can't imagine. But she primed it at a time when only Felicity was upstairs, so that she'd be the first to set it off when she came to dinner.

"I was sitting in a dark corner of the great hall. I saw Sibella doing this, and had no idea what was to happen, unless Pierce was meant to be jolted by some apt quotation. The gong went, Sibella came downstairs quickly and stood watching from the dining-room arch. I saw Felicity appear and suddenly I was afraid, it may have been ESP because for all I knew the tape held only a one-line zinger of the usual sort, but I was icy *scared,* and before I could speak she came past the armor and it let out this perfectly frightful scream, and—and my grandmother simply stopped walking and stood there, and then she—she crumpled and pitched over and came down the stairs like a big beautiful rag doll . . . and Belle had come from the kitchen and saw it happen, and I think she was paralyzed at the horror of it. . . .

"Then Belle shouted, everyone came running, but Grandmother was quite dead. I stayed where I was, unnoticed, till the police arrived. I was in shock, I guess. Even if I had told them what happened, of course they'd never have grilled Sibella or punished her, not at her age and with her clout; what's punishable by law at forty is a regrettable accident at seventy-eight if you're rich enough. Then, for some damnable legal reason, there was an autopsy." His voice turned altogether vicious, not Daniel's at all. "They cut her up," he said, bleak, furious. "They defiled her body, they made a despicable invasion of her privacy, Felicity who had been so proud and—and unsullied. They degraded her . . . you must understand, Laurel, that was as bad as her death. After that I thought a long time, and knew I had to destroy Sibella."

The old woman was staring at the floor, shaking her head. Pierce had his eyes closed and there was a waxen shine to his skin.

"She must have known that Felicity's heart was weak. So I thought, since they were twins, Sibella's shouldn't be any sturdier, I'll engineer the same finish for her. Listening now, Grandaunt? I set out to kill you in the fashion you'd used on Grandmother. Slowly, the potential shocks building. But it didn't *begin* to work. Damn it!" he cried, his voice blurring with static as it rose. "Even when I made the figure of Felicity and smeared the winding sheet with scarlet, to symbolize the autopsy, you only blinked and said something cynical, though it tore me up to see my own creation come falling in. You must have a heart of zinc. It was on that evening that I conceived the chandelier execution for you."

Pierce was saying to himself, "Mad, mad, mad, quite mad."

"Sherry tried to tell me last night that I'd been wrong about you, Sibella, but he simply doesn't know you. Felicity set me straight on you long ago. And Belle and I saw what you did. I hope you fry for eternity." Again came the off-on click. "Laurel, I'm sorry, my dear, but you had to know why I did those things.

"I've always claimed to possess no artistic talent. I had, I had—how odd, to use the past tense—but I was too lazy, honestly, to bother much with it. I didn't want people nagging me, as they did Wendy and Sherry, to whip up a figure of some actor or other. When Wendy admitted to you that the nameless scoundrel had made the dummy of Felicity, I bet that you'd suspect Sherry; and I think you did, for a while."

Oh, Daniel, you can't imagine how deeply and hopelessly I believed that.

"I like to work when I feel like it," said his voice, thoughtful, "to build vast sweeping bookcases, even to polish furniture and clean statues; *when I feel like it* is the operative phrase. I despise doing something artistic because I've been asked to, *told* to, and damn the mood I'm in. That's like being a commercial artist." He said it as though he were speaking of a streetsweeper in India. Poor Daniel had had his prejudices, like all the Sablecrofts!

"When I felt madly artistic, I went to the playroom, and under Wendy's tutoring, dabbled in papier-mâché and plaster. I was never as good as she, lacking practice. But I was satisfied with my ghost-image of Grandmother.

"When Wendy came unglued and began to threaten, and I knew that either she must die or I'd be thrown on the mercies of a world I couldn't cope with, I realized exactly how I'd do it. You guessed how—rather, you thought, for you don't guess, do you?—your 'dirty hands' remark hit me as hard as your later board in the belly!

"The smears of black between my fingers came from Wendy's hair, of course. You don't get grimy hands working on marble with spray and a rag. When I first noticed them, the police had been here half an hour. She'd put some sort of stain or dye on her hair because she was streaky gray in the front. I'm getting ahead of myself. You see, I had no time to write this part out." His voice abruptly turned hollow and different, and he said that now he was in our crescent room and had fixed himself up as I'd find him. "Let's begin again."

"Turn it off," said Sibella. Pierce jabbed a finger on a button. "Please get us three large Irish whiskies," she said, and he left us. "Laurel, I have to know one thing or I'll scream. There's enough to scream at, Lord knows, without a stupid question getting in the way of my attention to poor Daniel. What *were* those stains? You and I know, though a man wouldn't, that good dye does not come off hair, no matter how hard it's pulled. Were you fooling him when you—"

"No," I said. "I wouldn't have guessed either except for what I told you I'd found in Wendy's medicine cabinet. It was a big stick of some substance like mascara, I forget what the label called it, but it was recommended for beards and mustaches and for hair between dye jobs. It came off the stick rather grainy and dense, but I could see how you might rub it in and get by with it if nobody looked too sharply at you. Wendy had been depressed and confused, just sliding through the days, I knew, and she must not have done her hair for a while. That afternoon she looked in the mirror, I think, and saw the gray roots in front. She claimed to be in love with him—and she was vain of her appearance—so she must have used the temporary stuff then, just before she went to meet Daniel. Intending to dye it properly that night, I'm sure."

She said, "It's all so simple when it's explained to one. Thank you, Pierce." She sniffed the whiskey's bouquet and downed a longshoreman's slug. "Turn it on, please."

I sipped the liquor as the voice continued. Daniel said that it was getting along toward time for winding things up, and he'd light his final pipe before I thought of old Gilbert's preaching, jesting room and came to investigate. He'd already wired down his left arm, and would have to do everything singlehanded, but he'd manage. There was the comfortable, homely sound of a kitchen match striking, and a pipe being drawn on. I closed my eyes. I would *not* cry again. He said, "Sweeter than usual, I do believe—how nice!" I kept my lids clamped tight.

He said that he'd run a wire down the passage and along the base of the curved wall to set off the distant player and give us the signal when he was ready to leave. "The Cagney," murmured Sibella. Pierce inclined his head, saying it had been well chosen. I thought with a wrenching melancholy of how much silly fun Pierce and Daniel had enjoyed, topping each other with obscure quotations. There was an end to that now, too.

Daniel had discovered the rotten rungs when he'd started for the attic to oil the chandelier bolts. He used another entrance, but the rungs stayed in his mind. A fall was the most logical "accident" Wendy could have, with all the ladders, catwalks, and balconies of wood in this tropical climate.

The thought crossed my mind that falling deaths arranged thus, and the crushing of people with large dropped objects, are unconscious manifestations of a god complex—the superior being, punishing mortals for transgressions—of which Daniel had had an inkling but wouldn't accept its existence in his own psyche. I thought of him looking down from a porthole, my first week in the Hall, saying that the height made him feel godlike. He must have forgotten that at once. He hadn't wanted to think of himself as playing God.

Well, he'd collected a boxful of tapes at random and put them in the attic, avoiding the two weak steps. He'd cleaned the fifteen feet of ladder carefully, so that only Wendy's prints would be on it, which he later saw as an error of judgment. "Your neat little mind must have pounced on that as a definite oddity—who'd polished it so completely, and why? Luckily the police didn't think it strange. Sablecroft Hall hypnotized them." He took an axe handle and dented the top of the hatchway, where her head might have struck if she'd pitched out from her customary pose. Then he suggested to Pierce that it was time to clean the Moorish court.

His alibi—Sibella concentrating on her book, the big reading glasses, the taped noise of continual polishing and scrubbing, and my bits of thread unbroken on the passage doors (he'd seen them earlier in what he called "the game")—he knew was sound. He said that they all knew how Sibella hardly glanced up from a book: "When she reads, she *reads*."

Anyway, he went on, talking faster, there's a concrete slab under the house that everyone had always known to be solid, only it isn't. He discovered one of the secret entrances to it when he was ten or twelve, and there lay the vast maze of a three-foot-high crawlspace that winds beneath our feet.

As I'd complained, things were never what they seemed here. Why had the family so underestimated Gilbert's thoroughness? Tunnels and holes and pits in every room on the ground floor. . . . Because it's a truism that Florida has no cellars, no one but nosy young Daniel ever bothered to investigate the facts, which are that an endless sequence of electrical wiring exists down there, with scores of buttons like the one I'd found, and the labyrinth of low tunneling and other things I could discover at my leisure. I had, he admitted, even more of a genius for hunting than he, because I was more of a common-sensical plodder, no offense meant.

He'd already cleaned the crawlspace with soapy water, from the court to the lower passageway in the north wall, so he wouldn't get filthy creeping through it on the vital day. He'd spent a week on that job, going through Sibella's corridors and breaking my seals to give me something to think about. He assured Wendy that he'd abandoned the scaring and murder of Sibella, because she'd be dead in a year or two anyhow—

"Ha!" said Sibella loudly. "You'd think I was an elderly invalid!"

And he told her to meet him by the ladder at 2:00, for he needed her help with some tapes he'd rigged to baffle Pierce. He set the cassette to play its sounds of earnest toil, checked on Sibella at 1:57, and slipped down the hole into the underground burrow. At 2:00 he was with Wendy in the passageway, and by then Daniel was so wrought up that all he could think of was Sibella going to the court to speak with him, or Pierce or I coming in and wondering why he wasn't in view, or Sherry or Belle. . . .

"I remember only that Wendy demanded to know why *she* had to put the box in the attic, and I blustered my way through some fool excuse till she finally took the box and went up. I waited for her to hit those rotted steps and drop, and they held under her like steel bars. It was beyond belief. They were about as solid as a collection of spiderwebs, and they didn't crack! She was no heavyweight though—God!" he cried, "I'd give my soul if she were alive and here again!" shocking us all as we sat in horror-rigid stillness.

Wendy closed the trap and descended in her peculiar fashion, and this time a rung crumbled like the tinder it was. She floundered onto the next, which smashed too, and she caught the side bar and hung there shouting. The passage was lighted then, and the porthole shut. He helped her to the floor and took the axe handle from where he'd left it and struck her on the forehead before she'd emerged from her shock. He hoped, believed, that she didn't realize anything after she went through the steps.

"That blow may have killed her," he said steadily, "but I couldn't chance it. I sat her on the floor and got my fingers tight into her hair and jerked her head backward. When nothing seemed to happen, I was frenzied, and gripped harder at the front of her hair and yanked down and sideways, and her neck cracked like a pistol shot."

I thought Pierce would pass out. It may be that only Daniel's renewed control of his own emotions, calming his haunted, trembling speech, saved the fat man from fainting.

The tape told how he'd turned off the lights, opened the porthole and hefted the girl's body into it as Pierce and I, oblivious, worked below. Taking the axe handle, he went downstairs and back through the crawlspace, emerged in the court, leaving the handle below and dropping the cassette player beside it, and shut the sliding entrance by turning the "key"—the smallest marble faun, which was pivoted on its axis to open and close the trapdoor in the blue tile of the court.

"I'd done it," said Daniel. "Something I'd never wanted to do: commit the perfect crime. I had an airtight alibi in Sibella and in those sealed doors of yours, sweetheart. But I never noticed the black smudges between my fingers till the police were here. And I never imagined that even you could put so many small things together so carefully and logically until they spelled 'Daniel.'

"You may wonder how I extracted Micajah from your room so he wouldn't spoil things by answering his own taped meow from under the bed. I opened the hatch, shoved out the bookcase on the casters I'd fitted to it last week, and heard you in the shower. I called Micajah softly, and he walked behind the case and squinted up at me. We were buddies—I love that cat. But he wouldn't come close enough to sniff the sack of catnip I'd brought for him, and you'd finished your shower and I heard you coming; so I had to zip down the passage and go to ground.

"After some hours, in which I made a tour through Hell, my dearest, I put on an old black outfit that I'd worn in a magic show in high school. (The face is a hideous one, as you know, half devil, half foreshortened werewolf muzzle. It fits over the whole head, and the front's stiffened with heavy plastic, which was helpful when you unloaded those blanks at it.) A storm was coming up fortuitously. I doused my lights and waited till I could see pretty well in the dark. I got my player, one of the tiny boxes that runs a loop of tape, went downstairs and pulled the fuse switches for the locations I wanted blacked out, then crept to your door and began the mewing game.

"After a couple of the cries I tested your knob, and to my astonishment found you hadn't locked it. That was careless of you—or were you waiting for me with that revolver? I slipped the door open and Micajah barged out, I could see him like a patch of luminescence. So, close the door, down the stairs, settle cat on chair with catnip, back up once more, begin mews, damn dog appears in hall, scaring me witless in a lightning flash. I opened the door and shoved him in. A couple of seconds later I heard you talking to him. Then you came whirling out and locked the door behind you. I led you downstairs, and most of the rest you know.

"Get this pipe going again. . . . I was going to scare you into running outside, chivy you to the bayou, and drown you. Then I went out myself and saw nothing moving but rain, and realized you'd tricked me. Clever of you—oh, Laurel, I'd never have managed it! Love would have taken over, and I'd have hauled you out, yammering that I was drunk or crazy while I wrung you dry. I had no picture of the deed in my mind, just words, words. Drown Laurel, terrible accident, inexplicable; nervous girl fleeing awful house, lost her way!" He sighed. "I'm lying to myself. I was nerved up to it. I'd have done it but fooled nobody. We'd have had Jones and his lot crawling over us with warrants and truncheons and signals and codes—"

He sighed again. "The tobacco's gone. Last pipe." I heard it laid in the ash tray. "So I caught you on the catwalk. The words said *Throw her over,* and I moved to do it, and then I saw the little gun wavering in your hands and felt your terror, and I nearly stopped the whole charade. For you were putting your last pitiful smidgin of faith in that ridiculous gun that, darling, *I had given to you,* a sham, a useless prop that I'd stuck under Wendy's mattress for you to find. I knew you'd search her room—I know you pretty well, don't I? So here you were, high up in the night and the rain, having turned your back on those who would have truly protected you—Sherry and Pierce—and trusted your life to a silver illusion." He was quiet for a few seconds and then murmured, "'All is not true, all is not ever as it seemeth now. . . . Life is a loom, weaving illusion.'

"Well! There you lay, helpless, on your back with the futile revolver in both your hands, and I, loving you and regretting so much, stood over you and reached out like a monster on the late show, and you emptied it at me.

"You know, when an actor's killed in a movie, he has a certain leeway in how he dies—unless he's got a *very* sticky director—and most of them milk it for all it's worth. I certainly got the last ounce of simulated agony out of that scene, didn't I?"

"Yes," I said aloud.

"I wanted to stop it all then, and just lie there. But I was afraid. I didn't believe that I dared give up my life—which I find now is not a really hard task at all—so the black beast heaved up for its sequel, to kill you. And you laid me low with that railing before my fear could finish us both. God was merciful at last.

"Now I'm going to pour my last drink," said the taped voice

levelly. "Half cognac, half hydrocyanic acid—that's what they call prussic acid these days. I looked it up. Sherry was wrong about there being none here—I found a jar in the garage not long ago; Gilbert's gardener used it in homemade insecticide, I suppose. If one takes a massive jolt of the stuff, death is practically instantaneous, though I understand there may be 'loud cries and convulsions.' I'll strive against any such degrading exhibitions, I want this to go neatly. It's the last effort of my misspent life, Laurel, and I'll put everything I have into maintaining a calm demeanor. I'd hate to sit here looking like Lon Chaney when you find me. I hope the brandy will camouflage the taste. Oh, I won't live long enough to taste it, which is the cheerful thought for the day. I'll take a huge gulp."

There came a noise that harrowed me fearfully—the tiny clink of glass on glass as he poured the liquids into the big drinking globe. It was as though he were about to die again. I made a move to rise and turn the machine off, when Daniel's voice, steady and lighthearted, said, "Doesn't look half bad. Well, my dearest, this is it, as the chaps used to say tersely when they took off in their crates to engage the Red Baron. I'll alert you all now."

Muffled by the heavy walls of the hidden room where he'd talked this reel out, we heard again the voice of Cagney roaring that he'd made the top o' the world. Pierce began to cry uncontrollably. Daniel said, "Now Wendy won't be always there at the back of my mind, reproaching me with those lavender eyes. Don't play the other side unless you're alone, it's only a good-bye tape, a nonsensical thing that I started weeks ago—I must have known I'd be doing this soon, when someone had deduced what happened to Wendy—though I sure didn't know it *out loud,* as we used to say when we were kids, meaning 'consciously.' I think it proves that a part of me had absorbed Gilbert's lesson, 'Learn to die,' before he ever taught it to me. Die well in your fashion. You will erase this side, won't you, darling? I don't want my voice living when I'm dead. And whisper in my ear how you knew of the crawlspace? And forgive me if you possibly can?" A pause. "Forgive us our trespasses," he whispered. "Good-bye, sweet Laurel. Don't *quite* forget me."

I was afraid that the sound of his death would be next, but the tape whirred on, nothing more recorded, and Pierce shook himself and turned off the machine. He and Sibella began to speak, fragments of sentences that made no impression on my mind. I leaped up and ran back to the secret room. I stood across the little table from him, aware now of the length of wire with a switch at the end, the cognac flask, and an empty pill bottle that must have held the cyanide, all lying on the floor. I watched Daniel.

His face was not that of Daniel alive. It was Daniel stripped of all his conglomeration of movie roles, of all the masks after masks after masks that he'd put on during his lifetime; Daniel himself as he had been and had not known that he had been—a child. There was no cruelty, even innocent cruelty, in his own face. A child can lack imagination to such a degree as to be cruel, but this had been a nice, fanciful child playing a bad part, playing at being a tyrant, a godling, a righteous avenger . . . all its evil had been put on, like a grotesque false face of gauze slipped over a beautiful countenance in a spirit of play.

His imagination had stopped just short of recognition that his play was real. Until he'd tried to kill someone he loved, and realization had come to him; too late for Wendy, almost too late for me.

I laid my hand on his shoulder. The strange scent of the poison vapor was weaker. It was not the caressing of a dead body, wired bizarrely upright for one last wild joke; it was a farewell to poor, murderous, frightened Daniel, no longer dangerous or afraid. I said aloud, terribly sad, "You *had* to use the stage set you were born in, but you'd have been happier sitting in the orchestra seats gazing up at the screen, like Wendy—a little bored sometimes, but safe, safe."

"Laurel, what are you doing? Come away from that!" cried Sibella from the doorway.

That. Daniel. I blinked, emerging from my emotional mesmeric state. Daniel, who'd caused all the trouble and death. His charm had lasted, in spite of everything, including his own finish.

"I must tell him what he asked." I leaned and whispered in his ear. It would have been shabby not to let him know that I'd read in the green pamphlet from the public library, and even mentioned innocently to him, about its underground five-foot crawlspace, giving me eventually the clue to Sablecroft Hall's. It was the last thing I could do for him.

"He deserved to know, I suppose," said Sibella. "By his own

lights, he died rather well. Tell him this too: The scream that slew his grandmother was taken from *Psycho*."

I did so, my eyes drowning in tears, and what else I said to him in good-bye is no one's affair. Then I returned to the great hall, asked Pierce to erase the side of the tape we'd heard, drank the last of my Irish whiskey, and went to Daniel's room. I found the letter he'd written for the police. I fished a card out of my purse and went downstairs to dial a number.

"Hello," I said, "my name is Laurel Warrick. May I speak to Sergeant Quarterstaff?"

21

THE POLICE CAME AND TALKED TO US, AND EVENTUALLY LEFT with Daniel's body. Lieutenant Jones had been there, his camouflage of unemotional authority slipping badly when he first saw the crescent room, the skeleton on the hobbyhorse, and the upright corpse. Sergeant Quarterstaff had arrived too; unofficially, I believe, for he was in mufti. When I gave my statement, he stood near me, and once as I faltered he laid an unobtrusive hand on my shoulder and squeezed—he was a gentleman, and much concerned for me in this odd house which he referred to as "Sablecroft's Folly" and immediately apologized, face crimson with embarrassment. If he hadn't been married with three children, and I hadn't been in love with Sherry. . . .

The police didn't ask to see Sherry, which was fortunate because we still didn't know where he was. It turned out that he was at Belle's house, asleep with the exhaustion of sitting up all night talking with Daniel, after many months of half-enough rest. He slept for more than twenty-four hours.

Lieutenant Jones had allowed us to read Daniel's letter before he took it away. It was brief, admitting his guilt in Wendy's death and saying that he was about to take his own life with poison. He didn't mention Sibella, but said he'd killed Wendy because he'd loved her, she'd spurned him, and he'd undergone a spasm of temporary insanity, the jargon of which appeared to satisfy Jones completely.

None of us talked much for the next few days, being overly polite when we met, avoiding the great hall, and eating the relatively simple foods that Belle concocted for us. They were dispiriting times. I don't know about the others, but I was repelled by those still, staring figures that had seen the death which had begun everything, and when I had to pass among them, I could feel them thinking, their cryptic expressions hiding sentient, brooding remembrance. And I'd recollect myself blundering around them in the lightning flashes and the pitch of night, clutching at Nazimova and embracing the treacherous Disraeli, with a form in black moving beyond my reach. And we'd lost too many lives in Sablecroft Hall to relish the presence of multiple imitations of life.

On the fifth day, Daniel came back in a terribly small bronze casket, which we took to the family vault and slid into place beside Wendy's, while Pierce recited some sad verses from Job that made me cry again.

On our way through the staggering heat to the house, Sherry said, "Come to my room. I want to talk to you."

It was an intensely masculine room, which I'd seen only once briefly, full of pipes and old English sporting prints and albums of folk songs, and had that scent that such a den never loses, nine-tenths tobacco and one-tenth shaving lotion. He sat me in a leather chair and with one of the omnipresent levers opened the wall before me; the sliding panels had covered a collection of several hundred books on walnut shelves. "Oh, no more!" I protested feebly.

But these were his own, many of them from childhood. He ticked off categories—piracy, eighteenth-century London, animals, African history, warfare, general literature from Homer to Joyce. "This is the other half of my life," he said shyly. "You see I don't think only of movies, whatever your previous opinion. I love 'em as much as any Sablecroft, but I love to get outside and make things thrive in the skim of dirt we call 'earth' hereabouts, and I love to read and write." He took a new volume from a shelf and handed it to me. *Piracy off the Florida Coasts,* by one Sheridan Sablecroft. "My firstborn," he mumbled.

I looked up into his steady eyes, no longer the red and sunken eyes of the insomniac, but clear and as bright a green as Daniel's had been blue. "The others don't know?"

"I'll show it to them one of these days."

"Why," I said, as it slowly sank in, "you write! And this looks like a serious book."

"Written in what I hope will be a popular style," he said, remarkably ill at ease for Sherry. "I did my best. Always enjoyed the subject. Have centuries-old unpublished manuscripts, great correspondence file with all the experts . . . I, ah, want to be two things: an entertainer," tapping the book, "and an educator, historian—I suppose a scholar."

"*This* is scholarship."

"No, I mean serious historical work on the cinema. A series of definitive books. I'm halfway through the first one, Laurel. It's good. Modesty aside, it's good! That's why your cataloguing is vital. I spend days looking for facts I should be able to find instantly." In the past months, when he'd been grouchy, tired and antagonistic, I'd caught glimpses of the man I saw now—enthusiastically full of energy. I told him so.

"It was mainly that continual loss of sleep that made me so impossible. And worrying over you and Sibella."

"Even when you thought I was a despicable fortune hunter?"

"I did begin by suspecting that you meant to settle in and live off us without admitting who you were—"

"You branded me as an opportunist before you met me!"

"I am not perfect," Sherry said. "Not a man in a movie. I'm an ordinary man who jumps to conclusions, a man who's often wrong and admits it. If you'd rather have a flawless two-dimensional man, get yourself a projector and some films from nineteen thirty-six."

I laughed. "Sherry, I know you tried to bulldoze me for my own safety, but why did you lie? You said you doubted the story of a secret room full of valuables."

"So I do. You found a room full of pedantic lecturing. Laurel, I've told you only one lie—that I had insomnia. I had to say that or admit to the work I was doing, and I couldn't do that till I had concrete evidence that my ability wasn't pure surmise. I sold this a year ago," he picked up his book and regarded it anxiously, "but I had to have it in my hand, see? It only came out a couple of days ago."

"And you don't have insomnia. You typed at night."

"No one ever heard me because this room is absolutely soundproof," he nodded. "I worked most of each night, caught about four hours of sleep, and stayed up all day trying to look awake. I was typing, of all abysmal foolishness, the night Daniel set out to trap you. I ought to have known better, but I thought it would keep me awake till it was time to take up a vigil outside your door. So I dozed off and never heard the ersatz mews, the tapes, even the shots. I was wakened by your voice on the intercom in my room, and looked out at once, but when I saw everyone thronging down there, I waited to the last, to have a squint at Daniel as he left his room. Can you forgive me for sleeping, Laurel?"

I smiled. "Since your cheek was rammed into the typewriter keys, I think you were tired enough to be excused." This was my love, forever.

Eventually I went and got myself ready for dinner, talking nonsense to Micajah about how he must love his new daddy as much as I did, and Lord knows what. The gong gonged, and I walked on various cloud banks and ultimately came into the dining room and sat down, feeling a sweet-sixteen smirk on my face.

Belle served the first course in total silence. Then Sibella said, tasting the Taittinger's, "Have you something to tell us, Sheridan Todd?" in a tart voice, and I realized he wasn't looking any saner than I.

"Can't think how you guessed. Mrs. Warrick has done me the honor of consenting to become my wife."

"Oh, well done!" said Pierce, applauding.

"I see the alliance has already cleared up your eyes," said Sibella. "They've been looking like emeralds floating in rhubarb."

He took the book from under his jacket and handed it to her. There was a hushed interval. "I'll be hanged. Sheridan Sablecroft, eh? So that's what you've been doing at night all these years. I sometimes thought you were a closet drunk."

"Sibella!" cried Pierce. "I'm shocked! The boy is abstemious."

The second course came, and Belle was shown the book, and exclaimed over it again and again, and embraced Sherry and called him her baby, and disappeared, weeping with joy.

When we'd eaten, Sibella said, "Well, family," pouring herself champagne, "it's time we swept out the last mysteries and cleared the air. We've grieved, and now we'll recover. I've been breathing concentrated humbug too long! We are four honest Sablecrofts here, the last of the breed, and no need for keeping secrets among us. By the way, I hope you two intend to give me great-grandchildren," she growled. "You're the last chance for the race."

"We were just engaged this afternoon," said Sherry.

"Don't drag your feet. I won't last more than thirty years more! We were six and now we're four; gives me the willies to see us vanishing like the dinosaurs. If there is an *always,* there should always be Sablecrofts here." Micajah walked in, distracting her. "Hello, puss. You missing your old comrade? It's all right, animals needn't make moral judgments between bad and good people, or favor those who keep the law."

"I wish *I* didn't have to," I said. "I liked Daniel very much. I still do, now that I know about him. I'm sorry, Sherry."

"Don't be. We were always good friends, that didn't change even when I was ready to kill him to save either of you." His eyes darkened. "I'd find myself hoping that it was someone else, anyone else. But of course it was Daniel."

"I never knew which of you it was, not till the last day," Sibella told him. She fingered her tall glass, sighing. "I even was sure, sometimes, that it was you, Sherry." Then, looking into infinity, "Or I'd know it was Daniel, out to kill us all for greed. I did him an injustice there."

"We're speaking of a murderer," said Pierce, somber and sane. "We must not sentimentalize him. He killed poor silly harmless Wendy in brutal fashion, and nearly did the same for Laurel."

"I'm only saying that what he became in these last two years was wished on him by a force he could neither control nor understand." Sibella looked at Sherry. "You realized it was Daniel long ago. Was it because you saw him change after Felicity fell?" Sherry inclined his head. "You got jumpy about that time yourself. It was because you saw him giving way?"

"Yes. He kept it squeezed inside like a hot steel spring. You had to look close to recognize the awful tension. I can't do that, my emotions show whether I like it or not—which is healthier, and I'm grateful for it. No one but me noticed it because nobody really loved Daniel, intensely, personally, except Felicity, perhaps, and latterly, Wendy—who, poor girl, wasn't overly observant."

"We all loved Daniel," snapped Sibella. "We all loved one another here. Hell, I *still* love him, the wicked bounding sprite, and so does Laurel, more power to her!" She eyed Sherry hard. "You think I don't love you either?"

"You never said, but I guessed it." He smiled at her. "I agree, you liked Daniel, without actually noticing him. I liked him and saw how he felt, bugged or manic or moody. Sibella, most precious of grandmothers, you aren't geared to register that sort of thing."

"I'm not?" she said, honestly surprised.

"No more than Pierce, who's a friend to everyone, genuinely interested in their welfare and happiness, and takes them completely at face value."

Pierce moved ponderously to face her. "We've seen too many movies too often, my dear, you and I. We do tend to view individuals as types, I think. That was brought home to me only moments ago. Wendy and Daniel were satisfied if they were adequately entertained without much effort and could work in the house without punching a time clock. Since Sherry worked here too and spent time on the movies, we assumed without thought that he was firmly in their category. You can't deny that we were bowled over when Sherry brought us a book he'd written, researched, and sweated over for no one can guess how long! It would hardly have amazed us more had it been Daniel; whereas Sherry is obviously a man who must exercise his mind, while Daniel was happy to let his idle in low gear. We should have seen, we should always have known, but we didn't. How could I have failed to observe that Daniel was deeply affected by Felicity's death? Instead, I thought him almost callous about it."

"Was Daniel so different before that?" I asked.

Sherry said, "He was much as you knew him, without that nervous awareness, which, he told me the last night, was mainly dread of being caught. The real Daniel was a nice, erratic chap who enjoyed himself. The false Daniel was the 'Daniel come to judgment' who could kill. He was forced into that role, as Grandmother said, and it was unsuitable for him. Horrible miscasting," he said, perfectly serious in the terminology.

Everyone has his bag, I thought, and ours is movies, and I'd better be reconciled to it. "Forced by what?" I asked. "Felicity's death, is that what you mean?"

"Love and hate—love for Felicity, hate for Sibella."

"Behind everything was Felicity," said Sibella, her voice bleak, raw as a New England winter's ice. "When were you convinced beyond any doubt that Daniel was my would-be murderer, Sherry?"

"I knew it before, but it was nailed down when the dummy of

Felicity rocketed out the door. The blood on the robe—only Daniel had been abnormally preoccupied and bedeviled by her autopsy. He couldn't hide that from anyone who actually looked at him."

Sibella, face haunted, said, "How fortunate for me that he never knew *I* had asked for that autopsy. He blamed the police. If he'd known the truth, there wouldn't have been monkey tricks to scare me, there'd have been hands around my throat long ago." She turned her gaze to Sherry. "One last reference to my brief mistrust of you, boy. Your anger was obvious to me, Daniel's was hidden. He never seemed to have a malicious atom, although he was an elfin mischief-maker. Sometimes you're a brooder. Between Puck and Oberon, who'd carry a grudge, who'd kill for good reason? The king of night, every time."

"What good reason?" he demanded.

"The murder of Felicity."

"But you didn't murder her!"

"But I did," said Sibella.

"What?" shouted my true love, rising.

"Do sit down. So you see," went on Sibella carefully, "I considered that as you are a particularly moral creature, you might have appointed yourself executioner . . . as Daniel actually did. The motive, we now realize, was the deepest and oldest and ugliest in the world—hatred for love cut short. He loved Felicity and believed she loved him." She drank. "I never knew anyone but Belle had seen me tinker with that armor machine, though I did occasionally wonder, lately, if you or Daniel had done so."

"But Sherry was never close to Felicity," said Pierce, "while Daniel was."

"I didn't know then it was love avenged. I thought it was what Daniel said—justice wrought. For I did kill her."

"Though not on purpose," said an ashen Pierce.

"We'll never be able to say that for sure, will we? Granted, I didn't realize that she had a damned, moldering, threadbare heart, any more than she did. We never saw doctors! Conversely, she was seventy-eight, and it could have been expected. If I had a sneaking suspicion that that piercing skirl in her ear would drop her down dead, I wasn't aware of it. But Dr. Freud has taught us that we don't always know what we intend. Heaven's my witness, I'd wished her dead and ashes often enough since nineteen hundred!"

"Pure drivel," snapped Pierce. "I don't agree with all this subconscious twaddle. You never wanted to kill anyone."

"Don't be fatuous. Of course I have—time and again. Whether I intended to, God alone knows and may punish me if he sees fit. But I put the worst sound on that player that I could find, and it topped off Felicity neatly, didn't it?" As Pierce shuddered, unbelieving, she turned to her grandson. "A last word on you, boy, before we continue this completely unpleasant topic. You've lost a great deal of weight and fit your bones better. I assume you've dieted stringently for Laurel. That accounts for much of the evil humor, churlishness, tendency to be what we used to call a crosspatch. If I'd realized that, I'd have been slower to suspect dreadful things of you. How did you do it? You never ate much at all!"

"I used to decline second helpings politely, go to my room and gorge; wolf down halvah and marzi——"

"No-no-no!" I shouted. "Don't say it!"

He stared. "I don't mind admitting I was a furtive glutton. To paraphrase Thesiger in two movies, 'It was my only weakness.' "

"The word," I said, and spelled it. I motioned at the black dog Challenger, lying half-asleep in the shadows. "The attack word. It was on Daniel's tape."

"He told me everything that night. All but the word." Sherry grinned on the slant. "M-a-r-z— I wonder if Daniel knew my shameful secret? Bet he did. I can cure the dog quick enough now."

Sibella coughed. "As we've come to Daniel again, it's time I told you, all of you but principally Laurel, about my sister Felicity. Pierce, more champagne, please. Now we'll speak of the origin of our tragedy, the key to all things venomous and destructive under this roof."

Theatrical even for Sibella, I thought.

"True," Pierce murmured. "We used to say at home that an old death has cast a long shadow on this house."

"Scarcely Felicity's fault that she died?" I said tentatively.

"You think not?" whispered Pierce Poole.

Sibella leaned against the towering back of her throne as the fat man opened a second bottle. "We were twins. Not identical, but fraternal, though we looked alike. There, save for superficial tastes and such, the likeness ended. She was a cold, hard, selfish woman. I'm a touch despotic, perhaps, but not unkind, not vicious. There was nothing but bad blood between us from the day we were old enough to sit up and take baby punches at each other. Yes, we did. Mother told us so. Alfred Vane wasn't our first *casus belli* by a long shot. We always played tricks on each other, when we thought Gilbert wouldn't find out and wallop us. According to Daniel, the youngest generation believed that they invented the practical joke in our family. Why, the place was *built* for 'em, and Felicity and I achieved the worst examples!"

She sipped champagne from a fresh glass. "About once a year we managed a humdinger. It was we who'd tape the really bloodiest insults and make them come out of the walls, after the first recorders were installed twenty years ago or so. I suppose you and Dan and Wendy thought those dreadful vulgarities and hostile, unladylike yawps were always perpetrated by one of you. How very silly of you—it was she and I, slashing away at each other."

"May I say, as you likely won't, that you'd always let the feud drop until Felicity reactivated it," Pierce broke in. "She was . . . not a nice person."

"Some of my rejoinders hit pretty low. It was the only way to control her. If she'd had her way, our whole house would have been a continual chaos, everyone at the others' throats, with lies and arguments and contemptible double-dealing kept up day and night. She got away with that as a child in school, in the gangs of us that collected on weekends, but she never managed it at home. Father knew how to handle her, and I learned from him. Like all sneaks and bullies, Felicity was a coward, and could be domineered. By the time I was eighteen, she was scared of me, and didn't try violence often.

"I was the only person she feared after Father died. I was the only person she hated before nineteen thirty-three. But she never *loved* anyone in all her life, parents or husband or her own daughter, till Daniel was born. For some peculiar reason she doted on him, and if she was capable of love, loved him. Everyone, everything else, she despised. Being always in the minority, she couldn't effect much damage, and for most of her life was a harmless annoyance. Even the Great Danes couldn't abide her, and she was afraid of them."

My stomach felt cold. Felicity, my grandmother . . . *I* wished I'd never come to Florida, even to meet and love Sherry.

"On our seventy-eighth birthday, she played the last sordid trick she'd wreak while she was alive. We each took a large slice of our cake to bed with us. I put mine on my nightstand while I undressed, and a gigantic cockroach walked out of it, painted in black and gold—the colors of my favorite caftan—so I'd be sure to know it had been planted and wasn't a casual passerby. It was then I decided to use the new tape machine on her."

Pierce shook his finger. "You see, you meant only to strike back in retaliation for a cruel practical joke. Sibella," he said to me, "is not fond of, ah, palmetto bugs."

"I loathe them! A black widow would have been more welcome than that gaudy vermin. You may be right, I was unaware that Felicity had a weak heart, I only meant to hand her the worst fright of her miserable life. And I wasn't overly sorry when it killed her, but I *was* shocked.

"When an elderly person drops dead, with no wounds or suspicious circumstances, there's no autopsy. They put it down to coronary occlusion. Heart attack. But I wanted to be positive, so I asked that she be opened up."

Pierce winced. "What a delightful way to put it."

"She had, indeed, a bad heart. I had mine checked at once—after all, we were twins. The specialist said that when the rest of me finally died, they'd have to take out my heart and kill it with a club. His words, Pierce, not mine!

"Daniel made the natural error of believing that since we'd been twins, we'd have the same feeble engines in our breasts. He frightened me—yes, I don't want to die for a while—but he couldn't have stopped my ticker. Poor Daniel. He was his grandmother's grandson, and that was his misfortune as well as ours and Wendy's . . . but I'm glad he died with his illusions of Felicity intact and unspoiled."

"Why couldn't he see her as she was?" I asked, baffled.

"She wasn't overtly vicious or even her usual contemptible self in front of him. She valued his love beyond all else. So what he could grasp of her, because he saw her through veils of fantasy as the perfect woman, was only that she loved him . . . as his mother, Gloria, had not."

"Why?" I interrupted again, this being important to me. My own blood, after all. Gloria would have been half-sister to my dad.

"She'd been afraid to have children, hadn't wanted him, carried on like a lunatic through her pregnancy, and out of guilt, I'd guess, avoided him after he'd been born in spite of her. Gloria wasn't mean, as her mother was, but simply the coward that Felicity made her."

"A pretty unlovable line," I said with admirable restraint, since I was the last survivor of it.

"No, no, it was all Felicity. You saw what a fine fellow Daniel could be when he wasn't under her influence," said Sherry.

"Felicity," said Sibella, scorn spattering out with the name like a spray of hot sparks. "She ought to have been walled up—the curse of the Sablecrofts—like the fiend of Glamis Castle. She convinced that poor boy that she was the only soul who loved him, and in return he gave her all his adoration. Filthy! But she did lavish on him what he at least thought was real love—perhaps he *was* the only love of her life, and so she did her best to make him in her image. . . ."

Sherry said, "Laurel's fretting about the strain of madness in the breed. We're single-minded, darling, but not nuts. Pierce is eminently sane, Sibella too, and I'm not so bad, am I? Even Daniel wasn't crazy. In his position, a saint would turn malevolent. You thought it was a life of movies that made him go sour. It was Felicity, and the hate she taught him. 'Insane' is a word. He did insane acts, but was as normal as I. He was just given too much to bear."

"And Wendy?"

"He was fighting for his life and struck out as any cornered thing will. He knew he couldn't exist outside our rarified atmosphere."

"I think it would be termed 'insanity' by the courts." I said.

"All right," he said patiently. "In a normal family, then, Daniel's murderous fury would be called temporary insanity, maybe even attributed to an inherited taint of paranoid schizophrenia. But I swear on my knowledge of Daniel's ins and outs that he was not genetically crazy. He was so fixated on Felicity that he dropped one pose and took on another, as you'd put it—a murderer's domino. And if that's no less culpable, it's at least less worrisome for the rest of the family. Felicity, putting it mildly, was a bitch. No one else for generations of us was ever worse than eccentric. Stop stewing."

"Yes, dear," I said.

"And now may I go on?" asked Sibella frostily. "Thank you. I was married and widowed well before Felicity caught herself a man. The precise term, by the way, as if he'd been an unsuspecting fish. Her husband died in nineteen thirty-two. The next year Alfred Vane, the superlative film editor, who'd retired because his eyesight was failing, came from the north to argue and yarn with Gilbert. He was a most powerful and attractive personality. I was so glad to learn, Laurel, that his eyes did not wholly go."

"The deterioration was stopped. He still watched movies at ninety-five, though they were blurry for him. His eyes were no use for close work, though, after he was fifty-four," I said.

"Felicity and I were both mad about him, I with love—and a little tongue-tied if you can credit that—and my sister with brazen, unadulterated lust. He was fifty-five then, a great marvelous handsome gentleman with spectacles that he'd never wear, but fiddled with when he talked. I must say I thought it *low* of Felicity to make an open play for him, less than a year after poor Ryder had passed to a better world, where the naggers cease from nagging. . . . Well, Alfred was here for three months, and he made his choice, and when the baby was on the way, Gilbert pitched Alfred out. Eventually John was born, and Felicity took him north to Alfred, as I told you; and none of us ever saw Alfred or John again."

She stared into space and sipped from an empty glass. "Afterward, Felicity's hatred for me intensified," she said. "Her occasional jokes grew more savage, when she dared to play them. She progressed from hating me to loathing our father, her late husband, Alfred, her daughter Gloria, and the whole human race except Daniel, in whom she thought she saw herself reincarnated because he was an innocently mischievous boy. She tried to teach him not to trust anyone but herself, and succeeded to some degree, though he had sense enough to shrug it off sometimes. Pity he couldn't shrug off his total worship of the old wretch!

"She was a minority in the Hall, and never managed to turn it bad until she was dead. Then she did evil through Daniel, who wasn't himself evil in the least. It was her spirit that walked this house day and night as a kind of ghost—as a *presence* left here when she was dust, because of what she'd done and taught."

As she fell silent, I said, "I've been aware of a shadow going with me in Sablecroft Hall. Nobody else seemed to notice it, and I'm not superstitious—but was it Gilbert? Grandfather? Felicity? Or only my own secret, that I didn't dream of?"

"Daniel and Belle always thought it was Gilbert," she snorted. "It was never he who walked the place, but Felicity. Felicity, poking and eavesdropping and smirking and plotting, as in life. This was always a crazy house, but it became *insane* for a couple of years, which is far more wicked, less pleasant and mild, than *crazy*. You'll see it from now on, I think, at its best, Laurel."

She glared at her glass. Pierce filled it and she drank gratefully. I said, "I don't understand how my grandfather, who was one of the smartest men I knew, could possibly have chosen Felicity instead of you! He should have seen through a character like hers instantly. I wish he'd fallen in love with you!"

"Oh, didn't I explain that clearly?" she asked, all apparent concern. "I *am* sorry." Then she began to chuckle. "Oh, dear! You have to allow an old Sablecroft her punch line, Laurel. The baby whom Felicity took north to him wasn't hers. Gilbert would never allow me to see Alfred again, even though I was thirty-four years old. And there was no fear of Felicity doing little John a mischief—she hadn't the nerve for that. No, no! The baby was *mine*."

The room whirled and came to rest with an almost audible crack. "Mrs. Callingwood," I said hoarsely, "are you telling me that Felicity wasn't—"

"For heaven's sake, stop that young-Joan-Fontaine meekness! It doesn't become you at all. Call me Grandmother!"

"Yes," I said, weak with relief, "Grandmother."

22

SHERRY ANGRILY CALLED HER A TEASING OLD DEVIL, PIERCE SAID he'd thought she'd never tell me the truth, and I got up and kissed her for the first time, so that she did actually cry a little. Then Sherry put his feet on the oaken table and, pointing a finger at her, said, "One minute, Grandmother. I read Felicity's diaries before Daniel did, and they say—"

"I know what they say. I've spent three days going through the whole sixteen years of them." She put her elbows on the table, and Pierce unbuttoned his vest and expanded, and the three of them resembled a parody of an old English tavern painting. "I loathed my sister, but reading those diaries, I could find it in my soul to forgive her everything, even Daniel and Wendy. Dear Lord, what a sad creature she was! What a collection of pitiful lies and fancies! Sixteen years' worth of them, and who knows how many more hidden in her old room? Poor Daniel spent two years of his short life searching for something that's the most twisted tangle of falsehood I ever read. And Sherry, you and he both believed that Laurel was descended from Felicity. I'll wager it hasn't dawned on you yet that Laurel's your first cousin."

"That's all right, it's legal in Florida. Daniel told me he'd ascertained that, and I'd rather she shared you than was stuck with Felicity for a direct ancestor. But tell, tell."

"Naturally, Belle's always known the truth. She used to stand guard for Alfred and me. So has Pierce, except that he hasn't read the diaries." She gave Challenger a piece of cold chicken. "I can't put myself in the place of a woman who could write nothing but lies, day after day—was she kidding herself? Was she truly insane? Because I can certify that there's not a word of fact on any page of the things."

"For certain?" asked Pierce diffidently.

She looked at me, my very own grandmother, with her cap of chestnut hair and her family nose carved from fine bone and her tough, loving gaze. "Alfred and I corresponded all the years that were left. My information didn't come entirely from detectives, you see, though some did. For instance, when John was killed I heard immediately, as I told you, but poor Alfred wasn't able to write about it for months."

I said, "Granddad burned an enormous mass of letters on his ninetieth birthday. He wouldn't say what they were."

"He had a deep sense of privacy. He told me of that, and I agreed to burn mine when I felt death approaching. Can't bring myself to do it yet . . . besides, I've a while to go. When Gilbert was alive, Alfred would have his friends mail the letters from all parts of the country." She sighed heavily. "That love affair lasted all our lives. If we had married, it would likely have flamed out in a few years. Neither of us was designed for marriage. How fortunate that we knew it."

"And the diaries are *all* lies?" said Sherry.

"You can judge that if you remember how Felicity wrote of her pure love for Alfred Vane and how he returned it with passion; how they met three or four times a day in secret, with all the flowery details; and how I was ill with jealousy and took to bed for a week at a time, and put earwigs under her pillow. Ask Belle about those 'facts.' "

"Oh," I said faintly, "I'm so glad it was *you,* Grandmother!"

"So am I, dearest," she said. "Alfred and I turned out a pretty good line in people, didn't we? And poor wicked Felicity, romanticizing, playing out on paper the role she'd wanted and done her worst to get, like Miriam Hopkins competing with Bette Davis!"

"Have you thought of this?" asked Sherry. "If both sisters had been dead when those diaries came to light, as she likely thought you would be, there'd have been no one to know they weren't true. The Sablecrofts of the future would have thought her the heroine of the family, with every good trait in the register!"

"The old ghoul!" shouted Sibella, pale with fury. "We'll destroy them tomorrow. I pitied her living her pathetic fantasy life—I should have known better. It wasn't in character. She was stealing my life and making it hers for posterity. And there they hung in that stupid horse's gullet, and if Laurel hadn't come along to find that room, I suppose you'd never have told me about 'em!" she said to Sherry.

"By tradition we don't talk about our discoveries."

"She knew *I* never kept a diary," Sibella brooded. "The unholy witch! Nobody'd have known the facts at all. Not even John's child here."

I said, "How poisonously unhappy she must have been, to spend her life lying to books. What black despair she must have felt—"

"Not she, my dear," said Sibella. "Black glee, more like."

"She wasn't a whole person. We must feel sorry for her," said Pierce. "Laurel is right, as always: Felicity couldn't have had a thoroughly joyous day in her life."

"True. Very well, we forgive her, we burn her monument to Falsehood, and we forget her and all her deeds forever. Now was there something else? Ah, my will. I've changed it back; my attornies were here yesterday morning. Since there will be no more secrets among us, I'll tell you that Sherry inherits everything—"

"About the year two thousand sixteen," murmured my cousin, my love.

"To be shared with my granddaughter, Laurel Vane Warrick Todd Sablecroft or however you mean to style yourself. With the proviso that Pierce and Belle have a home here with anything they desire, unto eternity or later, whichever comes first."

"Hardly necessary to put that proviso in," said Sherry.

"I know! It wasn't much different before, but Daniel and Wendy were in the proviso. Daniel was too scatty to handle much money, and Wendy had no head for figures whatever."

"You mean I was in your will before I came here?" I asked, amazed.

"I always intended to bring you here and mate you with Sherry!"

"Fine mare that you are," muttered my fiancé.

"If you'd proved a dud, I'd have cut your share down to twenty or thirty thousand, I suppose. An academic speculation now. I think that's all."

Sherry took his feet off the table. "No. You must know what I plan for the Hall when it's in my care. It'll be opened to serious students of the cinema, to live in if they wish for a stated time of study. I know it's against your wishes, so you may leave it to Pierce instead."

"Open Sablecroft Hall, our home, to the *public?*" she roared.

"Not *en masse,*" he said patiently. "To scholars of the motion-picture art. It's criminal to keep it so private, just when many people are waking up to the enormous amount of factual material that's been lost, or hidden away in places like this—the data on the infancy, so recent, of our last-created art form. Much of it is here, locked away behind the double walls of this house, in a mass of paper like no other in the world."

"Welcome to Sablecroft-La," I whispered. "My name is Chang. . . ."

"Shut up, darling. This house is a—"

"Gold mine," I suggested helpfully, "of information."

"Do hush. It needs to be catalogued first, which will take years—"

"Your involvement in flicks has always been less emotional and more intellectual than ours," Pierce told him enthusiastically. "It's a splendid idea, eh, Sibella?"

"So long as I'm not here to see it!" But I thought her gray eyes flashed with pride in her grandson.

"Pierce is a naturally gregarious man," said Sherry intensely. "It's not people he dislikes, it's Out There. He'd revel in the association with other erudite buffs, wouldn't you, Pierce?"

"I do believe I would," said he, growing more excited by the minute. "What a marvelous conception!"

Sibella rose. "Pierce, there's something I want to show you."

"What? What? Oh, yes, of course," said Pierce, bounding up.

They turned to leave us alone, and we pushed out of our chairs and literally fell into each other's arms. As Sherry was kissing me, and I was kissing him, Sibella's voice floated back sedately. "Good night, grandchildren."

"Good night, Grandmother," we both said hastily.

I stood staring into my love's green eyes. "When will it be?"

"As soon as we can get the license. Have I said that I love you very much? That even if you *didn't* love me, I'd be content to live here, seeing you, hearing your voice in the mornings, never looking at another woman?"

"I love you, Sherry, and you won't have to limit yourself. You may kiss me sometimes."

He did. "Yes, I prefer it this way. I only wanted you to know how *very* much—"

"I do know. And now you can write whenever you like. When we leave Sablecroft Hall," I said slowly, "will it be all right? Or must you write here?"

"I've always found it perfect for concentration. All the books and manuscripts I need are here. But if you want to live elsewhere, we will. It hasn't felt quite like home to you, has it? Perhaps it'll be worse after what's happened. We can go anywhere you like."

"I love cold weather," I said wistfully. "Connecticut in the autumn. Even Maine in the winter."

"There's no better place for my work than here," he said, his lips in my hair, "but I can send for material I need. We'd visit Pierce, and—but there's Sibella. We'll win her to the notion gradually. She expects us to live here forever, and after us our children."

"Why should she want another generation of Sablecrofts, to sit and watch old movies?"

"I do more than that, so would my kids. But we decided neither of us wants children."

"Yes we did. Do you think we might change our minds?"

"I suppose it's possible. You'd make a terrific mother. The children of first cousins often turn out very well indeed. I don't know, by now I've no idea what I want in the line of kids versus no kids." He lifted me and carried me into the great hall. "We'll wait and see. Keeping in mind that Felicity was the only bad apple in the barrel, even if she did turn others rotten, I doubt that we'd need to worry about a mythical mad strain showing up."

"No. I love having Sibella for a grandmother."

"I am now going to carry you up the staircase," he said, as I nestled my head into the place where his neck met his broad shoulder. "I've wanted to try this stunt ever since Gable did it."

"Drop me and I'll be furious," I murmured, knowing he wouldn't. "Go on, try it." I closed my eyes. I'd love to have your babies, I thought, but I won't tell you that just yet.

More than two years have gone since that evening. Sablecroft Hall, no longer filled with the miasma of hatred or haunted by the evil influence of the dead, is alive again in the casual, light way for which it was meant. There is study and work and frequent laughter, and much love, and plenty of good intense talk about movies and other things. Sad memories don't often intrude on our thoughts, for the poison that seeped into everything while Daniel hated as Felicity had taught him is gone.

I kept Daniel's love tape: ten minutes of many actors speaking lines from many pictures, which took him weeks to prepare and remains in my mind the essence of Daniel as he really was. Unable to communicate as he wished on his own, he'd needed the other voices, the ready-made speeches, the exhalation of long-dead breaths to express his deepest emotions. He carefully chose all the performers he knew were my favorites.

The ultimate effect is of scores of them sitting around a huge table commenting on Daniel's character first—"Big man!" says the young Richard Widmark, with his paralyzing, psychopathic giggle, "ya squoit!" and Lee Marvin follows with "He's real mean, you know, out-and-out *mean.*" But E. E. Clive dissents: "Monster, indeed! Tush, tush!" Then I come in for some flattery. Laughton whispers, "How nearly a perfect woman she is." And there are others as well; but Ralph Richardson says, calm and wise, "She loves the other man," to which Robert Coote retorts, "The most obstinate young woman I have ever met!"

There must be sixty or seventy such excerpts on the tape. I shall keep it always . . . and some day play it for Sherry, when all the melancholy has gone for good and we can listen to it together as if to an old friend entertaining us. The end of it might have been sad and terrible, a combination of remarks about Dan snuffing out his own life and some famous dying lines from the movies, yet curiously the effect is cheerful, upbeat. "But at my back I always hear Time's wingèd chariot hurrying near," says Robert Newton. Colman does his marvelous bit from *A Double Life* on the old-time actor who used to die on stage and then, at the audience's request, get up and die again. "Here's happy days," says Bogart flatly. The very young Katharine Hepburn cries, "I'm not afraid—I'm not afraid! Why should I be afraid?" Edward G. Robinson *is* afraid: "Mother of Mercy, is this the end of Rico?" but George Sanders is nonchalant as, gun in hand, ready to shoot himself, he says, "Cheerio!" Dame May Whitty says, as from Daniel to me, "I do hope and pray no harm will come to you, and that we shall all meet again one day." And Fredric March exults, "Then there *is* a love which casts out fear, and I have found it!" There is a long silence, you almost think the tape is finished, till great Laird Cregar says with rich disgust, "Ye gods, did you ever *hear* anything so corny?"

It is very Daniel.

Grandfather Vane's library and mine have been taken out of storage and shipped to the Hall, where they belong. We had many items that Gilbert and his heirs did not.

The Great Danes all answer now to names of their own: there's Palmerston and Challenger, of course, and the harlequin, Roderick; the steel-blue is Ottermole; and the fawn with his black mask, Rudyardine. I really believe they're happier now than they ever were as nameless units in a pack.

I was right about the skeleton's room—at either end, behind the customary "solid" wall, I discovered a small hidden cavity with manuscript treasures in sealed, air-tight metal boxes. We also found the rest of Felicity's pitiful diaries hidden in her room where Daniel had so often searched at night, and we burned them unread. There are further secret rooms to riddle out, too. When I'm not cataloguing or busy elsewhere, I often search for them systematically. Time is not heavy on my hands.

I've even grown used to this frightful climate, to the extent that I'm making some repairs to the deteriorated stucco towers and buttresses outside.

The longer we are married, the more in love we grow, as it ought to be. I'm sure that Sherry will not mind leaving this vast house with its artificial, insular atmosphere and its omnipresent topic, if only to watch the seasons change for a while.

First, naturally, I'll have to finish the ordering and the cataloguing and cross-indexing, an enormous job. It will take many more years, but I don't mind that. I enjoy the work. And Sibella appreciates it.

I suppose that I don't want to move away while she's alive. I'd feel guilty about it, and I'd miss her. But then I'd miss Pierce Poole too.

Never mind, we'll leave some day. I haven't decided where I'd want to live, exactly, but I'm sure we'll find a place. We'll leave Sablecroft Hall. I truly mean it.

If I can persuade Micajah to go. The Hall, he thinks, belongs to him.

I must stop writing and dress for dinner. We're eating early tonight—Tibetan lamb à la Colman, one of Pierce's sautéed specialties—because there's an all-1937, Laurel's-request bill featuring *Lost Horizon,* one of my personal favorites. I suppose I've seen it a hundred times in my life. I wouldn't mind watching it a hundred times more.